THE CHILLING SOUND OF RIPPING METAL, THE HORRIFIED SCREAMS OF TRAPPED VICTIMS

Jerry Tanner couldn't believe what he was seeing on the television news report. And when he called to his wife, her reaction was even more frightening. She showed him a secret notebook, filled with her psychic predictions. A cold feeling rushed through Tanner as he read his wife's writing:

**THE GOLDEN GATE BRIDGE
WILL BE MADE TO COLLAPSE
WITH GREAT LOSS OF LIFE**

Farther down the page is the cryptic notation: *A politician will fall from the sky in flames.* When that happens a few days later, it becomes clear to the Tanners, and to the government, that America is under attack.

Jerry Tanner is a high-ranking scientist with a research institute. His pregnant wife, Eve, is a test subject. As the awesome attacks intensify, Jerry and Eve find themselves drafted as front-line soldiers in a new kind of war offensive.

Unfortunately it is a war that America is ill-prepared to wage, with a power once thought to be witchcraft...

"Fast-moving and terrifying. A chilling picture of a possible and horrifying future."
—CHARLES L. GRANT,
twice winner of the Nebula Award

"A fast-paced tale where fiction becomes stranger than truth. *Mind War* is a mind-blower."
—JIM BERRY,
author of *Beyond the Space of Time*

GENE SNYDER

MIND WAR

PLAYBOY PRESS
PAPERBACKS

To Nancy,
for her vision and support.

And to Laura,
who brings great joy.

ACKNOWLEDGMENTS

No novel is a solo effort. The writer, like a farmer, harvests ideas, techniques and needed information from numbers of sources. My editor, Sharon Jarvis, has been a prime source for all three. Her consummate editorial skill and tenacious creative support have been indispensable. In addition, I wish to thank Frederick C. Kniesler for his expertise in politics and international diplomacy; Phil Leonhardt, R. P., for vital pharmacological information, and Dr. Sam Zimmerman for needed medical data.

PROLOGUE

Like gravity and other natural phenomena, the phenomena we have been rediscovering and exploring in the laboratory have been around since the dawn of humankind's recorded search.
　　　　　　　—Russell Targ and Harold Puthoff,
　　　　　　　Mind Reach

"And so, with pleasure, I declare this Fifth International Conference of Physics . . . *and Paraphysics*"— the speaker's voice tightened like a noose around the words—"is officially in session. Thank you all very much."

Before the brief round of polite applause had a chance to die out, Channing Moreland and Andrei Sholodkin had slipped from their seats in the back row and walked out through the ornate though slightly musty marble foyer of the Goethe University Auditorium.

"Did you hear him, Andrei? I thought he was going to strangle on the words."

The small Russian shrugged. "Still, it's a big concession for them."

The day had grown unusually warm for January in Frankfurt. In fact, unusual weather had been commonplace in most of the world for nearly a year. Droughts

9

gripped rain forests, while torrents of rain soaked into deserts. As luck would have it, the most severely affected areas were the broad, fertile farmlands of Eastern Europe and Asia. Floods washed away acres of seed and the few crops that escaped drowning were baked to death by untimely hot spells. Ironically, while the East suffered, the West prospered. The vagaries of the jet stream moderated the growing seasons there, creating bumper crops.

It seemed more like early April than January as the two men tossed their top coats over their arms and strolled westward through the campus courtyards and walks. Both in their late sixties, they were an unlikely-looking pair. Sholodkin had the thick, stocky build of a Ukranian farmer. His totally bald head was concealed by a rakishly tilted black sable hat. He stood half a foot shorter than his American friend, whose angular lankiness seemed to belie his age. The crowds that passed them on the traffic-clogged Bockenheimer Landstrasse might have thought them two old war veterans at a reunion. In a way, they were.

It had been over twenty years since they stood as total strangers staring awkwardly at one another in the Stockholm anteroom. The two of them were about to share a Nobel Prize for separate, though related, research. Stalin's paranoia about the secrecy of research had prevented Sholodkin's papers on "Non-Hypnotic Distant Influence" from getting to the U.S., while Joe McCarthy's anti-Communist harangues had prevented Moreland's study of "The Physics of Psychology" from getting into the Soviet Union. As the Cold War thawed, the two men corresponded, then began to meet at conferences. Eventually they grew into a close friendship. Together, they had kindled the fire of excitement for the new and not yet legitimate fields of paraphysics and parapsychology.

It *had* been a war for them, fought alone on opposite sides of the world. There had been the battles for funds, the sniping attacks of colleagues, the politics and, perhaps worst of all, the indifference. And now they were two aging widowers who shared a small victory. The conference would include parapsychology, though conference president Metzieder had almost choked on the words.

As they stood waiting for the light to change, the small Russian tapped a Chesterfield from a battered pack and lit it, inhaling deeply. He coughed.

"Andrei, you know that's going to kill you."

He looked up at Moreland, his eyes tearing from the suppressed fit of coughing. "I've survived starvation at Leningrad in the war and more Stalinist purges than you Americans ever knew happened. I was sixtynine a fortnight ago. I walk two miles every day, and I'll die . . . when I die. Now, tell me about your work."

They slowed their pace as they turned onto a side street, where the crowd was thinner. Moreland was pleased with himself.

"I haven't had a chance to tell you about the new research center. The *Moreland* Research Institute. We managed to fund the merger of two smaller ones that had been established in California."

"I am pleased for you, my friend. Where is the new one?"

"In the western part of New Jersey. Lovely area. Very rural."

"So . . ." The Russian pointed a finger in mock accusation. "Now there will be no more letters bragging about warm California winters, while I freeze in Leningrad? That will be a relief."

Moreland gestured ahead to a dark cloud line skirting the tops of the distant Taunus Mountains. It had quickly dimmed the sunlight to gray, and there was a west wind freshening behind it. "With all the changes in upper air patterns, perhaps we'll get California winters in New Jersey. The way things are going, there's a chance that you'll get Black Sea weather in Leningrad."

Moreland paused, wondering if he should ask the next question. Would Andrei think he was probing? His own theory was that the Soviets had attempted to change the growing seasons with a weather alteration program. He'd had a hunch that Andrei knew what was going on, and it only took a second for Channing's curiosity to overwhelm his caution.

"Have your colleagues come up with some sort of handle on the causes of all this erratic weather?"

Andrei's nod was quick and curt. "Peak of sunspot cycle. Ionization changes. It will settle down in a year or two, at least that's what we think."

Channing had known Andrei too long to accept the statement. It had sounded like a memorized speech. There was clearly something in all of this weather business that Andrei knew and was not able to divulge.

"Well, with the East getting all of the rotten weather and the West getting all the good, I wonder if those Kremlin bureaucrats think it's an American plot to change the weather?"

Andrei's laugh was like a quick burst of energy being released. There was a twinge of irony in it. The laugh vanished as Andrei spoke.

"If our bureaucrats have secrets about weather, they did not confide in me." There was a hitch in his voice, as if a tiny sliver had been removed from a recording tape. Andrei was lying, and Channing knew it instantly. They had grown too close for the Russian to carry it off. Had the Soviets played around with the weather and messed up the normal patterns? If so, they'd created the problem instead of the solution.

The wind was steadier now and there was a chill in it. Andrei slipped into his top coat as they walked.

"What will your projects be, Channing? Or can't you say?"

Channing tried not to show surprise. Neither man had ever put constraints on what was discussed. His friend's caution saddened him. "Oh, distant seeing, precognition and some other things. I'm really enjoying all that nice fresh government money that's been dropped in our laps, and—"

"And getting rich?"

"And getting rich, a little anyway. It's exciting, Andrei. For the first time in years, people are taking the research seriously. What about yours?"

Andrei raised his hand, palm upward in front of his chest, as if he were balancing a delicate china plate on it. "They have resurrected the ghost of L. L. Vasiliev and placed a wreath on his tomb." Vasiliev had given his career to parapsychology research. He had been the nearly unrecognized Pavlov of the paranormal. In the 1920s he had founded the Leningrad Institute for Brain Research, devoting it totally to exploring the untapped potentials of the mind. His protégé and successor had been Andrei Sholodkin. "Of course, the old man is thirty years dead and the applause does him no good. But it does help us a little."

Andrei paused, frowning inwardly. He did not like having to be evasive with a friend as close as Channing. He could not tell him that the Leningrad Institute had blossomed to the size of a small university in less than a year; that where once access had been unchallenged, the halls now crawled with security people. "At any rate, old Vasiliev would have been challenged by the problems that we face, if he were still alive." He paused again, vainly trying to stop a question from popping out. In a second, his scientific curiosity overtook his sense of security. "We are having trouble maintaining psychological stability in our long-term test subjects, are you?"

GENE SNYDER

They've moved ahead that far? Moreland was
stunned. It wasn't the question's content that struck
him so much as it was its sophistication. Moreland's
research was like that of an earlier scientist trying to
prove the atom could be split. By comparison, Andrei's
question resembled a problem in advanced nuclear
warhead design. He had to answer somehow.

"It's something we haven't really wrestled with yet.
What kind of distances are your distant communications experiments covering now?"

It was Andrei's turn to pause. Asking the question
in the first place had been a mistake, and he knew it.
His answer to Moreland's counterquestion could border on treason.

"Vast ones."

The day was clearly colder now. The sun had vanished behind a wall of thickening clouds that boiled
across the Taunus and covered the main valley. Central European weather had always been fast-moving,
especially in winter, but the weather change that Andrei and Channing watched was uncanny. This was
the way things had been for more than a year, and
Andrei's comment about sunspots rang more and more
false in Channing's ears.

Together, they walked silently across Furstenburger
Landstrasse, past the looming concrete curves of the
I. G. Farben building and into the winding paths of
Gruneberg Park. They wove their way down a walk
lined with bright green laurels until they came to the
chessboard. It was a twenty-foot-wide tile mosaic where,
to the amusement of summer crowds, opponents played
in day-long matches with two-foot-high chessmen. Now
the board was littered with the flotsam of winter—
broken limbs and scattered leaves.

Andrei crossed the board, stepped onto a tile square
and turned to Channing with a sweeping gesture.
"Queen to king's bishop three."

Channing shook his head. "Fool's mate? What kind of Russian are you?"

"A troubled one, my friend. I think this is the last conference. At least the last one for us . . . like this."

Channing sighed. He'd been right about everything, and Andrei was confirming it. The Russians *had* been experimenting with weather control and they had failed. Somehow, it seemed that Andrei had been enlisted to bail them out. How? What was so secret that he'd lie to an old friend about it and then as much as admit he was lying? Channing could feel a great sadness inside. Woven into it was the dark foreboding of something that their years of friendship had managed to push away until now.

No! He wouldn't have it. Not, at least, until the conference was over. He strode out across the board. Reaching out, he gripped Andrei by the shoulder, the way the oldest child in an orphaned family might give strength to a younger brother. He could see the small Russian's eyes shine in the rising wind. Channing managed a smile.

"And where shall we go for dinner? The Kranzler Cafe with the string quartet and the arrogant German waiters? Or the hotel restaurant?"

Andrei's shoulders drooped as he sighed. "Not the Kranzler. It's full of old people . . . even older than us."

Channing's frown was comic. "Older than *us?*"

Their laughter echoed across the huge chessboard and was carried away by the growing storm.

1

These things that people accept as an external world . . . what appears to be external does not exist in reality. It is indeed mind . . . nothing but mind.

—Dr. Fritjof Capra,
The Tao of Physics

Trevor Lewis watched it happen almost every afternoon at five. The cold Pacific winds pushed the fog bank like gray ooze across the road level of the Golden Gate Bridge. The mammoth structure was one of the most impressive engineering feats in the world. It spanned the length of fourteen football fields placed end to end. It contained enough concrete to construct a skyscraper and enough intertwined steel wire to stretch out across the Pacific to Hawaii. There was something eerie about watching it simply vanish in the fog.

Lewis's cold blue eyes squinted into the distance where the dank wall had erased the Marin County side, almost a mile to the north. His eyes moved back to his tiny tollbooth, where he looked at the clock. *Half an hour. The fog will be perfect.*

"Lewis?"

He looked to his right in time to see Carl Thurman, his shift supervisor, gesturing and waving a *Reduce*

Speed sign over his head. The fat man's paunch jiggled as he waved. Lewis smiled a tight smile and made a circle with his thumb and forefinger. He thought it odd. In most of the countries of the world, the gesture was a wordless obscenity. But in the United States, it was one of understanding—even friendship.

Lewis reached down and pulled the sign from the rack at his feet. It had been filed between *Accident Ahead* and *Have a Safe Trip*. He ducked through the door and slapped the sign into its slot with a single practiced motion. He looked south and whistled through his teeth. A seemingly endless, unbroken line of headlights ground their way out of the Presidio Tunnel and crept north toward the fog-shrouded bridge. It was just getting to be one sweet-ass traffic jam.

He was lucky to be working the southbound lanes, where only an occasional car or truck crept in from the bridge. Monday morning in the same booth was another story. Drivers threw bills and coins at him as if he were a machine, silently blaming him for the slowness of the traffic. He smiled as he remembered the imagined signs he and Harris had concocted in a bar one night. *Boring, Isn't It?* led to *Who's Your Wife With While You're In Traffic?* He really wished he had one of those to slide into the holder when he went off shift—especially tonight.

He mechanically reached up and took a bill from the driver of a long-haul tractor. The driver's florid Irish face smiled down at him.

"Some kinda fog out there. Sure as shit glad I ain't goin' the other way, though."

"Yeah." Lewis smiled and reached up with the driver's change.

"Well, Happy Easter." The driver slipped the rig into a roaring first gear and accelerated southward away from the toll plaza as Walt Harris silently slipped into the booth through the other door.

In the three months that he'd known the man, Lewis had never seen him in a pressed uniform or with his wild black hair less than shoulder length. Conversely, Lewis always looked like a career soldier out of uniform to his coworkers. He drank with them but never revealed much personal information. The rumor was that he might be an ex-cop or someone just mustered out of the service.

Harris grinned at him. "Hi, Trev. Thank Christ we've got the quiet side tonight."

Lewis grinned back. *"You've* got the quiet side. I'm off duty."

He quickly closed out his cash drawer and slipped into his blue windbreaker. He tucked the cash envelope under his arm and clapped Harris on the shoulder.

"Have a quiet night."

He was already moving away from the booth when Harris answered.

"Happy Easter, Trev. See ya tomorrow."

Lewis waved. *You won't ever see me again.*

He turned in his cash and walked out into the small employee parking lot where his battered VW sat. He got behind the wheel and waited for the fog to thicken while he went over his mental checklist. Satisfied with everything, he started up the engine and pulled out into traffic.

Driving slowly in the right lane, he followed the sloping Presidio Drive south away from the bridge and the line of blinking tollbooths. A few hundred yards short of the Presidio Tunnel, he pulled off into a rest area. The parking lot was deserted, as was the observation deck that afforded an impressive view of the bridge when the weather was clear. The deck was always jammed with tourists in the summer, but for now the dime telescopes stood patiently at mute attention. He turned off the engine and took a few deep breaths. *So this is it—the culmination of everything.* It was odd that he couldn't sense any finality about it, only tension and a sincere desire to get things finished.

He picked up an empty gasoline can from the floor, got out of the car and quietly closed the door. He stared off into the gloom, seeing patterns of red-, orange- and yellow-lit fog swirl around the distant bridge super-structure. Suddenly, an unexpected wave of fear gripped him, shuddering its way up his back. His hands trembled and felt clammy. What was it? He pushed it away roughly. Confidence—total confidence was the key to everything. I'm a professional, he thought. The best they can get for this . . . job. For a second, his teacher's words flashed in his memory. *The more confidence you have in the technique, the more success you will experience. Prime yourself . . . build confidence. . . .*

Trevor took another deep breath and smiled to himself. The fear was starting to ebb. He took a few steps away from the car and placed the gas can on the ground, then moved several yards away. He turned and stared at the can, and in a few seconds he could feel a quiver move through his body. This time it was not fear, but something else . . . something more familiar—power. His breathing quickened and the cords in his neck stood out in grotesque relief as he stared at the can.

It moved slightly, sliding an inch or so to the right. The right side of the can lifted teeteringly clear of the pavement. Every muscle in his body screamed with tension as he reached out his right arm and jabbed at the distant can.

It lifted totally free of the ground, hovered for a second—

Unnnnh! A grunt erupted from deep in his throat.

The can flew aside, as if hurled by someone with great strength. It clattered against the car door and fell to the cement.

He was primed, powerful. He could feel the energy

surge through him like a flash of lightning. He turned and faced the line of telescopes and concentrated.

The one nearest to him creaked slightly. So did a second—and a third. The first one started to spin on its mount. Trevor laughed and turned away. The spinning abruptly stopped.

Now he was ready.

He grabbed the gasoline can from the spot where it came to rest. Then, hanging his head dejectedly, he trudged toward the roadway, like a commuter who'd run out of gas. He plodded between the cars on the traffic-snarled northbound lanes, then turned and started walking back toward the bridge. The gas can ruse had worked perfectly five times before and there was no reason to assume it would not this time. In his mind, his teacher's voice called out again to him.

Visualize the smallest possible fragment of the structure. Imagine the molecules as patterns of dots—or whatever you can employ most comfortably. Do this the same way in each of the six sessions.

Trevor smiled. For a split second, all he could see was that redhead from the singles bar. The dots had become her freckles, sliding down to the small of her back and fading above her warm buttocks. He let her freckles vanish from his mind like fireworks in the rain. *Complete the assignment, observe the results and get out.* He couldn't allow himself the luxury of anything else—not now.

A hundred yards short of the bridge proper, he veered away from the road on a path that would take him down the sloping Presidio hillside. He descended slowly through the rugged scrub until he was well below the glaring headlights and the traffic roar. Once he was in position, he gently put down the gas can and looked up at the looming superstructure that towered above him. His eyes traced the vague ghost of the support cable outline back down to the hillside, where it vanished into a deep, concrete caisson. Twenty-six thousand steel wires wound themselves into a spine that held the bridge erect. He closed his eyes and traced the cable into the hillside, until . . . *Yes. There*. The target point jumped out at him. It was time to start.

Breathing deeply, he closed his eyes. In seconds he could start to feel it. In less than a minute, his spine was tingling with energy rising up through him, growing stronger. In a minute, his whole body started to quiver, then shudder violently. Release. *Release!* it shrieked to him. He clenched his jaw and his breath hissed through his teeth while his pulse thundered through him at three times normal speed. *Another minute . . . a second. Nowwww!*

The dammed-up mental fire exploded out of him, flashing upward and pounding into the already weakened spot in the cable. A single strand parted, and another and a third . . . a dozen . . . a hundred. Yes. It was going.

The support cable is the Achilles' heel of a suspension bridge. It balances the incredible strain on the towers and stabilizes the road surface. When it is severed, the vertical wires are forced to carry ten times the weight they were meant to bear. As they give way, they put more and more strain on the support towers. Above Trevor, the southeast support cable was pulling itself apart.

Bleary and exhausted, Trevor grabbed the gas can and scrambled up the slick, craggy hillside like a spent mountain climber. In a few minutes, he was back at the observation platform, where he would wait and watch.

2

There is only one universal constant and it is change.

—L. L. Vasiliev

Dan Terrell's feet hurt from all the walking, and he was harassed by the crush of northbound traffic that had blocked him in and slowed him to a crawl. And driving Sue's unfamiliar Ford wagon didn't help things at all. It steered like a bus. But they needed it to get all the paintings to the gallery in time for the showing. Then they'd had to take rambunctious ten-year-old Tom and his eight-year-old partner in crime Amy with them after the sitter had called in sick.

Taking the kids had been a big mistake. After two hours of viewers and browsers, Amy was bored blue and Tommy had decided to take off and explore. Dan coralled him in the bookstore next door and took them both to the car until the showing was over. After Sue had spent another half hour greening up buyers and critics, she'd suggested a side trip to the De Young Museum. There they could have a quiet lunch while the kids could roam through the exhibits without shredding their good clothes. It was fun but it stretched out the day, and everyone was tired when they got into the homebound holiday traffic.

Dan glanced at the line of cars that crept ahead of him to the Presidio Viaduct approach to the Golden Gate Bridge. His eyes flickered across to Sue, once, twice. She didn't move. *Asleep.* His fiery little brunette had slipped out of her shoes and snuggled her feet near the heating vent. *The woman can sleep anywhere.*

Though he may have been a little miffed that there was no conversation to break the monotony, he was really glad she'd drifted off. It had been a momentous day for her. She'd worked for months to get her first showing, and he had watched as a hobby slipped into a profession. There wasn't a water color or an oil left in the Terrell home in Belvedere. Dan kidded himself that he might soon be able to stop hustling up annuity accounts for Western Equity and live on his professional artist wife's income.

Glad I got the petite artist sister instead of the tall, scientific one. Dan had only had one date with Sue's older sister before the woman who slept across from him had zeroed in. They were married a month later. After eleven years they were still in love, which Dan thought a major victory by the standards of modern American marriage.

The station wagon had crawled through the Viaduct Tunnel and the bridge was almost in sight. Dan watched as the incoming fog coated the windshield in a fine spray. He snapped on the wipers and thumbed the washer to clear the grimy mist.

In the distance he could start to see the bridge towers dimly. High above the roadway, the tower aircraft beacons flashed red once a second, creating intermittent crimson halos. Dan looked at the fog and then at his watch. His hopes to catch the last half of the Lakers game faded in the forest of brakelights ahead. In the rear-view mirror an even longer line of headlights crept slowly forward. Dan reached into a damp shirt pocket and fingered the toll.

"Gimme it. It's mine." Tom's ten-year-old voice threatened his sister in the back seat.

Amy grabbed for the pillow that her older brother had snatched from under her head. "Mommy said for us to share. Now, give it back."

Each held a corner of the battered pillow as they tugged it back and forth. "It's mine. You can have it when I say you can." Tom's thin voice had a shrill, thin edge to it.

Amy moved to her last resort. "Dadeeeeee! Tommy won't share the pillow. Tell him what Mommy said."

Dan checked the road ahead and turned his head back to them for a second. "Give her the pillow, Tom."

"But, Dad—"

"No buts. Give her the pillow. You can have it later. If there are any more fights, there'll be no TV for either of you." He waited a second and the rear seat fell into an exaggerated silence. Tom threw the pillow at his sister and sulked off to read a comic book by the light from the car to the rear. Every inch an eight-year-old young lady, Amy fluffed the pillow and, before retiring, stuck her tongue out as a sign of both defiance and victory over her brother.

Susan opened her eyes and stretched. Dan glanced over for a second as she arched her back, stretching the line of her breasts against the black blouse. Catlike, she stretched one shoulder and then the other, then looked across at her husband. "That battle didn't seem to last very long. What did you tell them? I was just waking up."

"Let's see. The rack, the wheel and dismemberment didn't have any effect." His voice lowered to a stage whisper. "No TV was the last. That one did it."

They laughed. She leaned across playfully and placed a hand on his thigh. His groin tingled. She snuggled her head against his shoulder and he could feel the smooth silk of her hair against his cheek. The drive home seemed longer all the time.

As they passed the observation deck near the bridge ramp, Dan glanced across the traffic to see a single car and a lone pedestrian leaning against one of the telescopes. He thought it odd that a tourist would be out in the March drizzle. He shrugged and let the thought slide past.

On the observation deck, Trevor Lewis zipped the windbreaker up to his neck and glanced at his watch. Soon.

Two hundred feet below, Stanford photography major Ken Frankovich knelt and gently adjusted the speed on the weather-capped Minolta. He had spent the better part of an hour getting the tripod into position and he wasn't going to let the fog stop him from shooting. The idea was to get a roll of shots that traced the looming underpinning against the dusk and fog. It would cement an *A* on his portfolio.

For Ken there were but two passions: skiing and photography. It was an excess of the former that had forced him under the bridge. He'd blown the written part of the midterm. *What the hell's essay writing got to do with* real *photography?* Even the professors who clucked at Ken's borderline academic average had to admit that he had the makings of a brilliant and dedicated photographer. His studies were artistically better than most of theirs and they knew it. So did Ken.

He inserted the plunger and squinted up. In a minute he could run off a roll to take into the darkroom tomorrow. He could hear the roadway traffic roaring above him and was glad he didn't have to head north after the shooting was over.

Almost a mile to the north, Bobby Collins's huge black ham of a hand gently slipped the stick into the third of the gas tanker's twelve forward gears. He eased out the clutch and gripped the wheel tightly with his left hand while his right flicked forward and snapped on the yellow fog beams. He glanced to the right mirror and snapped on the lane-change lights. He had five more gears to get through before he could coast on the downslope side of the bridge. If all went well, he'd drop off the rig in forty-five minutes and pick up double-time and a half for four hours' work.

Suddenly, there was a flash in the right mirror. A Challenger had ranged up on the right side and now the driver, no more than a kid by his looks, down-shifted to pass. Bobby could see that there were two couples and a guitar in the car. The two kids in the back passed a suspicious-looking paper bag back and forth between them. Bobby half sighed and half grunted. *Damn honky kids passin' on the right.* He wouldn't have minded so much if he'd been lugging cargo. But a half-full gas rig was dangerous. He'd be happy when he parked it downtown. Third gear screamed and Bobby dutifully slid the rig into fourth.

On the Presidio observation platform, Trevor Lewis's pulsar watch flashed ten past five.

Ken Frankovich had shot five exposures of the thirty-six on the roll, when something started to go wrong. A slight but nagging vibration was starting to wobble the image. He reached down and checked the tripod legs again, then peeked through the reflex lens for a second. It was still there, a little worse. *Tremor? Passing truck? Son of a bitch!* Then, as quickly as it came, it was gone. He nudged the focus and started shooting again. He had shot five more pictures of the underpinning when he started to hear it.

It was a low, ominous rumble from deep inside the Presidio hillside, where steel that was somehow no longer steel sheared away from concrete. The sound grew to a moan as the cable sagged, pulling free by a few feet from its bed like a tooth yielding to a dentist's pliers. A rain of tiny concrete fragments peppered Ken and he reached for the Minolta, pulling it from the tripod. He dropped to his knees, propped his elbows against the slope of the hill and flicked the settings, praying that they were right. He knew . . . deep inside. He could feel it. The bridge was dying, and he was getting it on film. This was Pulitzer Prize stuff, if he could only hold on for a few more seconds before he had to run. He got off five more shots of the disintegrating caisson when he heard the first explosion.

It sounded like a rifle shot. There was another, and a third. Three hundred feet above, two-inch-thick road support wires were exploding under a strain they were never meant to bear. Suddenly free of the agonizing pull, the wires whistled upward, lashing themselves into fragments that rained down, clanging on the roadway and the roofs of cars. Each explosion increased the pull on the almost severed support cable.

Ken furiously snapped the last few pictures and wound the neckstrap around his wrist. He was going to need both hands. He ran, skidded and slid down and to the right, away from the doomed superstructure. Like a fist, the concussion behind him pitched him off his feet.

With the shriek of a tortured, dying animal, the cable end had snapped free of the hillside. Anchored by the tower at the other end, the cable swung down and outward like a pendulum. Ken looked back in time to see it swinging down toward him. There wouldn't be time to move out of the way. He felt suddenly calm, almost euphoric, as he watched it gather speed. *What a hell of a shot that would ma—* The cable smashed into him like an express train, killing him instantly, and the force of the impact hurled his body out into the bay like a discarded toy. Snapped free of his wrist by the blow, the film-loaded camera tumbled away down the Presidio hillside and fell softly into a small bush.

Far above, Trevor Lewis was making observations and careful mental notes.

Sue Terrell felt the tremor before Dan and the kids did. *Earthquake?* The three of them had grown up with them, while she only read of them in books during her early life in New Jersey. *Dear God! On the bridge in the middle of an earthquake.* Her eyes flashed toward Dan as a wash of cold fear tightened her stomach.

Dan's eyes turned to meet hers. *Yes. I felt it too.* He glanced in the rear-view mirror. The image wavered and danced. Something was terribly wrong with the bridge. And they were hemmed in by a wall of traffic both ahead and behind.

In a few seconds, the bridge started to dance, slowly wavering from side to side. Cars ahead jammed on brakes, causing hundreds of rear-end collisions, most of them at low speeds. It only took a second's glance through the windshield for Dan to see that there was no way they were going to get off the bridge in that direction. In the distance forward, Dan could see a man running between the rows of cars, back past the station wagon. He had left his car and was trying to escape the bridge.

In an instant, Dan realized that if the sway got worse, there was a chance that the Terrell car might become a tomb for all four of them. He could feel Sue's hand claw at his arm with unusual strength. She was fighting the edge of panic.

"Danny? Honey? What—"

The cable explosion behind them slid the car almost a foot to the right. Like the floor in a nightmare funhouse, the road surface was starting to tilt slowly. Dan knew that the man who'd abandoned his car and dashed back across the bridge had been right. He stabbed at the seatbelt button and opened the door.

"Out. Come on." He pulled Sue across the driver's seat and half out the door before she realized what he was doing. He ripped open the rear door and grabbed Amy, who was half asleep on the pillow she'd won from Tom. Startled, the little girl started to cry. Dan pulled her to her feet and gripped her head in both his hands. It was getting hard to stand on the tilting road, and in the distance, through the fog, he could hear the scream of steel shearing. "Come on, Amy. Take my hand. Run with me." He grabbed her hand like a vise.

Sue had run around the car and pulled open the other door, grabbing Tom. She yelled across to Dan. "Ahead?"

"No. Back. It's only a couple of hundred yards. We'll run between the lanes. Come on. Quick!"

Amy pulled back against her father's hand. "I want Jennifer. Daddy, I can't leave Jennifer."

"We'll get another Jennifer. Come on." He half dragged and half pulled her as she started to cry. She'd had the beat-up rag doll since she'd been three, but Dan didn't dare go back.

With the support cable useless, the half-inch-thick vertical wires were unraveling or parting or simply exploding under the strain. As each one surrendered to the weight being placed on it, the next one had to bear still more. With the forces set in motion, there was no stopping the process. The stress was cumulative, with each wire parting faster than the previous one. With the wires collapsing, the entire mountainous weight of the center of the bridge span was placed on the towers that soared almost seven hundred feet up from the surface of the bay.

It was only a matter of minutes from the time that the support cable pulled free of the hillside until the incredible torque became too much for its twin on the other side of the bridge approach. With a sickening shriek, it too ripped free of its anchoring caisson and swung outward, smashing a hundred tons of steel into the already groaning south tower.

The delicate lattice of stress girders that stabilized the underside of the road surface started to bear weight from a direction that the bridge engineers had never expected. In a minute, they were starting to rip loose from their mountings and fell like a rain of steel into the bay. With much of the underpinning gone, and with the last of the wires shattering overhead, the full weight of half the bridge was starting to etch a death sentence into the concrete and steel fabric of the south tower.

The towers of any suspension bridge are not designed in a single piece. They're hollow so that they can carry their own weight as well as everything they're meant to support. Inside the south tower, twenty thousand coffin-like cells started to press inward on themselves. By the time a hundred of them had collapsed, there was not enough strength left in the structure to carry the weight of the inner stretch of cable. When that went, the roadway would have only a minute or two to live.

The Terrells ran single file and at a steeper angle every minute as the road seemed to sag farther. Dan and Amy passed the front door of a Cadillac a fraction of a second before the driver, wide-eyed in panic, hurled open the door to escape. Sue screamed as the opening door slammed into her. She and Tommy fell in a heap.

Dan skidded to a stop on the steep incline and tried to turn back. But in seconds the road had filled with drivers fleeing their cars and trying to make it to safety. Dan could make no headway against the growing sea of people. Dan could see that his wife and son were trying to get to their feet, when a man slammed into them from behind. In a second, two more people had hit the pile-up, trying to claw their way past. In a few seconds, Dan could see that his wife and son were hopelessly tangled in the midst of a dozen terrified, squirming bodies.

Falling from more than five hundred feet overhead, an outer section of the south tower impacted directly on the pile of bodies. Dan watched horrified as the steel snuffed out the lives of his wife and son. There was nothing he could do. Nothing. He scooped Amy up in his arms and started to run like a man running ahead of a tidal wave. A sea of humanity flowing southward was screaming and clawing its way off the bridge. Terrified of looking back, Dan plowed through them.

Bobby Collins was at midspan in the cab of the gas tanker when he felt the rumble. The roadway roared and lurched down and to his left. Bobby steered the rig slightly to the right to compensate. His high cab and piercing fog lights let him see farther ahead than anyone in a passenger auto might have. In the distance, the southbound roadway curved down, then back up like a banked racetrack turn. *Jesus Christ—the bridge.*

He drove the accelerator to the floor and slammed the screaming engine into the next gear. The downward slope was starting to help him now. The speedometer nudged up to fifty. The weird slope was still ahead. The only chance he had was to roar through it at top speed, before the rig ripped away from the tractor and blew up, incinerating him.

He drove the rig into the eleventh forward speed and leaned on the air horn. Directly in front of him was the Challenger that had passed him on the right earlier. He bounced his fist against the horn stud, creating a staccato pattern of sound. He saw the driver look in the mirror and gestured ahead. There was a good chance that the kid couldn't see the dip in the road looming up ahead.

Suddenly, the Challenger accelerated. The driver had seen it. He was going to try to get through the same way Bobby was. He watched as the small, light car hit the downslope into the belly of the disintegrating roadway. He knew a split second before they did that the kids weren't going to make it. The little car was too light and the sink hole that had once been a bridge surface whipped the Challenger upward and to the right the way a ski jump would hurl a skier skyward.

Bobby was a few seconds behind them and the road had tilted more. The speedometer was at sixty when he roared down into the sloping curve. He downshifted two gears, accelerating into the downgrade, knowing that the action might throw a tie rod or send a piston hurtling up through the hood. But the laboring engine responded, surging forward. He sideswiped a small car as he came out of the incline but he hardly noticed. *I'm gonna make it—I'm gonna live!*

He got to the other side before the superstructure started to fall. The next problem was slowing the truck down so he could negotiate the sharp turn into the Viaduct. Bobby started to run the big rig down through the gears. He might tear up a tollbooth, but, Sweet Jesus, he was going to live!

Dan Terrell was numb with exhaustion. He felt as if he'd been running up a mountain with little Amy crying in his arms. At six feet four, he had smashed through running crowds from behind, knocking them down and not looking back. He passed the bridge ramp and angled left off the road, falling forward and rolling down the embankment. His right arm smashed into something, and he screamed with pain. Amy slid away from him.

In a few seconds, both of them stopped moving.

The pain from the forearm was washing over him and he wasn't sure if he'd pass out or vomit from it. His breath came in hot, quick gasps.

"Daddy?"

He squinted through the pain, toward Amy. She crept up to him from a few feet below on the steeply raked incline. Her face was daubed with leaves and dirt. Her eyes were wide, uncomprehending.

"Where are Mom and Tommy? They—they were right behind us."

Dan reached down with his left hand and pulled her awkwardly up to him. The movement sent a flare of pain flashing through his right arm. He held her to him and pressed her hard against his chest to shelter her somewhat from the hideous sounds coming up from the Golden Gate. It would be more than an hour before the last of them drowned or were pulled from the cold dark water. It would be almost that long before they found the unconscious Dan Terrell still gripping his daughter.

On the observation deck, Trevor Lewis clung tightly to one of the ten-cent telescopes for support. He hadn't really believed it could work until he'd felt the first rumbling. And now he was overwhelmed by it. He pushed away the shock as best he could and tried to record in his memory the sequence and the details. They would become the fabric of his report.

It was three minutes after the cable pulled loose that he realized that the chances were good that the bridge might not fall, though it certainly would be crippled. He couldn't wait to see more, not with fire and police units moving onto the bridge from all directions. He started back to the small, bleak parking lot as he heard the first of them.

He started the VW engine and stopped himself from instinctively turning the lights on. He would ride dark until he got to the tunnel. Still rattled from what he'd witnessed, he let the clutch out too fast and stalled the VW at the ramp entrance. That was the first time that he heard the high-pitched roar of the screaming truck engine.

Bobby was frantically downshifting and rhythmically tapping the huge air-over-hydraulic brake system. He still had to lose more than twenty miles an hour in order to stop the trailer from slewing out and flying off the road as he moved into the dark, treacherous Viaduct turn. But the immense forces of momentum were challenging his brakes and gears. He was going to hit the curve too fast.

The eight tires on the trailer began to slide out toward the road edge. Bobby felt them start to go and decided to take a desperate chance. He jammed a foot down on the brake system and spun the steering wheel hard left. As air screamed from the brakes, the cab jackknifed against the side of the huge trailer. For a terrifying moment, nothing happened and Bobby thought that he and the trailer were going out across the observation deck and down the hillside together.

Unable to overcome the inertia of its movement, the trailer started to pivot outward. A scream of suddenly released air and ripping metal warned that the trailer was ripping free of the tractor. Bobby jammed his foot to the floor. The trailer ripped free and started to skid sideways across the parking lot of the observation deck. Suddenly, the tractor tires blew, skewing the tractor across two lanes.

As the cab spun and Bobby frantically tried to keep the skid under control, he could see the trailer starting to tumble across the parking lot. The little car! It was going to hit the little VW. He could see the man standing half in and half out of the door, watching the trailer bear down on him.

The huge metal tank struck the man, crushing him before he had a chance to scream. The tank rammed the VW and ruptured itself on jagged pieces of the engine. It was a fraction of a second later when the hot metal touched the high-test gasoline. The blast incinerated the remains of Trevor Lewis and turned the small car into hotter fragments of metal that sprayed out across the hillside.

Bobby was a hundred yards south when the cab came to a stop. He scrambled down and started to run toward the tunnel entrance, out of range of a possible explosion in the tractor's gas tank. He had gotten away with only some cuts and bruises. He was one of the few survivors.

3

We dare to contend that the development of parapsychology will sometime turn the whole of our civilisation to a new path.

—R. Kherumian,
French parapsychologist

Jerry Tanner reached down and tucked the blankets around his daughter Crissy. She reached up and gave him as crushing a hug as only a seven-year-old could. This was followed by a kiss that brushed the stiff-bristled beard that she couldn't remember her father ever being without.

"Yucch. Scratchy."

Jerry laughed. "Good night, Angel. Get right to sleep, now. You have school tomorrow."

Crissy was yawning and stretching as Jerry slipped out of the room and snapped off the light. He stretched upward and lightly tapped his outstretched fingertips on the hall ceiling. At six two, he could just manage to brush his long arms against the ceiling of any room of the suburban split-level where he and Eve had lived since just after they married. Daddy touching the ceiling had been an unending source of amusement to Crissy for as long as he could rembember. But now that she was getting to be a hefty forty-five pounds,

lifting her up so she could do the same was getting to
be a chore. He pondered spending the next seven years
doing it with the second Tanner child; a boy, the doc-
tors said it would be. He'd probably be heavier and
stronger than Crissy when he got to be her age. Jerry
pushed the consideration away for the moment. After
all, little "what's his name" wouldn't be born for four
months, if Eve's pregnancy went to term. *If.*

Since Crissy, Eve had started three pregnancies, all
of them ending in spontaneous abortion in the third
or fourth month. But this time, there was reason to be
optimistic. Eve was well into her fifth month, and according to Chet Kumasaka and two of the best obstet-
rics friends that Jerry's M.D. colleagues could round
up, this pregnancy had a better chance than any of the
others to date. Crissy was going to have a little brother,
and she'd put enough faith into it that she was getting
a case of sibling-angst, now that Eve's stomach was
starting to swell. Crissy's question had been asked with
some trepidation. *Are you and Mommy going to love
him more?* He made a mental note to give her more
time in the next months in addition to making things
as easy as possible for Eve.

As Jerry stretched again, he could feel the first
vague throbs of a headache start to slide up from the
back of his neck. Easter Sunday with Eve's relatives
had been about the same as all of the others spent
with the Lundquists—tense, tedious and a trifle boring. *Are you really sure about this pregnancy, Eve
darling? After all, you're thirty-five. That's getting a
bit old to have another one.* And then there had been
the polite yet thoroughly uncomprehending questions
about Jerry's promotion. *There must be a lot of money
to be made in all of that parapsychology stuff that
Jerry studies. Does "project director" mean that you'll
be making a lot more money? Will you still have to
work there with him?*

Jerry figured it was a trade-off. The extra manhattan he sipped his way through had been an anesthetic for the questions and the banality of the conversation. The headache he was starting to feel was an installment payment for the anesthesia. He shrugged and strode off to the bathroom in search of an aspirin. He felt like something of a hypocrite. It had been less than a year ago that he published *Consciousness: A Study in Human Potential.* It was there that he'd sung the praises of mental mastery of such things as headaches and allergies. While the book had done as well as many others on the same subject, it was clear to Jerry as he reached for the bottle in the medicine cabinet that he couldn't take his own advice.

He looked at himself in the bathroom mirror as he put the bottle back in the cabinet. The face that looked back at him was lean and angular, with piercing blue eyes and a well-trimmed black beard that was salted with flecks of gray. On the right side of his face, like the tip of an iceberg, a slender red scar protruded above the beard line. It was the reminder of a bout with a paranoid schizophrenic Jerry treated at a state hospital more than ten years ago.

The man, who was rather small and painfully thin, had never been violent before. So Jerry ordered him freed of restraints for the counseling sessions. It was a mistake. Jerry had only turned his back for a few seconds when the small man leaped from the chair and grabbed him from behind. They staggered across the room, knocking over furniture as Jerry tried to get the man loose. The patient repeatedly dug his nails into Jerry's cheek in an effort to gouge out an eye. The single scar, half concealed by his beard, was a reminder of that . . . and more.

In a final effort to avoid being either strangled or maimed, Jerry had lunged backward against the wall, slamming the smaller man into it to break the grip.

After the third bone-rattling impact, the patient fell limp to the floor. Seconds later, two attendants rushed in to find Jerry leaning over the desk and the patient lying on the floor—dead. The man's neck was broken.

The scar was a reminder of the dangers of over-confidence. Yet that ugly, terrifying incident, which still haunted an occasional dream, moved Jerry in the direction of success. Originally, the psychotherapeutic work was a way of gaining perspective on his first love, parapsychology. But it was also a hiatus born of hunger. Foundation grants were few and given with a degree of scorn. With the death of his patient, Jerry decided to go back to the guerrilla warfare of scrambling for grants. Perhaps there was an answer to psychosis hiding there among all the other fascinating unanswered questions. Anything would be better than counseling sessions with long-term psychotics who had been maintained for years on massive Thorazine dosages.

Jerry resigned from the hospital where the psychotherapeutic work was not only paying his bills but also feeding the research for the completion of his Ph.D. He threw out his unfinished dissertation and, girding himself for the conflict, returned to his dissertation advisor at the university. Doctor Collier sat forward in his swivel chair when Jerry made the pronouncement.

"You want to what?"

"I said, I want to change my dissertation topic."

The shock past, Collier sat back and folded his arms.

"What, pray, do you wish to change it to? I mean, considering that we are fairly close to getting the current one before the committee, isn't it a bit late to dump all the psychotherapy research and start fresh?"

"Perhaps it is, sir, but that's what I want to do. The new topic would be—" Jerry glanced at his notes. He wanted to get the wording right. "—The Psychological Relationship Between Right Hemispheric Brain Function and Parapsychological Phenomena."

"Are you serious?" Collier shook his head and stared at Jerry for a long second, as if he were a monsignor listening to the doubts in faith of a young curate. The brightest doctoral candidate in the department in a dozen years was speaking heresy and there didn't seem to be much that Collier could do about it. "Parapsychology is the darling of the lunatic fringe that hovers around the edges of true psychology. And the committee will not approve the shift of topic unless you get another mentor. Obviously, this is not an area that I am qualified to assist you in developing." Collier's tone carried the finality of the grave.

"Yes, sir. I understand that. You see. I've taken the lib—"

Collier could see it coming. "You've already got one?"

Jerry nodded with a touch of solemnity.

"It isn't Doctor Moreland, is it?"

"Yes, sir. Doctor Moreland."

That very same morning Jerry had asked Channing Moreland about assuming the advisory capacity. When he mentioned the topic, Moreland said nothing. The old man simply nodded and smiled. As the man who was considered the "senior crackpot" by his colleagues, Channing was pleased. He was gaining yet another disciple in Jerry Tanner. It was the beginning of a long and mutually profitable relationship for both men.

In the ten years that followed, both men's careers soared, thanks to Moreland's incredible diversity and Jerry's uncanny ability to devise research projects that forged clear, measurable links between hitherto unrelated fields. Channing saw in Jerry a carbon copy of his own abilities packed into a man thirty years younger. Together, they developed a presentation that won a mas-

sive grant. It was the seed money for the fledgling
Moreland Research Institute. Channing balked at using
his name for it until Jerry convinced him that just as
his Nobel Prize had helped open the treasuries of
the foundations, his name would attract research con-
tracts. He was right.

In those ten years, MRI doubled in size, then
doubled again. It engulfed the Western Research Institute, a leader in parapsychology and paraphysics research. Now it fully rivaled Rand in size and prestige,
working on dozens of research projects for the government and private industry. With management alone
threatening to devour all the time Jerry and Channing
lovingly set aside for parapsychological research, a
third member of the management triumvirate was appointed: Anton Deladier. The French Canadian had
been teetering on the top of the faltering Western
Research Institute when Channing offered him the
post of assistant director for management. Though
Deladier would have preferred to head the Paranormal
Research Division—of which Jerry had just been
named director—he accepted with considerable grace
the purely administrative post. His appointment would
allow Jerry and Channing substantially more time to
devote to the institute's new division and the myriad
projects that were starting to emerge from it. Channing
had known Deladier intermittently for more than thirty
years, and his stamp of approval was more than enough
for Jerry.

Moving down the hall past the master bedroom,
Jerry peered in to see that Eve had already gotten
into her nightgown and was starting to nod her way
to sleep while leafing through a paperback. Jerry could
not make out the title: There was a woman in an
eighteenth-century gown on the cover. Jerry felt it was
the kind of book that would irk the artistic sensibilities
of a ten year old.

After eight years of marriage, Eve Lundquist Tanner remained the most stunning woman Jerry had ever seen. It amazed him how they managed to retain the freshness in their marriage as they watched the relationships of friends and colleagues dissolving in dramatic numbers. She was tall and strikingly blond with sharp features and a dancer's litheness that made her sensuous despite the five-month fetus she carried.

"Sleeping?" His voice was a throaty whisper.

Eve turned to him. "Just resting my eyes." With the first threads of sleep pushed aside for a second, she smiled a half-inviting smile. "Why, Cap'n Butler, what didja have in mind?"

"Thank you, Scarlett, but I'm afraid I've got a headache."

She laughed explosively, reaching a free hand down to place it absently across her stomach.

"Just for that, I may get up and eat myself into a fat attack."

He shook his head in disbelief. "You're not hungry? Not after eating all day?"

She nodded. "I think I'd kill for chocolate ice cream." She shook her head. "Funny. I never had cravings with Crissy at all."

"Want me to get you some?"

She shook her head and kissed him lightly. Her lips were cool. "Nope. I can manage to get to the kitchen. Besides, you were just making sure I was bedded down. You want to get your procedures together for tomorrow, right?"

"Yeah." Jerry groaned to himself. Having a wife with whom he'd worked at the institute since their marriage meant having few secrets about work. Eve had started out as a paid test subject, whose ESP testing matrix placed her well into the "gifted" category. It was a matter of only weeks afterward that the institute had offered her a position as Jerry's research assistant, and it was two months after that that they were married.

As Eve moved in the direction of the kitchen, Jerry retreated to the den. He snapped on the TV for the basketball playoffs from the West Coast, and with the game droning in the background, he leafed through the testing parameters he would have to set up in the morning.

After reading a page or two, he noticed that the voice on TV had changed. The new voice was that of a somber-faced newscaster hunching over a mike in some foggy, dim, outdoor setting. For a second, Jerry couldn't detect any audio. Then somewhere in a distant studio, an engineer snapped on his mike.

". . . scene here almost defies description. The broken fragments of the support cable are still jutting out of the Presidio hillside and the entire road surface of the bridge is twisted and shattered like some massive and discarded toy."

"What the hell?"

Jerry leaned forward in his chair and peered at the scene.

"For more than four decades, the Golden Gate Bridge has been more than a monument to human engineering achievement. It has been the single, everlasting symbol of the city's pride . . . her self-esteem. And now, with a shattering suddenness, this incredible tragedy has left the city numb with shock and disbelief. There's no question that it will be days and perhaps even weeks before the toll in human life will be fully measured. . . ."

Suddenly, a uniformed figure strode into camera range. The announcer covered his mike and the two men conferred for a few moments before the uniformed man slipped back off camera.

"They're telling us that we have to move—right now. This area is about to be turned into a field hospital and morgue. This is Bill Peterson on the Presidio ramp of . . . what *was* San Francisco's Golden Gate Bridge."

Son of a bitch!

The camera snapped back to a studio shot. The announcer looked soberly up from his copy.

"And so, at least for the time being, all that we know here is that some sort of massive structural failure has totally crippled the Golden Gate Bridge. The initial speculation, and that's all it is at this time, is that there were upwards of a thousand cars on the roadway when all of this started, just over an hour ago. How many people were in the cars and just how high the death toll might go is still unclear. Emergency equipment is being rushed to the Bay Area from all over the state." The announcer reached up to his ear and pressed an earphone to catch an announcement. "In a few moments, we are told that we will have a statement from Governor Robert Tilden."

Jerry pushed himself to his feet and called upstairs. "Eve? Can you come down?"

"Did you win the basketball pool?"

"No. It's something else. Please come down."

Perhaps it was the note of urgency in his voice that told Eve Tanner that the time was suddenly wrong for witticisms. She came down the stairs quickly, belting a white terry-cloth robe against the chill of the ground floor. Jerry's tone had snapped her mind into full gear. She was all business. "What is it?"

Jerry pointed to the TV, where the scene had again shifted to the bridge. The twisted remnants of what had been a broad six-lane highway were visible in the background.

Jerry's eyes met hers. The only emotion he could not see in them was surprise. Something deep inside of her was searching for a memory. It was an ability Jerry had spent the better part of his career trying to harness. It was an intricate set of chemical messengers that activated a part of her mind that Eve could only fragmentarily control. It retrieved a shard of memory, or perhaps even an impulse fired from synapse to synapse. The look only lasted for an eye blink.

"The Golden Gate just collapsed—" It was Eve who had said it.

Jerry's own voice carried a sense of astonishment. "It was jammed with cars. How did you know? Did you hear it on the TV?"

He pointed to the carpeted stairs that led to the living room. The stairway might have reflected some of the words of the announcer. There was a chance that Eve, half asleep, could have stored what she heard, then played it back to herself as she saw the screen. The mechanism had been identified for decades as *déjà vu*.

Eve shook her head, then looked back to the screen. Some larger emotional impact was starting to creep into her subconscious, something that hovered just out of sight in a dark corner of her bedroom like a child's nightmare monster. She pushed it aside and turned quickly in the direction of the stairs.

Jerry reached a hand out for her. "Be careful on the stairs."

Her words were intoned, more a comment to herself than a response to Jerry.

"It can't be *déjà vu*. It was in the notebook."

She was back in seconds with a journal in which she made daily entries. She stopped and looked again at the TV.

He could see the material of the robe flutter for a second as a shudder washed over her. "Oh, dear God! Jerry? All those people." He walked out to the center of the thick, brown carpet that she loved to walk on barefoot and held her. He held his hand against the small of her back. Everything was bowstrings—spine muscles, everything. He held her until she moved away from him and looked up, tears in her eyes.

"It's here. Sweet Jesus, I could have saved them."

Eve opened the journal and pointed to a page that had been neatly dated in the upper left-hand corner of the margin, February 2, two months ago: "The Golden Gate Bridge will be *made* to collapse, with great loss of life."

He reached out his right hand and grabbed the phone from the small table next to the recliner.

Eve cocked her head. "Who are you calling?"

"Channing. I think he should know about the prediction. And I want to go through the rest of the notebook, if I may."

His eyes moved down the page to a small penciled note in the bottom margin. It had been scribbled, almost as an afterthought. "A political figure will fall from the sky to his death."

Jerry could feel a chill start to creep up his spine. It was something very primitive, some strange kind of elemental dread that couldn't be rationally explained.

"Channing Moreland." The voice at the other end was crisp.

"Channing, it's Jerry."

"Oh, hello. And a happy Easter. What's up?"

"Have you heard about the Golden Gate Bridge, Channing?"

"Yes. About fifteen minutes ago. Dear God, all those people . . . and on Easter."

"Channing, Eve predicted the event in her notebook. I'm certain it's a dead-on precognitive hit. She made the entry in February. I know she's on pregnancy leave, but I think it's something we should follow up right away."

"Agreed. Can you bring in the notebook Tuesday? And any others that we don't yet have a record of?"

"There's another thing, Channing. The entry says the bridge will be *made to fall*. That part of it is even underscored."

There was a slight pause on the other end. "Oh, I see. In that case, perhaps I should get on the phone. I would think Mike Grady might be the one to talk to."

Jerry was surprised that Channing knew the chairman of the National Security Council well enough to call him. But then, Channing seemed to have at least a casual relationship with half the population of Washington, D.C., after nearly half a century of pounding on doors for research grants.

After Jerry hung up, he curled his arm around Eve again. He punched the remote button on the TV and the screen went dark. He guided her to the couch, where they sat in silence for a few minutes. Then the strange chill came back. Jerry was conscious of it, like a wave of goosebumps sweeping across him.

Eve squirmed. "Jerry—do you feel it too?"

"Yes."

"It's not the prediction, not really. It's . . . something else, something sad. Whatever it is, it makes me want to cry."

He cradled her closer, feeling her shudder. In a few minutes, the chill that had formed around them like an icy cocoon vanished. It left them both oddly tired.

It was just after three when Eve awoke and moved away from the warmth of Jerry, who was curled against her back. Crissy was crying. She got up and shuffled toward their daughter's bedroom. It was ten minutes later when she slipped back into bed. Jerry, half aware of her getting up, stirred.

"What happened?"

"Nightmare." Eve said it through a yawn. She snuggled close to his back again. "She was being chased by monsters. Things were on fire. I got her back to sleep."

Twenty minutes later the phone rang. Jerry grabbed for it. The male voice on the other end had an official ring to it. The man identified himself as a lieutenant from the San Francisco police department. He regretted to report that Eve's sister and nephew, Susan and Tommy Terrell, were listed as missing and presumed dead in the collapse of the Golden Gate Bridge.

4

Pain makes Man think,
Thought makes Man wise,
And wisdom makes life endurable.
　　　　　　　—Okinawan proverb

The view from the executive suite at the St. Francis was breathtaking. Wednesday morning had dawned gray and chilly in the Bay Area; but by noon the view from the window was cheerier. Russian Hill was dappled by sunlight filtering its way through an intermittent screen of light clouds that swept it from the Pacific. The panorama was peppered with shades of light and dark, like a Seurat painting.

Michael Owen Grady nodded to himself. Yes. It was like a Seurat, or perhaps like an early Cézanne, with patches of color, indecipherable at close range, that coalesced brilliantly into a masterwork as the viewer retreated a few steps. But Grady could not retreat a few steps. It was ironic that he'd spent his entire career painting himself into the corner of *this* canvas. And, while the vista might be more pleasant than the one Grady had seen through the same window at dawn, the improved visibility did nothing to help him solve his problem.

In a way, Michael Owen Grady, Ph.D., national se-

curity advisor and personal friend of President Steven
Paulson, was a victim of his own success. He had become a crisis "fireman," darting from blaze to blaze.
Never in four years had he failed to quench any diplomatic or political conflagration that he stepped into.
Dozens of political cartoons had depicted Grady as a
leprechaun with a fire hose at the ready, seated on the
shoulder of a vast, hulking caricature of the President.
The contrast in sizes was just too convenient a ploy for
the political satirists to pass up. At five feet four, Grady
was dwarfed by the mass of Paulson's frame, which towered almost a foot above him. But no matter how he
was characterized, he'd been respected for his domestic
and international track record . . . until Paulson assigned
him to the Golden Gate disaster, demanding something
satisfying for the press by the end of the week.

Grady sighed as he turned from the window and
walked to the coffee table, which was covered by a small
mountain of blueprints and specifications. Around the
pile of clutter, three tired men sat in their shirtsleeves.
They drank coffee from Styrofoam cups as they stared
in silence at a heap of battered blueprints. Grady moved
back to the trio and sat in the large French provincial
chair, the one that somehow seemed too large for him.

General Carlton Biggs had spent most of the night
and morning being the spokesmen for his two colleagues. Though Leland Whittaker was the finest seis-
mologist west of Chicago and Otto Reinhardt was the
best structural engineer in the Defense Department,
they didn't have the kind of crisis fluency that Biggs had
when he spoke to Grady. Biggs had been the first black
general on the National Security Council, Grady's official inner sanctum. He had the ability to answer quickly,
usually with just what the Irishman was looking for.

As Grady sat, Biggs pointed to the topmost blueprint.

"As far as we can tell at this point, this has to be the
one. We'll know for sure when we pump it through the

computer model that Stanford's putting together." He shook his head. "But the model won't be ready to run until sometime next week. The programmers have to wade through every one of these." He ran a hand over the pile. "And the—" he looked for a moment at a notepad in front of him—"and the twenty-two hundred others that make up the entire set."

Grady folded his arms in a gesture of resignation. "The President wants something tangible to go with in the next forty-eight hours. If your estimate is that this is the exact area of initial failure, we'll simply have to take the gamble without computer verification. If we're wrong, we've lost a few days, and I'll only ask that in that case you all save me a place on the unemployment line."

They laughed explosively, more out of released tension than Grady's indomitable wit. Biggs opened the collar button of his tan army shirt and cleared his throat. "Doctor Grady?" He paused to let the tone of his voice prepare Grady for what was to follow.

"Yes?"

"There's something else about the consensus. While this schematic shows what we think was the initial fault area in the structure, we also believe that there's no way this could have happened without . . . substantial exterior intervention."

Grady blinked. "All three of you agree on that?"

Reinhardt nodded solemnly and Whittaker chimed in, glad for a second that his field was seismology and not engineering. At the moment, the risks of his profession were substantially lower than those of his engineering colleagues. His nod was little more than moral support. He was speaking out of his field.

"Why?" There was a touch of Grady's Irish in the question, a slight hint of a dare.

"At a depth of two to five feet," said Biggs, "the portion of the cable in question is stressed for what we'll call a stress/weight factor of ten. When the factor is exceeded in any way, the odds are in favor of cable structural collapse from sheer fatigue."

"The bastard just snaps. Right?"

Biggs nodded. "However, the calculated stress/weight factor on the bridge at the time of the event was an absolute maximum of five point nine."

Biggs put his hands back in his lap and waited while Grady paused, thinking. Grady looked to Whittaker. "What about seismic activity?"

Whittaker shook his head. "Not unless there was a tremor so slight that it dropped below the level of the monitoring instruments. In that case, the alterations at the bridge would not have had this impact. Simply, something too small to measure seismologically is too small to have done the damage." He finished, satisfied that he had extricated his field from the discussion.

Grady ran a hand through his thinning but still coal-black hair.

"A saboteur." It was a pronouncement.

Biggs shrugged slightly. "That's one of the possibilities."

"What are the others?"

"None of them comes close."

"Son of a bitch. Steve Paulson will have a coronary. He's got the Vice President arriving tomorrow night for the press conference Friday morning. That's when we're supposed to have this wrapped up. I guess that's out." He stopped for a minute and stroked his cheek delicately with his hand. It was an unconscious gesture, but one that Biggs had seen hundreds of times. Grady was flashing ahead in his mind to all of the other steps that the revelation of the engineers had created.

Biggs waited for the barrage of instructions.

"Carl, I want a second demolition team on site as soon as possible. I want every inch of the hillside combed for fragments or foreign residue. We'll need to place a higher priority on exact identification of every victim from both the dead and missing lists. I want a security check on every employee. Check it against the FBI listings of every potentially subversive bomb maker and crazy that they have. Also, follow up on every living survivor. We need a cross-check on everything that they saw and heard. We'll have to create a scenario from that." As Grady spoke in fast, clipped bursts, Reinhardt had slipped a calculator out of his pocket and was stabbing at the buttons. Grady was pleased to see Reinhardt react. He trusted the man in a crisis.

"Okay, Otto? How many are there?"

Reinhardt pressed the *total* button. "Two thousand three hundred and twenty-three. Do you wish to include such jobs as bridge painter?"

"I don't want to. But I think we have to, Otto. Murphy's Law, remember?"

Otto nodded as he pushed buttons. "Call it twenty-five hundred."

"What staff will be needed for the interviewing?"

Otto gestured vaguely. "How fast do you want it done?"

"Yesterday."

"Five hundred trained interviewers. They have to be able to feed all of the testimony into a central collection location. With five hundred, the raw data can be collected by Friday. It will take two or three days to machine and run for corollaries. A scenario can be printed out by . . . say, Monday afternoon."

Grady turned to Biggs. "Carl, get Chambers at the FBI. Tell him we need five hundred field agents. I don't care where he gets them. He's to have them here by tomorrow morning. Otto, you'll brief them. Assign them each five interviews."

Reinhardt nodded, resigning himself to more Styrofoam coffee cups and at least eighteen hours more without sleep.

"Mike?"

Grady's eyes snapped to Biggs. The general never used Grady's first name in a meeting. He reserved that for their private talks. It was a device to insure that Grady took him seriously. Grady braced himself. "Yes, Carl?"

"We can eliminate one part of the follow-up."

"Which?"

"The demolition team."

"Why?"

"There'd be more impact and concussion damage in the environment. The amount of explosive needed to do this job would have made a crater in the hillside. There is no evidence of a blast. There was no explosive used in this. It was something else."

Grady did not insult Carl Biggs by asking if he was sure. There was no question of it. Instead, there was another question to ask.

"Then what was used by this operative to carry out the severing of the cable?"

"I don't know. But there isn't a chance in hell that it was conventional explosives. We would have reports of a blast from Marin to Santa Cruz, given the amount of explosives needed for the job."

"I see. And there's no radiation?"

Biggs shook his head.

"What did the fucker use? A hacksaw?"

Biggs smiled. "Yeah. A big one. Seriously, explosives are out. Evidence would have been there immediately. It's got to be something else. If you want, I'll get Drawer D on the horn?"

"Drawer D" was Biggs's acronym for DAWRD: Defense Advanced Weapons Research Division. It was a small branch of the Defense Department and almost all of the projects it shepherded were farmed out to various research companies. "No. If we put it through the bureaucracy, it'll take ten times longer. Let me figure that part out. Let's get going on the interviews and see what we can manage to get into the computer."

Grady got to his feet, and all three men knew that the meeting was over.

He went to the coffee urn, poured himself a cup and stared at it for a second before moving across to the well-stocked bar and adding an ounce of bourbon to it. It was Grady's combination tranquilizer-stimulant. The alcohol kept him calm and the caffeine kept him going.

He had walked into the bedroom when he stopped suddenly at the bureau and slammed a fist down on the top of it. *Channing Moreland!* What an idiot he'd been to forget Moreland's call. He sat on the edge of the bed and picked up the phone.

Jerry Tanner had objected to Eve's flying to San Francisco. His concern was based on her pregnancy, but she wouldn't listen. She would not be deterred from looking after her dead sister's husband and lone surviving child, at least for a few days. They'd been on the flight from Newark International to San Francisco for just over an hour when she'd put her head on Jerry's shoulder and wept softly for a time. Her hand rested on her lap, as if to insure that there was still life there. It somehow counteracted a fragment of the sense of loss. Jerry curled an arm around her shoulder and could feel the sobs as they shuddered through her, almost soundlessly. In a way, he was glad to see her cry. It valved off some of the tension.

A few minutes later, she sat up and started to fumble her way through her purse for a Kleenex. She smiled unconvincingly and retreated to the ladies' room to repair her mascara.

Jerry watched her move down the aisle. Her gentle hip movement was still sensuous, inviting. He cherished the idea that it always would be something that intrigued him. There was still a mysterious quality about the woman he'd known for so long. She could be brutally frank with an evaluation of someone or a professional judgment of an idea. Yet she never divulged information without being asked. Nor did she lose her temper or cry, or rail or nag. She was a private person, in the purest sense, self-contained and yet extending a vital pseudopod of love and trust to Jerry.

He shook his head as if to dispel a muddled thought. How could such a woman seem so delicate and vulnerably feminine? He smiled to himself. If there was mystery in Eve it was something that he had needed and still did. If she was a private person, it was also because he needed someone who was private. In looking at her he could see large portions of his own personality reflected.

Jerry looked through the window. The Great Lakes were below, though Jerry couldn't be sure exactly which lake he was looking at. The huge sweeping curve of the shore arched northward, half obscured by intervening layers of clouds. His thoughts drifted along with it and stopped with the memory of Monday's conversation with Moreland. The old man had been genuinely struck by the tragic deaths. He had instantly assigned all of Jerry's project director duties to Anton Deladier, telling Jerry to take as long as was necessary to settle things on the West Coast. And, he asked, was there someone to care for Crissy? Chet Kumasaka had volunteered, as had Tom Hughes. Jerry was sure that Channing had not coerced them. He was not the kind of man who would.

Jerry had not mentioned the second prophecy to Channing, the one that he'd seen scrawled at the bottom of Eve's notebook page. It was too vague, too indefinite, not something that could be validated before the fact. But the bridge . . . the bridge was something else entirely. It was specific and tangible. He reminded himself that he would have to go to the scene at some time during his San Francisco stay. His curiosity was too great for him to stay away. There was one thing for certain. He did not want Eve to go there if there was anything he could do to prevent it.

Eve locked the door of the ladies' room behind her and stared at herself in the mirror, illuminated by the eerie fluorescent light. Her face was a disaster. Her eyes were hideously red-rimmed, and mascara had traced jagged lines down across the curve of her cheekbones. "You are a mess," she said to the woman in the mirror. She removed the eye makeup with a small dab of cream and began to reapply it.

She was not surprised that she'd cried, though she was surprised at the reason. The tears weren't for Sue or even Tommy. There was something else, some dark specter that sat in a corner of her subconscious and would not let go.

She couldn't define the feeling. It was what she'd felt when she'd first seen the newscast of the bridge disaster. It was an almost inconsolable grief that brushed by her. The feeling had returned after the plane took off from Newark Airport.

"Shit." She hissed the word through her teeth. She had started to cry again and the newly applied mascara was starting fresh jagged rivulets on her cheeks. She'd have to go through the process all over again.

Finished with the repair for the second time, Eve waited until the flush left her cheeks. It wasn't something to get upset about. It was something to get logical about, or at the very zenith of her ability it was something to get psychically intuitive about. She sighed. The zenith was something that she could rarely control. What was this grief . . . this fear . . . this *whatever* that had made her cry more in three days than she had in months? It was something that she had felt before, fifteen years in the past.

She'd been sitting in an art history lecture. Doctor Berkhoff, who was exceedingly knowledgeable and equally boring, was droning on to a class of twelve, less than half the normal attendance. It was an unusually warm Friday in November and Eve had guessed that the absent members of the class were managing to get the last rays of sunlight before the gloom of the long New Jersey winter settled in.

A student rushed in, more than half an hour late to class. Doctor Berkhoff interrupted reading his lecture notes and looked at the disheveled young man through smudged spectacles perched precariously on his nose. Eve could not help but catch the feeling right away. It was so immediate, so strong, so grief-laden. She knew. His words formed in her mind, it seemed, even before he mentally formulated them. A sob erupted from her involuntarily. The student looked at her for a second. The look in his eyes told her that he assumed she knew. He said the words slowly and with clear dramatic impact.

"President Kennedy was just killed in Dallas."

It had been the first time that there had been such an emotionally gripping precognitive reaction, that November 22 in Berkhoff's class. Though precognitive experiences had saved Eve's life as far back as childhood, the emotionally shattering tidal wave was rare . . . and now it had happened twice in four days.

She thought about the experience for a few minutes before deciding simply to file it away and do nothing. She'd wait and try to make sense of it later. It was better not to trouble Jerry with more of it now. He hovered overprotectively as it was. There was no sense in magnifying his concern, or even turning the scientist in him on to a new problem, one which he would clearly have trouble mustering the objectivity to solve. No.

She'd wait until it made more sense to her. Then she'd tell him.

It was four in the afternoon when the jet reached the stacked traffic pattern over San Francisco International. Under normal conditions, Wednesday would not have been an unusually heavy day for incoming traffic. But there were no such things as normal conditions, not since Easter Sunday night.

Without the Golden Gate Bridge, San Francisco was starting to slow down. Automobile commuting became lunacy. The Bay Bridge, the San Mateo span and the Bay Area Rapid Transit were filled to overflowing by the loss of the bridge.

At five-thirty, the flight from Newark touched the end of the runway. By six, Jerry and Eve had arrived at the meeting point, arranged in a call to Dan Terrell, Eve's brother-in-law. The normally forty-five-minute drive to Belvedere took over two hours in the thick San Francisco fog. It was half past eight when Jerry, Eve, Dan and his sister Rita finally pulled into Dan's driveway.

The Tanners had been asleep some two hours when Bobby Collins arrived at The Hangout. The bar was typical of those in the Mission District. It was too cramped to be comfortable, too dark to be atmospheric, and the music blasting from the jukebox was too loud. The place fit Bobby's mood in a way that the other three bars he'd been to that night hadn't.

Ollie Hampton spotted Bobby as soon as the huge, hulking black man came through the door. He got up from the tiny table in the corner and waved.

"Hey—*Bob?*" He cupped his hands and bellowed over the noise. Collins saw him and moved to the table, reaching out a hand.

"Hey, Ollie. What's hap'nin'?"

Hampton waved in the direction of the bartender as they sat.

"Ya know, man. Same old shit." It was clear to Hampton immediately that his friend was past halfway into an all-night drunk. Suddenly he remembered. The bridge . . . the news photo of the broken tractor . . . There'd been no name on the picture or in the story, but Ollie Hampton was dead sure the rig was Bobby's. "Were you out there?"

Bobby blinked slowly. "What? Out where? *There!* The bridge? Fuckin'-A right I was. Messed up m' shoulder. Sheeeeit, man. I get my ass outta one sling and inta another." Bobby shook his head for a minute, obviously building up a head of steam. Ollie started to feel that he shouldn't have mentioned the bridge. He reached a hand across the table and put it on the bigger man's shoulder. "Hey, brother. It's Ollie, man. S'me. Is last Sunday eatin' you up?"

"It ain't the bridge. It's today." Bobby's huge, ebony fist slammed onto the top of the table. "Goddamn that honky mother—"

Ollie started. The crowd at the bar quieted for a second. Suddenly self-conscious, Bobby waited for the volume to go back up before he went on, in a forced calm.

"Reilly." Bobby growled the name. Ollie knew. Nothing Andrew Reilly, senior dispatcher for their shipper, could do would ever be for the benefit of his black drivers. The man was the worst kind of redneck.

"What he do now?"

"I get kept in the hospital Sunday night, right? I don't get out till three or som'pin. I go home and take a drink and fall out after all the shit I went through. Then I spend most o' yesterday still havin' the shakes. Finally I go in today and that fuck Reilly's got me docked 'cause I didn't call in. I was real nice. I mean

. . . I never give him no shit before. No call for him to say that shit to me."

"What shit you mean, man?"

"He tells me, 'Go to the union,' then unda his breath calls me a dumb nigger."

Ollie could see what was coming. He looked like a man witnessing a streetcar wreck. "What did—?"

"I smacked the no-good mother in the mouth."

"No shit!"

Bobby nodded.

Suddenly, the chatter in the bar changed perceptibly. It was as if bar talk had strangely become a parody of bar talk, as if all of the customers were trying to speak in a way they thought would sound nonchalant. Bob and Ollie looked at the two white men in business suits at the door. One man stayed at the door while the other went to confer with the barkeeper. Cops. They had to be. Both Ollie and Bob knew it immediately, as did every other man in the bar.

Bob got to his feet and smiled a tight smile at Ollie.

"I'll see you around, man. You know what I mean?"

Ollie nodded. Reilly, probably with his jaw wired, would have reported Bob for assault hours ago. Ollie peered into his beer until a minute or two after Collins had gone through the men's room window. The cop at the bar turned and looked toward Ollie's table. He stopped and looked toward the front door. He wasn't sure if there'd been one or two men at the back table when he and his partner had arrived. He crossed quickly to Ollie, flashing an open wallet.

"My name's Jablonski. I'm a special agent working for the Defense Department."

He pointed back to the bar. "Bartender tells me you know a man named Collins? Robert Collins?"

"Who?"

The agent paused for a second. He knew he was starting to get the runaround.

"Robert Collins. He was one of the people on the bridge Sunday, and we're trying to find all of the people who were there. It's all a part of the investigation."

"Yeah, I know Collins."

"Could you put us in touch with him?"

"Yeah, well I could, but I ain't seen him. I heard he was on the bridge Sunday. But I ain't seen him, man, not in about two weeks now . . . or is it three?"

Jablonski tossed a card on the table. "Well, that's our number. It's pretty important."

Bridge, shit! Ollie knew they were cops. Bobby must have killed Reilly or something. "Yeah, sure man. If I see him, I'll . . . ah, tell him."

Jablonski had only been out of the bar for a few seconds when Ollie was tearing the card into small strips and winding the strips into a tortured cable.

It was eight in the morning when Jerry awoke to the distant ring of a phone. Someone answered it on the second ring and Jerry started to drift off again. A minute later Dan Terrell knocked gently at the door of the guest room.

"Jerry? It's a call for you—a Doctor Grady. He mentioned Doctor Moreland."

Jerry was rubbing the last of the sleep from his eyes as he picked up the phone in the kitchen. "Doctor Tanner."

The voice on the other end hesitated for just a second.

"Doctor Tanner? This is Michael Grady. I'm truly sorry to have to disturb you, especially at this time."

"That's all right, Mist—ah, Doctor Grady." Jerry was unused to hearing Grady referred to as anything but Mister or Presidential Advisor Grady. "You mentioned Channing Moreland to my brother-in-law?"

"Yes. I got a call from Channing the first thing Monday morning, which was right after the President tossed this investigation to my office. As it happens, we're going to need MRI to process all of the information we're accumulating. I called Channing back last night to officially retain the institute for the work. In the course of our conversation, Channing mentioned that you and Mrs. Tanner were here in San Francisco. He also mentioned why. Allow me to extend my sincerest condolences."

"Thank you."

"Doctor Tanner, I know that this is a terrible time to interrupt the arrangements that I'm sure you're involved in, but I'm going to ask if I can volunteer you, so to speak. We're going to need to assemble all of the information and evidence in a format that MRI can start to process immediately."

"You're going to want a simulation scenario, then?"

"Exactly, and we're going to need it fast. The President is breathing down our necks on this thing. He wants fast answers. I'm going to ask if I can impose on you to come out to the Presidio, so that you can brief Channing when you get back. Then, by the time you return to New Jersey, we'll have assembled a package of data that you can take back with you and the institute can start examining immediately on arrival. Is it possible for you to come out here this morning? I assure you that we wouldn't impose on you if there was any other way."

Jerry nodded wearily. "Of course, Doctor Grady."

"Naturally, the government will cover all of the expenses incurred in the trip out and back. I know that's not a fair exchange for the interruption at this ah, delicate time, but it's the best we can do."

"I understand."

"I'll have a car come out for you. Dr. Moreland gave me the address."

Jerry squinted up toward the clock. "I'll be ready."

The voice on the other end of the phone was gone.

"Jerry?" Eve stood behind him, still drowsy. "I'm going out there." It was not a question. It was a statement.

He turned and looked down at her. "I'm sorry, love. It's a mess out there. You're pregnant and there's no need for you to be there."

"I have to."

She went.

As soon as the government car emerged from the gloom of the Presidio Tunnel into the late morning sunshine, Jerry and Eve could see the barricades and police lines. There were over two hundred police and more than four times that number of government investigators. The latter wore white coveralls and, at a glance, Jerry estimated that they had been drawn from the ranks of the FAA crash investigating teams that followed in the wake of air disasters.

The entire area *did* look like a crash site. Multicolored chalk lines stretched in several directions and wide strips of engineer's tape had been pegged to portions of the road surface in an attempt to establish perspectives on the disaster. Jerry was certain that he would know their meaning all too soon.

The army colonel who'd escorted them slipped from the front seat and opened the door for the two of them. The three of them moved through the partially wrecked tollgate plaza and headed for the trailer that had become the on-site nerve center of the investigation. When they came in sight of the bridge itself, they stopped.

It was an awesome study in contrast. The day was magnificent. Fair weather clouds blew on brisk gusts of cool wind. Whitecaps dotted the waves as far as the horizon. To the north, the Marin hills were starting to turn green with the rains of the past week. But the thing that immediately drew attention to itself was the bridge.

The panoramas presented in the media were pale compared to the experience of viewing the damage firsthand. The south tower leaned at an angle toward the twisted and partially nonexistent road surface. The southern end of the six-lane strip had been torn apart, shredded by the snapping cables and falling girders. It was and would be totally impassable. More crews of white-clad men and women climbed like small white insects over the baroque sculpture of twisted metal. They were looking at the impossible, looking at the results of a force that could humble the proudest of man's accomplishments.

The colonel turned to them. "Every time I walk here, I stop and look, too."

Jerry looked at the man, whose gold slashes indicated that he was in the Corps of Engineers.

"Part of me looks and says that it couldn't have happened." He shook his head.

The colonel's brow furrowed. "Yeah. But it did. Doctor, Mrs. Tanner? We better get in to see Doctor Grady." He pointed in the direction of the trailer.

Grady rose from the small desk as the three of them came in. He registered only a moment of surprise when he saw Eve. "Doctor Tanner? I'm Mike Grady." He extended a hand while his quick blue eyes looked to Eve. "This is Mrs. Tanner?"

Jerry introduced Eve, indicating that she was a part of the research team that would be working on the bridge project. He wasn't lying. Eve had declared that she would come back to the institute for the project, despite any objection Jerry could raise.

Grady moved through the information on hand very quickly. They had established a time line for the events based on the first round of interviews with survivors. Grady said that the second round of interviews would be more thorough and would be completed by the time that the Tanners were ready to return the information to the institute.

Grady stopped talking for a moment, stifled a yawn and looked across the desk at the Tanners. "Can I get you two some coffee? I'm afraid I'm going to have to get some for myself. I've been living on it for the last week."

They both agreed and Grady moved from the desk to the percolator that bubbled in the tiny kitchen of the trailer.

Jerry conferred with Eve, then began, "Doctor Grady, we—"

Grady shook his head. "Jerry? It's Jerry, right?"

Jerry nodded.

"Call me Mike. I hate formality. I have ever since my ex-wife made it a habit to call me Michael."

Jerry smiled tentatively. "Well, ah, Mike, have you considered Pentothal or hypnosis on the interviewees who'll agree to it? Either one would allow them to sort out the jumble of memory. A lot will have been erased through shock and trauma, but the subconscious will have it recorded. It might help. But it will cost time and it's obvious that the investigation is under pressure. Presidential pressure, I would imagine, what with this being an election year."

Grady served the coffee and grinned broadly for a second as if it were a momentary respite from the pressure of the week. "I'm glad you know something about politics. Seriously, my personal goal out here is to come up with the right answers. All the President will want on a priority basis is a statement that Vice President Clearford will read to a press conference this afternoon or early this evening. The statement is simply going to be a status report, which will say that the investigation is proceeding as scheduled and that we're starting to nail down the cause of the structural failure.

After that, you two and Channing and all of the rest of the brain trust that he has back there in New Jersey can come up with the . . . *real* answers."

Jerry sensed something ominous in the pause.

"Real answers?"

"Right. And what we discuss from here on is, I'm sure I don't have to tell you, classified."

The Tanners nodded.

Grady pointed to a series of rough sketches pinned to a corkboard on the wall. There were four of them, each showing a different stage of the collapse.

"This is really conjecture at this point, but the part we're most clear about is that the southwest cable support abutment failed completely. It severed just inside the caisson and pulled out like a tooth from its socket. The rest was . . . well, dominoes. The real problem is—and this is why I've asked Channing to put as many people on it as possible—there is no natural reason for the cable to have pulled out."

Eve paused for a second with her coffee cup halfway to her lips. Her eyes riveted themselves to Grady's.

"In short, the engineers tell me that there was not enough weight or stress factor on any part of the bridge to rip the cable from the mounting. Strauss' original designs for cable stress and anchoring points allowed for an additional safety factor that does not appear to have been exceeded. We've managed to calculate that much from our preliminary computer run. It's—"

"The bridge was made to fall." Eve's voice was throaty and her words brought Grady's eyes to hers. The Irishman sighed and looked at her for a long minute before he responded. It was the thought that he couldn't get free of since yesterday at the Saint Francis.

"Exactly, Mrs. Tanner. We just don't know how. If there's any chance for a natural"—Grady said the words like a cancer victim clinging to the hope of a remission—"solution to this, I want Channing and you and your husband to find it. If it was made to happen, we want to know how. That's why I had to interrupt your visit and involve you in all of this."

Jerry looked at Eve. He wondered for a second, as he knew Eve did, if he should mention the prediction. No. There was no sense . . . not yet. He looked at Grady.

"Mike? Would it be all right if we toured the site?"

Grady gulped down the rest of the coffee and got to his feet. "I was going to suggest just that, but—" He looked at Eve and mentally tried to phrase his words before he said them.

"Perhaps Mrs. Tanner would be more comfortable here? I mean—"

Eve got to her feet. "I'm not in that delicate a condition, not yet at any rate. I'll go. If I get tired, I'll say so."

They moved out across the access ramp to a point from which Eve and Jerry could get another good look at the bridge. A dozen gulls climbed against the offshore breeze, then folded their wings and dove past them toward the dark water, diving for food. Jerry shuddered as he thought of the nightmare in the fog for Sue Terrell, little Tommy and the thousands of others. The fleeting thought of the food that the gulls might be diving for made him shudder even more.

Grady pointed off to the right, down the long Presidio slope, to a gaping hole in the hillside, where clusters of men collected and sifted grisly artifacts.

"That's the cable caisson aperture. We've collected metal fragments that I'll want you to take back for a detailed stress analysis." Grady moved back from the edge of the broken roadway and led them in the direction of a series of hastily assembled and labeled bins along the roadside. Jerry recognized them as the kind used for FAA investigations.

Grady turned to Jerry and Eve as they walked. "The search teams found a camera on the hillside early this morning. I think it was a Minolta, a professional model. It was quite a distance down the slope, and what appears to be a tripod was nearby. There's a chance that someone was snapping pictures when all of this happened, but we haven't been able to locate the photographer, not yet. Then there's also the chance that it was dumped from one of the cars. Anyway, there were a number of exposed shots on the roll, and they're being developed. We'll get the prints to you if there seems to be anything significant."

They had come abreast of the bins when Eve suddenly took Jerry's arm. Both men stopped immediately and Jerry looked down at her.

"Are you okay? Do you want to rest?"

She shook her head. "No. It's not that. That man—" She pointed to a man in white coveralls who was placing items in bins. "The thing he's carrying? Can I have a look at it?"

Jerry glanced at Grady, who immediately called to the soldier.

It was a battered, blistered lump of metal that might once have been a container of sorts. Grady looked at the red tag that had been tied to what remained of the handle. "They think it was a gasoline can. It has been badly burned. You see, there was an explosion back there not too far from the tunnel entrance. The trailer of a gas truck sheared loose from the tractor and blew up. We're still searching the area for more fragments. The truck driver was lucky. He escaped almost uninjured. We've been trying to reach him to get an interview. His truck has to have been on the road surface when everything started to break loose. Anyway . . ." He passed the can to Eve.

As she took it, she swayed toward Jerry and cried

out. Grady and Jerry grabbed her before she had a chance to fall.

She awakened on a bed in the trailer, with Jerry and Grady looking down at her. Grady had poured a shot of Irish whisky from a flask into a small paper cup. He offered it to Jerry, who shook his head. He looked down at Eve with concerned lines etched into his face.

"Welcome back. You gave us a scare."

She was clearly shaken, but managed a smile. "I'm sorry. But it wasn't what you think. It was the can. It was something about the can."

Jerry leaned close. "You *feel* something?"

She nodded, not yet able to find the words she wanted. Confused, Grady frowned at Jerry. "Feel?"

Jerry paused for a second, but could see no reason to hesitate. "Eve's a 'sensitive,' Mike. She sometimes can get powerful psychic impressions from inanimate objects. Technically it's called psychometry." He looked down at his wife. "Something specific?"

She nodded. "A man . . . a man speaking a foreign language. He's dead, I think. It has to do with the gas truck. And the can . . . it was empty. It doesn't seem to connect to gasoline at all. That part's fuzzy. The can seems more attached to water . . . something that holds flowing water. Perhaps a dam?"

"That's very interesting, Mrs. Tanner," Grady said formally. "But what does this have to do with the bridge?"

Jerry looked at him, eyebrows raised. "I think we'll find out soon enough, though you may regret it. You see, Eve predicted the fall of the bridge two months ago."

It was four A.M. the next day when Special Agent Jablonski's patience was rewarded. Bobby Collins returned, very drunk, to his apartment house in the Mission District. He was well past offering any resistance, and when they arrested him, he only made derisive comments about that "honky ex-boss." By eight A.M. he was delivered to Grady's team for interrogation.

5

*Negative energy is totally counterproductive and
perhaps even dangerous when it is allowed to
enter the realm of psychic growth. . . .*

—Madame Blavatski,
Russian psychic

"In this exploration of inner vastness, we em-
bark . . ." The speaker paused for a second, as if to
find the proper parallel.

He was Anton Deladier. He had given thirty years
of his life to merging paranormal research with be-
havioral technology into a mind control and programming system that was nothing short of brilliant. His
work along with Channing Moreland's, whose name had
become a household word as a result of his Nobel
Prize, had laid the groundwork for the massive Moreland Research Institute. As deputy director for administration under Moreland, he was in a publicity eclipse,
except to his colleagues in the field. Three hundred
of them were in this audience. And so, as far as the
small, slender French-Canadian parapsychologist was
concerned, eloquence was in order. Deladier was good
at eloquence.

". . . with Darwin on the *Beagle* . . . with Cook on the

Discovery . . . sailing toward this *terra incognita* of the human consciousness."

Unlike Channing Moreland, whose weathered Maine face betrayed his sixty years, Deladier, though only two years younger, had the face and body of a man in his middle forties. As he smiled, a gleaming row of white teeth split the deeply tanned face. His blue eyes were a mesmerizing contrast to the rest of the image. Each viewer in the audience felt an intensely personal contact. It made them hang on his words. Anton knew the effect. He played it like a master violinist might play a Stradivarius: lovingly and with practiced care. His ability to capture audiences came from skill as much as from talent. He had not given his life to research in his field without mastering a portion of it.

His hands moved out from his sides in a gesture that subtly blended benevolence and humility. "I regret that my colleague Channing Moreland could not be here tonight. I hope I have in some small way softened your anticipated disappointment at having to contend with a last-minute substitute. Thank you, very much."

The applause was abundant and enthusiastic. Deladier took it with a genuine smile. While it was true that almost half the audience had canceled bookings when it was announced that Channing Moreland was unable to speak, those who really mattered, as far as Anton was concerned, remained. The speech had been a coup of sorts.

He waited by the speaker's table for a few minutes as the crowd moved in the direction of the three elevators that served the Dinsmore Hotel's roof garden. They would take some time to disperse. The roof garden was made for small gatherings and cocktail parties rather than speaking engagements. But it was better than speaking in the main ballroom, which would have been half-empty. And the roof garden had its own special charm. Poshly placed on Central Park South, it had survived, while others of its status had drowned in rising prices and falling numbers of guests.

As the crowd milled around the elevators, Anton greeted a few colleagues who passed. As they exchanged pleasantries, Anton's glance swept the room. *Where is she?* Suddenly a hand was thrust into his. Startled, Anton looked up into the face of Tom Hughes, his coworker. Just thirty, Tom Hughes's sandy hair and chiseled good looks could have made him a model if he had not chosen academics and research instead. His boyish smile was contagious for men and irresistible for women. He nodded and flashed the best of the smile as Anton took his hand.

Seeing Hughes simply reinforced the memory of the recent defeat both of them had suffered in the appointment of Jerry Tanner to the parapsychology project director slot. It was not something that he really wanted to be reminded of and there were yet other reasons that Anton Deladier did not want to be encumbered by Tom Hughes on this night.

"You were brilliant, Anton. Absolutely brilliant. I mean I only got to hear the last few minutes of the presentation, but you had everyone on the edge of his seat." The man's grin widened into what Anton could only construe as an expression of hero worship. He mused silently for a second about how easily impressed the young actually were.

"Thank you, Tom. Glad you could manage to get here." Again Anton looked at the thinning crowd moving in the direction of the elevators. She was still not in sight. His eyes snapped back to Tom as the young man started to speak again. "Excuse me?"

"Are you staying for the rest of the program?"

"Oh, just for the things that Channing had been booked for. That will carry through tomorrow night, and I guess I'll go back home then. Are you staying?"

Tom shook his head glumly. "Afraid not. I have to

get up to Harvard this weekend and collect some research data from De Quincy's experiments."

"For . . . Doctor Tanner?"

"Yes. For our new and esteemed project director."

Anton nodded. There was an irony to the whole affair, though it was small compared to the larger irony of Anton's almost thirty-year professional relationship with Channing Moreland.

Anton could feel a small pinpoint of anger flare deep inside him. It had no business being there and still it persisted as it had for almost thirty years. He remembered how they'd spent nearly the entire weekend talking at the small conference in Portland, Maine. Moreland's university had sponsored it and Channing had hosted. He found Anton's ideas on behaviorism and ESP ability fascinating. They provided him with a fertile soil to grow the theories that later culminated in the Moreland Theory, which blended particle physics and the germ of Anton's own approach. It was followed by a massive U.S. government grant and, ultimately, the Nobel Prize, which Channing shared with a Russian doing similar research.

There was little question in Anton's mind that *he* could have been the man on the dais collecting the prize. The resentment and frustration had grown somewhat larger in the years since Gaby's death. It was her understanding that made him keep his sense of humor about the popular acclaim he never quite achieved. In his memory, Anton could still see her face. He pushed it away. The thought of Gaby only made him want to be rid of Hughes more. Luckily, he was spared having to dream up such an excuse. A matronly woman in her fifties took a few halting steps in their direction. It was clear that she wanted to say something but was unsure of how to approach him. Somehow, Tom assessed the situation quickly and decided Anton was going to be in for the woman's life story. He smiled his all-American-boy smile and looked at Anton. "Well, I have to start on Tanner's errand."

Anton watched Hughes head off in the direction of the elevators while the matron took another frightened step toward him. She was nearly his height in heels and though a little plump, was not too many years away from being what Channing Moreland might have called a "handsome woman." It would have been one of the few things that Anton would have agreed with Channing about.

"Doctor Deladier?"

"Yes." Anton smiled his podium smile.

"I have—ah, a slight problem. You see, I have something to deliver to Doctor Moreland—and, well, you're not him."

Anton could feel the ember of pain flash again. He pushed it aside.

"No."

"Well, I—ah, don't quite know how to handle this."

Anton reached out and covered her hand with his.

"Why don't you explain, as far as you are prepared to, and we'll take it from there." He again glanced around the now almost deserted roof garden. No, she wasn't there.

The woman, who had not volunteered her name, summarized her story.

"You see, Mister Deladier, my husband Charles was always a fan of this parapsychology business. He had what his family called a 'gift.' He could see things ahead of time. Well, I'm sure you know more about those things than I do, anyway . . ." Her hands clasped in front of her like a coloratura trying to reach an impossible note. "Well, Charles passed away recently."

"I'm so sorry." Dear Lord, Deladier thought, I hope she doesn't think I'm a medium who can contact her dead husband.

"It—it was cancer. A few days before he died—

that was last month—he mentioned something about a bridge being destroyed. He said it would be on Easter Sunday."

Anton could feel a tingle sweep through him. "Was it the Golden Gate?"

The woman moistened her lips and turned her head to the side slightly. She seemed embarrassed. "I'm rather sure it was the bridge he spoke of, Mister Deladier."

"Was there anything else?" he prompted. "I mean as far as your husband's 'gift' was concerned?" Secret contentions made before an event and proven afterward were as valuable as Confederate money after Richmond fell.

She nodded and reached into her purse. It took her only a second to come up with a battered envelope. Anton could see immediately that it had been prepared for a guarded delivery. It had been taped shut and sealed with a jot of wax. Either Charles was a cautious amateur psychic or no amateur at all. Anton could feel his curiosity being piqued.

The woman looked at him for a long minute, before she handed him the envelope. "This was for Doctor Moreland. Charles asked me to come to the conference and give it to him. He had been to two or three of Dr. Moreland's speeches at the Menninger Clinic. He seemed to think that Moreland would be the only one who could make sense of these *things*."

"Things?" Anton's tone carried the measured caution of a psychiatrist.

"Yes. *Things*. Predictions. That's why he sealed the letter. He mentioned something about predictions after the fact being useless."

Anton could feel his skin start to prickle. *Why did we think the same thing, this anonymous dead man and I?* He shrugged the sensation away. It was too mundane in his experience. He had loved the psychic and the occult since he was ten, when he had first felt a twinge of excitement when his sister had bought a Ouija board. At ten, he'd never asked, What will it tell us? Instead, he'd asked, what makes it work?

The woman held the envelope tightly. "Mister Deladier—ah, I mean Doctor Deladier, can you deliver this? I really have to get a plane home and I'm sure I can trust it to your hands."

He nodded, somewhat taken aback by the woman's sudden faith in him. "You can."

She was gone in the direction of the elevators a few seconds after she handed it to him. He watched her enter the car as he tucked the envelope into his jacket pocket. It would only stay there a few seconds. There was no way in the world that Anton Deladier could resist the kind of temptation that the envelope held. He'd known that as soon as the woman had mentioned the circumstances. He carefully sliced away the wax and opened the folded sheet of paper. He had just glanced at the first handwritten line, when he heard a woman's voice behind him.

"Anton?"

It was Rosemary.

Rosemary McGee was small, slender and stunning. Irish on both sides, she was raven-haired with a piercing blue-eyed stare that occasionally rivaled Anton's. Her features were sharp, with a sensuously angular quality. She looked more like twenty-five than thirty-five and the scars of her broken marriage had all but disappeared. Anton had helped the healing process.

They met two years earlier at the institute, where she was a programmer, working on the team headed by Tom Hughes. Though he was married, Tom was a hopeless womanizer and moved on Rosemary instantly. Still numb from the battering of her divorce, Rosemary spurned him and started to see Anton Deladier, himself recently bereaved, as someone she could talk to. Neither of them ever believed at the outset that the friendship would blossom into a December-May love affair. When they realized they were falling in love, he had her transferred from the computer center to his office staff. She advised him on programming matters and spent weekends with him. They managed to be sufficiently discreet so that the other members of the institute staff could only vaguely speculate on the liaison. Tom Hughes, ambitious and tied politically to the fortunes of Anton Deladier as a patron, dared not offer any objection to the transfer. Actually, Hughes was just as happy to see Rosemary out of the computer center, despite her incredible skill at devising programs. She was a constant reminder of one woman he was unable to conquer.

Anton folded the paper and slid it into the inside pocket of the natty Dior check sportcoat. He smiled down at her.

"You appeared in a puff of smoke."

She twinkled. "Magic. Actually, the puff of smoke was in the ladies' room. What were you reading, O Mighty Guru?" She took his arm and led him toward the elevators.

Anton shrugged. "It's not important. Did you see Tom Hughes? He was here earlier."

"That was the reason I retreated to the ladies' room. When that man looks at a woman, she can feel him breathing hard and drooling. It's uncomfortable. Besides, the chatter in the ladies' room is quite something to listen to. I think I'll take a recorder the next time. I bet you've become an instant erotic fantasy for more than half the women who were here." She paused and looked at him impishly. "I can't speak for the men, but there may have been some of them, too."

He folded his arms and looked fleetingly like a reproving schoolmaster.

"You are a bitch."

"You are almost right." She stepped close to him and tugged one arm from another. She folded it in hers. "I am a very horny bitch. I think listening to all that chatter in the ladies' room turned the trick."

Anton slid his arm around her slender waist. He could feel a small shudder flash through her as his fingertips slid across her ribs. "Why are we standing here?"

"The elevator, love." She reached out and stabbed at the button.

The bedroom of the suite was large and carried that easy sense of formal comfort that was possible only in vintage hotels. It was bathed in a sea of dark blue with tabbed curtains and blue walls complementing the lighter blue of the bedspreads and trim. Like a strange umbilicus, a trail of clothes, some his, some hers, stretched out to the large living room. They had dropped them as they moved from the door to the bed.

"Oh, my love." The words slipped from her in a breathy moan as she straddled his pelvis with her hips. Her hips moved upward, holding him more deeply inside of her as she felt the first swelling pulses of the orgasm start to sweep upward, swirling her along with it. As it grew, it loosened her grasp on control and her fingers dug deeply into his shoulders. She leaned forward, and her ebony hair swept slowly across his chest.

She moaned again as the first of several tidal waves swept over her, and she leaned further forward, pressing her erect nipples against Anton's chest.

As the pulses ebbed, she moved smoothly to the side and under him. His body slid over hers without losing contact. His orgasm exploded like a lightning flash, blending deliciously with the waning pulses of hers. She knew in that moment that she was as close to Anton as she would ever be; as close to opening the inner recesses of her lover as she would ever approach. As the violent series of shudders rocked him, he mumbled something in French, fragments of *Québecois*. "Ma petite . . . ma Gabe." It was the name of his dead wife. It was the ghost that Rosemary could never fight; the specter that she could never dispel. It was something she had learned to accept in the same way she had learned to accept the other darker recesses within Anton Deladier.

Later, spent and glowingly warm, they curled under the comforter. Rosemary traced a line with her fingertip along his chest. She could see the part of him that was lazily satisfied coexist with the part that had drifted away, deep in thought.

"Ten dollars for your thoughts," she whispered.

"Ten dollars?" His voice mirrored the mental distance.

"Inflation."

They laughed.

He raised his hands from her and cradled them behind his head. "Today's the fourth."

"Right. Now, let's work on the day of the week."

"No. I'm serious." There was no question that he was. She had learned some time ago that his gesture of putting his hands behind his head was a transition away from lovemaking to other things. She sighed.

"Yes it is the fourth. It is Thursday, and it's somewhere between eight and nine at night. Where do we go from there."

"Back thirty years."

"Hmmm?"

"It's an anniversary."

She could feel the slightest tension start to build in him and for a painful moment, she thought it might be the specter of Gaby again, reminding him of their anniversary. She took a deep breath and asked.

"Whose?"

"No one's, really. It's the anniversary of an event, like Pearl Harbor or Bastille Day."

"What event?"

"Hmmm?"

"What event?" She craned her neck up and looked at him. "And stop working on my curiosity."

"It is the thirtieth anniversary of an appearance I made before a House committee."

"An important one?"

"Very."

The House committee chamber was nearly empty. The visitors' gallery, often crammed with the press for the far more prestigious hearings of what was rapidly being called the "McCarthy Committee," was totally vacant. Just under thirty, Deladier sat in front of the committee table opposite four men. There was no need of microphones. The hearing outcome was spoken softly by the young congressman who had assumed the chair. The duty was distasteful; something befitting the role of freshman congressman.

"Doctor Deladier, the committee has come to a decision as regards the funding for your proposed project." The chairman, himself within a year or two of Anton's age, stopped and poured himself a glass of water.

"Considering all the facets of your proposal and the presentation which I for one am willing to admit was . . . brilliant, the committee is left with a very difficult series of decisions to make."

Anton had lost and he knew it. The rest was frippery as far as he was concerned.

The chairman went on. "Unfortunately, despite the fact that the kind of parapsychological research you propose is unusual, it is not unprecedented. What I mean is that the committee would see your project as duplication of effort in federally funded projects. We have already invested a substantial amount of research funds in the similar project being conducted by a Doctor Channing Moreland."

Rosemary could feel the bitterness of the years still inside him. "Some anniversary. Was that the first time you'd heard of Channing?"

Anton slowly shook his head. "We'd met at a conference in Maine several years before. It had been an exciting meeting, really."

He paused and she knew that there was something else coming; something more than the fact that Channing Moreland's career had proceeded to eclipse Anton's; something more than the fact that the Moreland Research Institute might well, if the fates had willed, been the Deladier Research Institute; something more than the Nobel Prize going to Moreland and making him a household word in parapsychology research.

"He certainly has come a long way since then," Anton said, suddenly coming out of his reverie.

"Who, Channing?" Rosemary asked, puzzled.

"No, the chairman."

"What about him?"

"I'll give you back that ten dollars for my thoughts if you can tell me who he was?"

She giggled. Let's see . . . Groucho Marx . . . Richard Nixon . . . Father Divine?"

"Steven Paulson."

She thought for a second, allowing the impact of what he'd said to settle.

"And that's responsible for the building of the Moreland Research Institute?"

He shook his head as if he were dismissing a foolish question, but when he spoke there was a gentleness in his tone.

"No. Not really. Paulson knows little about it. It was simply the seed. It let Channing go on and pyramid the research funds into a Nobel Prize. He was able to take the things I'd given him at the Maine conference and put them together with the kind of research he'd been doing in paraphysics and sub-atomics. He shared the prize with Sholodkin, the Russian from Leningrad. It could have been mine if he hadn't gotten that seed money first." His tone was somewhere between anger and resignation.

"There were a lot of lean years that followed. They ended when Moreland offered me the assistant direc-torship. And then—" he paused as if to look for a word. It was unusual, something Anton Deladier was not used to doing—"there's dear Doctor Tanner."

"Jerry Tanner?"

"The same."

"He's too young to have been at the committee hear-ing, isn't he?"

Deladier smiled tightly. True. Though, at the same time, he's a young Turk. He's Channing's fair-haired boy and I think he's trying to ease me out . . . assimi-late my job with the rest of his duties. Channing might be pulling the strings on that."

"You're sure?"

"It feels right. Assigning Tanner to a job that Hughes should have gotten was the first of several steps. Soon, they'll give me an assistant . . . then move me out. I've always been an irritant to Channing. Years back, when he offered me the job, it was only a matter of pity. Or perhaps his guilt."

His face, which had grown serious, split into a smile as he looked down at her. "Of course, this all may be the paranoia of an aging *Canadien.*"

"For *aging,* you're not bad." It was a mumble against his chest.

She deftly pushed herself up from the bed and Anton could see her delicately conical breasts sway as she strode nude toward the bathroom.

Anton lay on the bed, half-covered with a sheet. He could still feel her warmth. As long as it lasted, it kept the depression at bay. In that would lie a vision of failure and old age. *Perhaps there was no reason to shoot so high.* And yet, there was a part of Anton that would not let it go: that notion of ruthless competition that had put him a constant career second to Channing.

He sat up suddenly. The phone! It was in the middle of its second ring when he'd noticed it. He'd turned off the one in the bedroom earlier so that it wouldn't interrupt.

"Doctor Deladier, this is Chet."

Instantly Anton could see that there was something wrong. Chet Kumasaka was one of the M.D.'s on Tanner's project. There was no reason in the world for him to call except that there was a storm brewing at the institute.

"I can assume that something is ready to blow up? Mongol hordes have invaded the institute and are pillaging?"

"No. Just a fast-moving government project. Apparently it's blank-check stuff. It's the real reason you had to take care of Moreland's lecture. He's called an emergency meeting for eight-thirty tomorrow morning. I've already taken the liberty of canceling all of his speeches—and yours—at the conference. All I know is this has something to do with the Golden Gate investigation."

"Eight-thirty, you said?"

"Yeah. Sorry. Look, I've got a whole list here. I have to get through it and try to get home before Kim files for divorce. The Golden Gate and then this new thing have just erased most of tonight. I'll see you in the morning, Anton."

"Chet? Wait!"

"Yes?"

"What 'new thing'?"

"I haven't got time. Check the TV."

He was gone. Anton hung the phone up and walked back to the bedroom. Rosemary had come from the bathroom. "Who was that?"

Anton sat on the side of the bed. "Kumasaka. Channing's called a meeting for the morning—eight-thirty." She groaned and half put the pillow over her head.

"Something vital?" Her words were half-muffled.

"I think so. I'm canceled out here. I'll probably have to go back and get things set up. That will mean getting to the institute at seven. . . ."

He paused as he watched her get up and reach for her bra and panties.

"Enough. If you've got to be there at seven, I might as well go home now." She laughed. "I do eventually want to get some sleep without being molested. Are you going back tonight?"

He nodded. "You've got the longer drive," he said. "Go now, and I'll try to get some things together here." It was a way of saying he understood.

It was less than ten minutes later when they kissed at the door and she strode off in the direction of the elevators. Anton closed the door and headed back into the bedroom to dress.

He was in his shirtsleeves when he remembered the "new thing" that Chet had mentioned on the phone. He snapped on the TV.

The news was the same on all the channels. The Vice President of the United States was dead. Albert Clearford had been touring the site of the Golden Gate Bridge disaster when his helicopter exploded and fell from the sky like a torch. There were no survivors.

Something flickered in the back of Anton's mind. He walked to the closet and pulled the envelope from his pocket. He opened it again, this time the envelope and wax seal completely. It was there! The first item on the list. *"CLEARFORD WILL FALL FROM THE SKY TO HIS DEATH."*

His eyes moved quickly down the rest of the handwritten items on the small sheet. They were scrawled, growing wilder with each item . . . as was the tone of the statements. The later ones seemed to be a coded gibberish compared to the prediction about Clearford. But Anton knew if there was a way to make sense of it, he would do it. *He* would . . . not Channing Moreland.

He folded the paper and placed it in his wallet. There was a lot to be done.

6

When the impossible has been eliminated, whatever remains, no matter how improbable . . . is possible.

—Sir Arthur Conan Doyle

The Moreland Research Institute was vast and unusual. Formerly the Weatherstone Mansion, it had been built just off what was to become Interstate 78. It was a touch of New England in the middle of more than a hundred acres of low rolling hills and stone walls. The English manse had been built at the turn of the century by Carlton Weatherstone. According to rumor, he'd been a real estate wheeler-dealer who'd amassed a fortune after the Panic of 1898. He'd bought up land on Long Island and created what would later become the King's Point–Sand's Point that Fitzgerald immortalized as the "East Egg" and "West Egg" of Jay Gatsby. It was there that he constructed estates for families including the Strausses and the Vanderbilts. His fortune assured, Weatherstone, a small, dark Welshman, set out to create Graymoor, his own landmark, far away from high society. The house had three floors, eighty rooms, and a massive basement and wine cellar. Landscaping was done to remind Weatherstone of Wales.

Ironically, after a trip back to his homeland with his wife and only son in 1912, he booked a return passage with the people for whom he'd built many of the homes that had made him a millionaire. The Astors, the Vanderbilts and the Strausses surrounded him and his family on the voyage home . . . on the R.M.S. *Titanic.* Dying intestate, with the only possible heir in the same watery grave, Weatherstone's white elephant of a mansion created a problem for Hunterdon County. They came into possession of the estate and eventually turned it into a museum. It was to remain that way until Moreland saw it. Around the old house, the Moreland Research Institute was constructed.

The eighty rooms of the original house remained as administrative offices, labs, briefing rooms and resident staff quarters. But like the iceberg that struck the *Titanic,* the bulk of the complex was invisible, vast, below the surface. Three subterranean levels accommodated an additional research complex that seemed impregnable. At the bottommost layer, some fifty feet under the surface and perhaps a hundred yards distant from the house itself, lay perhaps the largest computer in the Western world, rivaled only by that of the Pentagon and the mountain cavern North American Air Defense complex in Colorado.

Channing Moreland's briefing room would have made a television network president green with envy. He had kept the drawing room that Weatherstone had so lovingly cherished and had added the sixteen-foot oak dining room table. Jerry remembered that during the evening staff meetings and the briefings that went long into winter nights, Channing had set a wood fire in the twelve-foot fireplace, making the place look like a setting in a Dickens novel.

But this morning there was little atmosphere. The morning sun slanted through the large windows and the room seemed to dwarf Channing, Jerry and Eve as they sat around the too-large conference table. Perhaps, Jerry thought, it was the fatigue and the jet lag combined with the energy and intensity that Channing was pouring into his briefing.

"I wasn't really surprised to get the first call from Grady, especially after what you told me about Eve's notebook prediction. It was the second call that threw me a bit. That was the one that came in after Eve got such an intense set of impressions from *that*—" Channing pointed to the battered, blasted lump of metal that sat in the middle of the conference table like a baroque centerpiece. "When Grady said that you were bringing it back along with photos and samples from the bridge cable, I put the metallurgy, computer science and half of your parapsychology group on twenty-four-hour duty. I'm glad I did, considering everything that happened after the Vice President's death."

Jerry reached for the coffeepot that sat on a tray near the gas can. He refilled his coffee cup and quickly took a sip. The last thing he wanted to be was fuzzy-headed, while Channing was so alert. "Then, Grady called right after the crash?"

Channing nodded. "Within an hour. He asked if we'd take on the additional investigation of the Vice President's death. I agreed and he sent an air force jet east with samples from the wreck and some others that match the ones from the bridge. They got here yesterday about noon and I've had them in analysis ever since." He looked for a second at his watch. "Tom and Anton should have preliminary findings any time now." He paused and looked across the table at them. The mask of the tough scientist cracked for a second. There was a touch of fatherliness beneath it.

"How are you two holding up?"

Eve Tanner managed a weak and unconvincing smile. She had gotten off the plane from the coast only to be plunged into intense research by the new crisis. After a call to her cousin Marcia, who was taking care of Crissy, she and Jerry had sped to the institute without even seeing their daughter. Eve felt herself pulled in two or three directions at once. At this point all she wanted to really do was to escape with Jerry and Crissy somewhere, anywhere, for a few days. After Sue's and Tommy's deaths, the jet lag and the baby, she was bushed.

Jerry was not feeling much better, but he was ready to muster whatever energy he had. He sensed the crackling urgency surrounding the events of the last five days. Michael Grady, a pragmatic and cautious man, was clearly alarmed by the bridge's collapse and by Eve's seeming knowledge of it. His alarm had been more than intensified by the death of the Vice President. And Channing, whose exterior blended energetic enthusiasm and scientific calm—well, it was a strange and unusual combination in Channing. Jerry had known him for a long time and he could tell that beneath the facade, something was eating at Channing, something Jerry couldn't quite penetrate . . . something frightening.

As for Moreland's question, Jerry knew he could afford honesty. "Channing, my brain feels like the bottom of an old parrot cage."

A laugh exploded out of Eve. She was on the verge of giddiness.

Channing sat back in his chair and smiled. "For me, it's just senility."

Jerry took a deep breath. He could start to feel the coffee doing its job.

"Does Grady buy our approach, Channing? It didn't seem like he did when we spoke. He's just a little too tough-minded to buy the, what do I call it, esoteric approach."

Channing shook his head. "I don't think he does.

But he's pragmatic. We're not the only ones working on the investigation. Grady said that much on the phone. I'm sure that samples were given to Rand . . . to the Stanford Research Institute and perhaps a half dozen others . . . not to mention the in-house government agencies. He'll get all of the results and massage them together in his mind and present the best case he can to the President.

"There are two reasons why we were included on all of this. Well, three, maybe. The first is that I've known Grady casually for a number of years. I don't pull punches and I don't like bureaucratic doubletalk. He knows that and I think he likes it. The second reason is that the institute has gotten big enough and diverse enough to handle several investigations at once. The third reason is timing. I called Grady Easter Sunday night, after you called me. He knew from the call that we'd be the first to be ready to accept such an investigation. He made the offer before I got a chance to mention the prediction. I'm glad I didn't, as things turned out. The prediction seemed to have more impact coming from you and Eve on the scene." He pointed to the lump of charred metal in the center of the table. "The gas can was icing on the cake. I think it was that combined with all of the other things that propelled Grady into asking us to take on the investigation of the helicopter crash that killed the Vice President."

Suddenly, a thought struck Jerry like an express train. "Oh, Jesus H. Christ!"

Eve's head snapped toward him as did Channing's.

"I forgot. In all the madness . . . I just forgot. Damn it. That's inexcusable."

"Forgot what?" Channing asked.

"The other prediction . . . the one on the same job."

Eve's jaw hung slack for a second before she shook

her head with a vehemence that betrayed the anger she felt at herself. "I did too . . . totally."

Channing looked from Jerry to Eve and then back again. "What are you two talking about?"

Jerry answered. "There was a second prediction on the same page in the notebook. In the chaos of the last few days, I'd forgotten it. We both had." He turned to Eve. "What was the exact wording?"

"A political figure will fall from the sky to his death," she said.

"I see," Channing said, nodding to himself. He paused. The technique was one Jerry recognized. Channing's lightning-fast mind was moving through all of the ramifications of the prediction and how it might best be used in his dealings with Grady. With the institute on the verge of making a large leap in terms of government credibility, the information would have to be dealt with carefully. Very carefully.

"I'm sorry, Channing," Jerry said quietly. "There's no excuse for it."

Channing shook his head. "Einstein used to forget his socks . . . and where his seminars were supposed to meet."

"I'm not Einstein," Jerry said sheepishly.

"Yes, but—" Channing started to nod to himself. "Perhaps it's better this way. I don't want to inundate Grady with too much of the kind of thing that his pragmatism might reject. Also, the general nature of the prediction could easily have meant a political leader in Outer Mongolia or Tanzania. It didn't even say an American political figure. No, it's better in a way that you didn't remember it, both of you. I'll put it in the hopper." He made a quick note on a yellow pad in front of him. "Perhaps I can use it later.

"About this." He pointed to the gas can. "Perhaps while we're waiting for some of the test results, Eve . . .

could you see if you can get any more impressions from it?"

She was sure there was little chance of getting any more impressions. The baby was sapping her strength. It made her vulnerable in a way she didn't want to be. She swept her hair back from her face in a single gesture. "I don't know, Channing."

Channing looked at her and smiled. "Try, Eve. Any shred would help."

She picked up the can gingerly.

Nothing.

She tried staring at it. Shaking it.

Again nothing.

Frustrated, she dropped it on the table with a clatter. "Sorry, Channing. There's nothing."

"I know, Eve. I know yours is not the kind of ability that bears much pushing. It's just that any other scrap I can give to Grady would help. So far, all we have is something to do with a dam or water and a man speaking a foreign language."

"A dead man, Channing. I think, a dead man," she added.

"Yes. A dead man." He shook his head. "It all seems like something out of Ian Fleming."

Suddenly, the conference room door flew open and Anton Deladier strode in with Tom Hughes in tow. Bleary-eyed, unshaven and tieless, Tom showed the results of several days of intense, mind-bending work. He carried a thick sheaf of computer paper under each arm. Anton, as usual, was impeccable. His blue suit was freshly pressed and perfectly fitted. It made him every inch the picture of a senior executive. The *Canadien*'s face was grim.

"Channing?" His voice was a low rumble—a dirge.

"Yes, Anton. Sit down, please. You too, Tom. Have we—?"

"I'm afraid we have. Perhaps it would be better if Tom briefed. He's the computer expert."

"No. This one belongs to Rosemary McGee. She plays that computer like a piano."

Tom managed a not-too-sincere smile, brushed a shock of sandy hair from his forehead, then riffled through a few pages of one of the stacks of paper. "I requested the analysis program and she produced results faster than I've ever seen before." Tom cleared his throat. "The results are highly unusual—almost unbelievable. I think the computer might be on the blink or there's an error in the program . . . my part of it, not Rosemary's."

"Knowing you, Tom," said Channing, "I'm sure that the program is perfect. And you know as well as I do that the company technicians gave the hardware a clean bill. What's the bottom line?"

"This is the run on the bridge steel sample. And this"—he patted the second pile of papers; Jerry was sure that he was treading water, unsure as to how he might launch into the results—"is a check run. They're identical." He pushed one across the conference table in Channing's direction. "The sample of the helicopter steel, or rather aluminum, is still on the high-speed printer. It'll be up in a few minutes."

"Tom?" Channing said. There was a slight edge in his voice. "What have we got? Get to the point, please?"

"The results indicate structural change . . . at the molecular level."

Channing was thunderstruck. There was just no such thing, not within all his experiences. Mechanically, it was still theoretical. Molecular alteration was the black hole of particle physics. And naturally there was only one way it could have been done. "Radiation? Trace or background?"

Tom shook his head. "No radiation at all."

"Son of a bitch." It was an intoned whisper. It was the first time Jerry could ever remember hearing Channing swear, especially in the presence of a woman. He did not look at Eve, nor did he apologize. The thoughts that were starting to form in his mind were too important to let him stop and speak.

"What is the nature of the alteration?" asked Jerry.

Tom looked down at his papers. "The sample was altered in atomic number, gross weight and valence. The structure of the steel was . . . well, softened, or made more brittle. We can't be sure. Two samples analyzed separately reacted differently. One was putty-like. The other was brittle, like china."

Channing looked up slowly. "So there were, in actuality, two alterations to achieve two planned effects?" It was not a question so much as a statement that Channing was making to himself.

Jerry realized what was going on. If some natural force destroyed the Golden Gate Bridge, the force was something that civilized man had never come in contact with before; something that required the development of an entirely new set of physical laws. The possibilities were enormous. And terrifying.

"Dear God." Deladier shook his head; it was a gesture somewhere between astonishment and incredulity. "Basic change at the molecular level, without any irradiation. How long did alchemists look for that secret? A thousand years?"

Jerry appraised Deladier. Compared to the other three men, Anton was alarmingly alert and fresh. There was not the slightest trace of fatigue in his dark, aquiline face. And what went on inside the enigmatic French Canadian was a mystery. There was no way for Jerry to get a clue as to what went on in that brilliant mind.

And Tom Hughes, sitting quietly next to Anton, seemed out of his league. He'd come in prepared to blame it on malfunctioning equipment rather than open his mind to other possibilities. Jerry was glad Tom did not get his job during the power struggle between Deladier and Moreland. Deladier fought intensely for Tom Hughes, but Jerry got the appointment. It was just more fuel, unfortunately, for the rivalry between Moreland and Deladier that went back almost three decades.

Tom scratched his head. He knew nothing about metallurgy or particle physics.

"Channing, I—"

Channing cut him off and gestured in the direction of the ream of computer paper that laboriously detailed the nature of the change in the sample. "Is there any chance at all that the sample could have altered simply by torque, pressure or perhaps stress?"

"If I may, Channing," interrupted Anton, "I don't see that there is any way in the world that a stress of G-force could have done this, not even over the bridge's life span of forty years. It is simply *not* common metal fatigue. A sample of exactly the same tensile strength and composition was run through the computer as a control. Bert Carruthers in the metallurgy lab did two sets of double stress tests and he ended by throwing up his hands. He said that the sample wasn't worth getting him here at four in the morning. As far as the sample is concerned, what happened to it is . . . well, unprecedented." He glanced at the gas can in the center of the table. It looked like a centerpiece in a surreal dream. "Is that related to the sample?"

"Yes and no, Anton," Channing said. "Let's hold off on that for just a few minutes. What I want to establish is what the change is related to. I mean, is there anything within the framework of our research that mimics this change? Some psychokinesis or paranormal force?"

Anton slowly shook his head. "Just offhand, I don't know. But . . ." He turned a cold, blue-eyed stare to Jerry. "Perhaps Doctor Tanner might help here. After all, he directs that area of the institute's operation."

It wasn't exactly an ultimatum. It was a mild challenge. Jerry tried to sweep the fatigue and mental fuzziness away as Channing looked to him.

"Effective metal distortion, either real or apparent, was around long before Uri Geller started bending spoons and stopping clocks. People have been doing that for centuries. But this is the material equivalent of something like genetic engineering. It's like altering DNA. To alter properties *that* radically, I'd say the odds are that the process was not natural."

He paused to let the impact settle. "And if it wasn't natural, it was controlled, directed and . . . carried specific intent."

Deladier rubbed his chin. "We have to eliminate outside, sophisticated technology. We have to consider satellite systems . . . and . . ."

As Deladier rattled off the possibilities, Jerry, Eve and Channing already knew. It was even dawning on Tom. There was a set of new rules for the game. They would have to learn them quickly if they were going to compete.

". . . in short, there are dozens of things that have to be checked before we can develop a paranormal line of inves—"

There was a sharp single knock at the door.

"Come in," Channing said.

Rosemary McGee came in quietly and placed another sheaf of computer paper on the table in front of Tom. She flipped it open to a marked page she knew he'd be looking for. "It's the third time we ran it," she said, half to Channing and half to Tom. Everyone in the room knew that given Rosemary's brilliance with the computer, there would be no errors in the read-out. She flashed a quick smile to Anton, then looked to the others. "It's the helicopter sample," she said quietly, then left.

The room was silent.

Tom looked up and his eyes met Channing's. "This one's aluminum . . . so the testing conditions are a little different. But . . ."

He looked back to the page for a second before his eyes returned to Channing.

"The changes in the helicopter sample are identical to those from the bridge."

"Structural alteration," Channing said. His voice was that of a man who wanted to be contradicted, who wanted to be told what he was thinking was wrong.

"Yes, Channing. At the molecular level."

So there it was. The five of them sat in silence for a moment.

Channing took a deep breath, exhaled, then spoke. "We're going to have to order some priorities . . . and rather quickly." He turned to Eve. "I'm afraid we'll have to go back to this." He pointed to the gas can. It may be our only other major clue."

Eve nodded. "I know."

Anton looked to Channing. "Channing? What—?"

"Oh, I'm sorry, Anton." He quickly explained the encounter that Jerry, Eve and Grady had had with the can at the bridge. Then he turned to Eve.

"Eve, could you go over the impressions you got from the can again?"

He didn't ask to have her examine it again. And for a reason he couldn't quite articulate, Jerry was glad he didn't.

Eve nodded, pushing a curl away from her face with the back of her hand.

"I got a strong impression of water in connection with the can—flowing water. Another image was of something that stopped the flow of water. Perhaps a dam. The last was that the can might have belonged to a man. I think he's dead. And there's an outside chance he spoke a foreign language. That was all there was." She looked to the dour faces of the four men who looked back. "This way to the egress."

They laughed briefly, and as the laughter died away, they were confronted with the truth. The images were tiny fragments of energy, perceived by Eve and translated into symbols, probably by the right side of her brain. Everyone in the room, with the exception of Tom, knew how fragile and cryptic the symbols were. The right side of the brain was artistic, but effectively illiterate. It simply shaped the images into symbols, using the most convenient framework it could find. The symbols were usually associational and, aggravatingly, they rarely made sense to the logical, mathematical left hemisphere of the brain. Channing, Jerry and Anton knew that they needed a stronger connection, an anchor of some sort. Otherwise, all that was left was a guessing game, leading to the wild-eyed speculation that Channing knew would be futile.

"Anton?" Channing's voice sounded somehow older. "Assume for the moment that the images Eve got were coherent to the sender—"

"Then," Anton interrupted, "we have to reconstruct the sender from the message rather than simply trying to identify him."

Channing, grateful for Anton's quick mind, despite the power struggle that had recently raged between the two of them, nodded. He looked at Eve.

"Eve? Could you—?"

He stopped. Eve was staring at the can. There was suddenly something odd about it—something that wasn't there before. She knew before Channing started to speak that he was going to ask her to pick the can up again. Inside, she didn't want to, though she couldn't understand why, nor did she want to appear uncooperative. She nodded absently in Channing's direction and then looked back to the can.

Suddenly, the sight of it repelled her. *Why?* A slight shudder ran through her as she felt the repulsion. Jerry saw her movement and leaned close to her.

"You okay?"

She nodded, took a deep breath and exhaled. She looked worried but rubbed her hands together as if to spark some small fire between them. Jerry remembered that her hands always got cold during an experiment.

She had managed to dispel the strange feeling that the can had started in her. And, satisfied with the warm tingling in her fingertips, she reached for the can like a surgeon reaching for an instrument.

She had only held the can free of the table for a second when it happened.

The power ripped outward and smashed through her like an explosion. Fire . . . pain . . . get away . . . away . . .

She screamed as her hands flew away from the can and it fell, clattering along the table. She started to slump forward over the table.

"Eve!" Jerry dove for her, catching her a split second before her head hit the polished maple tabletop.

Channing was already on his feet, heading for the phone.

"This is Doctor Moreland. This is an emergency. Tell Doctor Kumasaka to come to the conference room immediately. And tell him to bring a stretcher."

Eve was still unconscious when Chet Kumasaka arrived with the stretcher and two nurses. He was a small, powerfully built second-generation Japanese-American, who hefted Eve onto the stretcher with an ease that betrayed great physical strength.

"She passed out," Jerry said. There was fear in his voice.

Chet nodded as he lifted an eyelid, then took Eve's

pulse. "Looks like primary shock. I'll have to get her down to the dispensary and into a bed. I don't want to take any chances with her being five months pregnant."

Jerry hung close to the stretcher as Chet and Tom Hughes carried it to the door. He was shaking visibly and the color had drained from his face. *God, why did I get her in on this?* He looked back to Channing. "Channing, I'll be—"

Channing nodded. "Of course." He still stood at the phone. He looked down at it, then back up to Jerry. "I think I'd better call Mike Grady."

Normally, the forty-five-minute drive to the White House was a time of relaxation for Mike Grady. On most days, he'd be able to look at the Maryland hills bursting with spring and feel a tranquility.

Not today.

Today, he hunched forward over the portable desk that had been built into the back of the Mercedes 600 and tried to make sense of what was in front of him. The difficulty of the task was compounded by the fact that he'd gone almost three days with only an occasional cat nap. The first day and a half had been spent on the bridge investigation and the last was spent on the crash of Al Clearford's helicopter. He was frustrated. After all, he was a National Security Council senior advisor. How was it that he was suddenly a nursemaid to the Federal Aviation Administration and the U.S. Army Corps of Engineers? He shook his head in frustration, looking for an answer that he already knew. President Steven Paulson assigned him to head both investigations for the simplest and most insidious of all reasons—politics. Grady was a nationally known name and was considered by many to be the finest intellect since Henry Kissinger. He was known to be able to reduce massive intellectual problems to their most crucial essentials. Grady's name lent respectability to the investigation of both calamities, and speedy results for both could do nothing but enhance Paulson's chances for a second term.

But as he sat, riding through the Maryland hills, Grady found himself not caring a whit about Paulson's chances for a second term. He was going to a national security meeting and coming from a marathon meeting with General Edward Forrester, the Air Force Chief of Staff, and Mortimer Hathaway, the chairman of the FAA. He took a second to close his eyes and let the film of the accident play again in his memory:

The Vice President's modified Bell UH-1 helicopter had been descending slowly at about eight feet a second in the gathering darkness of the Golden Gate. Suddenly, it lurched slightly to the left, as if it had been caught by a sudden gust of wind. The rest happened very quickly. In a split second, the rear of the craft started to yaw to the right. In just over a second, it was in a fast, horizontal spin, like a berserk, overwound toy top.

Below, people scattered in panic. The audio portion of the video tape was lost as a mike cable was severed. The helicopter fell just over thirty feet before it exploded.

General Forrester punched the rewind button of the cassette player. "Do you want to see it again, Doctor Grady?"

Grady sat in the swivel chair at the far end of his office. Mortimer Hathaway, a man in his sixties, with more rotary-wing pilot experience than anyone in Washington, sat quietly next to Grady, looking down at a clipboard.

"No, General," Grady said. "Three times is enough. Now we need some answers." The general nodded solemnly and came across the large office to join the other two.

Grady swung his chair around so that he faced both

men. "General," he said, "you've got what—ten thousand hours in the air?"

General Forrester nodded. "Give or take a hundred, sir, in fixed-wing aircraft."

Grady turned to Hathaway. "Mort? You've got almost the same in helicopters, don't you?"

Hathaway looked up from the clipboard and nodded. "Just about."

"Then let's start putting conclusions together, shall we?"

Both men nodded and Grady could see a slight reluctance in both of them.

The two looked at one another for a second as if to come to a silent agreement about who would speak first.

It was Hathaway.

"It's usually best in cases like this to lay out the things that are immediately obvious from the evidence —in this case, the video tape. The first lurch that the ship took is something that could happen to any chopper, given the kinds of winds that blow through the Golden Gate area. The *UH-1,* we call her the Huey, is designed to take those kinds of shear forces in stride. This ship, especially, would not have been fazed by winds. She'd been modified with computerized trim tabs that made instant corrections in rotor pitch and tail-rotor angle. I think the general and I are in agreement that the first lurch is not a part of the event proper."

"Then where does the confusion start?" Grady asked.

"Well, there are two places. The first is where yaw converts to lateral spin. We think linkage failure at that point—"

Grady raised a hand. "I'm sorry. I'm not a pilot. Could you simplify?"

Hathaway nodded and folded his hands on his clipboard.

"It's Newton, Doctor Grady. The spin of the rotor creates a tendency for the entire helicopter to spin in the opposite direction. The tail rotor acts like a stabilizer. When the tail rotor fails, the ship immediately starts to spin. The action of the chopper in the film indicates its tail rotor failed."

General Forrester cleared his throat and interrupted. "We are fairly sure that there was a linkage failure there, Doctor."

"Why?" Grady snapped.

"At no time in the event are parts of the tail rotor seen to break or shatter. The prop just stops spinning. That means its power source, the linkage to the engine, malfunctioned."

Grady looked to both men. "You both agree on that?"

They nodded. "But," said Hathaway, "I'm afraid that brings up another problem. You see, the chopper had just completed a five-thousand-hour check, which included a complete inspection of the linkage assembly. All of the steps were verified. It just shouldn't have happened."

"I agree that it shouldn't have," Grady said. "Nevertheless, it did."

Forrester gestured to Grady. "Another thing that has us, well . . . confused is the explosion. You see, there was no reason for it."

Grady raised his eyebrows. "There wasn't?"

"What I think the general means is the tanks were topped off minutes before takeoff. It's the fumes in a tank that explode. The gas burns after the initial explosion. The less room in the tank for fumes, the less danger of explosion."

"You're saying the bird should have blown up on impact and not before?" Grady's question was carefully put.

"Exactly," Hathaway said. "There was not enough

centrifugal force to rupture the tanks, even in the middle of a spin. And we have to eliminate fuel leaks, as they were checked and double-checked in the just-completed routine maintenance."

Grady shrugged. "What about a hot piece of steel from that broken linkage you spoke of?"

Hathaway shook his head. "Unlikely, from the characteristics of the explosion. We agree on that, don't we, General?"

Forrester nodded. "True. The bird blew apart like she was—"

"Sabotaged?" Grady said.

Both men sat silently for a few seconds before Hathaway spoke.

"We can't conclude that, Doctor. Though, to be candid, it has entered our thinking."

"All right, what can you conclude?" Grady was starting to detect a bureaucratic shuffle from Hathaway.

"Probable mechanical failure . . . followed by a question mark. I'm afraid that's all we can say at this time."

Grady shook his head in the back of the Mercedes. He really shouldn't have expected more from them. Caution was their business. Still, their answer was not one that the President could comfortably present to the American people.

He opened the file of test findings on the bridge and helicopter samples that had been fed in from a half-dozen research institutes over the last twenty-four hours. Next to them, he placed the sheet of notes hurriedly scribbled when Moreland had called, just before he left the house. He read the notes again, then skimmed the reports. Dear God, he thought. Will old rock-headed Steve Paulson be ready for this?

Still, Moreland's data were the same as the other institutes; it was the conclusions that were different.

At least Moreland *had* conclusions, while the others just presented the data and scratched their heads. And dammit, as wild-eyed as they sounded, there was a rightness to them that Grady couldn't dismiss. He leaned back on the plush seat cushion and folded his hands behind his head. He would have to spend some time assembling a way to present all of this.

The traffic on the beltway inbound to Washington was starting to build. Grady thumbed the intercom. "Carl?" he said to the driver.

"Sir?" the gray-haired man in the driver's seat responded.

"How late will we be, do you think?"

"Perhaps ten to twelve minutes, sir. I'm sorry."

"That's all right, Carl. It gives me time to catch up." Grady reached to his briefcase and removed a tape cassette from it. He slipped it into the player and put the earpiece in. Alice Conner's voice was pleasant and soothing and Grady often wondered if he'd hired her for her sexy voice. He must have, he mused. She was horse-faced and sixty. But there was no one else in Washington who could manage to get an up-to-the-minute onto a cassette and into his car before seven-thirty in the morning. He pressed the play button.

"The following material is classified top secret and carries a security credibility of A-Two, unless otherwise specified.

"Soviet Premier Kharkov today committed twenty million tons of Soviet wheat to the African nations of Chad and Mali. In return, Premier Mgoyu of Mali and Prime Minister Aquilli of Chad granted the Soviets exploration rights for uranium and petroleum deposits in the areas now called the New Sahara. Both leaders made sure to indicate that this commitment to the Soviet Union is in no way an alteration of their neutral status as Third World powers."

Grady stopped the tape and scratched his chin for

a second. What the hell was Kharkov doing? According to the weather patterns and satellites, the Soviets had the poorest wheat crop in a quarter of a century. How could he commit twenty million tons of grain that he didn't have to spare? He snapped the tape back on.

". . . in a related happening, Premier Han T'sing of the People's Republic of China and India's President Jarawal Chanon indicated that they had reached a tentative agreement on the food crisis. Indian volunteers are marching northwest toward the Chinese border in the first stages of implementing the open lands and food agreement signed earlier this month. They will be joined by another group of laborers, whom Han T'sing has called rural émigrés. The total force numbers nearly five million. They will set up a bipartite area exclusively for food growing. The best estimates are that the area to be used is on the border of China's Tien Shan Province . . ."

There was a pause in the tape and the sound of a stifled cough. When the voice resumed, there was a less formal tone to it. "Sorry, boss. It's after midnight and this old girl's voice is starting to go. The chances are that this material will be included in Defense Secretary Clayton's cabinet briefing tomorrow. I'm glad you have to sit through that one rather than me."

Grady chuckled to himself. The chances were that Secretary of Defense Clayton would take ten minutes to say what Alice had crammed into less than one. Grady could not help but dislike the man. Clayton was an intellectual lightweight who fumbled his way through briefings and reports to the President. On a score of occasions in the four years of the Paulson administration, Clayton had made sloppy, inept mistakes that Grady as national security advisor had to rectify. God protect me from the vagaries of "practical politics," he thought. Clayton had held a full third of the convention votes during that hot summer, four years ago. The late Albert Clearford had controlled another third. Steven Paulson, our esteemed President, was the third man in the triumvirate. So Clearford and Clayton swung their votes to Paulson, enabling him to win the nomination in exchange for the plum appointments. Paulson couldn't stand either of them and thus had risen the star of Michael Grady. In the roles of national security advisor and ambassador without portfolio, Grady had supplanted both of them, though it was not something he'd come by easily. He'd have just as soon stayed at Harvard after his divorce, until he'd discovered that while academia suited his intellect, it was not nearly enough for his Irish sense of adventure. And so, he'd taken the job.

The tape stopped and Grady peered through the windshield to see the trees of Lafayette Park in the distance. Carl had shaved minutes from the driving time.

The Cabinet Room in the East Wing always reminded Grady of the inside of an expensive wallet. Everything visible, it seemed, was decorated in dark, rich wood grains and deep-stained leather. The glistening mahogany table was a twenty-foot-long sweeping oval that gently reflected soft, indirect lighting from the ceiling.

Grady raised an eyebrow as he walked into the room. He was surprised to see how few members of the cabinet and national security staff were there. Secretary of State Wilson Masterson, a bright, though rather brash black man, sat near the end of the table. Near him was Mordecai Jasper, the President's secretary of agriculture. Thomas Carlucci from HEW sat quietly at the table with Andrew Clayton from Defense, who was droning on in his part of the briefing as Grady thought he might.

At the head of the table sat President Steven Paulson. He had been called "the Farm-Boy President," and his six-foot-four stature, broad, thick features and shock of reddish hair testified to it. His hair was just starting to slide into gray at the temples and it contrasted with the trimness of his physique. When he spent time at his farm retreat in Minnesota, he exercised daily by lifting bales of hay and riding horses; he looked ten years younger than the fifty-five that Grady knew him to be. His homespun features had set every political cartoonist in the nation working on their sketchpads for four years. They tended to paint him as a dumb boy, out of place in the White House. Grady knew him to be far from that. Paulson enjoyed playing the role of bumpkin—it gave him an advantage. He had one of the finest minds in the country and tended to be harsh and abrupt with slower men. Though Grady sometimes was angered by the fact that Paulson's brilliance was more often than not directed totally toward practical politics and his approach was aggravatingly narrow, he knew Paulson was far from the bumpkin he pretended to be.

Paulson nodded to Grady, acknowledging his arrival, while Clayton was droning toward the end of his briefing.

"And so, Mister President, it would seem that the Soviets are prepared to make substantial concessions in their quest for a hundred million metric tons of wheat. . . ."

A huge plume of bluish smoke shot from the top of Andrew Clayton's pipe. Grady thought that he could be measured by the speed of the puffs; as they slowed, Clayton came to the end of a briefing.

The puffs were almost finished when Paulson interrupted. Grady groaned to himself. Clayton was in for a grilling about the things he'd mentioned in the briefing. Grady and the others would now have to sit through it.

"Ah, Andy, what's the excess wheat, real and projected, that we have available for, say, the next twelve-month period?"

Another puff. They were starting to speed up again. Grady could see that the question had Clayton tensing for an answer.

"Something on the order of seventy million metric tons, Mister President, though Mister Jasper of Agriculture"—Clayton gestured to the secretary of agriculture with his pipe—"might be better able to refine those figures."

"They're about right, Andy," Jasper said from the other side of the table.

The puffs stopped. Clayton had failed to toss the ball into Jasper's court.

"Then where are they going to get the other thirty million metric tons or so?" asked Paulson.

Clayton cleared his throat. "We think that they'll cancel their projected wheat sale to the Chinese. China, in turn, is banking on the rural émigré thing with the Indians to get a fast crop of something like sorghum. We assume that they'll artificially process it into some staple that will tide them over until their rice and wheat crops start to come in. We can assume then that the Soviets can get along domestically on the seventy million tons that we have as surplus."

"Will this deal, I mean selling wheat to them—and understand me, I don't favor it at this time—will it mean any gain in immediate or long-term defense capability?" Paulson asked the question as his huge frame hunched slightly over the end of the table.

Clayton smiled. "Sir, the concessions that could be wrested from Premier Kharkov in a SALT negotiation could give us a defense advantage for four or five years. I must emphasize that the Soviet need for wheat is urgent. Rationing has already been planned, or so the latest intelligence information indicates."

"How much?"

"Excuse me, Mister President?"

Grady recognized Clayton's technique as simplistic. So, he was sure, did the other men in the room. The secretary of defense was treading water, asking for the President to repeat the question. It was a cheap shot. But Grady was puzzled. Paulson was reaching for something. What was it?

Paulson cleared his throat. He was growing impatient. "I mean, Mister Secretary, how many nukes will we have to trade away to get how many conventional weapons from the Soviets?"

The question should not have been hard, thought Grady. Nuclear capability was the direct domain of the secretary of defense.

A huge jet of smoke shot from Clayton's pipe. "That would depend on Premier Kharkov, Mister President."

"I guess so." Paulson's voice was icy. Clayton had shucked the question badly and everyone in the room knew it. Clayton placed the pipe in an ash tray in front of him. He glanced to Secretary of State Masterson, who glanced back. "Ah, Mister President, I understand that Soviet Ambassador Gregory Luboff contacted the State Department this morning. I'm not sure how Mister Masterson interprets that action, but I would take it as a gesture of good faith. At this point, I would recommend that the President see Mister Luboff."

Masterson smiled, while Paulson's face started to redden. Grady folded his arms and closed his eyes. Clayton had again tried to toss the ball to another court. This time Masterson had been the intended recipient. Grady could see that Masterson's white, even-toothed smile had widened. He knew that the ploy would not work.

As Paulson spoke, his voice was tight, angry. "Goddamn it, don't corner me Andy. Let Luboff cool off for the rest of the day. The Russians need us more than we need them, at least for the moment."

Paulson turned to Jasper, from Agriculture.

"Jazz, if we sold the Russians seventy million metric tons of wheat, how would that alter our price supports on wheat at home?"

Jasper's answer seemed to form even before Paulson had completed the question. Next to Grady, Jasper knew Paulson better than anyone in the room. They'd met when Paulson was a freshman senator from Minnesota, who'd squeaked into his seat in a close election that filled a retirement slot. They'd cosponsored enough farm bills to get the support of every farmer in the state. Ultimately, it had put Paulson in the governor's mansion, and he'd been astute enough to stay with his expert.

Jasper folded his hands on the table as he spoke. "Any sale of more than twenty million tons would require that we go to the Congress to get raised supports. The chances are that we wouldn't get that before the fall session. And that makes it a campaign issue, Mister President."

Paulson's eyes locked on Clayton again. "What if we offer them twenty million tons, Andy?"

Clayton picked up the pipe again. "The less wheat, the fewer concessions won, Mister President." There was a tone of mild rebuke in Clayton's voice.

Grady could see that Paulson was starting to ride the edge of losing his temper.

"Mister Secretary," he queried, "what about the other twenty million tons that the Soviets have just committed to Chad and Mali?" Paulson cocked his head to the side, waiting for an answer.

Clayton was lost. "The oth—?"

Grady interrupted. It was clear that Clayton had not heard the information that Grady had gotten from his tape on the way to the White House. It was equally clear that the President *had* heard the news. "Excuse me, Mister President. Andy, Premier Kharkov committed twenty million tons of wheat to Chad and Mali in exchange for oil and uranium drilling rights in the New Sahara. At least that's the way Reuters presented the story. It couldn't have happened more than three or four hours ago. I think what the President's asking is—" Grady's eyes flashed to Paulson, who smiled. It was clear that the President didn't mind Grady getting Clayton off the hook. "How can the Soviets commit wheat they do not have, and are not likely to get, from us at least? I'm wondering that if they get a sale from us, will they be back for another soon?"

The President turned to Jasper. "What about that, Jazz?"

Jasper shook his head. "They'd consider themselves lucky to get one sale from us, Mister President. And if we sold them, say, a hundred million tons, it would double the domestic price of wheat here, in an election year. But, I'm damned if I know another place they can get it. Argentina's barely able to meet her domestic needs. So's Canada. It stumps me. It's as if Kharkov's trying to squeeze us, and he's got nothing to squeeze with . . . if you know what I mean."

Paulson hunkered forward over the table, like a man more comfortable in the role of professional football linebacker than President of the United States. He took a deep breath and exhaled slowly. "Very well, Gentlemen, I'll come up with a proposal for either a wheat sale or some alternative. That will be all for this morning."

Paulson's eyes met Grady's and there followed a quick nod that went unnoticed to any of the others in the room. The nod said "Stay," as Grady knew it would. As the rest of the men left the room, Grady went over a mental set of notes. The President beckoned Grady to the end of the table and the two sat quietly for a few seconds before the President spoke.

"You were generous this morning. That's not exactly like you."

Grady smiled. "And it's not exactly like you to pin Clayton down like he was a bug, either. I guess I just wanted to cut the horseshit and get on to business. I'm sorry, Steve; lack of sleep gets me that way."

The President rubbed his face in his large farmer's hands. "Yeah. Mike, if you added our joint sleep hours since last Sunday, they'd equal what one man should get in a night. I get testy. I guess I should thank you for shaking me loose of Andy. But that man is such a zero, I get pissed."

Grady arranged papers as he responded. "Think of your poor Irish friend. Most of the time I have to do his work for him."

"Touché. Now, what have we got on the bridge and Al Clearford's helicopter? I want to get something out today if there's a chance. I need something to start boosting my Eagleton poll . . . fast."

"Steve, the whole thing is pretty complex. I'd better start with these."

Grady opened a briefcase and removed a pile of eight-by-ten glossy prints. Six of the prints had been numbered in sequence and Grady spread them out across the table. The quality ranged from sharp to grainy, as if the photographer couldn't get the proper adjustments. The photos seemed to be of the underside of the Golden Gate Bridge.

"Where did we get these and what are they?"

"The search crew found a camera on the Presidio hillside. A tripod was close by. As close as we can figure, the photographer may have been Kenneth Fran-covich, a student at Stanford doing a photo project."

"You're not sure?"

"Well, the camera is his but he's missing. As you can see from the progression of shots the chances are good that he didn't make it out from under."

The President looked at the fifth and sixth pictures. A huge, dark shape filled the frame of one and totally obliterated the other. There was little question that they were looking at the photographic record of the last seconds in the life of the photographer, as well as the bridge.

Paulson shook his head. "Morbid."

"What, Steve?"

"A death's-eye view." He looked up at Grady. "What can we gather from these as to the cause?"

Grady had been waiting for the question. He pointed to the first photo. The curving underpinning swept outward from the dark mass of the hillside. Above the latticework of struts, the fog-softened light haloed a distant road surface. It was a creative, beautiful shot. "At this point in the sequence, it seems that there's nothing wrong at all. However, here"—he pointed to the second shot—"the main support cable has already parted from the caisson support and from the position of it, we conclude the break was several feet inside the hill. This was verified later." He moved to the next shot. "Here, the cable is starting to swing free, heading down the hill. It was only a few more seconds—two and a half, according to the photo analysis—before the cable—"

"Smashed him like a bug, didn't it?"

"Yes."

"Well, like I say, Mike, there's irony there, but what do these mean to the problem—what caused the cable to part?"

"Steve, the first thing we tried to do was eliminate

the things that couldn't have happened." He took a deep breath. He was committed to Moreland's solution and he knew it. Now he had to sell it.

"According to the finest bridge engineers and architects we could muster, and given the photo evidence of the way the cable parted, we come up with a problem. The bridge could simply not have collapsed through natural erosion, earthquake or simple metal fatigue. When Strauss built the bridge, he built in stress safety factors of twenty and thirty to one, or so they tell me. We examined the original plans and programmed them into a computer against all of the weight and shear forces that would be needed to break the cable. When we added the estimate of car weight, we still needed a force of hundreds of tons to part the cable that way."

After pointing to the second picture again, Grady gathered the glossys up and slipped them back into his briefcase. He removed a folder stamped TOP SECRET that he held in his lap as he talked. "Given that hypothesis, at the negative end of things, we had to look into the metal itself." He unrolled the long, thin strips of paper and laid both out on the table. Next to each, he placed a picture: a microscopic cross section of the samples.

He pointed to the strips of paper as he spoke. "We ran a spectrographic analysis of two cable samples. One is from the point of the metal failure. The other is from the opposite cable on the Marin County side. When we saw the differences in the read-outs, I ordered an electron microscopy done on both as a follow-up."

The most striking contrast appeared on the microscope shots. The one labeled "Marin" looked like a shot of lunar mountain peaks; a tiny microcosm of an endlessly jagged and forbidding set of metallic hills and valleys magnified three thousand times. The second photo was totally different. The surface was smooth, like polished glass. There wasn't a detectable flaw in it.

"The metallurgists tell me that steel's strength and flexibility are created at the rolling plant. The long chains of molecules that were forged in the furnace are piled up on one another again and again. The blacksmith did that in the shop with a hammer a hundred years ago. At any rate, when you separate this grade of steel by pulling or shearing, you get this result." He pointed to the hills and jagged peaks.

The President pointed to the other shot. "And when do you get this one?"

"That's just it, Mister President. You don't." Grady cringed at the way he had to put it. Still, it was the best way he could think of.

"Come on, Mike. What are you saying?"

"Initially, we thought that it had been melted, in much the same way as delicate incisions are made with surgical lasers."

"And?" Grady was starting to see that he was trying Paulson's patience. It was something that he did not want to do. But he really had no other choice.

"And, going back to the earlier photos we saw, there is no way that a laser with that incredibly fine precision could manage to cut through so much steel fast enough to create the effect shown in the pictures. To make a long story short, Steve, the steel wasn't ripped, pulled apart, cut or melted. It was . . . well, altered."

Paulson's look stopped Grady. He was getting the idea. "Sabotage, then?"

"Sabotage." Grady's voice was just above a whisper.

"All right." Paulson spoke slowly, like a man arranging the terms of a delicate treaty. "What kind of weapon and who used it?"

"We don't know of a weapon technology in the

world that can do this at this time, Steve. And, that should tell you that we haven't any answer to the second question either."

Paulson got up from the table and crossed to a table. He opened an ornate cigar box that in actuality contained a telephone. "Millie, see if Andy Clayton has left the building. If he hasn't, send him to the Cabinet Room, please."

The woman's voice had the slightest touch of Scandinavian in it. "Yes, Mister President. A messenger just arrived in a huff looking for him. I think they're just down the hall. I'll send him up now."

Paulson looked to Grady as he hung up. "Let's see if Clayton knows if there's any kind of system. He's Defense. He should."

"He won't know, Steve."

"Wha—? Didn't you brief him on this."

"No."

"Well, why the hell not, Mike?" Paulson calmed for a second. His voice was quieter as he resumed. "Look, I don't have any illusions about Andy Clayton's abilities. I told you that when I first appointed you to the National Defense Council operation. You know that and I know that. In addition, Andy Clayton is one of the more obnoxious men that either of us knows. But if there's a chance that he knows of something experimental that might have been able to do this, let's get his input."

Grady shook his head slowly. "He won't know of anything, Steve."

Paulson reached up and ran a hand through a thick head of sandy gray hair. "For Christ's sake, Mike. What makes you so all-fired sure?"

"Ultrasonics, subsonics, heat or stress . . . nothing could have done to that steel what we see in the photo. It isn't steel any more, Steve. It's an isotope, damn near another element. And there isn't the barest trace of radiation that might account for that. Something got into the structure of the steel down at the molecular level and—I don't know, ordered the damn molecules to rearrange themselves."

"Jesus Christ, Mike! What do I do? Go on TV and tell the American people that the bridge was done in by some sort of medieval alchemist?"

"Steve, you can tell them anything you think you can make them believe. All I'm saying is that's what happened to the steel, and—"

Paulson was on his feet and pacing across the room. "My God, Mike. You're the last person in the world I'd expect this kind of crap from. I put you on this because you were the best man for the job, bar none, and I knew you and I could trust you. I'd even been looking for a delicate way to ask you to fill Al Clearford's spot, at least until the convention. If that isn't a vote of confidence, I don't know what the hell is. But this shit . . ."

Grady got to his feet and stretched as tall as his five-foot-four frame would allow.

"Mister President, if the trust you mention is still there, allow me to finish what I started to say. If it is not, then I'll have my resignation to you in less than an hour."

The men stared at each other for a long minute.

Paulson folded his arms. "I'm sorry, Mike. Go ahead. Finish."

"There are only two places in the world that we've been able to find cross sections like those." He pointed to the pictures on the table. "One is in psychokinesis experiments done with psychics in test labs."

"You—"

Paulson was interrupted by the phone. He opened the camouflage cigar box and snatched up the handset. "Yes. He's on the way up, then? Very well."

He turned back to Grady. "Psychokinesis? Psychics?" His tone was more confused than unbelieving.

"That's right, Steve." Grady pulled two more photos from the case. He laid one of them next to the one of the bridge sample. The President looked at both for a second. They looked like prints from the same negative.

"It's impossible. I mean it's got to be a coincidence."

"Why?"

"Because all of that stuff is bullshit, Mike. That's why. It's got about as much credibility to me and to the public as the tooth fairy. Can you imagine what would happen to my Eagleton, Harris and Gallup ratings if I started saying that the Golden Gate Bridge, perhaps the finest engineering marvel of its time, was crippled by—" he looked for the right word—"by witchcraft? No I can't accept this."

"Steve, for God's sake! We've eliminated the impossible. What remains is this."

"No. We have not eliminated the impossible. Witchcraft is one of those things that you eliminate first; it sits on top of the impossible list. I never knew you went in for that kind of thing, Mike. No, I'm sorry. I can't accept that."

Grady took the other photo from his lap and slowly placed it between the other two. Together, the three prints looked like mirror images of one another.

"What's that?"

"A sample from the tail-rotor cable of the Vice President's helicopter."

Paulson stared at the three shots. "Identical?"

Grady nodded gravely. "Exactly."

"Is there any chance that—"

Grady could see where he was headed.

"Steve, they were done on separate microscopes. There were over two hundred prints and all of them were run through a computer. They are absolutely identical. All three samples have undergone a molecular alteration, what you called alchemy. There was no trace of radiation in any of them. My conclusions coincide with those of the Moreland research team. The bridge and the helicopter both fell victim to a force we cannot identify or duplicate, therefore we can classify it as 'paranormal'!"

Paulson stared down at the pictures as he spoke. "Let me get this straight, now. All three shots are— what did you call it? Paranormal?"

"The process seems to be."

"And there's no other way to duplicate it?"

"Not exactly." He pointed to the third picture on the table. "This is the enlargement of a small piece of steel wire bent and broken without physical contact and at a distance of several feet. The sample wire was under a bell jar and the protocols were rather severe. That, Moreland's research team has been able to do for several years, when they can get the right sensitives and the right timing."

"They can't do it on command, so to speak?"

"No. It's whimsical. Some subjects seem to have the skill and some do not. And no one has ever been able to have any impact on a three-foot-thick steel cable buried in a caisson or a moving target like Al Clearfield's helicopter."

"And that's the best consensus?"

"That's it."

"A form of sabotage?"

"Right. One against which there seems to be no effective or meaningful defense . . . except—"

"Except what, Mike?"

"Except what you would say was more witchcraft."

Paulson spread his hands in a supplicatory gesture. "I'm sorry I ever mentioned the term."

"There are several people who work at Moreland's institute. One of them, a woman named Tanner, predicted the fall of the bridge. She also predicted the fall of the helicopter. Her husband heads up the psychic research team for Moreland. He's kept a statistical record of her what shall I say . . . predictions for the past several years. Eighty-three percent of the things that she has predicted have been right on the money; statistically significant, Moreland calls it. Her prediction about the bridge said the bridge would be *made* to fall."

"Aside from these predictions of hers, and the fact that according to her there would be volition in the bridge catastrophe, what else supports the sabotage angle? I mean, what did she say about the helicopter."

Grady shook his head. "I spoke to Moreland about an hour ago. He says that her prediction was too general there to be considered meaningful. All she said was that a political figure would fall from the sky to his death. She didn't consider it important enough at the time to bring up, simply because of its general nature. Actually, I'm linking the bridge to the helicopter because of the samples and the fruitless session that I spent with General Forrester and Mortimer Hathaway from the FAA. They threw up their hands . . . mechanical failure followed by a question mark. The metal sample in the picture came from the rotor linkage area, which according to them simply could not have failed—though it did. And the chopper simply could not have exploded before it hit the ground—which it did, at thirty feet. When I put all of that together, I come up with sabotage, and whoever's behind it has a whole new set of rules."

Paulson clasped his hands behind his head and looked to the ceiling for a second.

"Assuming that any of this is true and not just a bad script from some science fiction movie, is their an operative involved? Or more than one. A team of them. What do they call that—a coven?"

"It's quite possible that there is a team or a single individual at large at this time. As far as Moreland's people know, the chances are that the saboteur or saboteurs would have to be in close proximity to the object concerned. There seems to be a relationship between distance from the target and force exerted. At least that's what I'm told."

"So someone has to be up close to the target?"

"We think."

"Okay, Mike. Here's the big question. Why? What's the motive? If something is all that powerful, some nut or some extremist group of weirdos, why haven't they made demands or claimed credit, like terrorist groups?"

"Perhaps because they haven't provided us with a sufficient enough example of their power. Perhaps they'll knock out another target and then claim credit . . . make demands. I don't know."

"Do you really believe this?"

"I have a healthy respect for it. I can't say I embrace it. It's the single thing that all of the evidence points to. I can't dismiss it. I . . ."

Paulson shook his head, more in confusion than in disbelief. He was a man at sea, fighting a logic that said it was all hogwash. "I just don't know, Mike."

"None of us does, Steve. That's what's so frightening about it. But I can tell you one thing, Steve. I get the feeling that we might have to learn fast."

It was just over an hour after Eve Tanner had passed out that Jerry watched her start to slide up from unconsciousness in the institute dispensary. Chet Kumasaka looked on from a few feet away.

As Jerry looked down at her, the weight in his stomach was starting to lighten. "Hi," he whispered.

"How? I mean . . . where am I?"

"That's a corny line." He leaned down and kissed

her gently. After a moment, she pulled back. "How long was I out?"

"About an hour."

Chet moved closer. "And no getting out of that bed, at least for a little while. Got that? What you experienced is exhaustion. Jet lag, pregnancy and emotional upheaval are just too much for a woman who's five months pregnant. So stay put."

Eve placed a hand on her stomach. "Is? . . ."

Chet nodded. "Fine. I checked all the fetal vital signs. Its and yours are normal." He looked to Jerry. "Shall you tell her or should I?"

"Tell me what?" There was fear in Eve's voice.

"You're being honored," Chet said. "I'd like you to be the first overnight guest in my hospital. Just a precaution."

She turned to Jerry. "I can't. Crissy . . ."

He shook his head. "I already called your cousin. She'll look after Crissy for another day."

"But this is silly," she said.

Chet frowned in mock seriousness. "You toss my hospitality back in my face, after I spent years building this dispensary into the best ten-bed hospital in the county? Do you want me to lose face? Have my ancestors rolling in their graves. I might have to commit suicide. One night here saves my life. Don't be silly."

"Oh, Chet." She smiled. "I'll stay. At least"—she patted her tummy—"for this one."

There was a knock at the door. "Evita?" The voice was deep and leathery, like a man's. The pronunciation was Castilian. It was Maria Munoz.

For a woman close to seventy. Maria got around under her own power quite well. She'd taken to Eve and Jerry soon after she was contracted as a test subject at the institute. A widow, she'd fought her way out of her inlaws' and grandchildren's attempts to mum-

mify her in an expensively disguised senior citizens'
community. She had adopted them as cronies and
there was little that they could do about it, not that
either of them would have wanted to dissuade her.
She was five feet three and alarmingly thin. It had
been something that her family pestered her about.
She could eat like a farm hand and never put on an
ounce. There was compassion in her eyes that were
black as coal.

"*Pobrecita.*" She came over and brushed Jerry
aside as she moved to Eve. She fussed over her like
a preening pigeon. There was a loving quality about
all of it.

"I came as soon as I heard." She spoke Oxford
English, without a trace of an accent. Her use of
Spanish expletives was more a dramatic affectation
than anything else. Maria's abilities in Rhine card
experiments and psychometry tests were phenomenal,
as were her talents in precognition. The old woman
maintained that she'd taught herself to be psychic.
She had to, she'd say. Her late husband had been a tal-
ented wine grower but a terrible businessman, inca-
pable of defeating the larger California wine growers
in the marketplace. Maria had honed her psychic
capabilities to help him, and by the time the man
had a fatal coronary, she had managed to triple the
sales from their Napa vineyards. It was the idea of
trainability that had spurred Jerry to bring her to the
institute. If she could train herself, could she train
others?

Maria looked from Eve to Jerry, then back again.
"Has he been beating you again?" The words dripped
with mock venom.

Eve managed a weak smile. "Mercilessly . . . day
and night."

The old woman turned to Jerry and smiled, display-
ing a row of straight, strong, though somewhat yel-

lowed, teeth that she bragged were her own. "Beast!"
She couldn't maintain the pose of anger any longer
and burst into a broad peal of laughter. "Seriously,
now. Tell me what happened. Is the baby all right?
Are you?"

Eve started to speak, but Jerry cut her off. "Chet
wants her to rest. You know Eve. She insists everything is okay. She passed out in the middle of a psychometry reading. She—"

"Is she mute? Let her tell me." Maria turned to
Eve, who was sitting up in the hospital bed. Eve's
tummy pressed against her pulled-up knees. Jerry
thought how stunning she was, even exhausted and
in the middle trimester of pregnancy. She moistened
her lips before she spoke. "There's an artifact from
the Golden Gate disaster. I—" She paused and Jerry
watched a well of tears she could not fight back spill
down her cheeks. It was the first time that she had
allowed herself to think about the bridge and Sue
and little Tommy. It was the kind of delayed reaction
to the death of a loved one that Jerry had seen before,
but it was different when he had to see it in Eve.

Maria reached out with skinny, bronzed arms and
held her. "Now, now, *pobrecita*. Let it out, all of it.
Sí. Let it out."

In a couple of minutes, Eve had composed herself.
She wiped her eyes, which had streaked with the
remnants of mascara. She looked to Maria, who sat
gingerly on the edge of the bed.

"It was the gas can. I held it and something happened. I don't quite know what it was. Perhaps it
was the . . . family I lost there."

"I heard and had not been able to see you to tell
you how sorry I was. I lit a candle for her and she
is in my prayers, she along with the little one. If
that is any comfort. It might be best if you did not
deal with this gas can again. Perhaps I . . ."

Eve shook her head. "Be careful if you do. There's something about it. Something I'm not sure of. I had opened up my walls. You know what I mean. Whatever it was, hit me like a fist. It pulled the can away from me. I've never experienced anything like it before. The odd thing is that I'd touched it only a few minutes earlier and gotten nothing."

"There was physical pain?" the old woman asked softly.

"Some. But it was more like a wave of emotion. Anger . . . terror. And it simply pushed me away. If you deal with the can, you'll have to guard against it in advance."

Maria looked up to Jerry, but before she could speak, Chet Kumasaka came forward, carrying a surgical tray with a small tablet cup and some water. "Time to break this meeting up." He handed the small cup to Eve. "Take these with this water." Eve paused for a second. Jerry could see the concern in her eyes. Apparently, Chet could too. "Don't worry. They're safe for the baby. It's an analgesic, nothing more." Eve looked to Jerry for a second. It was not a look that asked for help, only one that reassured.

Jerry kissed her goodbye and left with Maria, while Chet stayed to check Eve's vital signs. Jerry and Maria spoke quietly for a moment in the hall before Chet came out, closing the door behind him. He started to speak to Jerry and stopped, apparently in deference to his oath of confidentiality. Jerry was a relative; Maria only a friend. If there was something about Eve's condition that had to be mentioned, Chet would only mention it to Jerry.

Chet kept things general. "No more excitement for her. With her history of miscarried pregnancies, I want to keep things as calm as possible."

Jerry shook his head solemnly. "No more psychometry?"

"No more nothin'." He pointed to Maria. "Or I'll turn her loose on both of you."

Jerry smiled. "Okay. Okay! Anything but that."

Maria looked up at Jerry, her craggy features scrunched together. "This gas can, it is very important or you would not have asked Eve to do it in the first place. Correct?"

Jerry nodded. "She decided to do it on her own. I wish to hell now I'd jumped in and overruled her. If I had, she'd be mad as hell, but Channing would have listened to me and all of this wouldn't have happened."

"I should hope he would have listened. He's old enough to know women in love have no common sense. And pregnant women in love are *totally* unable to make rational decisions."

Jerry smiled down at her. "You mean you, the driving force behind the Munoz Wineries, admit to being irrational during those, how many—five pregnancies?"

"Seven. Two did not go to term. And, yes! I admit being totally out of my mind when it came to common sense. But it is clear to look at me that all of that is well past. Now I have one foot in the grave and in that position, I have a lot of common sense. So let me take a look at this gas can that is so important. And don't start fussing over me, Jerald. Now that Eve has told me what to be careful of, I can protect myself."

Jerry agreed and they went up to the conference room.

It took only a few minutes to assemble Channing and Anton, both of whom came from staff meetings. The speed with which they arrived testified to the importance of the task and the considerable respect that both men had for the carefully nurtured psychic ability of Señora Munoz.

The old woman sat, dwarfed by the large leather chair. Her traditional black dress made her look like one of the fates or a Goya sketch of a woman in mourning. She looked to Channing, then Anton and finally Jerry. Jerry could feel a lecture coming on. She loved to lecture them, especially Channing.

"Doctor Moreland."

Channing smiled winningly. He also could feel the tones of a lecture. He didn't mind. "Yes, Señora Munoz?"

"I will examine the artifact and try to tell you my impressions. You will do nothing to interrupt or impede my activities and you will ask no questions until I am ready for them. Is that clear?"

Channing nodded, his smile not quite as broad as it had been.

"So." She rubbed the palms of her hands together in much the same way Eve had. Jerry wondered if Eve had learned the gesture from the old woman. Satisfied after a few seconds, she reached for the can.

The whole thing took only a few minutes. Maria, eyes tightly closed, cradled the can to her like it was a small child being comforted after being hurt. When she put it down, she opened her eyes and looked at Channing. "There are impressions, but they are faint . . . distant . . . not the type to have such a dramatic impression on Eve Tanner. Therefore, it must be some other force than the can that created the impact. I sense something to do with water . . . this might have to do with the bridge disaster. I also see a man . . . I am sure it was the one who owned the can. He wore a uniform and spoke a foreign language . . . not Spanish. As for the rest, there is something to do with a leader . . . an American President, which one I do not know. He seems to be connected to large rocks . . . stones. This I do not understand. That is all there is, I'm afraid." She turned to Channing.

Channing sipped from a glass of water before he spoke. Fatigue was etched in his face. "Señora Munoz, would you say these images relate to a past or a future event?"

She thought for a second. "Future."

Channing slid back in his seat. His long, slender hands remained on the table. Jerry could see that they had grown white-knuckled. A sinking sensation deep inside Jerry swelled upward from his stomach to his chest. It was a cold, hard lump of fear, the like of which he had not felt in years. His eyes stayed on Channing and watched as the old man blinked.

Anton Deladier broke the silence. "Channing?"

"Yes?"

"The impressions we have from the gas can. The water does not have to be connected to the bridge. It could be another disaster at another structure connected with water and a president. All of that might attach to a stone building. The Lincoln Memorial and the Washington Monument are both by reflecting pools. The Jefferson Memorial is not far from the Potomac Basin. The—"

Jerry's head snapped to Anton. "No, not stone. Stones . . . rocks. It was plural, wasn't it, Maria?"

She nodded.

Jerry leapt to his feet. "Jesus Christ! Stones, rocks . . . boulders. Boulder Dam!"

"But—" Anton tried to interrupt, but Jerry cut him off.

"Anton, the other name for the dam is Hoover Dam."

Channing studied Jerry's face for a moment before he nodded in resigned agreement. "I'd better call Mike Grady, right now. He'll have to know."

There was a light tap at the door of the White House Cabinet Room. President Paulson waited a long minute before he responded. His eyes met Grady's.

"All right, Mike. I agree. For now, let's keep things about this between just you and me."

Grady nodded, relieved that he did not have to put up with explaining the whole hypothesis again to Clayton.

"Come in, Andy," Paulson said.

Andrew Clayton strode in and, seeing Grady, stood awkwardly at a distance. His mood seemed an odd blend of curiosity and agitation.

Paulson smiled a purely political smile. "I'm sorry, Andy, I brought you up here on a false alarm. Mike Grady had the answer I was looking for. My apologies."

"Oh, I see." Clayton nodded tersely. "Well, in a way, I'm glad to be able to watch you for just a second, Mister President." He held out a photocopy of what appeared to be a cablegram. "It was sent over from the State Department just a few minutes after we went into the meeting. It relates to the things mentioned in the briefing. It's from Premier Kharkov, personally."

Paulson took the copy and looked at it.

"Dear Mister President:

"As I am sure you are aware, I would not normally attempt to communicate in this manner unless the matter for discussion was of consummate importance. As it happens, I must speak of such a matter. I am certain you are already aware that the vagaries of the weather, and what my advisors tell me is sunspot activity, have caused vast, swift alterations in climate in most of the Eastern Hemisphere. As a result, last fall's grain crops, as well as those just harvested from the winter cycle, were dramatically diminished. While fortune smiled on most of the countries of the Western Hemisphere, the grain crops in Europe and Asia were disastrous. I am taking this opportunity to personally request that an international meeting be negotiated, in which your country and mine discuss the possibilities of a sale of American wheat surpluses to the Soviet Union. I assure you that the Soviet Union will be most eager to accept terms of sale within responsible limits and is prepared to make an offer substantially above the going international rate for such a transaction.

"Allow me also to express my sincere condolences on the lives lost in your recent bridge disaster. However, as I mourn that loss of life with you and the other members of the civilized world, I can see the same number of people dying daily in the Soviet Union—from starvation. Double that number might die daily in both the People's Republic of China and India. These estimates are not what you Americans might call scare tactics. They are estimates of wheat supply versus mouths to feed.

"All of this will start to take place before midsummer, unless we make some arrangement for a more equitable reallocation of food. I ask you as a world leader to reach out to us in a gesture of humanitarianism, as well as in the cause of world peace. Again, let me extend my condolences on the death of your Vice President. Mister Clearford and I had spoken on a number of occasions and I found him to be intelligent and articulate; a human yardstick for the measurement of accomplishment in diplomatic negotiations. And once again . . ."

A quiet buzz told Paulson that the phone in the cigar box was ringing. He looked up to Grady. "Mike? Would you?"

Grady moved to the phone.

"Grady." He paused for a second in surprise. "Yes, put him on. Good morning, Doctor. . . ."

President Paulson looked up from the end of the cable to Clayton. Confused, he asked, "Did the Soviets translate this or did we?"

"The Soviets, Mister President. That was the way it came off the telex. We confirmed content as accurate by asking for a second transmission. The Kremlin confirmed accuracy. The photocopy was made from the second transmission."

Paulson nodded. "Okay, Andy. It looks as if you were right about how desperate Premier Kharkov was. I'll get more to you by tomorrow morning. Meanwhile, you warm up Ambassador Luboff for a small gettogether here. Make some copies of that and—" Grady ended the phone conversation and slowly came back to his chair. His expression was grim. He sat and listened. "—white out some of that gibberish at the end of the page. There are a couple of scrambled words in the last two lines. I'm sure that our friend the Premier is mistaken about U.S. geography."

Clayton took the cable and left.

Grady looked at Paulson. "Was the end garbled?"

The President nodded. "It was a last offering of condolences. They were sorry for the loss of American lives 'on the Colorado.' I'm certain Kharkov meant, 'in California.' They must have coded it wrong when they sent the transmission."

Suddenly, Grady looked like a man who'd been struck by something ominous . . . something terrifying.

Paulson leaned forward in his chair. "Mike? Are you all right?"

Grady waved away the concern with a weak hand. He nodded and looked directly at Paulson. "That garble at the end of the cable? It said 'on the Colorado'?"

"Yes. Why?"

"The call was for me. It was Doctor Moreland. One of his psychics predicted . . . that there would be another unexplained catastrophe. It—"

"It what?"

"It would be at Hoover Dam."

Paulson cocked his head to the side. "I . . ."

Grady caught the President's eyes and held them. "That cable. The garble at the end might not have been a garble at all."

"I don't understand."

"Hoover Dam—the next—the next—" He didn't want to say the word. "Target."

"What about it?"

"Steve, Hoover Dam is on the Colorado River."

The President sat, like Grady, in stunned silence for a minute. When he spoke his voice was just above a whisper. "What do you think? Send in the army? A batallion of engineers? Shit. A fortune teller?" There was still a tone of skepticism in Paulson's voice, though his reaction had been more positive than Grady had any right to expect.

Grady shook his head slowly. "I don't know exactly what to look for, Steve. I don't know what to do if we find anything. And I don't know what to do if we don't. I do know we're going to have to rely on More- land and his group."

Paulson shook his head, as Grady had. "Fly up there, Mike. Get all the data and get back as soon as possible."

Grady nodded.

Paulson shook his head again. "Witchcraft . . . Jesus!"

In the dispensary at the institute, Eve Tanner's breasts rose and fell slowly, as she slipped into a deep sleep. Beneath her eyelids, her eyes started to flicker back and forth in a rapid-eye-movement dreaming pat- tern.

Suddenly, she thrashed, sat up and screamed.

In a few seconds, Chet Kumasaka lunged into the room.

"Eve? What is it?"

Tears streaked her eyes and she shook violently, trying to speak through racking sobs.

"All th—those people . . . drowned. All of them."

He took her by the shoulders. "That's over, Eve. There's nothing we can do about it. Nothing. The bridge was—"

She pulled away from him. "No! Not the bridge . . . the dam . . . the big one. It's going to break and they'll all drown."

7

*Above this energy threshold, at very high ener-
gies, everything changes.*

—Dennis Postle

It was rumored that Herbert Hoover himself had
christened the dam system The Corks on the Colorado.
He had seen the completion of the largest dam system
in the Western world and then saw it bear his name.
But the Cork was more than a single dam; it blossomed
into the largest single, centrally controlled power-pro-
ducing dam complex in the world. Capped by the mammoth Hoover Dam at its northern end, the Hoover
system created hundreds of cool lakes in the three
hundred miles of the Colorado River. Six associated
dams diverted the water, and the power that their
turbines generated created the Imperial Valley, one of
the largest food-growing regions in the West. There
was little question that the Cork had been a success.

An army helicopter descended near the side of the
chiseled gorge, south of the massive lower wall of the
dam. The dam appeared like a manmade mountain
placed in the path of the fast-flowing Colorado, then
hewed and smoothed like an Old Kingdom burial vault.
It arched its curving back against more than a hundred
miles of Lake Meade. The south spillway sloped over

seven hundred feet down to the lower power station control building. The structure spilled outward along the banks of the river to house turbine engines that gathered power from the waterflow that roared through huge underground spillways. It was awesome.

The helicopter's passengers got the full impact of the panorama. General Harry Briggs, obviously sleepy from being roused in the middle of the night by a presidential special advisor, yawned as he watched the scene unfold through the open side door of the Bell *UH-1* helicopter. The Huey, as the pilots called her, was the same model that had been turned into a flaming coffin for the Vice President, though unlike her ill-fated sister ship, this Huey was not built for executive comfort. But Briggs didn't mind the bumpy, wind-blown ride. He'd logged more than five hundred hours in such helicopters in Viet Nam. He simply buckled up a belt against his lean, tall frame, ducked his bald, bulletlike head forward into the wind and dozed.

For Lieutenant Walter Fox, the general's aide, the helicopter ride was not quite so placid. He was far more used to flying a desk than an aircraft. He was small, plump and, behind his thick glasses, had the beady eyes of a bureaucrat, all set in a round face that was growing greener by the minute. It was all Fox could do to keep his stomach where it was, by sheer force of concentration. Anton Deladier and Maria Munoz both simply stared out the open door at the dam. It seemed so huge, so impregnable—it was hard to believe that anything short of a nuclear weapon could disturb it. Still, as a target, it was impressive. For if anything did destroy it, the results would be more than a catastrophe —there would be an almost immeasurable cataclysm.

With more than a touch of lingering anger, Anton looked at the old woman who'd fought her way into the mission. She was professionally qualified for this— she was the best sensitive in the history of Moreland's

program. But Anton simply felt that she was old and
pushy and was liable to keel over from high blood
pressure. It was not professional jealousy. It was simply that the old woman was a pain in the ass to have
along.

As for Maria Munoz, the view of the dam was a
victory. The immensity of the structure and the havoc
that sabotage could wreak there justified the chances
she was taking with her frail body. Even if she didn't
make it through the mission, she would have died
doing something meaningful . . . something important.
In the moment that she first saw the dam, she had
questioned her decision. But it was too late to do anything about it.

The helicopter set down in a swirl of sand near the
new administration building. Sitting off to the west of
the gorge, the structure was three stories of blinding,
burnished aluminum. The glare from the structure
was so intense that Deladier and his entourage squinted
involuntarily as a flash of reflected sunlight blinked
across the helicopter's skin. On the pad, Roger Henderson, the Department of Conservation's chief engineer
for the Man Management Division, stood waiting,
shielding his eyes from the stinging sand grains. Like
General Briggs, Henderson had been awakened by a
call in the middle of the night. He was well used to
inspection tours and visits, but this was something different. He had not expected to cope with a detachment
of Mountain Rangers and Navy SEALS, the equivalent
of Green Berets—experts at everything from underwater operations to scaling mountains. In addition,
a batallion of army troops showed up in the dawn hours,
blackening the sky with helicopters. They set up a field
operation and patched their phone lines through the
Hoover Dam switchboard. Their self-contained headquarters was less than a quarter of a mile west, still
on federal land and within sight of the administration

building. The Navy SEALS had been flown in by chopper less than an hour ago. Henderson expected they'd been relayed in by a jet from either San Diego or Treasure Island. Through the early morning hours, Henderson let the rumors circulate among his staff members. Before the arrival of the military, speculation had run to things like a bureaucratic shake-up, with President Paulson shifting control of the dam complex from Conservation to Interior or another cabinet agency. After the troops arrived, the rumor mill went into high gear, spinning out everything from a terrorism scare to Martians. Henderson hadn't listened to any of them. Instead, he'd ordered fresh computer read-outs on every phase of the dam, engineering inspection reports and a generalized VIP briefing for the arriving team. As he walked to the chopper in the swirl of dust, he was as prepared as he could be . . . he hoped.

The sight of an old woman emerging from the back of the helicopter was a surprise. Henderson peered into the intense glare to see if she was a recognizable congresswoman. He reached the party and extended a hand to the general.

"General Briggs?"

"Yes. Are you Henderson?"

The engineer nodded and then, to avoid shouting over the whirr of the blades, led them off the landing pad. With a roar and a final roiling cloud of dust, the helicopter lifted behind them. Briggs and Henderson waited a few minutes longer; when he was sure he could be heard, Briggs pointed to the civilian in the blue suit next to him. "This is Doctor Deladier. He'll be running the operation."

Anton introduced Maria Munoz by name only. Maria just smiled. Lieutenant Fox, still pasty gray from the flight, trailed the trio in the direction of the administration building.

The briefing room was large and plush in an ultramodern style. An oval briefing table surrounded by swivel chairs dominated the center of the room, while affording a magnificent view of the dam through a specially designed antiglare picture window. One entire wall of the room was an aerial mosaic map of the dam complex, taken by satellite. Hoover and the other dams in the complex were noted by circles and arrows, which led back to a series of explanatory keys off to the side. Two visual scanner computer terminals sat quietly in the corner of the room, flanked by related teleprinters.

The room was a refuge from the heat and grit of what was fast becoming a spring heat wave. Henderson seated the four visitors and made sure that all the needed briefing materials were at the end of the table. He took a seat and smiled at Deladier. "Now, Doctor, what can the Hoover complex do for you?"

Deladier opened his briefcase and removed a form. He passed it across the table to Henderson. "Mister Henderson, before we start, I'm afraid you'll have to read and sign this document."

Henderson skimmed the National Security secrecy document and looked to the doctor. "I believe I still have one of these on file from the time when I was in the service."

"You will still have to sign a new one, I'm afraid." Deladier's tone was gentle but firm. Henderson pulled a felt-tipped pen from his jacket pocket and scrawled a signature on the document, then passed it back to Deladier, who smiled and slipped it back in his briefcase.

"Mister Henderson, the document simply assures what is said in this room cannot go any further than the five of us here. If it does, then all five of us, you included, risk federal prosecution. Do you have any further questions before we begin?"

Henderson paused then shook his head. "No, not

really. I am anxious to find out what this is all about and to know how I might help."

It was clear from Henderson's expression that all he was concerned about was getting the four of them back onto the helicopter, along with the rangers, SEALS and the rest of the army detachment they brought with them.

Deladier settled himself in the chair and looked at Henderson. "Your attitude will be very helpful and I can assure you that when we complete our . . . business here, your assistance will be mentioned to your superiors, including the President." Henderson smiled, as Deladier expected he might. The best way to assure the cooperation of a public servant was to tell him he could score points with his boss if he did a good job.

Deladier looked to the others around the table. "I guess we should get right to it. Mister Henderson, General Briggs is the deputy commander of the U.S. Army Corps of Engineers. He and the troops that have been flown in will assist you and your people. Señora Munoz will be working with me as you will. Now, as to what we're here for. . . ."

He turned to include the general and the aide, then paused. "General, has the lieutenant signed the security document?"

The lieutenant nodded.

"Perhaps then, General, we could allow you to use your discretion as to what parts of the briefing the lieutenant might need to know?"

Briggs nodded. He turned to Lieutenant Fox, who had fully recovered from the flight. "Walt? Get yourself a cup of coffee. Be back in say—" he looked to Deladier—"half an hour?"

Deladier nodded and the relieved lieutenant left the room.

"General, Mister Henderson, I'll make this brief. We

have reason to believe that some sort of sabotage operation might be enacted against the dam system." He paused to let the impact of the statement sink in. Henderson looked incredulous. Briggs' brown eyes, deep-set in a leathered face, narrowed like a poker player who suspects he's being bluffed. He would listen to more before he made a comment.

Henderson spread his hands. "Ah, Doctor . . . how?"

Deladier looked to Maria for a split second. He detected a slight shake of her head. He agreed. *"How* is something that we are still determining. The chances are that we will be determining that for some time."

Henderson was still incredulous. "Well, is there a time frame? I mean when would—? I mean . . ."

Deladier shook his head. "I'm afraid we don't know that, and—"

Suddenly, they could all feel it. It was a slight vibration in the table top; something that had slid up from the floor. Far beneath them, a dull, deep-throated roar was starting.

Deladier stopped in midword. Something flashed across his face that could only have been fear. Even poker-faced Briggs shifted slightly in his seat. In a few seconds, the roar was louder, clearer, more ominous.

"It's only the sluices."

"The what?" Deladier jumped on Henderson's words.

"The sluices, Doctor. The spillways. The master computer is programmed to activate the spillway system and engage the secondary turbines to augment peak power-usage times." He looked at his watch. "A lot of air conditioners go on in Vegas in the early afternoon. We boost our power output based on a profile of increased power demand at this time of the day. The lower dams in the system react to the same computer signal and automatically open their spillways so that the level of water flow is consistent. In about an hour, cities from Salt Lake to Tucson will up their demands and we'll increase flow again to beef up the power grid."

Deladier interrupted. "Why an hour from now, if they're east of here?"

Henderson pointed to the window. Past the walls of the east side of the canyon was Arizona and north a few miles was Utah. "Utah and Arizona are on mountain time. We're on Pacific. The computer is keyed to clock times."

Deladier nodded.

"Doctor, you mentioned sabotage?"

"Yes. Perhaps the best thing for you to do is to give us a quick sketch of the system." Henderson was on his feet before the words were spoken. If it was to be a briefing, he was prepared. He walked to the curtains at the far end of the room and pulled the cord at the corner. They parted, revealing a large satellite mosaic map of the entire Hoover system. Arrows and captions marked landmarks and for the first time, Deladier could see the extent of the complex. It stretched along the length of the Colorado, turning the river into a series of irregularly shaped lakes, each created by the backflow of the dam just south. Henderson was pointing to the northernmost cork in the river, Hoover itself.

Henderson had clearly pushed the thought of sabotage to the back corner of his thoughts for the moment. He was good at briefings, and he knew it. He picked up a metal pointer and moved it along the map. "Hoover is the uppermost dam in the complex. It controls the flow of Lake Meade, which the dam's construction created back in 1936. When we release spillway flow here, it affects the dams south of us all the way to Yuma. The next link in the dam chain is Davis Dam. That's just over sixty miles south. She increases flow five minutes after we do, so that the water level in Lake Mojave remains constant. Then, there's Parker. Fifty miles below that, there's the new Johnson Dam, and further on the Imperial and Laguna Dam complexes. The key to the whole thing is a constant flow. It's a single computer-controlled operation, responding to seasonal changes in river levels and power demands from the Southwest power grid."

Deladier pointed to the aerial map. "Hoover, being northernmost, is then the focal point?"

"Absolutely. It creates the largest body of water behind it. We're the cork in the bottle so to speak. Lake Meade stretches all the way north to Overton, that's more than sixty miles. None of the southerly dams creates that size backflow. Hoover's over seven hundred feet high and more than twelve hundred feet across and she's built at the narrowest point of Boulder Canyon. As I mentioned, she's the cork in the narrowest point of the river."

Henderson paused, watching Deladier cock his head to the side. "What, Mister Henderson, would happen if the cork were—removed suddenly?"

Henderson looked at the map and then back to Deladier. "*If* that were to happen, and I'm assuming that what you're talking about is the partial or complete failure of Hoover"—he looked back to the map as if to try to visualize the impossible—"and if there was sufficient time to activate the safety systems, the lower dams would throw open their spillways to accommodate the water surge. But . . ."

"Yes?"

"Well, if you're anticipating that someone will come along and blow Hoover up, then something on the order of twenty million cubic acres of water would be released all at once." He paused and shook his head. "None of the lower dams in the system could hope to accommodate that. The high walls of the canyon would increase the speed of the water. By the time that it reached Lake Mojave, well . . . it would increase the lake's depth by more than fifty feet. If Hoover went, Davis would go too—so would Johnson. It would be dominoes, Doctor. I'm afraid it would resemble the Vaiont case in '63, but on a much larger scale."

"Vaiont?"

"Yes. It's a similar gravity arch dam in Switzerland. Vaiont is newer and just over two hundred feet higher than Hoover. She's built on a reservoir fed by mountain streams in the Alps. In the spring of 1963 there was a huge avalanche at the opposite end of the reservoir. It built a tidal wave that swept across the top of the dam, topping it by more than a hundred feet. Luckily the dam held, but the wave flooded the lower areas of the valley, killing several hundred people. As a result, the silt released pressed against the upper apertures, totally negating all of the power generating capability of Vaiont. Vaiont was rendered totally useless. Not counting lives and property claims, the loss to the Swiss government in the dam alone approached a billion dollars."

"Mister Henderson? Is Lake Meade substantially bigger than that Swiss reservoir?"

Henderson nodded. "About ten to fifteen times bigger, Doctor."

The four of them were silent for a minute. Deep below, the tone of the roar shifted, indicating some adjustment of the spillway gates.

"Doctor Deladier?" Henderson started back to the table. "I have to mention that a sabotage attempt on Hoover Dam would—well, I don't say that it is impossible—but short of a nuclear weapon, there isn't much that could blast Hoover out of existence. We've got more than three and a quarter million cubic yards of concrete out there. I don't see how sabotage could be carried out. There would have to be literally hundreds of coordinated charges placed to all go off at once, and that's something that simply could not be hidden. The security staff would be on to something right away."

He paused, realizing that he had simply glossed over one point, a terrifying point. "Is there a chance of a nuclear weapon, Doctor? If there is, then I retract my statement."

Deladier shook his head reassuringly. "Not to our knowledge, Mister Henderson. If that were the case, we could probably find such a weapon in rapid order, simply by using radiation detection equipment. No, we believe that an entirely new . . . ah, weapons system might be at work here. It would be one that is triggered, perhaps, from a distance, and the only indication that the dam would get would be immediate structural failure. There is a chance that such a weapon might have been used over a period of time to weaken the structure."

"If that's the case, Doctor, we'd know about it. Every stress factor that relates to dam safety is on the computer. It registers stress information from sensors imbedded in the concrete. We get a daily read-out on all of them. When something is wrong, the computer prints it out and we have a team look at it. Cracks, fissures, canyon erosion, everything is profiled. Any long term attack or sabotage—anything—would have to show. Before you arrived, I ordered a read-out on all systems." He pointed to a pile of computer paper on the table. "It's all there. Everything is in order, as far as the computer can tell us. So this weapon you mention would have to be something extraordinary."

For the first time in the meeting, Maria Munoz spoke. "It is extraordinary, Mister Henderson. Very extraordinary."

By late afternoon, the lower west wall of the canyon was in shadow, making the east side stand out in stark relief. Along both corners of the dam structure, teams of Army Rangers on scaffolds, bosun's chairs and rappelling ropes were going over every inch of the dam face at the point where it intersected with the canyon wall. Henderson had explained that the points where the dam structure interfaced with the canyon were the weakest part of the gravity arch structure. It was at that point that the millions of tons of water compressed the concrete against the rock. If there was a failure, it would probably occur there. On the dam's northern side, Navy SEALS scuba teams played flare lights against the margins of the structure, searching for underwater faults. Deladier and Briggs had turned the conference room into a headquarters-communications center. The mosaic map had been shaded for areas already checked by both teams and by computer sensors. A two-way radio set sat on the center of the table surrounded by books, papers and piles of computer read-outs. Henderson seemed upset that Deladier had little faith in the computer sensing apparatus. The man wanted every inch of the dam eyeballed for anything abnormal.

Deladier had shucked his jacket and rolled up his sleeves. He stared at a spot on the map that Henderson had just marked as checked.

"Negative so far, Doctor. Everything that the teams have checked mirrors the computer read-outs."

Deladier nodded. "Very well, Mister Henderson." He looked to General Briggs, whose jaw furiously worked over a large wad of gum. It was clear that the general was starting to agree with Henderson. Both men were beginning to think that the doctor and the old Spanish lady were on a wild goose chase.

"General, how long do you estimate before the teams complete the entire check?"

Briggs stopped chewing for a second. "At least another twelve hours, Doctor. Starting at first light in the morning, they will—"

"First light?"

"Yes. First light. I'm afraid that this kind of operation could only be carried out in daylight. Oh, there's a chance that the SEALS on the north side of the dam could work through the night, but I don't think that they could stay underwater that long. And as for the Ranger teams, the artificial light that they could carry with them at night would be insufficient to carry out the kind of inspection that you are requiring. We'll probably have to pull them out of there in about forty-five minutes; after that it will be too dark."

Deladier paused before he spoke. Mentally he weighed the possibilities of the need for speed with the risks of a night operation. He wasn't really sure what they were looking for. "Very well, General. Pull the teams off the operation, then. They can start at first light in the morning, I assume?"

"Yes, sir. With luck, they'll have seventy percent of the search completed by nightfall tomorrow."

Deladier, obviously troubled, turned to Henderson. "Will the com—"

"Deladier, are you there?" The voice of Maria Munoz crackled from the small radio on the conference table. She had usurped the general's aide and a jeep and had been driving along the road surface on the top of the dam.

Anton reached over and pressed the talk switch on the microphone. "Yes, Maria."

"It will be here. I am standing at the spot."

"Where is it? Are you sure?"

"I am on the roadway on the top, near the middle and I am very sure. It will be here and . . . soon."

"Very well. I am on the way."

Deladier reached for his jacket. He looked at the two men, who were obviously confused and exasperated. "You have both been very patient with all of this. I have to ask for more of that patience. General, you can call the teams off the cliffs now. Have any SEALS who are in the water near the center of the northern wall get clear of the area. In fact, get them out of the water completely."

Briggs nodded and left. Deladier turned to Henderson.

"Mister Henderson, please come with me. What's the quickest way to the center of the upper roadway?"

"It's by jeep. We can take mine. It'll only take a minute to get there. But Doctor, what is Mrs. Munoz referring to? I mean, how can she know where something is going to—"

"Maria Munoz is a psychic, Mister Henderson. She is one of the most skilled psychics alive. If she says she's found where the sabotage will take place, I believe her."

Henderson's mouth fell open in amazement. Before he could object, Deladier grabbed his jacket and turned to leave. They were at the door when Henderson's phone rang. He reached for it angrily.

"Henderson—where? Thank you. Keep me posted."

He hung up and looked at Deladier. "The computer sensors have picked up a structural weakness."

"Where?"

"In the middle of the upper roadway, where Mrs. Munoz is. But it's crazy."

"Why?"

"It's the strongest part of the dam. I mean it simply can't happen there. It *cannot*." Roger Henderson's tone was that of a man who could not accept the fact that his dam was in trouble.

"Believe it, Henderson. It's happening right now. Let's go."

The sun had dipped below the rim of the canyon by the time Henderson's jeep screeched to a stop on the still warm macadam. Maria and Lieutenant Fox stood a few yards away.

Deladier approached the old woman; she stood with her arms folded and her eyes tightly closed. Seeing her concentration, he stopped and waited. Lieutenant Fox stared at her then turned to Deladier and Henderson. It was clear that the young man was totally bewildered.

The old woman's eyes opened and her outstretched hands traced an invisible line in the road surface.

Anton approached her. "Where?"

She pointed to the same invisible arc in the road surface. "Here, or within a few feet. I had the young man stop the jeep as we were driving across the top. It was something very strong. I've never quite felt the same kind of sensation, Anton. There is a huge force at work, right here . . . even as we speak . . . It . . ."

She stopped and pointed off a few feet. *"There. You see? There."*

Anton hunched down on one knee. Yes. It was there. A hairline crack in the macadam. It was only a few inches long, but as Deladier watched, it seemed to grow in both directions, like an inchworm, slowly, but with a relentless steadiness. "Henderson. Come here."

Henderson looked down at the crack.

Without looking up, Deladier pointed back toward the administration building.

"Is this what the computer was reporting?"

The engineer shook his head. "No. It couldn't be. There are no sensors close to here." Deladier watched for a second as Henderson's mind seemed to race through the locations of the sensors. "The sensors were registering something below here, though. Perhaps fifteen or twenty feet down. It might be related, though this seems to be only a surface crack."

Deladier watched as the engineer pulled a felt-tipped pen from his shirt pocket and marked the ends of the slender crack. They watched the ends for a second. The crack did not seem to advance. He looked to Deladier as he hunkered down next to the crack.

"How did she . . ." He shook his head. "Never mind. It doesn't matter."

Somehow he'd managed to accept it. Deladier admired the man's flexibility. He'd spent a career trying to convince the scientific world that what people such as Maria could do was more than sleight of hand. He had just watched Henderson accept it as a fact, concerning himself with effect rather than motivation or cause. The dam was his child and Maria had committed herself to helping. It was enough.

"Another one." Lieutenant Fox's voice was shrill. He was on his hands and knees some twenty feet away. Before the two men had a chance to run over, the radio in Henderson's jeep had started to squawk. He trotted back and grabbed the mike. "Henderson."

There were a couple of clicks and then a loud blast of static. Briggs was on the other end trying to manipulate the unfamiliar controls. It took a minute for him to get the squelch and the gain adjusted. "Henderson? Briggs. The SEALS just reported in from the north side. They were making the last dive when they came up with a large set of fissure cracks at the ninety-foot level. Commander Morressey says his guys report that they seem to be getting larger by the minute and . . . hold one." The radio went back to static for a few seconds. There was an edge in Briggs' voice as he came back on the line. "Henderson?"

"Yes?"

More static.

"The shit's hitting the fan down here. Either that computer of yours is fucked up or there are ten or eleven just-reported areas of pressure irregularity. I'm pulling the rest of the SEALS out right now and I'm getting my men off the canyon walls. And . . . there's something else crazy."

"What?"

"All of the anomalies seem to be across the middle

of the span. I've got my tickets in civil engineering too. It can't happen that way."

Henderson looked at Deladier as he answered. There was a mixture of fear and resignation in his eyes. He was a man trying to cope with what he knew to be impossible. The middle of a span in a gravity arch dam was the last thing that was supposed to go. It had been an engineering concept since the Romans spread dams and viaducts across Europe. And how? Why? There'd been no floods, no gales, no earth-shattering quakes.

"General?"

"Yes? Wait!" This time the general held onto the mike, with his thumb on the talk switch. Henderson and Deladier could hear what was going on in the briefing room. There was the chatter of the computer terminal and a bell. It chimed like a wire service heralding a flash to all the stations on the line. Henderson's stomach fell.

"Henderson?" The general's voice was tense.

"I heard it, General. What letter does the computer use to identify the class of the emergency?"

"It says L or LIMA."

"Is there a lead time estimate on the right corner of the page?"

He could hear Briggs rip the paper along the perforation. "One hundred twenty-four minutes, plus or minus six," Briggs said breathlessly. "It's the doomsday estimate, Henderson. We have just over two hours before the dam goes completely."

Maria Munoz came slowly across to the jeep. In the distance Lieutenant Fox was sliding slowly sideways across the road like a man frantically looking for a lost wallet. Suddenly, his head snapped up and he looked off toward Deladier and Maria. "There are three more over here," he said in a frightened voice.

Maria looked up to Deladier. "It is what we thought," she said simply.

Deladier rubbed his chin. "Can you do anything to stop it?"

She shook her head. "I don't know. I can try. I know what Eve Tanner felt now. It almost pushes you away, it is so strong. Let me try." She raised her hands and formed her bony fingers into what looked like a child's cat's cradle. "It is like a web, converging at the center of the structure. All of the cracks . . . faults are moving toward one another. I think when they merge, all of this will . . . go."

Deladier looked out over the south canyon. He could hear the shouts of NCOs pulling in rappelling lines and ordering the Rangers off the crags. Hundreds of uniformed men on either side of the canyon were scurrying like so many spiders back up their slender threads to safety. They moved with a slow, deliberate rhythm. Many of them had been in harnesses for hours, dangling precariously over the seven-hundred-foot drop. They were weary.

Suddenly, Deladier could hear a shrill voice screaming into a bull horn.

"Swinggg Lefteftefteft." The voice echoed back and forth across the canyon. And as Deladier peered into the gathering darkness, he could see a soldier trying to free his rope from an outcropping of rock. On top of the wall a man was yelling to him with a bull horn. Confused for the moment, the soldier pushed off the side of the face propelling himself to the right.

"Noooooo. Leftefteft," the voice screamed.

Anton and Maria could see a flicker of movement. The rope parted.

The soldier hung in the air for a fraction of a second before falling. His scream echoed all the way to the bottom, where his body smashed into the roof of the power turbine building. Hundreds of feet of rope snaked its way down behind him, covering his shattered body like a grotesque shroud.

All movement stopped for a long second. Then the bull horns squealed to life again as more orders were shouted. Deladier looked down to Maria as the old woman crossed herself.

"Señora Munoz? If you could manage to work at a distance, you could go back to the administration building. I'm certain this area will be jammed with engineers and technicians in a few minutes."

"Certainly. I would prefer it."

Deladier turned and cupped his hands to his mouth as he called out: "Fox!"

The young man turned suddenly, still on one knee, and scrambled to his feet. He started to trot toward Deladier and Maria. "Yes, sir?"

"Take Señora Munoz back to the building. I am sure General Briggs will need you."

Deladier started to move in the direction of Henderson's jeep, then stopped. He looked to the far end of the roadway. Rangers were scrambling down from the rocks and moving into formations just off the road surface. He could see two army trucks roaring into position across the span of the road. On the far side, more soldiers deployed quickly. It appeared that the dam road was to be blocked on both ends. Only enough room was left for a single truck width to pass. It was obviously something that Briggs had ordered, though Deladier couldn't be sure what orders had been given.

He ran the last few yards to Henderson, who was barking orders into the radio. The engineer looked up as Deladier approached. Anton pointed in the direction of the receding jeep. "She is going to work from the administration building. I think she can at least predict the pattern and location of the cracks that are now appearing. If she can do that, can you take advantage of it?"

Henderson ran a fast hand through his close-cropped hair. "Maybe. I . . ." The roar of a high-powered outboard engine drowned his words. He looked north to the vast expanse of Lake Meade. A second outboard roared to life and then a third. Three pickup boats sped into the waters of the lake. In each a man with a bull horn yelled to SEALS in the water. They kept shrieking the same word. "Recall!"

Henderson and Deladier could see heads start to bob out of the water, as wetsuited men in scuba gear started to pop up in line. Each boat circled until it could line up with a team of four or five divers. Then, the men who wielded the bull horns dropped them and held out what Anton could only think were large rope nooses. The nooses were held over the sides of the boats and one by one, the divers hooked arms in them and were pulled into the boats like netted fish.

Henderson looked to Deladier. "That's Briggs' order. He's getting them out of the water as fast as possible. If the dam goes, they're all dead. I told Briggs to get my people out here with an emergency sealing compound. They should have a team ready in a couple of minutes. He'll send them out in an army truck." Henderson pointed to the activity at both ends of the roadway. A line of soldiers had spread out across the road, shoulder to shoulder. They moved forward slowly, a step at a time, looking down at the road. It was clear that they were looking for telltale faults in the road surface. When one was found, the man finding it would stop the line and yell to an officer at the rear. The crack would be marked with paint. Anton could hear their voices faintly. The number of cracks was growing. The soldiers' shouts were becoming a rhythmic litany. "Here . . . here . . . over here . . ."

Henderson pointed to them. "Briggs ordered that.

He thought it would give us a pattern to work from." He swept his arm out in the direction of one of the approaching lines. "Those Rangers have set up a road-block. Briggs has them sealing off all the access roads to the damsite. They'll hold until the state police arrive."

Deladier shook his head, emphatically. "No, Mister Henderson. The state officials will *not* arrive. I cannot allow any of this activity to leak to state officials or the public without contradicting my orders from the White House. Let the Rangers continue to hold the road. They can say that there is a toxic chemical spill or maneuvers if they wish. I don't care what ruse is neces-sary to divert the flow of traffic. Washington will have to come up with something. For now, though, we can only allow army, federal and Moreland Institute per-sonnel in here. It absolutely must be that way."

Henderson shook his head in anger and disbelief. "But what about everything south of here? Everyone in the Imperial Valley will have to be gotten to high ground. If we don't warn them—" Henderson's voice rose shrilly. "We'll kill a lot of people. You'll have to order me not to warn them."

"There's still time to decide. You said your team is coming out with a compound?"

"Yes. But, it's pretty new; we only added it to the safety program last year. It's an epoxy resinous cement. You open the can and trowel it on then spray it with aerosol. In about four minutes, the stuff is rock hard. The trouble is we don't have a whole lot of it; we'd have to send a chopper for more. And it's only for surface problems—it'll be like an expensive Band-Aid."

Deladier turned away thoughtfully and squinted into the deep shadow that had overtaken the west side of the dam canyon. A truck was bearing down on them.

Henderson waved to them to speed up and the driver gunned the truck ahead.

Anton started toward the jeep. "You start them on the patch job. I'm going to see Briggs. I'll have him send the copters for more."

Henderson again brushed his hair with his hand in a nervous gesture. "Have him warn the downstream stations. They're supposed to have the sealer ready for use on a moment's notice, but the crews down there usually only trot the stuff out for federal inspections." Henderson did not wait for an answer. He turned to the approaching truck. It had traversed the growing cracks when, deep inside the dam structure, there was a painful groan, then a growing roar. Henderson watched in horror as the truck swayed for a second, then pitched into a pothole that had not been there only a few minutes before. The driver gunned the engine but the truck was stuck fast. Several men scrambled out as Henderson rushed to their aid. Deladier grabbed the communications mike and stayed with the jeep.

The road surface was eroding. It was soft and crumbly inside the pothole; the concrete underlying the macadam should have been as firm as steel. Something was turning one of the most massive structures in the world into a sand castle that an invisible tide was crashing in to dissolve. It could not have been a more haunting nightmare to Henderson.

He ran to the rear of the truck to his white coveralled technicians.

"Pull a drum of that stuff and pour it right into the hole!" he shouted.

One of the men looked oddly at him. It was the army driver. "What about my truck? I have to get it back. I'm on a trip ticket. Who'll sign it?"

The question was so unbelievably banal Henderson lost his temper.

"Listen, soldier," he bellowed. "General Briggs will personally sign for your truck. Now, get the hell over to the wheel that's in that pothole and flatten the tire."

The man looked confused. "Why?"

"It'll be easier to turn over that way. It's leverage. Now, do it."

The soldier did as he was told.

Henderson looked to the three men who were wrestling with the drum. "Stop. Get the drums out, then turn the truck over. After that, pour the compound all around the bottom of the truck body. We'll want to seal it to the road." They stared at him dumbly for a second. "Get the hell moving. Get started!" Henderson ran back to Deladier. He was starting to puff. In the last five years, his job had kept him behind a desk; he cursed himself for not getting more exercise.

"Deladier?"

Anton put the mike down. "The helicopters will be off the pad in a minute. Briggs also ordered your people to call the other dams, but they wouldn't without proper authorization from you." Deladier shrugged. "I took the liberty of persuading them otherwise. The message has already been sent." He squinted off in the direction of the men who were turning over the truck. It rocked back and forth, then hung precariously for a second before toppling with a crash to its side. He turned back to the puffing Henderson. "Are you going to wedge it?"

Henderson's eyebrows went up. He was surprised at the quickness of Deladier's mind. His respect for the man grew a bit. "Yes. Or something like that. I'm going to use the sealant to affix the truck to the road surface then add support to the truck. The dam is thinnest at the top. If I can prevent a breech across the roadway, I can stop it from peeling down like a zipper."

"What will you use for the rest of the support structure?"

"Wood. It's flexible and relatively portable. There's a visitor's area under construction up at Lake Meade National Recreation Area. We have to commandeer lumber."

Deladier nodded quickly.

"I'll have Briggs send those Rangers on the far side for them. With luck, they will arrive here when the rest of the epoxy resin does."

"Okay, and—"

"Deladier?"

It was Briggs' voice on the radio jeep. Anton recognized the deep basso. "Yes?"

"Señora Munoz wants—"

"First"—he relayed Henderson's instructions quickly and precisely—"get your Rangers up to the Meade recreation site. . . ."

It was a minute later when Maria Munoz came on the line. Her voice was deep and steady. "Deladier, there are other locations . . . two of them along the road. Neither—neither of them is as large as the ones we saw first. But they are speeding up. The general says these new soft spots will cut the LIMA time by half. We have less than an hour now."

Henderson, who was a few feet away, cursed under his breath.

Deladier breathed deeply and spoke into the mike. "Look, you'll have to try to . . . stop the others if you can. Can you do that, Maria?"

Maria did not pause nor get irate at the use of her first name, though she had never expected it from him; under other circumstances she would have reprimanded him. Now when she spoke, her voice sounded old, and frail, and tired—like she had suddenly come abreast of the enormity of what she had to face. "I will try, but I don't know."

"Very well." He snapped off the mike.

There was a shout from the men pouring the sealer into the nooks and crannies of the truck. The wind brought the stench of the sealer to Anton. It almost gagged him. It was a rotten-egg smell and the sour smell of vinegar together. The aerosols were starting a chemical reaction with the viscous sealer. Henderson coughed.

"We're going to need gas masks for this." The engineer covered his mouth and nose with a handkerchief. His movements were uncoordinated; his breath ragged.

Anton coughed several times before he managed to get his handkerchief to his face. It afforded him only a small degree of relief. He reasoned that although the compound was apparently exquisite in its bonding ability, it was clearly not made for such extensive use as it had just seen. It was obvious that gas masks would be needed for all personnel in the area when the helicopters started to arrive with tons of it. The wind had subsided momentarily and a thickening cloud of grayish gas clung like an expanding halo around the overturned truck. The men in the cloud were coughing now and grabbing for their handkerchiefs, but none seemed so suddenly and so severely afflicted as Henderson, who was now staggering in a dead man's weave. Henderson stumbled a few feet from the front seat, wheezing in a desperate attempt to breathe. Deladier pulled him up to a sitting position. He was past speech and his hand went out clawlike to Deladier and pointed in the direction of the jeep's back seat. Deladier seemed to understand immediately and grabbed Henderson's discarded jackets. He patted the pockets until he found what he was looking for. It was a double-barrelled pump—a vapolator. Henderson was an asthmatic and the fumes had started a seizure.

Anton yanked it from the pocket, losing precious seconds fumbling with a tear in the lining. Ripping the vapolator free, he ran back the few feet to Henderson, who was clinging to consciousness by a thread. He pushed the tube into Henderson's mouth and pressed the release once . . . twice. It was on the fourth jolt, at least one past what Deladier thought might be an overdose of ephedrine, that the chemical started to open Henderson's severely strictured bronchial tubes, allowing them to feed precious oxygen to his blood stream and on to his brain. By that time, a slight wind had come up in the wrong direction. Anton started to press his handkerchief to his nose again, forcing away the urge to gag.

Henderson pointed to the vapolator. "Use it . . . once . . . twice . . . now."

Deladier did use it, surprisingly finding a surge of energy hitting him almost immediately. A body rush washed over him for a few seconds before he pushed himself to his feet and stumbled to the jeep and the radio. He was trying to raise Briggs when three Rangers appeared like specters running in the gloom. Their faces were grotesque. The masks they wore made them look unearthly in the failing daylight and the toxic fog. The first man ran past Deladier and immediately headed for Henderson, over whose head he slid a mask. The second man passed a mask to Anton, who pulled it over his head and breathed deeply against the gasket after covering it with the heel of his hand. The action created a seal of mask against skin and cleared the mask of fumes at the same time. Deladier managed to get three or four deep breaths to clear his head and get back to the radio. He was starting to yell through the muffling effects of the mask into the microphone when the third soldier ran to him, pointing to the nose piece of the gas mask. The man reached across then unsnapped a plastic flap from his own and then pointed to Deladier's.

Anton felt for the snap and did the same.

"Briggs? Briggs? This is Deladier." The voice was much clearer now. Deladier had never seen the flap before or if he had, he'd forgotten it.

"Briggs here. What the hell's—?"

"Listen. Have everyone in the area use gas masks. If we don't have enough, get those without one into the administration building and turn up the air conditioning. Then get more masks. Get a hundred—all you can. Make sure that those helicopter pilots have them, and get them to use the downdrafts of their rotors to push this gas away. Henderson's had an asthmatic seizure, but I think I know what he was trying to set up. Can you get down here? I need an engineer here who knows what he's doing."

There was a crackle in the signal. "On the way . . . out."

In the corner of the briefing room, oblivious to the shuffle of papers and the voices of tense, frightened engineers and administrators, Maria Munoz sat alone. She had been breathing deeply for several minutes before she could feel the sensation of total calm start to spread outward from her chest through her trunk and slowly move to her limbs. Once the process started, it took less than a minute for the wave of warm calmness to envelop her. With a final, carefully controlled breath, she arrived. There was nothing that could touch her now, not unless she willed it to enter. She was totally in control, and gaining more power with each second.

Had she been attached to an encephalograph, her brain waves would have been traced by the pens in the deep, sweeping waves characteristic of a theta state. A sleep researcher who did not know her would have said that she was in the second stage of deep sleep, hovering above a plunge into the *terra incognita* depths of delta: the sleep of the yogis; the sleep from which there was no memory and over which there was no control.

They would have been partially right. While Maria's brain hovered between theta and delta, firing signals from cell to cell at a rate of two to six a second, another part of her, the part that Jerry Tanner and Channing Moreland and Anton Deladier would have called her consciousness, sat at an imaginary control board, as one might sit at the control terminal of a computer, typing in programs and observing visual displays on a color screen.

Playing over the imaginary keyboard, Maria scanned the dam surface. It appeared to be a white wall, scarred with two crimson latticeworks. As she watched, the two seemed to creep outward like a spreading malignancy, enlarging the lattice, deepening the lines. She reached out tentatively with a mental finger, trying to erase the lines. *No!* She recoiled, suddenly in pain as if she'd been burned. In that second, an observer might have seen the slight flutter of an eyelid and an encephalograph might have registered a spike that almost took Maria up to a beta state: full wakefulness. It was strong, whatever it was. Terribly strong. There was clearly no way that she could get into the webs and erase them. She would have to do something else.

On the road surface, Briggs' jeep stopped a few feet away from Deladier. After he got out, two Rangers helped Henderson into the jeep and drove him to the administration building. The general turned to Deladier. The masks the two men wore made them look like two mutated rodents, frantically attempting to communicate. They had to shout.

"I ordered the floodgates opened to relieve some of the pressure," the general said. "What did Henderson have going up here?"

Deladier pointed to the overturned truck and the

thinning cloud of noxious fumes. "The truck was the first weld point. He was going to use timber to create a lattice of them. The sealer would hold all of it together. Would it work?"

Briggs looked at the truck and then at the rest of the road surface that was now a fast growing web of dangerous cracks and soft spots. "Who the hell knows? I've never seen anything like this before. It might, if no more soft spots develop."

Both men looked up and to the south. In the distance they could hear the high-pitched whine of helicopter rotors. More epoxy was arriving.

Briggs shook his head. "If the breaks happen further down than the surface, the timbers at the top won't help. I see Henderson's logic, but lowering the level of the water will do the same thing. We'll have to spread the sealer over the entire road surface and let it seep into the cracks. Then we'll lower Rangers down the front face of the dam to patch any soft spots." Deladier nodded in agreement and then started off in the direction of a group of Rangers, who stood waiting for orders.

The webs had metamorphosed into two scarlet blobs. Maria reached an imaginary finger down behind them, preventing them from merging. There was no question that when and if they did merge, the dam would crumble. She knew enough to avoid direct contact. It repelled and stung her to touch the red part. *Something* was clearly aware of her presence. Maria could sense it. She couldn't be sure that she wouldn't come under attack. If she did, then the energy she spent on defending herself would be energy diverted from protecting the remaining portions of the dam.

Breathing deeply, Maria balanced concentration and relaxation with the skill of a woman who knew the danger of psychic assault. Her consciousness sat at the console, creating an imaginary bubble around herself. It was a protective amoeba, constructed of an energy she could manipulate far more easily than she could define. With this armor intact, she looked back to the imaginary specter of the dam. The scarlet cancer was starting to eat its way into the blue border she had created. She'd slowed it only for a few moments.

She retraced the blue sweeping strokes, adding strength to them. Again and again, she layered a protective coating on the still uninfected parts of the dam. She had been working for five minutes of objective time when she felt the first slashing, searing bolt of an energy that Channing Moreland had spent a lifetime trying to define and measure smash into the bubble that surrounded her. The bubble groaned, bent, but held.

The power of it was awesome; the like of which Maria had never felt. Whatever was attacking the dam knew of her presence, knew of her attempts to defend it and sought to sweep her away with the same force that it exerted on the structure itself. It would have meant terror and screaming nightmares to a person less skilled, less disciplined.

She refused to give into fear . . . until the second blast of energy battered the mentally constructed bubble.

The scene at the top of the dam was like a Halloween nightmare. Teams of soldiers and technicians, their gas masks giving them the appearance of strange, buglike aliens, moved through the dense clouds of toxic fumes, spreading the viscous syrupy liquid into the now chalky spots on the road surface. Above them, two helicopters, which had just delivered the sealer, hovered noisily, using their rotors to blow the fumes downstream, helping the teams get some measure of safety and visibility. Some fifty men spread the ooze across the entire road surface with brushes and spread-er rakes. Upwind of them, still others spread an aerosol fog across the goo, creating more clouds of white, opaque gas.

Deep within the walls of the canyon, the computer to which Henderson had given instructions before his seizure passed signals to switches and flashed corre-sponding messages to the downstream dams in the system. On the road surface, Deladier could feel the rumble building beneath his feet. It was only seconds later when the downstream spillways erupted in huge torrents of water. The structure was trying to lower the pressure on itself, trying to lower the pressure of Lake Meade's billions of gallons of compressed energy in the form of water. Every inch of water level lost reduced the stress on the dam by some twelve hundred square feet of surface area. Deladier could only guess at how much water pressure the twelve hundred square feet represented. He had no idea if the lowered pres-sure would have any impact at all on what was hap-pening to the millions of tons of concrete that was somehow being changed in the dam structure.

General Briggs, who had been trying to scream into two radios through the muffling of the gas mask, got out of Henderson's jeep and moved briskly over to Deladier.

"An attack of some sort. Right? Some method of sabotage?"

The question made Deladier think of Maria. He didn't know if her silence on the radio was a sign of progress or imminent disaster. "Yes. An attack . . . by a weapon system. That's the theory."

"How long?"

"What?" Deladier leaned in toward the general to cut through the noise of the helicopter rotors.

"How long does it last? I mean, do they run out of ammo or power or whatever?"

"I don't know."

"You don't know?" There was an edge to the general's mask-muffled voice.

"No. It's all theory. We just don't know."

"Well, here's a theory for *you*. If some mysterious power is causing all this to happen and it has no end, we'd better start arranging terms."

Deladier leaned in further. The men were almost mask to mask. "Terms?"

"Yes, Doctor. Surrender terms."

Maria Munoz shuddered in her chair. She could feel another wave of *something*—a powerful, physically painful jolt smashed into the invisible barrier she had built around herself. For a second, it broke her concentration and her eyes snapped open.

The room had filled with ten or fifteen men or women, obviously from Henderson's staff. They were a mix of electrical technicians, engineers and administrators. They huddled around several computer terminals, some maps and a radio. No one took any notice of her. Henderson sat at the end of the table. He was still florid and weak from the asthmatic seizure on the road. Maria could hear him cough as he tried to bark questions and issue orders. She took a minute to compose herself, then closed her eyes and breathed deeply; again willing herself into a deep, meditative calm. She scanned the dam with her mind, seeing it in the simple, symbolic terms that the right side of her brain could understand. The angry red spots had waned, lightening in color shade by shade through the amber ranges and into the yellow. They were fading quickly now, as if the damage was starting to repair itself. Self-regeneration? She wondered. It was something she'd never experienced before. In a few seconds, her eyes opened. When she spoke, her voice was frail.

"Mister Henderson?"

The din in the room overrode her.

"Mister Henderson!"

She watched as Henderson got to his feet and pushed past a few members of his staff as he headed toward her. The man was not a "believer" and she knew it. But he was a pragmatist. If she had anything to contribute, he'd listen.

"Yes, Mrs. Munoz?"

"It is over."

"Over?"

"Yes, there will be no more—" she looked for a word, taking care not to use symbolic terminology— "cracks . . . for now."

There was a rustle in the group that surrounded Henderson. The looming figure of the engineer silenced them with a glance. "For now?"

"Yes." The old woman nodded tightly and managed a tepid smile. She was bordering on exhaustion. "As far as I can tell, your repairs will hold. . . ."

She seemed to stop in the middle of a thought as though holding back something that she didn't want Henderson to know. He wouldn't let her.

"For how long?"

"Forever, Mister Henderson, if . . . all of *this* doesn't happen again."

Henderson nodded solemnly. He hadn't the faintest idea what had dealt the dam a near fatal blow, but he never wanted to see it again.

The briefing room, chaotic only a moment before, had fallen silent save for the chatter of the computer printer dutifully reporting alterations in water flow and corresponding flow alterations in the downstream dams. Henderson turned to his staff.

"Get Briggs and Deladier. Tell them Mrs. Munoz says the attack is over." Several people in the room looked at him oddly, as if his bout with the gas had done something to his brain. "Do it!" He bellowed.

The man lunged for the radio. Henderson coughed. "And I want a revised repair plan in two hours. Now, everyone get on it."

Maria closed her eyes and again let her consciousness slip down to the level where she could function best. She started to explore the scars on the dam, looking for the possible origin of the attack. Her curiosity had made her forget the protective "egg" with which she'd shielded herself earlier. She could feel it start to build. It was vast, dark and terrifying. The power probed toward her. She worked quickly to reconstruct the shell of energy that would protect her. She built layer on layer of imagined energy in a cocoon as the painful, almost incendiary probing lashed at her. It only took a few more seconds for the sinister energy to find her location.

"Mrs. Munoz?" Henderson looked at the old woman who gritted her teeth. She did not answer. "Mrs. Munoz?"

She moaned.

Suddenly, everyone on the room could feel it; the tingling eeriness that comes before an electrical storm.

Maria Munoz moaned again, like a woman in pain.

The room started to vibrate, ever so slightly, as if a distant engine were set into motion.

Henderson looked at Maria and his eyes widened in disbelief. He took a step backward. There was a faint but nevertheless discernable glow outlining her entire body.

"Do you see that too?" a voice called half in fear and half in confusion from the back of the room. Henderson nodded, his eyes riveted on Maria.

The glow brightened, swelling like a huge globe around her. Inside the globe, a guttural moan rose to a scream.

The room was vibrating faster now. A water glass

flew from the table toward Maria and smashed harm-
lessly against the energy field.

A woman cried out and pointed to the ceiling.
Plaster was starting to flake down across the room. In
the distance there was the agonized wail of metal
girders under strain.

The room went insane. It shook like a soul in torment. A rain of books, charts and papers flew in all
directions. The table flipped over, barely missing Henderson and Lieutenant Fox, who dove out of the way
at the last second.

An arc of blue flame leapt from the computer console and struck the man who was sitting near it. The
bolt of energy threw him screaming across the room
and smashed him into the far wall. His scream stopped
suddenly. The machine exploded in a shower of sparks
and started to burn.

From the floor, Henderson could see that the light
surrounding Maria had deepened to purple. It crackled with sparks and Maria could no longer be discerned
in it.

The room continued to shake violently and Henderson was suddenly terrified that the building would collapse.

"Look out!" a man's voice screamed from behind
him. He ducked and narrowly avoided being hit by a
chair that flew through the air in Maria's direction.
It hit the blue-purple globe and bounced off.

Suddenly, Henderson saw something move to his
right. Fox had gotten up on one knee. The young army
officer had lost his glasses and was covered with
mortar.

"Get down!" Henderson yelled to him.

Fox looked at Henderson as if the man were speaking a foreign language. He got to his feet and started
toward the terrifying globe of purple light that had
been the old Spanish woman.

"Get back!" Henderson shrieked.

Fox reached Maria and reached out as if to embrace the globe. It was as if he had grabbed a high tension wire. He was thrown backward at incredible speed and smashed like a rag doll into the huge picture window. It shattered outward and Fox's body fell the three floors to the helicopter pad.

Henderson looked back to Maria—the globe of light was starting to fade. In seconds it was gone.

Henderson scrambled to his feet and made his way to the chair in time to catch the limp form of Maria before she slipped from the chair, unconscious.

He yelled to the people in the room: "Get a doctor."

It was fifteen minutes later when Maria's eyes fluttered and she slipped up from unconsciousness. She looked up at Deladier and Henderson from the make-shift stretcher she'd been placed on.

"I am all right," she said unconvincingly.

Anton nodded. "Just rest."

The old woman shook her head. "No. Jerry and Channing must know. *Madre de Dios!* It is so strong . . . so strong. God help us . . . it is so strong."

8

The relevance of the paranormal in understanding the nature of man and life is clear.

—John Taylor

"*In other Washington stories, President Paulson today appointed his chief national advisor Michael Owen Grady to the head of a committee assembled to investigate the recent Hoover Dam incident, in which major structural damage was done to the dam by spring flooding. The floods, it is rumored, were due partially to federally funded construction on the upper river. Grady has been quoted as saying that he'll appoint nearly the same staff as is currently investigating the Golden Gate Easter Sunday disaster. As an investigating group, says Grady, they are moving forward with considerable speed on both projects. California governor and presidential hopeful Rob Tilden commented that, quote, 'the President doesn't seem able to invest any confidence in his staff and others. He has Grady running the country.' Vice President-designate Andrew Clayton was not available for comment.*

"*Internationally, another series of civil disorders is reported in several Soviet cities this morn-*

ing. Moscow watchers in Stockholm report that the rising price of bread supported by the Kremlin sparked the unrest. Kremlin spokesmen remained silent. An unnamed source in the Department of Agriculture here at home says there's a chance for a considerable jump in U.S. wheat prices.

"In a quick roundup of sports . . ."

"Turn it off, Mike."

A solid week of spring rain in Washington had prompted Steven Paulson to move many of his smaller meetings, generally solo talks and small group briefings, into the second floor den. It had been rumored that President Ulysses S. Grant had had the room built to accommodate his late-night drinking and poker parties. An inner room, void of windows, the den had been designed to keep the noise of revelers in, while keeping the bullets of potential assassins out. Since Grant, it had been metamorphosed into an auxiliary pantry, a maid's area, a sewing room. In the first year of his administration, Steven Paulson turned it into a comfortable retreat that offered greater seclusion and comfort than the Oval Office.

Following Paulson's redecorating suggestions, the den glowed in the richness of fruitwood panels. The roll-top desk gave the room a nineteenth-century air, despite the presence of an intricate panel of phone sets and a futuristic switching console. The rest of the room was decorated in leather. Two ten-foot leather sofas faced one another across a massive coffee table. The latter had been left by Teddy Roosevelt and the very size of the thing seemed to testify to the size of Teddy's ego.

Grady crossed to one of the three television sets that lined the far wall. He turned off the middle set with a snap.

Paulson sat in his shirtsleeves on the opposite couch,

leafing through a red-bordered report and shaking his head. "What's the rating on the report, Mike?"

"A-Two, Mister President. Almost total accuracy."

Paulson looked at Grady over the top of the report. "And so, we verify the shortages and the first impact starts, internally. And Ambassador Luboff this morning made his third attempt in as many days to get an appointment on my calendar."

"Will you see him?"

"Of course. It would be too much of an affront not to."

"How much wheat are you going to deal for?"

"That depends on what your psychic geniuses can pull together for me. If we get something tangible out of this morning's meeting, something we could count on for a defensive weapon, I'll sell fifty million tons and take the gold teeth from that son of a bitch Kharkov at SALT in September. If we've got our butts in a sling as far as all this psychic stuff goes, I'll deal the hundred million and play it as a humanitarian gesture. But I'd hate like hell to have to do that. I want something big at the SALT summit. The timing's perfect."

Both men recognized that a September summit would have a profound influence on the November election.

"Are you dropping Clayton?"

"I'd love to. But he carries too much Southern vote. I might have to hold on to him to beat the Golden Boy from California. Shitty business, politics."

The President looked at his watch. "Let's get your people in here. I have to deal with Luboff this afternoon or tomorrow at the latest. Stay after this meeting, there are some things we'll have to talk about."

Minutes later, the White House protocol director, Jake Carpenter, swept Channing and Jerry into the den. Grady waved the tall, young White House staffer away and made the introductions himself. Among the things that Channing and Jerry carried with them was a portable cassette projector and a screen. They were easily set up in seconds, after which the four men sat on the facing couches.

Paulson looked across at Channing. "What is it? Thirty years, Doctor Moreland?"

Channing flashed a winning smile. "Thirty this year, Mister President."

"My goodness. Well, I guess it wouldn't do for either of us to say that the other didn't look a day older . . . Gentlemen, let me get right to the point. Mike Grady said that it was very important that I meet with you, especially before I meet with the Soviet ambassador. I have to confess that I was impressed, if that's the right word, by the . . . ah, predictions of Mrs. Tanner and the others at Moreland Research. Past that, I'm afraid I'm just a Minnesota farmer who gets a little skeptical when someone starts to suggest things like attacks mounted through . . . psychokin—"

"Psychokinesis, Mister President. It's the ability to move or alter the properties of matter using only mental energy."

"Yes. As I said, when that esoteric a subject arises, experts have to help. You come more than highly recommended by Mike here. He says you've moved through the available material on both the Golden Gate and Hoover with exceptional efficiency."

Channing and Jerry smiled nervously.

"And now that we've established that the two of you are both efficient and experts, it's your show."

Channing glanced quickly at his watch. A half-hour. A half-hour to brief the President of the United States on the work of a lifetime. "Mister President, I usually deal with the physics of things and Dr. Tanner handles the psychology. I'll ask him to start and I'll try to fill in the physics of all of this as it pertains to our investigation."

Paulson nodded and his gray eyes moved to Jerry, who'd been eyeing the President's body language since they'd walked in. There were two contradictory forces at work in the President, though Jerry was sure that Paulson was not fully aware of them. Though Paulson's remark about being a Minnesota farmer was in one way sarcastic, all of its ramifications were probably true. Although Paulson graduated among the top five in his class at Harvard Law School, he was still the son of a farmer and his upbringing was tough, pragmatic and somewhat unimaginative. The intensity of the President's glance indicated a man with a real interest in problem-solving. It was the "closed four" position of his body: legs crossed and turned slightly away from Jerry and Channing; that denoted the close-minded quality that could not allow him to accept anything parapsychological or paraphysical without rock-hard evidence. Jerry was glad that he had set up a demonstration, just in case.

"Mister President, the parasciences we study have been around as long as man. If we separate out the work of charlatans and superstitious zealots, we still come up with a considerable volume of evidence that man has a latent ability to divine future events accurately; to detect information from inanimate objects; and to alter the properties of matter. These abilities are called precognition, psychometry and psychokinesis, respectively. There are some other skills that we call 'distant seeing,' and 'distant influence.' They're of equal importance, but I'll get to them as we move on."

Paulson nodded cautiously.

"As far as we know at this time, all of these skills are controlled by the same areas in the brain; hitherto untrained and unrecognized in potential. Simply stated, we believe that man has, in reality, two brains; and one of them has gone begging for eons."

Jerry took a pen and sketched hurriedly a cross section of the brain, seen from above. He darkened in the corpus collosum as the brain's fiber barrier that separated the two.

"In essence, we know almost nothing about the function of the right hemisphere. Even the best brain surgeons in the world can say only that the right side has something to do with artistic function and aesthetics." Jerry pointed to the line drawn through the middle of his brain sketch. "The reason for our ignorance of the right brain is a communications problem. Although the fibrous barrier between the two"—Jerry avoided the technical term—"admits information from one side to the other, each side speaks a different language. And so, the right rejects much of the information that the left side has to offer."

Paulson raised a hand. "Wait. Is this a division of labor problem?"

Jerry smiled. "Exactly. In fact, that's probably the best way to put it. The left side controls all of the cognitive functions. Math, reading, conscious thought, memory . . . a great many things, and simple ones too. When you tie your shoes, it's the left side of the brain that makes it possible for you to carry out the task. With all of that control rooted in the left side, there was no need for the right side to learn how to read, write or communicate in a manner that the right side could comprehend.

"The right side contains all of the possible controls for PSI functions, but it hasn't developed them. Because the right side of the brain cannot communicate in a conventional manner, it sees and acts intuitively, which the left side cannot translate or make use of. Therefore, man hasn't developed the conscious control of these functions. Except for certain individuals."

"And those are the ones you and Doctor Moreland are studying?"

Jerry nodded. "We also feel that all of the PSI operations that the left side can control can be trained . . . in *anyone*." Jerry paused to let the statement sink in.

"Our contention is that everyone in the world has the raw material . . . everyone. All that has to be done is to train it so that it can function in a way that works voluntarily and on command. It also has to be trained to accept what the left side tells it. At this time in our research, we believe—as have Eastern religions for centuries—that individuals in an alpha state can control these functions. An alpha state is akin to twilight sleep and can be brought on by trance."

Paulson shook his head. His body language was still in a closed four: antagonism, disbelief. "Okay, Doctor Tanner. I've got all of that. But, how does all of the training account for Mrs. Tanner's ability to see in advance what happened at the Golden Gate . . . and Al Clearford's death? I mean those things are well outside the range of probability?"

"That, Mister President, is because probability is a left-side function of logic and cannot admit the possibility that the right side has anything to contribute. The chances are that the same thing is at work when 'psychics' have to perform in front of witnesses and in many cases in rigid, sterile lab conditions. The right side of the brain starts to . . . feel uncomfortable, if you will, and allows the left side to obliterate its signals. It is only after the right side is allowed to get in charge that it can get results. Historically speaking, psychics do poorly on rigidly controlled tests after a period of time.

"There are hundreds of factors. But what we're interested in is how all of this can be made to work, in the light of left-side logic. Logic tells us that we cannot see the future. But the chances are that the right brain can extrapolate information about future events and distant occurrences by integrating all of the known possibilities and intuiting the right one. Past that, we know little. Eve, my wife, has worked on building her right-side ability for at least the last ten years. She's retrained the left side so that it does not always impede what the right side intuits. The chances are that the right side of her brain saw the bridge tragedy as something that *had* to happen. The left recorded it as data and she retained it. The gas can that we found at the scene was something that triggered the same intuition again and she saw the dam as a possibility. The reason that the predictions are fuzzy sometimes is that the right brain is illiterate and only speaks to the left in dream images and visions."

Paulson nodded. Jerry could see that his body language had softened slightly.

"Okay, Doctor. Assuming that all of the theory is correct—and, by the way, you explain all of it well—how does this become a weapon? How does someone knock out a bridge or a dam with it?"

"That's psychokinesis or PK. It's another right-side ability we're just starting to explore." Jerry's eyes darted to Channing for a second; it was really Channing's area he was about to explore. Moreland got the idea immediately.

"Go ahead, Jer. You're doing fine." Channing looked to the President. "Doctor Tanner is concerned about my sensibilities. PK is my specialty. But he can do a better job of briefing on it that I can."

Paulson nodded impatiently. "Okay, Doctor, how does it become a weapon?"

"Mister President, consider for the moment that all matter"—he tapped the top of the immense coffee table—"all of it is not as solid as it appears to be. Rather, it's moving, vibrating at a rate set by the elements that it is made of. In essence, all matter is frozen energy, moving in a predetermined pattern. We believe that it is possible for the right side of the brain to generate a signal that is measurable on a number of scales. This signal relates to the molecular glue in the element."

"It . . . dissolves the glue?"

"Exactly, Mister President. It's really a fairly mysterious process and we don't know much more than conjecture and theory. If I can take a minute"—Jerry pointed to the small projector that he and Channing had brought with them—"I can show you what we mean."

Paulson nodded and Jerry cranked up the film cassette.

The boy was nine or perhaps ten. He sat at a table in a stark, antiseptic room. The camera drew back to reveal a complex apparatus, mounted on the table top.

Jerry froze the frame. "His name is Jeffery Cuthers. He's ten and he's from Newark. We've been working with him at the institute for just under a year. He's sitting in a Faraday cage: a kind of psychic isolation chamber. No detectable signals can get in or out."

The bar was stainless steel. It looked to be about a half-inch thick and just over a foot long.

"The bar is mounted on a pedestal, which has been bolted to the table, which, in turn, is bolted to the floor. The pedestal is covered with a glycerin bubble and the whole thing is covered with a bell jar. The protocols are as rigid as we can make them. The read-outs that you'll see on the bottom of the screen will be heartbeat and respiration."

Jeffery might have been any black child from the Newark ghetto except for his striking blue eyes—the heritage a plantation owner gave his great grandmother who was a slave. Painfully thin, Jeffery eyed the steel bar and leaned forward toward the table, resting his elbows on the edges and his chin in the palms of his hands. His blue eyes narrowed in concentration.

The film jumped.

"For the sake of time, Mister President, we've moved

ahead to a point some five minutes into the experiment."

Jeffery was ragged. He looked like a child in the midst of a nightmare. Bathed in perspiration, the boy rocked back and forth rhythmically. His small black hands balled into tight fists, which were held tightly to either side of his head, like a boxer defending himself against the onslaught of an opponent.

Numbers flashed across the bottom of the screen.

HB . . . 160 . . . 165 . . . 175// RES 37 . . . 42 . . . 50 . . .

Slowly, almost imperceptibly, the shape of the bar was starting to change. The left end was starting to reach slightly upward from the horizontal, while the right end had started to bend slightly toward the camera.

The film blinked and Jerry pressed the hold button again.

"At this point, we stopped him. The stress is considerable. Look now."

The bar had been transformed into a bizarre modern sculpture, twisting up and out in several places. It wobbled slowly forward and backward on the small pedestal. . . .

Jerry snapped off the projector. "The metal continued to alter in shape for fifteen minutes after Jeff was taken from the Faraday cage."

Paulson stared at the blank screen for a second. Jerry opened his briefcase and removed a thick plastic bag, like the airtight commercial bags, but larger. He opened the top and pulled out a twisted snake of metal. He handed it across to the President.

Paulson took it silently and turned it over in his hands for a few seconds, before his eyes moved up to Jerry's. "The same one, I assume."

"The same." Jerry gestured to it. "You can try to

bend it, Mister President. It's a pretty natural thing to want to do. I always tend to want to."

Paulson did, halfheartedly, as if to assure himself that all of it was real. It wouldn't budge. He handed it back to Jerry.

"I'm . . . impressed. And a little confused. You mentioned earlier that a twilight sleep, I think you said, was the basis of all of this. The little boy— Jeffery? He was far from relaxed."

Channing cleared his throat. "Mister President, if I may?"

"Of course, Doctor Moreland."

"The child's brain was relaxed. His brain waves were in a high-amplitude alpha mode."

"You're saying that his brain was asleep while the rest of him was keyed-up like a bowstring?"

"That's correct."

"Then how does he do it. How does he make the separation?"

Channing darted a glance at Jerry. "Part of it he came to us with. He had a raw skill. But for five months he could only affect metal by laying hands on it. By last week, he was able to have the same effects in the experiment, from a table on the far side of the cage. Oh, and by the way"—Channing pointed to the steel snake still in Jerry's hands—"the steel isn't steel anymore . . . not strictly speaking. It's an alloy—lighter, more brittle."

"But *how?*"

Channing gestured to Jerry. "Through Doctor Tanner's training program. The child came with a great potential. Jerry simply applied a training sequence over a period of time."

Paulson gestured to Jerry. "You said *anyone* could do this?"

"We think so. Though we've had a great deal more success with distant seeing than with PK. PK requires a great deal more development, because of the balance of tension and relaxation."

"Wait, wait. Distant seeing?"

"Yes, Mister President."

Grady reached over and touched Paulson on the shoulder. "Steve, perhaps I'd better explain this. After all, I was a test subject."

"You?"

Grady looked to Jerry and then to the President. "It was that day you sent me up to the institute. Moreland said anyone could do it. I think I believe him."

Paulson smiled tentatively. "You mean if you can, anyone can?"

"Something like that. Jerry, do you have the sketches and the photos?"

Jerry dug them out of the briefcase. He passed three sketches and the Polaroid photos across to the President.

"Jerry convinced me to do this. A demonstration is the best way to dispel doubt. If after you see these, any doubts remain about the validity of all of this, I'm sure Jerry and Channing can arrange a demonstration for you, Steve."

Grady laid out the sketches and the photos on the coffee table. It looked to the President as if the sketches were made of the subjects of the photos. One shot showed the eighteenth-century facade of a Georgetown townhouse. Paulson recognized it as Grady's. The second was a view of the reflecting pool as seen from the Lincoln Memorial. The third was of an open field somewhere. Paulson guessed that it might be in the Maryland mountains.

"I made all of those sketches while I was sitting in a lab at the research institute. The target locations were given to one of the staff members at the institute who was flying to D.C. that morning. He opened three sealed and randomly selected envelopes. Each stated a location where he was to be at a predetermined time. He was instructed to take photos and bring them back with him. Jerry here had me relax in the lab while he asked me to try to imagine where the man was. You can see how the sketches match with the photos, given my rotten sketching."

Paulson shook his head. "I don't know, Mike . . ."

Tanner and Grady exchanged glances. "Steve? I'm a believer. I did this. I know that there was no possible way that it could have been faked. Jerry and Channing have an operative somewhere downtown if you want to carry out the same demonstration." His eyes went back to Jerry, who quickly glanced at his watch and nodded.

"No, Mike. That's not it. It's just that I'm getting a lot of input here and I need time to absorb it." Paulson reached up and kneaded a tight shoulder muscle. "The trouble is that we don't seem to have the time for me to absorb anything before some decisions have to be made. Do *you* know how you did it?"

"Not really. I thought that my imagination was wandering. I felt at one point that the sketch was totally fantasy. As it turns out, none of the three were."

"All right. Say all of this works. And I accept for the moment that it does. What is the range of this distant seeing?"

Jerry folded his arms. "We're not sure . . . not precisely at any rate."

Channing interrupted. "Mister President, experiments have been carried out at a range of twelve thousand miles, with an eighty percent accuracy rate. As far as we know, it will work at any distance, and there does not even have to be a person on the scene. All that has to happen is that the subject be given the locale and be *led* there verbally by the tester. It's a positive feedback approach. Encouragement usually increases the accuracy rate for distant seeing. We—"

"Excuse me, ah, Channing."

"Yes, Mister President?"

"You said a twelve thousand mile range with eighty percent accuracy?"

"Yes, Mister President."

Paulson turned to Grady. "Mike, neither you nor Andy Clayton has ever briefed me on any of our research that's been that sweeping."

Grady started to answer, but Channing cut him off. "Mister President, the reason you got no briefing is that *we* haven't done the research. The Soviets have. Their research operation is headed by an old friend of mine . . . a colleague of sorts. His name is Andrei Sholodkin. Some years back, we shared a Nobel Prize. He is, in my opinion, the world's foremost expert in this area. Much of the research that the institute is now doing is based on Andrei's techniques as well as his protocols."

Paulson got to his feet and moved across to the rolltop desk. "Let me put this together." He paused a second, then turned back to the group on the sofa and asked shrewdly, "What is the connection between . . . PK and distant seeing?"

Channing Moreland's hand quivered slightly. Jerry noticed that a thin film of perspiration covered the old man's forehead. He was perhaps too old, Jerry thought, to be under such intense pressure. Apparently, Grady also noticed. He spoke before Channing could.

"Steve, let me address myself to that question, if I may. It's the part of things that I've been in close touch with in the last weeks."

"Very well." There was a touch of formality and distance in Paulson's tone. Grady recognized it as the discipline of a trial judge on the bench. He remembered hearing the President characterize it as his "this-is-what-I-get-paid-to-do" attitude.

"Doctor Moreland mentioned that PK altered that piece of steel at the molecular level. Numerous metal samples from the Golden Gate support cable, the tail rotor assembly of the Vice President's aircraft, and metal reinforcements in the Hoover Dam structure show exactly the same characteristics as that piece of steel that you saw in the film.

"Last week we managed to complete the reinterviews with the Golden Gate survivors. I took Doctor Tanner's suggestion and had as many interviewed under hypnosis or pentathol as possible. We got lucky. One of the witnesses who we'd had trouble locating was a man named—" Grady opened a file folder on the coffee table —"Robert Collins, a truck driver. He was on the bridge surface when all hell broke loose. We'd missed Collins on the first set of interviews. It seems that he'd had a bit of local trouble. An assault charge lodged by his former employer. So he wasn't anxious to speak to federal investigators. At any rate, we managed to smoothe things over with the plaintiff, and Collins in return agreed to a pentathol exam.

"It seems that in the moments after Collins had driven his gasoline truck off the bridge, the trailer sheared loose and skidded across the observation deck platform. It smashed into a VW that was either parked or trying to get out of the way. Collins remembers seeing the driver and the car incinerated when the tank blew up.

"I assumed that as his was the only car incinerated and that as the gas can that Mrs. Tanner saw at the scene was also incinerated, there might be a connection. We went over the wreckage again; there was nothing to really find, just a heap of melted metal. But we did find a small metal tag in the parking lot. It was an employee's bumper tag for a toll taker named Trevor Lewis.

Then a search team found an unclaimed and badly charred skull and we assumed it was Lewis' because no other victims were burned. Investigation revealed a jackpot. Trevor Lewis never existed, not before a few months ago, at least. His entire background seems to have been a clever cover, developed over a period of time. The coroner who checked the dental work says Lewis had a hinged tooth hollow on the inside. It contained traces of shellfish toxin. . . ."

Grady stopped and took a deep breath. "And a number of the other teeth seem to have been made of stainless steel."

"Jesus Christ." Paulson's voice was a barely audible whisper. He knew as well as Grady what stainless steel teeth meant: Russia! They were the only ones who still used them. Paulson looked for a second like a man who'd just been read his own death sentence and didn't believe it.

"Is it blackmail, Mike? Russia wants our wheat? And if this man Lewis died, then who is continuing the attacks?"

Channing stood up. "I last spoke with Andrei Sholodkin in January. I was given the clear impression that an 'experiment' along the lines of distant PK was the next step in the development. I have to add that it was something that Andrei did not want; I'm sure that he had no choice in the matter. Just as I'm sure that Russia has trained *many* operatives."

Paulson crossed quickly to the couch. There was a sense of efficiency in his movement that had not been there before. "The Soviets must be responsible for all the disasters. If the metal samples are all in the same altered state, then the same forces are at work." He stopped for a second and rubbed a large gnarled hand through his thinning hair. "Bluntly, how many of these fuckers are operating?"

"Steve, the number doesn't matter. We would have no way of apprehending them. We only pieced together the theory on Lewis from hunches and lucky breaks. We have no concrete leads on the helicopter crash or the dam. Channing's test subjects think that whatever hit the dam hit it from a distance—a great distance. If the Soviets have perfected what we saw that little boy do in the film, and they can do it from a distance with the aid of distant seeing . . . well, we're going to need a crash program in order to muster any defense at all. Jerry and Channing here tell me that they can assemble the staff and the subjects to make a start at it. Time is the problem."

Jerry interrupted. "Mister President, we're not even sure if a defense can be developed. It's possible that there is no defense except the strong development of an offense. Something like a nuclear stalemate."

"I'll settle for that, Gentlemen. Consider that you have all of the resources that you will need as far as government funds and cooperation are concerned. We need results. We—"

A quick tap at the door stopped Paulson in midword. It was followed by the young, alarmingly calm face of one of Paulson's press aides. Grady hoped for the young man's sake that the issue was vital.

"Mister President, excuse me, sir. The press release?"

"Ah . . . yes. Release it right now."

The young man nodded and was gone. It was that quick. Grady was curious but decided to wait.

"Now, Gentlemen. How long will it take until you have a defense?"

Jerry and Channing looked at one another for a minute. It was as if the enormity of the task had just struck them. How could a deadline be put on a lifework?

Jerry shook his head slowly. "I don't think we can say, Mister President."

"That's not acceptable, Doctor Tanner. I need something to work with. Don't tell me it will be years. If that's so, we'd might as well not worry about it."

Jerry's eyes met Channing's fleetingly. The old man was distant. He seemed almost catatonic for a second or two. His voice's strength startled Jerry. If the old man had reserves, he'd just started digging into them. "Two months for results. Three for something really operational. I agree if it goes past that, we've lost."

"Two months."

"Or three, Mister President."

Paulson closed his eyes and breathed deeply. The burden didn't ease. "I might be able to stall that long. Perhaps we'll all get lucky."

Grady stayed on with the President after Channing and Jerry left. He went to the roll-top desk, where he quickly jotted down a scribbled set of notes. "Hang on for a minute."

Obviously satisfied with what he'd written, he moved to one of the easy chairs and sat. Grady chuckled his thin Irish laugh.

Paulson looked at him quizzically for a second. "No, Mike. No puns, no witticisms—not now."

"No, Steve. I wouldn't. It was just an hour ago, we were going to deal wheat to Kharkov for a summit . . . SALT concessions . . . a second term."

"The stakes went up. The game's the same. There's even an outside chance . . ." Paulson sat forward. "What do you have on this Russian genius Sholodkin?"

"Scientifically?"

"Politically."

"He's not in the party. If that's what you're after."

"Do you remember Kharkov's telegram: '. . . on the Colorado'?"

"Are you saying he's a shill? A pacifist?"

"Perhaps one of his people?"

"So that garbled line is Sholodkin's warning rather than Kharkov's threat?"

"I have to consider that it's possible."

"I don't know. Let me put a feel out through NSA. There's a chance I can get something. Not to change the subject, how much wheat will you want to deal to Luboff?"

"As little as I have to . . . enough to buy us three months. And there's something else I'll need. You're going to be the Leslie Groves for the operation."

Grady thought for a second about Groves. He'd managed the entire Manhattan Project for almost four years, juggling large corporations and weaving the greatest security blanket in the history of the Western world around the operation. But Groves had every resource of the country at his disposal and that was in wartime. Secrecy was the order of the day. This was forty years later; Grady didn't have that kind of elbow room.

"Groves had more clout, Steve. So did Roosevelt, for that matter. He was in his third term."

"It doesn't matter about the term, Mike. If everything I just heard is true, then we flop in the next sixty to ninety days. There won't *be* an election. As far as clout for you, the only way you'll have that will be as Acting Secretary of Defense."

Grady winced. "Oh, shit." His tone wasn't anger. It was resignation.

Paulson actually smiled. "I know. You hate politics. I have to fill Clayton's slot fairly fast. You need muscle to do this job. It would be for less than six months. After that all of us might be out of work—or dead. Besides, you owe me a favor, after not preparing me for what those two were going to say."

"If I had, you'd have said it was all bullshit. You know that as well as I do. Tanner had someone downtown with a camera all through the meeting against the possibility that you might have needed a demonstration with you as a test subject. That's how he convinced me. No, Steve. I owe you a lot, but springing that on you was necessary."

"In the same way that springing this on you is necessary?"

Grady nodded. "I guess. All right. I'll agree to it . . . if I can move some of Clayton's people aside. We won't be able to afford harassment from appointees loyal to him."

"It's your show. Do what you have to. Just remember we have to have perfect security—perfect."

Grady took his pad from the coffee table. I guess I'd better get a statement together for the press."

"Right."

Paulson walked across and snapped on all three of the TV sets. One carried a five-minute news brief. He snapped off the other two and turned up the sound on the newscast.

"Along with the announcement, White House Protocol Director Jackson Carpenter characterized Doctor Grady's reaction as pleased. He quoted Grady as saying, 'It's an exciting and challenging responsibility; one that I am proud to accept.' "

Paulson turned off the TV and turned to Grady. "Jake Carpenter's probably released the rest of the acceptance. He'll have a copy for you on the way out."

The two men stared at one another for a long, tense minute before Grady spoke. "Mister President, you are a son of a bitch. You had that appointment ready before Moreland and Tanner got here. That was the release you were talking about when that youngster dropped in."

"Right. Congratulations, Mister Secretary. Or will they call you Doctor Secretary."

"Kissinger clarified that when he was appointed in Nixon's second term. The media asked him what he wanted to be called. He said he didn't stand on ceremony. 'Your Excellency' would be fine."

The two men laughed.

9

*And for a fleeting second . . . I was not sure if
I was a man dreaming I was a butterfly, or a butterfly dreaming I was a man. . . .*

—Lao-tzu

The flames were licking upward hungrily through
the windows. Firelight cast grotesque shadows of running forms on the brick wall across the street. In the
distance, she could hear explosions or gunfire. They'd
been getting closer for hours. And then there was a new
sound. Deep, guttural and male. They pushed through
the door and amid whispers and deep-throated laughs
they splayed the harsh beams of flashlights across the
darkened room. Feet ran past her. She could hear the
sound of shattering glass in the other room.

In the last second, she could see the boot coming
at her. She tried to dive out of the way and cover her
stomach with her arms. It hit and everything exploded
in pain. . . .

The twinge of pain brought her awake with a gasp.
She was curled in a tight fetal ball in the middle of the
bed. Beneath her, the sheets were damp with her perspiration. She reached down and guarded her stomach
with her hands.

A dream. He's all right. The pain was in the dream.

She reached an unseeing hand out to feel for Jerry's back, just for the security of it. He wasn't there. The clock radio on the night table read 2:07 A.M. Eve stretched and rolled over. After a quiet moment and two or three deep breaths, she could feel the pressure on her chest start to ease. Her adrenalin subsided and her heartbeat returned to normal. A tiny flutter just beneath her fast-disappearing navel surprised her, and after a second or two, she smiled. The surge in her endocrines had awakened him. There was another flutter and the barest hint of a kick. She thought of a cartoon fetus, pounding a pillow inside the womb, settling in after its sleep was disturbed. *My nightmare or his?* She mused over it for a second until a sense of urgency told her the probable cause of the nightmare: the pillow that the baby had thumped before going off to sleep—her bladder.

She trudged down the hall in the half-light that seeped up the stairs from the den. The bathroom light was harsh and her eyes reacted by snapping shut. She relieved her cramped, painful bladder of its contents and then looked at herself in the mirror. Her sharp features and deep blue eyes were softened by sleep. Unfortunately, they weren't softened enough. *Damn!* She was totally and irrevocably awake . . . again.

It was a blessing and a curse. Even as a frantic teenager, she'd needed only a few hours of sleep a night, while her sister Sue had needed a solid eight. When they'd shared a room at the summer lakefront cabin, Eve could jabber about boys until three and then be up with the birds. She'd bang around getting dressed to face the dawn, while Sue groaned and pulled a pillow over her head. Eve had always complained that her sister wasted her life in bed.

She suddenly realized that she thought of Sue in the past tense. It had only been a month and already . . . in the past tense. A slight flicker of guilt flashed distantly, like fireworks in a rainstorm. As it evaporated, Eve realized that she'd adjusted, adapted—coped. And for what it might have meant to Sue's memory, she was playing a role in avenging her sister's death.

She snapped off the light and started back down the hall. The light still burned in the den. Jerry'd been at work from just past eight. Eve tied the belt loosely over the top of the bulge in her tummy. In a month, she realized, she wouldn't be able to belt it at all. She went quietly down the stairs to the den.

"Hi."

Jerry took off a pair of black-rimmed reading glasses and squinted across the room at her. Perhaps it was the cheeriness of her greeting that told him.

He looked up in a kind of mock supplication to the gods then glanced back at her, managing a grin. "Oh, God. Don't tell me. Bright-eyed and bushy-tailed. Full of ideas and rarin' to go—right?"

She scuffed a bare foot across the deep shag carpet. "Shucks, Doctor Tanner, you see through me just all the time. I just here to turn a fast trick so that I can pay the rent."

He pointed to the prominent bulge under the robe. "We did that a few months ago, remember? If you don't, try thinking about it when you can't see your feet any more."

He was surrounded with note pads, reference books and reports. Hunched over a small work table in jeans and slippers, he wore a black T-shirt that carried a single, ornately printed word. SHRINKS! It had been the institute's ill-fated softball team that had died of lack of interest more than a year ago. The shirts were the only artifacts.

Jerry's eyes were red-rimmed and he needed a shave. He had been pushing himself brutally since the trip to D.C. and the Paulson-Grady briefing. He was under intense pressure from the President, from Channing, from everyone. But Eve knew that the worst pressure was that he placed on himself. He'd spent the better part of the last year helping Channing with operations and reports and now, with a double load, he was pushing himself even harder.

He smiled at her as she came across the room to him. "What woke you?"

"A scary dream. Amazing what a little pressure on the bladder can do to the subconscious."

"Speaking of the subconscious . . ." He pointed to the pile of papers that surrounded him.

She nodded. "Yeah, I noticed." She picked up a volume from the top of the pile and read the title: *Experiments in Distant Influence* by L. L. Vasiliev. "The Einstein of Soviet parapsychology."

Jerry folded his arms and laughed. "You always get this eloquent when you can't sleep at two in the morning?"

"Just when I sleep alone."

He nodded and raised an index finger like a basketball referee indicating a foul shot. "Touché, Tanner."

Her looked changed. It became empathetic, compassionate, strangely defenseless. "Oh, honey, I didn't . . ."

He moved the index finger to his lips. "*Shhh.* It's okay. It was a bad line. But the 'Einstein of Soviet parapsychology'?" That's something you could sell to Anton Deladier."

"No, I couldn't either. It's bad business to sell back what you've stolen. Especially, selling it to the man you stole it from. I remember Anton using the phrase a year or two ago on the rostrum, somewhere." She looked at the book again. "Isn't Vasiliev Anton's strong suit? I seem to remember he was lecturing about the Leningrad Institute and Faraday experiments the night he coined the phrase."

"It is his strong area. He might even know more about the Soviets than Channing."

"Why are you doing his work for him, then?"

The question was not accusatory. It stemmed from a deep commitment to brutal intellectual honesty that burned inside of Eve and always had. She liked to put the right peg in the right hole. Jerry's greatest strength was in the evolution of applications based on his own theories and some of Eve's. The leg work of research was something that he dragged his way through. It put more pressure on him and took him from her. She wanted to know why.

"The man is brilliant. I give him that."

"But?"

"Yes. But. He has a temperament to match. He managed to get himself bent out of shape twice today. I guess it was yesterday by now. First, he was pissed at not being included in the Paulson-Grady briefing. An hour later he was chewing into Channing in a staff meeting." Jerry paused and shook his head.

"What about?"

"Me. At least that was what the subtext was all about. After saving the dam, he must have really wanted to head up Grady's task force. When he heard that Channing appointed me, he boiled over. It's probably an extension of his not getting the PSI director's post. He can't forgive me or Channing for either."

"Were you sitting there?"

"About three feet away, across the table. You would have been proud of me. I didn't hit him with the water pitcher."

"What did Channing do?"

"He just listened and nodded. It was more to let Anton blow off steam than anything else. The meeting was over a few minutes later and Anton stormed out, still in high dudgeon. The whole thing started when Channing asked him to work up a summary of Vasiliev's research. We were going to put eight or nine of them together for the major researchers of the twentieth century. I'd drawn Wilhelm Reich in the raffle, which was logical. I know something about him. I think Anton said something like: 'The approach is infantile. We're feebly trying to reinvent the wheel without competent management. We'll never find the answer. . . .' It went on for a while. This," he said, pointing to the mass of books and papers, "is the bottom line."

"You do both his and yours." There was an edge in Eve's voice. The last thing in the world Jerry needed was more pressure.

"Yeah. At least until Anton's feathers unruffle. And there isn't time for ego trips, not with everything we've got to do. Channing asked me to make a start on it. He said that Anton's always been a little bitter. I think Channing nosed him out for a grant thirty years ago or so. He's hung the failure of Western Research on it. Channing thinks it's a convenient rationalization." He rubbed the backs of his hands against his eyes.

"And Channing?"

"He's more pressured than I am. I'm trying to put the management of the project together to take some of his load." He exhaled audibly through his teeth. "A lot of work."

She got up from the sofa and moved across to the big recliner-rocker, which he'd made his night headquarters. "So you do half of Channing's, all of Anton's and all of your own. Doctor Tanner, you are out of your mind." She slipped onto his lap and curled her head against his chest. She reached up and took the pair of reading glasses from their perch on his forehead. He couldn't read without them and she knew it. She tossed them across to the couch.

"Break time," she whispered and slid a hand up his chest under his shirt. Her slender fingers kneaded his wiry chest hairs for a few moments.

Jerry thought for a moment she'd gone to sleep and had started to consider carrying her up to bed, then coming back down. Suddenly, she looked up at him again. She got to her feet and started out of the den.

"Where?"

"Getting some coffee. You can do two people's work. I've seen you. But, I don't know about three, and I'm too awake to go to bed. So I'll get some coffee and we'll work together. Until you crash, that is."

Jerry smiled. There would be no deterring her. "Maybe an hour."

She brought the coffee back and they began. She pieced together all that she know of Vasiliev's works and Jerry added all of his information. They reduced the body of information to research topics and outlined the key elements of each topic. A casual observer, perhaps, would have been surprised at how Eve and Jerry could slip from personal to professional with such fluid ease. It took them just under a half-hour to list twenty areas, all of which would need research. Each of the twenty could have become a key factor in the mastery of PK over distances. Or the key to the technique might be in a merger of two or more. All of the available information would have to be crossindexed and run through a concordance procedure that could matrix the similarities. The odds were that Jerry could get those on a computer. He made a note to give the outlines to Rosemary McGee. If there was a way to construct a quick program for almost anything she'd be the one who could deliver. He wondered to himself whether he should mention Anton to the woman. Jerry had known of their relationship for some time. Eve didn't. Nor did she really know Rosemary, not personally, at least. He dismissed the idea. Better to brainstorm Vasiliev with Eve.

By just after three, they had started to pound through the corollaries. Both of them mentally ran through any corollary information relative to spinoffs to Vasiliev, exclusive of Sholodkin. He was Channing's to explore. Together, they took an idea, and turned it so that it was visible from all angles. It was becoming almost aggravating how much Vasiliev had spurred.

The Russian innovator, who'd been almost a foster father to Andrei Sholodkin, had started research in distant communication as soon as he'd founded the Leningrad Institute for Brain Research. The core of his thesis was a wave theory. Distant communications experiments between Leningrad and Vladivostok had shown him that the speed of communication in a successful experiment was so great as to be unmeasureable on the best recording instruments of his day. It was the nineteen-thirties, and his measurements and calculations suffered from long trips by courier on the Trans-Siberian Railroad. With these impediments, Vasiliev assumed that the speed was instantaneous and PK as well as distant seeing were signatures in a large electromagnic waveform. He hypothesized that the earth was being struck by constant waves of energy that, as Wilhelm Reich later characterized them, were "neither electric nor magnetic, but carried the properties of both." Reich had called the wave "Orgone energy." Vasiliev saw this wave as a carrier for the telepathic signal that was overlayed on it. He theorized that the sender emanated a electrical brain-wave pattern on a wavelength of just under a hundred meters. This "brain radio" signal overlayed itself, hitchhiking, so to speak, on a freight train. It moved so quickly to a distant target that communication seemed instantaneous. And neither the sender nor the receiver was aware of the carrier wave that sped through the atmosphere, any more than a person on the street might notice radio waves coming from a radio transmitting antenna.

Did PK have the same kind of signature pattern? If it did, and Vasiliev claimed that almost all paranormal brain activity did, why couldn't Jerry get PK to work at a distance? Or was PK something else entirely. Was the human brain the bullet or the gun?

It was nearly four when Jerry saw Eve stifle a yawn with her hand. They hadn't gotten very far. They would, with Channing and the others, have to look for a philosophical premise, rather than a technique. It was frustrating.

"No, we can't do that either," Eve objected. "There isn't the time. We have to practically apply Vasiliev's theory. We have to just assume that there is a signal and look for ways to use it, detect it . . . and deflect it!"

"Eve, if the theory's wrong, the applications won't matter a damn. We'll be doing apples and Sholodkin would have been doing pears. We have to know if Sholodkin is working off of something unrelated to Vasiliev's work." He stopped and looked at her as she sat next to him, knees curled under her on the floor. "And you're right. There isn't time. We just have to assume that Sholodkin *is* doing a variation or a direct derivative."

"Wait, Jerry—we're stupid. Our own experiments have the answer . . . or a key to it. PK effects carry on after the subjects stop sending, right?"

"For as much as half an hour. Maybe longer."

"Does a single radio signal hang around that long . . . when it's riding a carrier?"

"No." Jerry was tired. He wasn't quite sure where she was going.

"Then there is no wave . . . not for PK. It's got to be resonance . . . vibration. An internal human radio signal that gets amplified by something in the endocrines. That's why PK sensitives get so agitated. Every hormone in the body jumps. The chances are that you have to get an adrenalin spike going before any vibration will be emitted. The left brain creates a frequency and the endocrine system probably boosts it. At a point, the harmonic resonates with the same pattern as the target. That's why metal keeps bending after the subject stops bending it. If the cable on the bridge was a tuning fork, Trevor Lewis simply tapped it with the right resonance and let it shake apart. If the molecules vibrate in the metal, wouldn't that be what causes—" she stifled another yawn—"the steel to turn into an alloy . . . to change at the molecular level?"

Jerry tried to look enthusiastic. He jotted down a note to check the work of Cazzamalli on human wavelengths and Kajinsky on the nervous system as a conductor. "It's a brilliant suggestion. Are you after my job?"

She patted her tummy gently. "I'm a little tied up, right now. Maybe later. And for a brilliant suggestion, your reaction is pretty dour, fearless project director."

"No, not dour. It's just that it will take us a month to set up the tests on that and maybe another month to get any results . . . if there are any to be gotten. The whole thing is a crap shoot, with this kind of time deadline. And it won't give us the sophistication to zap a moving helicopter or start to shake apart something the size of the Golden Gate or Hoover dam. We need an early-warning system, a burglar alarm,—and then something to stop the burglar with."

"I'm the burglar alarm. So are you, and Maria, and Channing and everybody else at the institute. Distant seeing is the burglar alarm. All we have to do is to flood Sholodkin's lab with distant seeing experiments. We'll collate the results. There's a chance that we can get early warning of the targets and perhaps something on technique. The PK side of the experiment can start using what we find as soon as possible. If—"

It sounded like a moan.

They looked at one another in silence for a second.

Another moan, like a sob.

Crissy.

Eve got to her feet. Jerry started to follow, but she waved him off as she headed for the stairs. "I'll get her. I'll be back in a few minutes. She probably just needs to be held."

Moving quickly up the stairs and down the house's main hall, Eve snapped on the hall light and let the reflected light illuminate the child's bedroom. Crissy was thrashing and mumbling. Eve woke her gently. As soon as the seven year old realized that Eve was holding her, she started to cry in earnest.

"Mo—Mo—Mommy?"

"*Shhh.* It was just a dream. It's gone now." Seven and eight were the years of night terrors and there was nothing to do but be quietly reassuring about them.

"It was—was—"

"Try to forget it, Sweetheart. It's gone."

The tow-headed little girl shook her head.

"It was fire and monsters and running and—and—"

Eve rocked her back and forth. "I'll stay with you for a few minutes and maybe you can get back to sleep. You have a big day at school tomorrow."

Eve cradled the child in her arms for a few minutes. The little girl pressed her head to her mother's breast. "You won't let them hurt us?"

"Who?" she whispered.

"The monsters. The ones in the fire—with all the lights . . . those bad men." Crissy started to sob. Eve shushed her and stroked her hair.

Finally, Crissy drifted off to sleep. Eve felt a cold, tight knot hardening in her stomach. *The bad men. The fire and the chasing.*

The same dream? She shuddered. What was it?

She quietly left the room with the knot tightening. Her nightmare had been shared—rerun in the mind of a seven year old.

She thought of mentioning it to Jerry. It was also the same dream that Crissy had had the night that Sue and Tommy were killed. No. Jerry had enough. This would be hers to figure out . . . once she stopped being frightened.

She went back down to the den.

Anton Deladier sat quietly in his living room, surrounded by piles of occult reference books. On the coffee table in front of him was a photocopy of the battered list of predictions he'd gotten from the woman in the hotel. He had spent every spare minute for weeks trying to decipher the baroque scrawl and the cryptic phrases. He yawned as he opened another book and scanned a marked page.

Suddenly, he sat up, eyes wide. *Yes. That's it. The eagle . . . the bear . . . and that's it!* He had the key and he knew it. His mind raced ahead. He'd get into the computer center early and set up a secret program on it. No one would know . . . not even Rosemary. He smiled broadly as he thought of the thirty years he'd waited for revenge. He held the key now. And soon Channing would pay, along with Tanner.

It was only a matter of time.

10

The simple truth, writ large by the whole history of science, is . . . that which yesterday appeared as supernatural is today accepted as natural.
—L. L. Vasiliev,
Experiments in Distant Influence

It took Jerry two days of battering, pestering and generally harassing the MRI staff to gather all existing information on resonance and vibration as they related to PK and other psychic phenomena. The results of the search were both positive and negative. On the positive side, there was a massive volume of data on vibration and resonance, especially when Jerry added to the research the information provided on the harmonics of metals, courtesy of the metallurgy lab. It was the very wealth of data that was available that started to create difficulties. While the exact resonances of almost all metals were available in one form or another, the research on the impact of mind on metal was poor. Most papers written on the subject were totally theoretical, with little true experimental groundwork in evidence. Jerry felt like a man starving in a desert. He was surrounded with an abundance of canned food and water and he was without a can opener.

He spent the better part of Thursday morning in his

office at the far end of the parapsychology lab, skimming the most promising of the information. He knew that he was over his head with most of it. He was not a physicist and a great deal of the data was pure physics. Boiled down to what he could begin to understand it told him that everything in nature vibrated at a specific rate. It ranged from trees to bridges to people. The vibration was created by the action of molecules, presumably moving in response to either decaying orbit patterns or the actions of the electrons themselves. Past that, chemists and metallurgists threw up their hands. What the true causality of the vibration was had been a mystery. True, more examination by electron microscopy was being done every day. Indeed, it was going on in the same complex where Jerry worked. And, sadly, it might go on for years before any breakthroughs were made. Jerry didn't have years. It was a race, and his opponent had dashed from the starting blocks ten, perhaps twenty years before. Jerry would have to come up with one of two things: luck or a miracle. Ironically, he believed in neither.

Of the things that Jerry *did* learn, perhaps the most important was that a natural vibratory rate could be used as a weapon. The follow-up study on the fall of the Tacoma Narrows Bridge was a clear indication of that. When Galloping Gertie had been constructed, her designers and engineers ignored the factor of sound resonance in the superstructure. It was fatal. Once the winds that constantly wailed through the canyon she spanned reached a certain velocity, the entire bridge would hum. The wind moving across the struts and cables created a sound at the proper pitch to activate the natural harmonics of the steel. After a lengthy period of humming, Gertie started to gallop like a skittish horse under a saddle for the first time. The road surface bucked up and down five and six feet at a time. It was only a matter of weeks before the road was impassable. Shortly after that, Gertie fell, ripped apart by forces that altered the weight-bearing capability of her design. But how did the human mind create that vibration? *How?*

Jerry turned his back on the pile of papers on his desk and stared out the window. He liked the view. The rolling hills and farmland were turning green. Fair-weather clouds dotted the sky and a line of apple trees adjacent to the main lab building had just burst into pink and white. He was tempted to bolt from the office and run out into the field and then keep going. But he knew that Grady would find him. Grady had assigned more federal security men to the project than there were researchers. He slammed his hand down on the chair arm and grabbed for the phone. It only rang once before it was picked up.

"Logic systems. Doctor Hughes' office."

"Alice? This is Jerry Tanner. Is Tom at his desk?"

"No, Doctor Tanner. He's out sick with the flu. He called in several hours ago. He said he thinks he can be back on his feet by tomorrow."

"Alice, how sick is sick?"

"Well, he said if he felt any worse, he'd be dead. And he thought that to come in would expose everyone on the staff. He said that the last thing that we needed here now was an epidemic. I agree with him. Can I get someone else for you?"

Jerry thought for a second. "I don't know. I've got a pile of information here on my desk; I realized that the fastest way to collate it into some understandable order might be to use the computer. "What I need is someone to look at it and come up with a quick and dirty program that I can use to extract what I'm after."

"Well, I'm sure whatever you need, Daniel can do it. He's built for things like that. If there aren't too many variables, that is."

Jerry was always amazed at how MRI's computer department constantly referred to their computer as a person. While it was clearly easier to refer to a system formally known as Digital/Analog Integrated Electrical Logic System as "Daniel," the computer folks in the basement of the complex had turned him into a person, another member of the staff.

"Alice, honey, I got nuttin' but variables up here. I need someone who can gather it all up and come up with the time estimates for results fast. Who's the front runner in that department?"

There was silence for a second on the line. Jerry could almost see Alice hunched over the desk, chewing on the eraser end of a pencil as she thought.

"Well, if you want to know what *I* think, the best person to do that isn't in this department any more. She's"—a split second before Alice said the name, Jerry knew who she'd mention; it was someone he'd thought of several days earlier and forgotten in the crunch of information gathering—"Rosemary McGee."

"Thanks, Alice. You're fantastic. If I ever leave Eve, you'd be the one I'd leave for."

Alice giggled for a second. Jerry could see all of her two hundred or so pounds jiggle in his mind's eye. "Doctor Tanner, you are a rogue."

"I know. Thanks again."

He broke the connection and started to dial Anton Deladier's office number when an incoming call interrupted him.

"Parapsi. Tanner."

"Jerry? This is Mike Grady. Have you a moment?"

"Yes, Mike. What's up?"

"First, you have a touch tone phone, correct?"

"Yes."

"Would you please depress the asterisk button on the bottom of the phone? Depress it three times. Wait a second between each time."

Jerry did as he was told. For a few seconds after the last tap of the button, he could hear electrical connections being made and broken. When the sounds stopped, Grady's voice seemed ever so slightly more distant, though still quite clear.

"Now, if we could wait just another second or so. . . ."

Another voice came on the line. It surprised Jerry. The voice was efficient and also sounded a trifle bored. "Delta, Delta . . . Mike-Romeo-India security monitor. What is the precedence and clearance of this communication, please?"

"Clearance JCS. Precedence Flash Override."

Both men waited an additional few seconds. Jerry could hear the sounds on the line again. "Cleared for traffic. Please use a triple break at the end of this conversation."

"And now that we've gotten that out of the way, what—"

"Mike?"

"Yes, Jerry?"

"Excuse me, but what the hell was *that* all about?"

"I'm sorry. I didn't get a chance to explain. But I wanted to make sure that we were on a secure line before we started. It's a scrambler system. As we speak the conversation is getting routed through the STRATCOM system. That's Strategic Communications Command. It's being scrambled into word fragments and then reassembled on the other end. Detection is always possible, and there is nothing in the world that we could do to avoid being overheard if anyone wanted to go to a hell of a lot of trouble. What they couldn't do is understand a word we're saying. The computer that controls the scramble system uses a random pattern. It would take years to reassemble the conversation, even for a computer. STRATCOM erases the scramble pattern from memory as soon as it reassembles the words. In other words, this is now one hell of a secure phone line. I've taken the liberty of having the system keyed to your home line as well as Doctor Moreland's and my own. When you need to get in touch fast, just pick up the phone and break the signal three times. After that, dial the number nine-nine-nine. Then break the connection with the asterisk button . . . again, three times. The STRATCOM operator will identify himself or herself as DDMRI. That identifies the line as one between the institute and the Department of Defense. Say who you are and ask for me. Ask for the President, if you have to—but it's easier to get me. The operator will know my whereabouts twenty-four hours a day. Have you got that?"

"I think so."

"Tell the operator, should there be any confusion, that the precedence is Flash Override and the clearance is JCS. That stands for Joint Chiefs of Staff. That will get you through. You can reach Doctor Moreland at home in the same manner. Simply ask for him by name; the STRATCOM operator will handle it. Just don't do it unless there's an emergency. All hell breaks loose when that code is used. I mean they follow me into the john with a phone."

"You mean you don't want 'I'm Joe. Are there any messages for me?' "

Grady laughed. He paused and then said soberly, "The President has scheduled a meeting with the Soviet ambassador for Saturday morning. Is there anything that I can tell him? Can we make the kind of impression that we are hoping to make?"

Jerry looked at the mess on the desk. "I'd be less than honest if I said there was . . . yet. I've got a mountain of information here on my desk. If we can get it all sorted into a meaningful order, the chances are that there will be something. But, as I said when we met at the briefing, it's going to take time."

"And luck?"

"And luck. What I could use is all of the intelligence information you can get me on the Leningrad Institute for Brain Research, especially data for the last three years. I assume that what I have on my desk is heavily screened by the KGB or someone before it gets out of the country. So if there's an agency that you can call on to get me the most up-to-date information, we might get a lead."

"I'll put someone on it. Is there anything else that you need?"

"Time. And I know you can't get me that."

Grady sighed. "I'll tell the President that you're working on things."

They hung up and Jerry waited a few seconds for the line to clear. He switched the phone to the other ear and dialed a number.

"Doctor Deladier's office."

"Rosemary? It's Jerry Tanner." He outlined the problem as succinctly as he could. "Do you think you can come down and look at it?"

There was a pause on the other end. "Well, that creates a ticklish situation. I mean, it sounds urgent, but I'd have to get released from here so that I could devote time to it . . . I mean getting Daniel cranked up and everything."

"And to get that, we need to get Deladier's permission?"

"Yes. Perhaps if you spoke to him."

"Is he in the office?"

"Not just now. He's off doing some research. I believe it's on the same project that you're working on. I could try to reach him?"

Jerry thought for a minute. He'd have to clear it with Channing. But he could do that later. This was too important to wait. "Rosie, get someone to handle whatever you're doing and come on up here, as soon as you can. I'll take responsibility for all of it."

"Very well, Doctor Tanner. I'll be there in a few minutes."

As Jerry put the phone on the cradle, he realized that his hand was sweating.

In order to avoid a scene over appropriating Deladier's assistant, he'd have to clear things through Channing as soon as possible. He tried all three extensions and found them all busy; the chances were that Channing also had two or three calls backed up. He reminded himself to call as soon as he got the chance. He looked at the notepad on top of the pile of research materials on the desk. He flipped through the pages to the latest entry. It was Jerry's practice to keep all of the pages of the most current notepad and file them after the pad was used up. He had started a fresh legal pad on Monday and he was almost finished with it. It was only Thursday. He tried to calculate for a second the number of pads he might go through in two months' time. Too many. If he kept going through them at this rate, the chances were that he'd need two or three more filing cabinets in the office.

He eyed the numbered notes.

1. Have Morey run Jeff through the PK training experiments.
2. Do the same with Tim Schyler.
3. Can we set up a joint experiment?
4. Measurements? Protocols?

He stabbed at the intercom switch. "Morey?"

His voice boomed out across the lab on a set of loudspeakers. Sensitive mikes near the speakers allowed anyone in the lab to answer, without interrupting what they were doing. The voice that answered was tinny, with a New York accent.

"Yeah?"

"Can you come in?"

"Yeah."

Morey Kellers was the best lab technician Jerry had

been able to find in the ten years that he had worked with Moreland. Kellers was only five feet five and that was small to carry two hundred pounds. Spectacled and prematurely balding at forty, Kellers could pass more for an out-of-shape Brooklyn cabbie than a master lab worker. But he was clearly the latter. He'd held five jobs in ten years by the time he interviewed with Channing and Jerry. He'd left each job when he thought he'd mastered it. Boredom set in for him fast after that, or so he said. He was blunt in the interview. He'd said he didn't believe a lick about PSI or any of the other "fuzzy" sciences that the then small institute purported to investigate. He said if he got bored, he'd give notice and that would be that. He'd been with them for eight years and boredom had not yet been in evidence.

Morey came into the office, plopped down in the chair across from Jerry's desk and put a coffee mug on the arm. He balanced a clipboard across a folded leg and pulled out a pen. It was then that he saw the pile of things on Jerry's desk.

"Holy shit. Busy, huh?"

"Right."

"I'm up to my ass in alligators out here and from the looks of that pile, you're gonna want ten or twelve crazy things set up and ready to go . . . let's see when? An hour ago, right?"

"Exactly, Morey. And all of it has to be done total vacuum, bombarded with hard radiation and oh, we'll need three hundred Rhesus monkeys to carry it out."

Morey smiled a gap-toothed smile. "Fuck you, boss."

They laughed. It was their standard opening gambit. Morey insisted that Jerry spent most of his time asking for the impossible and Jerry complained jokingly that Morey was never around when things *really* got busy.

Jerry glanced at the page of notes. "Are you set up for Jeff Cuthers?"

"It's Thursday, isn't it?"

Jerry nodded. Morey put the small boy through his Faraday PK experiments every Thursday afternoon. The scheduling usually worked out just right. His mother would drive the boy out to the institute after school and she'd wait until Jerry and Morey finished the experiments. It usually meant that the three of them worked an hour or so late on Thursday. It was probably silly of him to ask. Morey never missed a scheduled commitment and screamed like hell if an experimenter showed up late.

Morey looked at his clipboard, which had been spattered with coffee. The stains matched those on Morey's lab coat. "Today, he works eight feet from the bell jar and we're working with five-eighths-inch standard-length stainless."

"You're part right."

Morey squinted at Jerry over his spectacles. "I knew it. We have to get the Rhesus monkeys, right?"

"In a manner of speaking. Can we manage to get the Schylers here at the same time?" He was referring to the Schyler twins, both paranoid schizophrenics.

"The loonies? I don't know. I'll have to call Hunterdon Psychiatric. There shouldn't be any problem, not if there's someone to pick them up and take them back. Why?"

"Can we set up a parallel experiment with Timmy Schyler?"

"At the same time?"

"Right—and the same object metal. What I'm looking for is three set-ups, really. Run them first through separate Faraday boxes, with the normal protocols. Then put them in the same box and let them work on the same piece of steel. I'll want separate monitors on each of them."

"What kind of results are we looking for?"

Jerry shrugged. "I don't know, quite."

Morey nodded and took a sip of black, greasy-looking coffee. He tended to boil it up in the lab several times a day. It would, according to Jerry, remove the rust from an iron bridge and ultimately Morey's stomach. Morey ignored the warnings. After he gulped some of the coffee, he carefully balanced the cup on its perch on the arm of the chair. "Oh. It's going to be one of those we're-not-sure-where-we're-going-but-we'll know-if-we-get-there things, right?"

"Sort of. I want to see if there is any difference in the reaction of the metal when two of them work on the same piece. We can use the individual PK-altered steel as a control and the joint one we can measure for differences. Can you set it up?"

Morey rubbed a hand across his bald pate. He shook his head several times.

"There are several questions. But . . . I'll get the answers. The most important thing is—now, remember that a Faraday is small. Both of them are small. Do you want to take the risk of putting the loony in the same box with the kid?"

Jerry paused. Timmy and Jack Schyler were identical twins; both eighteen and both incurably ill. They were institutionalized at a nearby psychiatric hospital, and their visits to the institute were considered by their psychiatrists to be therapeutic. Identical to the last detail in their appearance, the boys were both blond, lean and close to six feet tall. They were perfectly normal as far as all outward appearances were concerned. There were only two unusual characteristics about the twins. The first was that one of them, Timmy, was an extremely gifted psychic, while his brother Jack seemed to manifest no psychic ability at all. As Jerry was aware, the average person dragged in off the street managed to manifest *some* measurable if erratic ability in one or another of the areas of parapsychology. But Jack Schyler did not manifest a single skill in any of the tests administered. This was significant. "Null-PSI" was the term that had been coined to describe such a condition. An absolutely negative PSI condition was as meaningful to the research as was a superior one. It was as if one of the boys balanced the other, although in over a year of work with both of them, neither Jerry nor Channing could determine why.

But that was not the most unusual thing about the Schylers. Rather, it was the fact that when they were together, they were docile, almost sane. However, when they were separated, for even the briefest period of time, both of them turned into raving madmen more appropriate to Hogarth's "Bedlam" than to a lab. Jerry, Channing and Morey had learned the truth of their condition from bitter experience. They had separated the boys for only a few seconds in the early stages of an interview. As a result, an entire office was terrorized and several of the staff were hurt. It took all three men plus two burly attendants from the psychiatric hospital to get them back under control. As soon as each came into the presence of the other, everything was eerily tranquil again.

As a result, Morey was forced to build another piece of apparatus into every experiment; a TV camera and monitor screen. Jack would sit glued to it like a child to Saturday morning cartoons. As long as he could see his brother on the screen, all was well. The device had been Morey's idea and the staff psychiatrists at Hunterdon were eternally grateful. It allowed them to interview and treat each separately. All they needed was TV, and the hospital was equipped with them for security reasons, anyway.

Taking no chances that *his* lab might suffer the same fate that one of the interview rooms had, Morey took great pains to insure that the TV monitor was always working flawlessly. A back-up monitor had been installed and was ready to be snapped on in seconds if need be.

Jerry looked at Morey. "Restraints?"

"That adds another set of parameters. If the results are different than before, can we say that the restraints were a part of it?"

Jerry nodded. Morey was right, as he usually was about such things. For a minute, Jerry silently considered setting up something totally different than the Faraday box. But that would add dozens of potentially uncontrolled and unmeasurable outside influences that might have a totally disruptive influence on what they were testing. The Faraday box had been around for more than a hundred years, since Michael Faraday, the inventor of the dynamo and the theorist of the laws of electrolysis, developed its design. It was a simple lead- or copper-wrapped box, which effectively shielded everything inside from almost all electromagnetic emissions. Vasiliev had used it as a safeguard in testing distant seeing in the twenties. It ultimately proved to have little impact on seeing, influence, or person-to-person telepathic communication. Stanford had used it to isolate test subjects and to test PK in an electrically measurable environment. Jerry had been using it as part of experimental procedures for at least four years.

"Why use Faradays at all, Jerry?"

Morey hardly ever called Jerry by his first name. It was usually "Doc" or "Boss." When Morey used the name, his logical guns were normally loaded.

"Why not?"

"What I mean is, what will you be able to determine with both of them in the same Faraday? Let them conduct the independent controls in duplicate boxes. We'll use the same TV rig we always use to keep Jack from going loony. In addition, Timmy can have the same environment he's always used to. When they work together, put them outside across a table. That way we gather additional data. Simply, non-Faraday PK data as well as joint PK feedback in all of the telemetry. If we get anything significant, we can move either or both of them back to the boxes to see if the results alter. That way, with two sets of experiments, we can remove a whole set of random variables. What we don't eliminate can be screened through other procedures. If it works, we keep doing it until all of this flap is over. Then we go back and try to assess the data." He smiled to himself. "Of course, there's always the chance that nothing will happen. In that case, we haven't lost any ground." He folded his arms and again smiled a gap toothed smile. "See? Now, aren't you Ph.D.'s a bunch of dumb shits?"

Jerry rubbed his beard. "They're either going to have to give you Channing's job or fire you. You know that?"

Morey waved a hand, missing the coffee cup by a fraction of an inch. "Channing can have his and you can have yours. I *would* be willing to trade salaries with either or both of you and stay in the same job, though. I like setting up protocols."

There was a tap at the door. Jerry was still shaking his head at the burst of logic he'd just experienced from Morey. "Come in."

"Doctor Tanner." Rosemary McGee was really a stunning woman. Jerry had always thought so. Jerry could see Morey look at her as he always had; as if she were a filet mignon and he was a starving man.

"Yes, Rosie. Come on in." Both men rose. Morey even steadied the coffee cup. "And since when have I been Doctor?"

"I guess since the . . . promotion."

"Well, I'm still Jerry. Wouldn't it be a blow to that

feminism of yours if you called me that while I still used your first name?"

Morey smiled at her and started to the door. "I don't know about you two, but I have to start moving furniture. What about it, Doc?"

Jerry didn't have to think to answer. After all, the whole thing was a crap shoot, anyway. "Try it. Like you said, what the hell?"

"Four o'clock?"

"Four o'clock. I'll try to gather up the brain trust and get them there." Jerry sneaked a quick look at his watch. "Sit down, Rosie. Coffee?"

She sat in the same chair that Morey had vacated. She waved the coffee away, wrinkling her nose. "I've had six today—I'll be awake for a week."

Jerry didn't really know where to start. He talked about the resonance theory and worked his way up. Rosemary rested an elbow on a knee. It was a position she liked to assume when she thought. "Vibratory rates and resonances, you said?"

He sat behind the pile and nodded solemnly over top of it.

"Well, as far as that's concerned, most of the basic data is already in Daniel. All we have to do is ask him for it. But it seems to me that you want more than just lists of frequencies and angstroms."

"Yes. What I'm after is—" He tried to think of the term. The miniworld of the computer and the attendant experts carried with it its own dialect. There were times when Jerry saw job applications where the box labeled "Languages" was filled with comments like "FORTRAN . . . COBOL . . . BASIC, . . ." when their original intent had been to list French, Greek, etc. "—an interface."

"Oh." Rosemary sat up.

"What I need is any connection between the theoretical approaches to PK, specifically resonance, and the actual resonance information about stresses and breaking points. I'm training PK into sensitives who already have a demonstrated capacity. To date, we've trained them so that they can work at greater distances by getting them in an alpha state and simultaneously increasing endocrine activity. But all of this has been done by the seat of the pants. I don't know the real connection. And, as far as I know, the only man who might have a real game plan in the area is Andrei Sholodkin."

"At the Leningrad Institute?"

Jerry was surprised for a second. But it was reasonable that Anton spoke to her about it. After all, they were lovers.

"Right. What I need, in effect, is a concordance that says, most of the probable connections are in electromagnetism . . . or resonance . . . or I don't know, drinking tomato juice, or something."

She laughed a deep-throated laugh, warm and full, a sensuous laugh. Despite the fact that Deladier could be a colossal pain in the ass, the man did have exquisite taste in women.

He smiled. "Can you do that?"

She smiled back. "Of course."

"How long will it take?"

"About ten years."

"How about a little less than that. Say . . . a week?"

"No. Seriously, it will take perhaps three weeks, assuming that we have a priority with Daniel over other experiments."

"Rosie, you can have Daniel all to yourself for that three weeks. This has priority over everything else."

She leaned back and looked at the ceiling intently for a second, as if she'd found the secret to the universe there and was trying to read it without her glasses. "That's challenging—having Daniel all to myself for that much machine time."

"You make him sound like a stud."

"He's much better than that, Jerry. He's interesting to talk to."

"Touché. You hear on this side of the desk the crumbling sound of a collective male ego. We've been supplanted by machines."

"Not entirely. Daniel wouldn't do much for you on a cold winter night."

"That's reassuring."

She took off her glasses and peered across at Jerry. "Is all of this cleared with Ant—Doctor Deladier?"

He shook his head. "I tried going through Channing. All of the lines were tied up. We have a brainstorming session in about half an hour. He'll be there and so will Anton. I think so, anyway. I'll settle it there. There shouldn't be any problem."

"Not like Monday?"

It was an invitation to explore further—one offered freely. Jerry did not waste time. "Can you help me with something else?"

"No." She'd pulled the rug out from under him. "What I mean, Jerry, is, I have trouble enough separating the professional from the personal as it is. You know what I mean."

"Rosie, I just want to find out why the man dislikes me so intensely. After that, I can try to manage."

"That's fair." She said it as if it were unusual in her experience. "He doesn't dislike you as much as you might think. In a way, he has a lot of respect for your professionalism. It's another problem, more one between Channing and Anton."

"Channing thinks highly of him. He says that if it weren't for Anton, the chances are that he wouldn't ever have managed to get where he is. He says that he took off from a lot of Anton's early research. Channing gives Anton a great deal of credit, publicly and privately."

"That's just it."

Jerry realized in a sudden burst of perception. "Oh. Not enough. He takes it as being patted on the head?"

She nodded and looked down. "Things have been tense. That's why I asked for you to clear all of this. If we have to get this thing with Daniel done, I'll need some domestic tranquility."

"Then let's explain what the experiment's about at the meeting. Both of them will be there. Or is that too awkward? Uncomfortable?"

"Both, yes. But I think it has to be done."

They arrived at the meeting a few minutes after Channing. Anton sat at the back of the table. His face remained an impassive mask as he saw the two of them enter.

Surprisingly to Jerry, Rosemary crossed the room and sat next to Anton.

Jerry couldn't decide if it was a war council or a peace gesture. It took Channing fifteen minutes to get the preliminaries out of the way. He looked to Jerry, who wished he'd managed to brief the old man on the phone.

"Jerry? Are there any new developments?"

"Yes, Channing." He explained the rest of it: Rosie, Daniel—everything.

Channing looked to Anton as soon as Jerry was finished explaining.

"Anton, do you have anything to say? After all, we're horsetrading Ms. McGee away from you for some time."

Anton turned to her and they conferred silently for a second or two.

"Channing, I believe that the move is a good one in one respect and a poor one in other respects. Ms. McGee's real professional strengths are in the area and for that I applaud Dr. Tanner's choice of her for this. I also can applaud her willingness to participate

and, of course, as the director, you can assign her anywhere on whatever priority you wish . . . at least during the present emergency."

He paused and took a sip of water from a glass in
front of him.

"I question the logic that brought him to the conclusion in the first place, though. I think that the general consensus in the area is that we have basically
four forces at work. Gravity, electromagnetism, nuclear
energy and radioactivity. I think monopolizing Daniel
—not to mention Ms. McGee's time—for this project
alone is, based on its potential payoff in terms of what
we're after, badly thought out, at best."

Channing had to look to Jerry. He sat between them
like a judge at a debate in the few minutes that followed.

Jerry gestured with a pencil as he spoke. "It is clear
that PK experiments in or out of the Faraday environment have little effect if any on the properties of
objects altered. Also, the same experiments say that
the internal electrical potentials of the room or the
cage are not altered in the slightest by PK, or vice
versa. Alterations in gravity are thoroughly unusual
in anything but huge planetary masses. Radioactivity
alterations would have been noted in the first experiments with PK, decades ago. A Geiger counter was an
integral part of the protocols for men from Vasiliev
to Reich and others. That leaves nuclear—which is the
level of change the metallurgists report. If the change
is nuclear, and the curve of nuclear energy is a constant—"

Both Channing and Anton knew where Jerry was
headed at the same time. The chances were that both
of them also knew that Jerry had Anton's argument
soundly beaten. There was a case for harmonics monopolizing Daniel's and Rosemary's time for the following three weeks.

"—and it would have to be or there'd be a nuclear blast, then we must explore other influences on the nucleus. The most prominent of these is using the natural harmonic vibratory rate of the molecule to alter the properties as we see currently in the post-PK samples."

Channing looked at Anton. "He seems to make a good case."

"I disagree." Jerry could see the French Canadian start to redden, then carefully calm himself. "I suppose, though, we'll have to see the results."

He pushed himself away from the conference table. "If you will excuse me, I have to get back to a project. I'll have my report put in a memo, Channing. You'll have it this afternoon."

He moved quickly out of the room, so quickly that Rosemary was clearly surprised. She quickly got up and followed. After a few minutes, she returned as Channing was adjourning the meeting. She crossed the room to stand by Jerry.

"Jerry?" Channing still stood at the head of the table. "It sounds good to me. Go ahead with it. I'm afraid we'll have to afford to be at variance with Anton this time." The old man started to go. "Oh, I'll be there for the PK this afternoon at four. Perhaps Ms. McGee would like to be there also? After all, what she'll be gathering will be a function of all of this."

Jerry looked at her. She smiled at both men. "I wouldn't miss it. I was going to suggest it in any event."

As Channing left, Jerry and Rosemary remained for a second alone in the empty conference room. She took a deep breath and exhaled, apparently releasing some of the tension that the meeting had developed. "He's right. He is deeply into something. It wasn't a dodge or anything like that."

"What's he working on?"

She shook her head. "He wouldn't say, but that's nothing. He never does, until he's sure of his findings. It's a habit with him."

She moved across to the other side of the table and gathered her notes.

"Oh, another thing . . . he'll be there for the PK this afternoon, too. I thought that it might take you some distance toward bringing him out of this angry mood he's been in lately."

Morey was ready to go precisely at four, as he'd said. The large, windowless lab area had been reorganized in a very short period of time. The two Faraday cages had been moved to the center of the room and all of the electrical connections had been made. Morey was hounding the technicians to double- and triple-check calibrations and settings. Jerry and Rosemary were the first of the observers to get there. He took her to meet the Schylers, about whom she heard; the disastrous first encounter with them was legendary. Jack was laconic and absorbed with the picture of his brother on the TV monitor in front of him. Tim must have seen Jerry in the reverse image on his monitor in the box. The voice was high and thin. "Afternoon, Doctor Tanner."

Jerry waved to the camera. "Hi, Tim." He pointed to Rosemary. "This is Ms. McGee. She'll be working with us today."

The boy greeted her with exactly the same tone as he had Jerry.

Morey, minus the coffee cup, strode purposefully across to Jerry as he and Rosemary spoke to Jeff Cuthers, the child whose psychokinetic power had impressed President Paulson when he saw it on film.

Morey took Jerry aside a few steps.

"Okay, boss. Where's the brain trust? We're running late."

Before Jerry could answer, Channing came in, closely followed by Anton. *Had the two been talking?* Jerry wanted to see it as a hopeful sign. He turned to Morey. "There they are, hot shot. Now, how did you set up the second experiment?"

"Large lab table. There."

Jerry looked at it and understood.

"One at either end?"

"Right. A single bar in the center, using the bell jar and the glycerin bubble. I had the table bolted to the floor, same as the box. Past that, I've got some trembler sensors on the floor so we can sort out background from anything meaningful."

Jerry was pleased. He noticed that Channing and Anton had taken up positions near one another, but were still not conversing. Well, there was still a chance.

The first experiment went as predicted. Both pieces of metal altered shape and resembled the one that had been shown to the President. It was in the second experiment that all hell broke loose.

11

We have met the enemy . . . and they is us
—Pogo

It took Jerry and Morey the better part of a day to reconstruct what actually happened. And even after all of the factors were analyzed, there were still a considerable number of questions left unanswered.

Morey had run the initial parallel Faraday experiment like a finely tuned watch. Both subjects registered considerable adrenalin spikes and other endocrine activity. Little Jeff managed to turn a eighteen-inch-long steel rod into something resembling a Calder sculpture. Timmy Schyler characteristically turned his rod inward on itself. Both Jerry and Morey had noted the marked similarity of shapes each time the subjects were tested. The locations of the bends in the steel were always the same, though none of the test subjects seemed to have conscious control of the creation of a new shape. As the experiment ended, Morey retrieved the data from the paper tapes and punched the computer record into memory. He respotted the lab with the help of some of the technicians. It took only a few minutes for the second experiment to get underway.

Morey walked back to Jerry after checking the last item on his list. He gestured in the direction of the observers: Rosemary, Channing and Anton. The latter two had said nothing to one another or anyone else since their arrival. Jerry decided to try to change that and went over to them.

"Anton? Channing? This is the first of a planned series of experiments outside of the Faraday. The design here is a joint experiment. We'll have Timmy and Jeff sit at opposite ends of the table." He pointed to the table that Morey was doing some last-minute fussing with. The bell jar was the exact duplicate of the ones that they'd just finished working on. Their chairs were set at the same distances that they had been in the boxes. "The conditions remain the same except for the fact that the boxes aren't used and the subjects are jointly going to attempt to alter the shape of the same object. Essentially, the existing characteristic shapes and how they are altered in this experiment will indicate if teaming is possible. In addition . . ." Jerry pointed to the apparatus that seemed to straddle the bell jar. It looked for all intents and purposes like a department store electric eye. But everyone present, with the possible exception of Timmy and Jeff, recognized them as laser readers. A ruby light beam of low intensity measured the vibrations of the metal as it stood at rest. With this vibratory rate as a jumping-off point, the laser recorded and fed to the bowels of Daniel all of the measurable alterations in the vibration of the steel. It was primitive. Jerry was willing to admit that. But it was a place to start.

"So we hope to learn something that we might be able to feed across to Rosemary for the larger Daniel resonance report."

Both men nodded politely, though neither would comment. Jerry could understand that attitude in Anton. The man kept his own counsel about such things and Jerry was sure that all he was waiting for was the smallest anomaly. He'd use it to destroy the decision made by Channing about Rosemary and the utilization of Daniel. Channing, however was uncharacteristically quiet. Jerry assumed that pressure was the answer, or perhaps it was the presence of Deladier.

Morey was in the last stages of taping down two parallel lines on the lab floor. They created a corridor some three feet wide that everyone present knew not to cross. They were the sight lines that allowed the Schyler brothers to see one another.

Jerry and Morey seated themselves at a small, makeshift control table that was covered with TV monitors and print read-outs. One set was a videotape monitor with a two-camera attachment: the same rig that had been used to let the Schylers communicate earlier. Another was a schematic representation of the laser reader while still another was a TV scanner from Daniel of the vital signs of both subjects.

Three of Morey's assistants monitored the official record. Morey oversaw them and this left Jerry to observe and troubleshoot.

Jerry looked at Morey, who nodded. "Okay. Let's get started."

They were three minutes into the experiment when the first visible changes started to appear in the metal bar, which lay cocooned under the bell jar and glycerin bubble.

Jerry glanced at the visual display stopwatch that snapped off seconds in fractions. He checked it against the hand-held watch that he wore on a lanyard around his neck.

"It's early." It was meant more as a comment to himself, but Morey, who heard it, nodded. They spoke quietly, so as not to disturb the concentration of the subjects.

"Very. Nearly three minutes on average. Whatever is happening, it's happening twice as fast as it usually does."

"Vitals?"

Morey leaned across and peered at a scanner manned by one of the lab techs.

"High for both. Higher than in the box. Something's going on."

Jerry could feel a twinge of excitement. Perhaps they had something? If nothing else, the speed of the metal alteration that they were watching was enough to justify the other things that he'd seen that day.

At four minutes into the experiment, the speed in the change of the metal was marked. Something strange was starting to happen. Little Jeff's Calder pattern of bends and twists was starting to reverse itself, while Timmy Schyler's was turning inward ever more intricately.

Jerry talked in whispers to Morey, who sat next to him. "Vitals?"

"Higher on the kid than we've had. Recommend termination in two minutes."

Jerry nodded. When experiments were underway, Morey assumed the role of medical officer, monitoring vital signs and making judgments about them. Chet Kumasaka had said on many occasions that he was not needed when Morey was around.

A technician whispered something to Morey, who immediately got up and moved behind the man's position, looking at readings over his shoulder. He came back to Jerry with some speed.

"We're starting to get something. The laser reader is getting an altered resonance in the steel. You just might have had your head on right when you thought of that. But I still recommend that we terminate in"—he looked at the clock—"about a minute and a half."

Jerry nodded, all the time still watching Timmy and Jeff. The little boy was perspiring heavily, and with his hands pressed against the sides of his head, he was rocking back and forth in his chair. Timmy's face was reddening, turning scarlet. His hands were extended out over the table—muscles tensed. His hands and fingers moved in jerky motions, as if they themselves were the force altering the shape of the already tortured steel.

Suddenly, Jerry heard something pop. In a second, he could smell the acrid odor of burning coaxial.

"Shit." It was a comment hissed through the teeth by one of the techs. Morey was on his feet in seconds and hovering over the man's shoulder. He looked back to Jerry. "Burned-out relay in a TV scanner."

Jerry still watched the two people at the table. As he turned to answer, he noticed that Channing had walked up behind him. Rosemary was a few steps away. "Go to a back-up. Termination remains the same."

He wasn't about to cancel in the middle, not before he'd gathered all of the possible data.

Another pop. A third. Suddenly, at the back of the lab, an oscilloscope that should have been turned off for the duration of the experiment exploded.

Jerry pushed himself to his feet, causing Channing to back away a few steps. The last thing that the old man was going to do was to be underfoot.

"Morey. Terminate!"

The table moved. Every piece of apparatus was suddenly alive with smoke and sparks. Morey tried to yank a cable from a power source. He was lifted off the floor and thrown backwards by a blue, flashing surge of power. He flew into Moreland and Rosemary, bowling them over. Jerry kicked a chair out of his way and started for the master power switch at the other end of the lab. He didn't make it.

While Timmy and Jeff sat in their chairs, frozen like grotesque mannequins, the lights in the lab went out. Jerry stumbled into a lab table that was in an unaccustomed position and fell to the floor. "Hit the master switch!" he screamed.

As he tried to get to his feet, there was another sound of a small explosion followed by the shattering of glass.

"Everybody stay where you are. There are flashlights in the cabinet near the outer door. I'll get the master switch." Jerry managed to get to his feet. He couldn't understand why the emergency lights hadn't kicked in when the power went off. They were well engineered and tested regularly. In the distance he could hear an alarm bell clanging. It sounded like it was coming from the other end of the building. In seconds, another alarm chimed. In less than a minute, there were a chorus of them and the sound of footsteps running on the floor above. It was then that Jerry heard something that made him freeze in terror.

It was a guttural, animal scream. Then there was a second, but not from the same place in the room. *The Schylers. Mother of God!*

Unable to see one another, the twin paranoid schizophrenics were starting to go berserk in the total darkness. "Channing? Deladier? Get those two tied down. They're starting to freak out." But the chaos that erupted behind him said that it was too late. He crashed forward in the darkness, moving inexorably in the direction of the master switch, while the primitive screams of the Schylers blended with the crashing of lab equipment and the yells of the others. Suddenly, he remembered the little boy.

"Somebody get Jeff." Someone answered, but Jerry could not make out who it was in the din.

He was only a few feet from the wall, or so he reasoned, when he heard yet another sound. It was an animalistic growl, deep-throated and terrifying.

"Watch out, Jerry!" It was Rosemary's voice. Apparently, Jack Schyler, in a frantic attempt to get to his brother, was on a collision course with Jerry. Jerry took another step in the direction of the switch

before he was hit from behind. It must have startled
Jack as much as Jerry, for the mental patient attacked
immediately.

He grabbed Jerry with incredible strength. His
fingers were like steel springs around Jerry's throat.
They fell to the floor in a heap. Jerry jabbed an elbow
into Jack's ribs, once . . . twice, with no effect. He
tried to pry the fingers loose, but they squeezed with
a grip he couldn't break. Jerry bellowed for help and
thrashed more violently. It was the nightmare of the
mental hospital all over again. The viselike hands on
his throat . . . crushing the life from him. . . .

Slowly he drifted back up from the blackness and
tried to open his eyes. The bright lab lights were still out
and the lab was eerily lit in the glow of emergency
lighting. He squinted up at the frowning face of Chet
Kumasaka.

The hulking figure of the Japanese-American doctor
reached a hand down to Jerry's throat. He kneaded
the larnyx slowly, professionally, with thick, stubby
fingers more suited to a Sumo wrestler than an M.D.

"What—" Jerry's voice was a painful, rasping whisper.

"Shut up and stay still, at least for a few minutes.
That kid put a good-sized dent in your windpipe."
He kept kneading as he spoke. "The esophagus and
the larynx are pretty elastic. They can be massaged
back into shape. But I haven't done this in a few years,
so stay still, okay?"

Jerry stayed still.

It was a few minutes later when the normal lighting
system snapped back on and Chet helped Jerry back
to his feet. He was dizzy from the sudden movement.

"Move slowly for a while. That brain of yours got a
little oxygen starved. Breathe deeply and don't get your

head lower than your waist, or you'll be back on the floor. Got that?"

Jerry nodded. "Sure." His voice was still raspy. It frightened him for a second. Chet could see the fear.

"Your voice will come back. It's just bruised. I have to get to the others."

Chet moved to the center of the lab, which Jerry could see was in a shambles. Channing and Anton were leaning over Timmy Schyler, who seemed to be unconscious. Rosemary was with Jeff, cradling the terrified boy in her arms.

Jerry took a few slow steps in her direction. "Rosie?" His voice came out like a croak.

She turned to him, knowing what he was going to ask. "He's okay, Jerry. Just scared." Jerry could hear the sound of sirens in the distance. The chances were that the ambulances from Hunterdon would arrive in minutes. Morey was just getting to his feet.

He was gray and moved slowly. He was wrapping a roll of gauze around an ugly-looking burn on the back of his left hand. In addition there was a nasty gash on his forehead that was just starting to turn purple. Jerry and Morey moved to one another like two somnambulists. Jerry reached for the bandage that Morey was trying awkwardly to wrap around his hand. "Let me do that."

Morey held out the hand and Jerry started to wrap it. "For a minute there, when you flew away from that console, I thought—"

"I was lucky. It was an arc. I jumped more than flew. Good thing I wore my crepe soles today." The jolt of electricity had thrown him too fast to do systemic damage, at least that was what Chet had said. But he, like Jerry, had been warned not to move too quickly.

"What about the Schylers?"

"Both okay, I think. Tim passed out at the table

and fell backward. When the emergency lights came on, Jack was knocked out. You'll never guess who smacked him and got him off of you?"

Jerry shook his head. The action made him dizzy.

"Deladier."

Jerry looked across to the French Canadian who was helping get Jack Schyler back on his feet. He'd thank him later.

"Could we save any of the data?"

"I haven't looked."

They moved to the center of the lab, where the experiment table had held its position, secured by bolts. Miraculously, the bell jar was intact, though the glycerin bubble had dissolved. Jerry pointed to it. "Morey?"

"Yeah. I saw."

There was no rod under the jar. The stainless steel sample was gone. It had been disintegrated, shattered into filings and small shards. Something . . . some force of incredible capacity had been unleashed in the minutes of insanity in the lab.

It was well past seven in the evening when they started to make sense of it. The Schylers had been moved back to the hospital and Jeff's mother had retrieved the child. She'd shepherded the boy out of the lab, threatening to sue for damages. Channing and Anton together had spoken to her about the difficulties that were encountered. They'd explained that what had happened was a million-to-one shot, something that could never again happen. The little boy, still frightened and in shock, had pleaded with his mother to be allowed to come back. By the time she left, both Channing and Anton seemed to think that she'd been somewhat mollified.

Jerry had gone to thank Anton, but Deladier had brushed him aside. The testing protocols were atrocious, he'd said. He'd spent a full five minutes railing about what a disaster Jerry'd made of things. Channing had come over to the pair and tried to mediate, to no avail. Anton said he thought Channing's judgment was as poor as Jerry's and stormed out.

Jerry had remained with Morey after the others had left, and it was dark outside when they'd managed to get things together. Morey sat across a lab table from Jerry looking at a pile of read-outs from Daniel.

"Doc, it's a new ball game."

"I know, but how?"

"Every circuit in the place shorted at about the same time. It looks like electron flow was accelerated, or maybe interrupted. That's a guess. As far as the sample is concerned . . . well, that's the damndest thing I ever saw. The larger pieces have the consistency of peanut brittle and it looks like a whole bunch of other properties were altered. It'll take a few days to get that together. The scary thing about it is that the steel doesn't conduct electricity the way it should. It's the same thing as the wiring and the circuits. If the circuit breakers hadn't popped, every wire in the building would have burned out."

"From the experiment, you think?"

"One hell of a coincidence if it isn't."

"But how?"

"Good question. We've got results here, and it looks to me like they are a function of resonance— like we talked about before. But with all of the craziness that went on, how do we know what factors were at work?"

"We don't. We'll just have to set it up again."

12

Power corrupts, absolute power corrupts absolutely.

—Lord Acton

For Steven Paulson, the day had gone sour early in the morning. The balance of the day did not hold any promise either. The wire services had buzzed with the news of renewed unrest in a number of Soviet cities. It had come in response to the rumor of rationing that would take effect across the Soviet Union within a month. As the rumor spread, Czechoslovakia and Poland, whose wheat crops had suffered from the same adverse weather as the Soviet's, started querying the United States through their respective embassies about wheat transactions. American wheat speculators watched wheat futures soar. Agriculture Secretary Mordecai Jasper had spent ten minutes on the phone with Paulson warning him that price controls might have to be placed on the sale of wheat abroad, lest the price become so prohibitive that a panic would ensue.

In the Oval Office, Paulson met with an National Security Agency briefer who warned that there was a chance of trouble between the Soviets and the Chinese. A fairly good intelligence report from a source reportedly within the Kremlin had told of a sternly worded

243

note sent from China's Premier Han T'sing to Premier Igor Kharkov. It demanded that the Soviet Union honor her commitments to the People's Republic, or he could not be responsible for the consequences. It appeared that the open lands agreement that China and India had implemented was not going to be enough to stem the tide of hunger. Moreover, the nearly five million Chinese and Indian rural émigrés who frantically tilled the fields in the program were perilously close to the Kazakh S.S.R. border. The NSA briefer mentioned that the Soviet Premier could easily see them as a massive army of humanity, sitting strategically on his southeast flank. It was an added incentive to get foreign grain as soon as possible.

Domestically, the rumor of a Soviet-American grain deal had broken in the first editions of the *Washington Post* and *The New York Times*. Paulson was certain that every major daily would carry a similar story by the end of the day. Paulson's chief political opponent, California governor Bob Tilden, wasted no time in turning the story into political fodder. He'd held a press conference in New York at eight-thirty in the morning to say that he considered that if the President sold quantities of wheat abroad, he would make the cost of domestic supplies prohibitive and massive profiteering would result. He accused Paulson of poor crisis management and demanded a TV debate on the issue.

In addition, Grady had phoned in a report that there had been an accident during an experiment at MRI and it would take them some time to get a handle on exactly what was happening there. Paulson had heard all of it before ten-thirty in the morning. And his scheduled appointment with Ambassador Gregory Luboff was at eleven. Paulson called protocol and told them he'd be in the Rose Garden and that he was to be informed when the ambassador's car entered the grounds.

By the time the limousine carrying Luboff was swinging into the South Portico, Paulson knew what he had to do.

Ever the master of protocol and procedure, Gregory Luboff was more than a little surprised when the President was not at the portico to greet him. Conventionally, a sitting President met ambassadorial level diplomats in person, rather than sending the chief of protocol. Being ushered into the Rose Garden was also something that he was unused to. Such visits were almost exclusively conducted in the Oval Office. It disarmed Luboff, all of this change in routine. And *that* was what Steven Paulson wanted.

The two men approached each other in the midst of scarlet blossoms. The warm sun had moved the temperature into the eighties. Paulson could see that the Russian was starting to sweat under his dark serge suit.

"Mister Ambassador, what a pleasure to see you again."

Luboff's smile matched Paulson's. It was neither excessive nor was it perfunctory. It was adequate. Both were.

"Mister President, it is always a pleasure. I trust your health is good?"

"It is, Mister Ambassador." Paulson shortcut his way through five or six more formalistic pleasantries. "I wish to express my regrets about the kind of briefing that I got this morning."

He watched the Russian's single eyebrow furrow in the wrinkle above his nose. "Mister President?"

"I mean the food-rationing problem."

Luboff smiled hesitantly. The President's remark forced him to start an entirely different set of thoughts. Paulson was overloading his system in a number of ways: the unusual meeting place and the alterations in routine. Luboff decided they were designed merely to soften him up.

"Thank you, Mister President, but I am certain that the Soviet Union will manage to cope with this small crisis." Again he smiled. It was broader than before.

Paulson paused a few seconds. Luboff had taken the lead line. There was no question that the Russian would move immediately to the subject.

"It is with something more than this immediate disturbance that I must now be concerned, Mister President. For there will shortly come a time when such disturbances all over the world will become commonplace and both of our countries may well suffer considerable loss."

The Russian was being proper, occasionally eloquent but thoroughly unimaginative. Paulson decided to make another jump.

"Mister Ambassador, exactly how much wheat are you prepared to buy from the government of the United States?"

Luboff blinked twice. Paulson had won another round and pressed on.

"What I actually mean, Mister Ambassador, is: How much time will it be before you solve the weather problem that you managed to have backfire?"

"Ah, Mister President I—I carry with me a communiqué that clarifies the terms of possible sale. But I don't know if I am familiar with it enough—I only received it this morning—to quote the exact tonnage."

It was a good play for time. Paulson headed it off.

"Estimate in millions and don't bother to count higher than fifty million metric tons. That is as far as we are prepared to go with any sale."

Luboff's frown deepened a fraction. It told Paulson that the Premier had ordered him to get more . . . perhaps a hundred million tons. That was in line with Moredecai Jasper's estimates. The old bastard had been right again.

"Let me show you the rest of the Rose Garden,

Mister Ambassador. We can talk and stroll." Thoroughly off balance, the Russian used the walk to regain his composure. The two men strolled through the garden, Paulson with his hands deep in his pockets and Luboff with his clasped behind his back. They spoke quietly, like two philosophy instructors walking in a symposium. The casual viewer would have been astonished to know that they were deciding the fate of millions of lives. Nor could either of the men allow himself the consideration of the number of lives involved. The fisherman in the midst of boating a huge school of fish cannot afford to stop and count the numbers, lest he lose the rest.

"Mister Ambassador, the United States is willing to help the other nations of the world in resolving the growing food crisis. However, we do make the point that the alterations in the weather patterns was in large measure a function of clandestine experiments with the jet stream flow. You have created the problem for the majority of the world's population; the United States is well within its moral rights to refuse you grain and sell it to the other countries whose crops these experiments devastated. It is also in order that we demand a considerable number of concessions, as regards SALT and the possibilities of a summit meeting." He stopped and looked at Luboff. The Russian was listening—smiling, but now he was also flushing. His hands tucked behind his back had been clenched into fists. If he could be pushed further, then Paulson would have a better chance of succeeding.

"You see, Mister Ambassador, we are actually in a position where we can ask for any concession and you and the Premier will have to at least consider them. But that is not exactly what we had in mind."

Luboff gestured with his left hand, which Paulson thought he wrenched from the sweating palm of the right one. "Mister President, I am afraid you have the advantage on several counts. I am a diplomat, and will confess to being nothing even resembling a scientist. I know nothing of . . . weather research . . . nor of anything that could cause such changes, short of natural forces. I have come prepared to discuss the possibilities of a sale of a quantity of wheat. That, it is obvious, that you know. Moreover, I believe that the amount that the Soviet Union had in mind was something on the order of the number that you mentioned, perhaps a hundred million tons. Aside from that, I'm sure that negotiations could resolve the price in possible cash and perhaps concessions. We—"

"Mister Ambassador, I'm pleased to see you come so swiftly to the point." Paulson's smile glistened. "You understand that the United States would require that the purchase be made at the current market price? Past that, we would have no demands, not at this time, in any event."

"Yes, Mister President."

Luboff seemed both surprised and pleased. Paulson expected that he would. He did not have to use the hole card he'd come to the White House bearing.

"Of course, there will be a fifty million ton differential in your needs and our export capability, but I'm sure that the Soviet Union will be able to solve that 'small domestic problem.' Aren't you?"

"Yes, indeed, Mister President." The Russian rankled as his words were tossed back to him.

"We can leave to your staff and mine, Mister Ambassador, the specifics of delivery and payment. I assure you that the United States will expedite shipment of the wheat with characteristic efficiency."

"That will please the Premier, Mister President."

As if by an unspoken cue, the two men started back through the Rose Garden in the direction of the White House. They spoke of small things, insignificant things. It was more the talk of diplomats than the haggle of merchants. Paulson noted that Luboff's hands were no longer clasped tightly behind his back. They moved freely at his sides. The Russian was obviously practical enough to avoid looking the gift horse in the mouth. However, he was not so gullible that he was put too far off guard. The diplomatic small talk was simply a diversion on Paulson's part. It was a device designed to put the Russian at ease. Luboff was a master at diplomatic small talk. In fact, he'd been known to go on for hours with it. It was the Russian's device for wearing down the opposition over a period of time. Paulson's approach to him had been one that prevented him from taking that advantage. He allowed the Russian the luxury of it only after the impact of his statements had been felt. Luboff was feeling far more comfortable and was eloquent in his appreciation of the humanitarianism of the people of the United States of America. It was only when Paulson was sure that the Russian was totally relaxed and was starting what were obviously parting remarks that he sprung his hole card.

"I trust you will convey my best wishes to the Premier. Tell him the United States of America stands ready to assist in this time of crisis, short only of wreaking economic havoc in the domestic and international markets."

"I am certain, Mister President, that the Premier will be pleased and reassured by the readiness of your country to assist in this crisis."

The Russian started to extend a hand to shake. He was certain that the President had finished, or so it seemed.

"Oh, there was one more thing, Mister Luboff."

"Yes, Mister President?"

"I wonder if you can bear another message for me. It's personal rather than diplomatic in nature."

Luboff stared at him for a second. He could sense

something. Paulson knew that he might but hoped Luboff would not guess any more than that.

"I believe a dear old friend of mine knows a personal acquaintance of the Premier's. I wonder, if you have time in your very busy schedule, you might convey mutual greetings through the Premier?"

The Russian paused for a second. Paulson could see the slightest hint of confusion on the man's face. Luboff had been moved to a corner, but he didn't know it.

"Of course, Mister President. I would be most honored to convey such a message to Premier Kharkov."

"Tell him that Doctor Channing Moreland of the Moreland Research Institute conveys his warmest greetings to Doctor-Academician Andrei Sholodkin of the Leningrad Institute for Brain Research. Both Doctor Moreland and I would be pleased if you would do that."

The Russian's face flushed ever so slightly. In a matter of seconds, it was gone, replaced by a cool diplomatic mask. But the signal was enough for Paulson. Luboff had come armed with a threat. The Russians *had* demolished the bridge and arranged for the other disasters. For Paulson, the reading of the Russian's body language was crucial and formed a Pyrrhic victory of sorts. He had succeeded in making Luboff play the hole card and had at the same time realized that it was something the U.S. could not yet beat. Like the easy concession of the wheat, it was something designed to buy time. It was like saying: "Yes, we too have a nuclear potential." It was simply designed to make the Russians think before they did more. At least it would be, if Paulson could make Luboff believe the rest of it.

"I . . . I would be pleased to carry that message to Moscow. I assure you that I will mention it in my conversation with Premier Kharkov later today."

Clever, Paulson thought. "And would you also convey the fact that both Doctor Moreland and I are aware and rather impressed with the Golden Gate operation, despite the fact that the motif was rather transparent, at least to *our* psychics."

Paulson reasoned that the statement would move the Russian in either of two directions. The first would be confusion and the diplomatic doubletalk of denial. The second would be an admission of sorts. He secretly hoped for the latter as it would allow him to carry out the rest of the gamble.

"The what? Mister President."

"The Golden Gate operation, Mister Ambassador."

"Mister President . . . I'm afraid I—"

"In fact, Doctor Moreland informs me that to muster the power to achieve that goal, as well as the others —the helicopter and the dam—your capability in terms of applications must have reached a parity position with ours in the area."

Luboff spread his hands out in a gesture of confusion or even supplication.

"Mister President, I pride myself on not having the need of an interpreter. To be candid, using one always allows both parties to formulate the proper and, shall I say, the most diplomatic responses, while the questions are being asked. But perhaps it has been presumptuous of me to do this. Perhaps my command of English is not as considerable as I might have thought. For this, I apologize. I am thoroughly confused and cannot effectively respond to what you say.

"I do not personally know Academician Sholodkin, though most Russians would be pleased to admit that they know him by name. He is one of the Soviet Union's most honored men of science. But how a greeting sent through me and the Premier to Academician Sholodkin can relate to the Golden Gate? We have already conveyed to you our nation's condolences on the recent disaster and attendant loss of life in the Golden Gate Bridge catastrophe. We grieve for this as we grieve for the world's poor and her starving populations. But dams? Helicopters? I am sorry, Mister President. These leave me totally unable to respond intelligently. I regret this."

Paulson nodded tersely. "You are a master diplomat, Mister Ambassador. I am merely the son of a farmer, thrust into the White House to carry out the wishes of the American people. Those duties that bind me to the position also require that I speak plainly about grave concerns of the American people and government. This sale of wheat is nothing more than a gesture on our part to maintain the world's view of both of our nations as both powerful and benevolent. It is, of course, regrettable that our countries must, on occasion, face one another across a gulf of distrust. It is equally regrettable that the arms race over the past several decades has forced us both to escalate our research for new and more devastating weapons systems.

"But, faced with the realities of the situation, you *will* convey to the Premier the message that I have outlined. If the context is alien to you, I am sure it will not be to the Premier or to Academician Sholodkin. Please inform them that should another such 'event' take place at any time in the future, the United States will be forced to retaliate. Is that clear, Mister Ambassador?"

Luboff's brown eyes narrowed as he looked at the President. There was no confusion in them now. "I shall convey what you have said to the Premier. Again, despite this—message, I wish to thank you for your willingness to assist at this time of crisis."

"Good day, Mister Ambassador."

Paulson waited until Luboff was out of the garden before he breathed. He had just played the biggest bluff of his life. It was a brand of brinksmanship he did not have a stomach for. He took off the light blue sport jacket and rolled up his sleeves. Moving slowly through the trellises, he examined the early-blooming roses like a farmer might look at a money crop. His hands traced the lines of the stems and the soundness of the roots while his mind raced through the options that the action just taken would offer to Igor Kharkov.

At the worst, Kharkov might sniff out the move as a bluff. In that case, he'd allow the wheat sale to be completed, then he'd move against them with something spectacular. Assuming that the shipments and payments were completed by the latter part of June, Grady and Moreland's people had a small breathing space. Still, they would not have the two or three months he'd promised them. At the outside, they might get six weeks. That was the worst eventuality. The others offered greater latitude.

There was the chance that Igor Kharkov, with the Chinese nipping at his east, would be forced to assume that a balance of psychic capability existed. If that were the case, Kharkov would complete the wheat deal, then send his researchers in Leningrad back to come up with heavier guns, so to speak. Clearly, then, both superpowers would have to rapidly escalate development of "psychic" weaponry.

Kharkov had still another alternative. Paulson was facing an election. The Premier could hold off and see if Bob Tilden were easier to deal with. Paulson laughed to himself. There'd be a fat chance of that. The election was six months away. And Tilden would probably come out against the sale to the Soviets because Paulson was for it. The chances were, with Tilden creating a potential campaign issue about the sale, Kharkov could alter either of the last two strategies and move in strength . . . psychic strength? He wondered at the phrase for several minutes. It was so alien to him; something that he might have laughed at a few years earlier . . . might have even snickered at a few weeks ago. Suddenly, it had the power to change the face of history, in the same way the power of the atom had.

"Mister President?"

It was Jake Carpenter. The man had stood there for perhaps five minutes before speaking; he looked concerned. "You have a call from Doctor Grady that will be coming in in four minutes, sir."

Together, they started back toward the Oval Office. Paulson looked down at the young man who'd been the media wizard of his first campaign. Jake didn't look to be over forty; he might have passed for a younger brother of the President's, or perhaps a close cousin. "How come Appointments didn't come out with this?"

"Will Reilly wanted to come out to the garden with the message but I asked him to wait. You looked like things were serious with the Soviet ambassador. I told Doctor Grady what you were doing and he agreed to hold. Then I had to find you out here. I'm sorry if I interrupted your thinking."

Paulson smiled. "A President's thinking is made to be interrupted, Jake." He sat down behind his massive desk and waited; he picked up the phone on the first ring.

"Mister President?" Grady's voice sounded weary.

"Well, Mike, I played the hand."

"And?"

"I guess we'll see. One of the things I gleaned was that Luboff would have used psychic warfare as a club if he'd been pushed to the wall. At least, that's the way it felt. When I mentioned Sholodkin and Moreland in the same sentence he really got flustered. I'm sure Kharkov has the message by now. Unfortunately, the earlier we finish the delivery of wheat, the earlier he'll move again."

Grady coughed. "I agree. I can't see him doing anything before that—he really needs that wheat. But that won't get us the two months we need, will it?"

"No, it won't. I thought of that earlier. Something more like six weeks. We can't delay delivery any more than that without Kharkov getting suspicious. You're elected to tell Moreland that."

"I'm sure he'll love to hear that, Steve."

"Just tell him to come up with a miracle—we need one."

13

It is like the pool that becomes peaceful, quiet any evening when there is no wind; when the mind is still that which is immeasurable comes into being.

—Krishnamurti

Eve and the others sat in a long row of recliner chairs that ran down the center of the lab. They reminded Jerry of statuary marking some ancient Egyptian or Persian city. But few ancient stone figures wore electrodes pasted to their scalps.

The mass of electrical connectors moved tiny brain signals to a permanent record on an electroencephalogram tape. The tapes' pens scratched similar rhythms across the crawling sheets. It was the frequency of alpha; the rhythm of the ancient Hindu meditative syllable "om." It was the key to most of Zen, of Buddhism, of countless other disciplines. It was the motor noise of a mechanism that man had either newly discovered or rediscovered.

Jerry and Channing moved slowly down the row of chairs, glancing at each tape to see the familiar seven-to fourteen-cycle-per-second pulse. Satisfied that the subjects were ready, they moved quietly to the end of the lab, where a tape played a quiet, almost subliminal pulse. The tone, broken into ten beats every second, used the principle of synchrony to reinforce the alpha brainwaves of the six who sat in the chairs.

Channing had explained it to Grady by saying, "Try walking down the aisle of a supermarket, listening to a Sousa march. You will fall very quickly into a martial step. The same would be true of any rhythm that you heard. The alpha pulse allows the brain to have a companion pulse to feed upon. Many primitive religions use chants; actually, quite a number of the more sophisticated ones do too. The chant is usually in an alpha-compatible overtone. A modern strobe light will do the same thing through the optic nerve. It's really quite simple."

Grady had folded his arms and cocked his head to the side. "My Irish father, Doctor Tanner, would have said, 'If we're so damn smart, why ain't we rich?' "

Jerry and Channing came back to the table, and the six volunteers who waited there moved into place. Morey, Chet, Kumasaka, Rosemary, Tom and two other staffers acted as "coaches," leading the subjects in a distant seeing experiment. In other parts of the building, other labs that had been conscripted for the Moreland-Tanner project were carrying out similar experiments. A total of forty subjects had been put through hypnotic conditioning and a complex series of psychological and parapsychological tests to determine basic PSI index levels.

Originally they had started with a hundred psychics gathered from various college campuses and research facilities all across the country. What they needed were skilled PSI subjects who could carry out distant seeing and some marginal level of PK. Characteristically, far more of the subjects had been able to manage the latter and fewer still could do both. Thus the numbers were cut by forty percent. That was six weeks ago.

It had taken three weeks to move the subjects from

the more conventional experiments, where a runner would be sent to a distant location with a Polaroid camera and would return after the experiment with photos to match with the sketches of the same location made by the subject in the lab. The results of these more conventional distant seeing exercises were astounding. More than eighty-five percent of the sketches and photos had some correlation with the sketches. This was made more impressive by the constraint that Channing imposed on the experiment. He required that all matchings be "double-blind." What this meant was that the random set of photos and sketches were matched by a totally disinterested party, who knew nothing about the experiment.

As this phase of the testing developed, Channing and Jerry decided to expand the distance covered in slow stages and to use the aid of a coach to guide the subject to the location. Today was a vital day in the testing series. The psychic experimenters were trying to see inside the Leningrad Institute.

Channing nodded to Grady, who waited sitting on the corner of a lab table. "The experiment will only last fifteen minutes. But it will be some time until we get something useful."

"Why so brief?" Grady asked.

"It's a factor of boredom. When the subject gets restless looking at the same distant landscape, the hits diminish quickly. Fifteen minutes seems a good average. The results will take perhaps an hour to run through the double-blind system. We can wait for the rest of the report in my office."

The coaches leaned close to their charges, whispering instructions and repeating coded phrases that would assist the subjects with positive feedback. Jerry noticed that Eve had begun to sketch something. She was the fourth of the six to start. In a matter of a few more minutes, all six were sketching—images, visions, pictures projected on the insides of their eyelids. No one in the whole institute could be sure of how it was operating; they simply, pragmatically, knew that the technique worked . . . most of the time.

"Jerry? Are you coming with us?"

"Oh. Of course, Channing." Something had struck him, something tingling through the recesses of his memory. A large number of subjects . . . like a primitive dancing circle? He tucked it in a mental file folder for later examination.

Unlike a number of other rooms in the Weatherstone Mansion, Channing Moreland's office had not been modernized. Rather, it had been restored to what the original builder had envisioned as his den-study. The Persian carpet spread out gracefully in front of a huge fireplace that Grady could have walked under. The windows were lead glass, sliced with Tudor braces. The furniture was turn-of-the-century massive and was clearly meant to last a hundred years. Just off the office, Channing had built a kitchen and a small bedroom. There were times when he was working on a particularly nagging problem that he stayed overnight. Grady took a seat in a huge leather British club chair that seemed to dwarf him; Jerry sat in a matching chair. Channing had abandoned coffee for tea and the three started to establish their perspectives on where the now sizable experiment stood.

Grady jotted a note in a battered notebook before he asked his questions.

"Channing, assuming that you can get something from that group down there about the Leningrad Institute, how much faster will that make the overall development?"

"It's hard to say. I'm not trying to be evasive, Mike. If we can get a glimmer of their apparatus, we can tell some things about the thrust of their experiments. At least it's a handle."

Jerry stretched and yawned. "Sorry. I spent two hours asleep in my office chair this morning . . . There's a bright side in that we have the threads of something quite new. Unfortunately, there are no signposts. In the experiment with Cuthers and the Schyler twins, we had a powerful PK outburst of energy. Every electrical circuit in the building blew. Whatever was either created or enhanced could have moved outward like a bubble. When we tried to duplicate the effect the following week, we got nothing. We examined every factor and we still couldn't make it happen a second time. In scientific terms, it remains phenomenological—and that does us no good at all."

Grady laughed to himself. "You created a force that you cannot create again and you have no idea of how the force works. I'll have to find a diplomatic way to tell the President about that. We're dragging our feet as best we can on the Soviet grain shipments, but things are getting tight in Moscow. My people think that Kharkov is close to declaring martial law. We're not sure just how much wheat he has in reserve, but there's a chance that he shipped some of it to cover some of his commitments in Africa and Eastern Europe. That tightened the rationing structure some, perhaps close to their World War II rationing level. With them in that position, we can't afford to stall for too long. We have another three to four weeks, no more.

"Channing? You said you'd get a handle if this distant seeing experiment yielded something. You mean something about PK, don't you?"

"That's the idea. Perhaps ten years ago, when I was a bit more privy to Andrei Sholodkin's work, my friend and sometime colleague was examining the underlying principles of PK. He went through electromagnetism. That had been his mentor Vasiliev's approach. He was unable to prove anything conclusive except that if electromagnetism was involved at all, it was not the dominant factor. That's something that we've witnessed in the lab also. It was obvious that the Faraday had little impact on the experiment with Schyler and Cuthers."

"Channing, wait." Jerry chewed on the end of a pencil. "There is another random factor at work; one that we haven't hit on. It simply means there was something in the experiment that we have not duplicated. What came out of the experiment was vital in terms of the way the steel was altered. It was the same as the bridge, helicopter and dam."

"You did it, but you don't know what you did. Like I said before." Grady looked around the room. "Channing, is there a chance for some coffee."

Channing got to his feet. "Of course. There's always some brewing in my kitchen. Jerry?"

"Hm? Oh, no." Again, Jerry could feel the glimmer of something in the past. But, it was not ready to come out of its file yet.

Channing went for the coffee and Grady looked at Jerry. "When was the last time you slept?"

Jerry had managed to shave before Eve arrived for the tests. He knew that she'd come not so much to be a test subject but more to get a chance to see her husband, who was living five days out of every seven at MRI.

"I told you, I got two hours this morning."

Grady looked quickly at his notebook. "Did the other brother have anything to do with that experiment? The twin, the one that had to be in sight of his brother?"

Jerry shrugged. It was something that he had wrestled with and still had no answer for. "It could be, but Jack Schyler has no PK ability. He also flopped at all of the distant seeing experiments. The only thing that I can see is that Jack might have created an observer-interference axis."

Grady looked querulous.

"Oh, I'm sorry. Observer interference is a problem in all of this research. It's especially true in PK. Many times when there is pressure to perform, often in the face of severe skepticism, the subject cannot perform."

"They choke?"

"In a way. But it's more complex than that. If PK happens at the molecular or even the atomic level, the forces at work are really very subtle. They may cause test subjects to exert mammoth amounts of energy, but the point of impact of the energy is down at a sub-microscopic level. It's possible for an observer to interfere with the energy transfer and impede the experiment. It's the same in distant seeing. If the coach was telling the subject that he or she could *not* see anything, the chances would be that they would not."

"If Jack impeded Tim, then how did the circuits burn out and the metal . . . well, dissolve?"

"Perhaps the interference assisted in the change of the metal. It might have shifted greater power to little Jeff. Given the mental state of Jack Schyler, we cannot be sure if he was setting out to obstruct or help, or if he was involved at all. We just know that when we put it all back in the same positions with the same people, it didn't work the same way. We can get a subject to alter a steel bar now—in or out of a Faraday. They can even do it at a range of several feet. But what we saw in the lab three weeks ago . . . that was a hundred times more power than we've ever seen in any PK experiment. It must be close to what Sholodkin is using. And it has to do with setting up some resonant harmonic with the target metal. I'd bet anything on it."

There was a light perfunctory tap at the door and Eve Tanner came in. She was now obviously pregnant and tired from her brief excursion in distant seeing. She sat in a small love seat near Jerry. He moved across to join her. The look on her face was disappointing. "Nothing?"

"Absolutely nothing. It was gray sludge. I think everyone in the lab got the same thing. Never happened that way before."

"What way?" Channing came back to the cocktail table with coffee mugs. "I'm sorry, Eve. I didn't hear you come in. Coffee?"

"No, thank you, Channing. Caffeine and kicking don't mix. It seems *he* always wakes up just when I'm ready to go to sleep. What I was saying was that I don't think one of the six of us got anything. Maria was next to me. She started to get some doodles and then it went blank."

Jerry looked to Grady. "Negative results are often as significant as positive ones. If no one in the experiments in any of the labs got results, then that's a radical departure from the norm. Perhaps Leningrad is jamming the signal?"

"Perhaps. Eve, was there any pressure, a sense of fear, of foreboding?" Channing seemed to dig into his memory for the wording of his question.

"No, Channing. It was just black out there."

Grady sipped at the coffee. It was the consistency of molasses. He began to regret that he'd asked for some. "Could that be your observer-interference phenomenon, Jerry?"

"I don't think there's any question of it. Channing?"

"I tend to agree. If there's an energy bubble or a wave . . ."

Moreland stopped to look through the great Tudor windows. A magnificent late morning sun, which had seconds earlier patterned the Persian rug in dapples of light and half-shade, had gone rather suddenly. It was too dark for just a passing cloud. It was more like a squall line or a towering thunderhead, moving rapidly.

"Were there thunderstorms predicted? It's pretty dark out there."

No one seemed to know. It had been some time since any of them had stopped to hear anything as mundane as a weather broadcast. "Well," he said as he sat back in the huge club chair, "that's one of the fifteen percent that they can't predict. Eve? You said there were no results for anyone?"

"No, and I don't think we can count Maria's doodles. Chances are that someone is jamming all of this. Though I've no idea how."

"I know how." Jerry shook his head exasperatedly as he spoke. "They did it with the same mechanism that allows them to knock out bridges while we can't do much better than small pieces of steel from two or three feet—"

They stopped and stared at one another for a second. The rumble was clearly not thunder. It was something else, something ominously closer.

The lights went out.

In the distance a chorus of alarm bells started to clang.

"Wait!"

Channing went for the phone. He tabbed in a coded number.

"This is Moreland. What—injuries? I see. Well, thank God for that. Get a crew on it. We're on the way."

He hung up and turned back to them. "Second floor lab. No one was working there. A sample blew apart. Jerry—it was one of the kind you used. It was a set-up for this afternoon, laid out under a bell jar and everything. It exploded."

"What about the lights?"

"The circuits blew—the same way they did a few weeks back, or so it seems."

Grady gestured to the gathering darkness through

the window. "Perhaps lightning. It's been known to strike as much as eight or ten miles from the storm."

"Did you hear a thunderclap?" Jerry asked.

None of them had.

"Well, what I felt was a rumble, like an earthquake through the foundation. That's what we felt with the Schylers and Jeff Cuthers." Jerry got up and turned to Eve. "You stay put. You hear?"

Eve nodded. She didn't want to take any chances with the baby.

The lab was a shambles. The metal sample had blasted outward through the bell jar sending shards of glass ripping through everything in range. Jerry managed to find a Petri dish, usually used to develop a culture. He scraped some of the fine metal filings and glass shards into the dish and sealed it with some tape from the supply cabinet in the lab. He used his pen to scratch an identification mark on the tape but stopped—not knowing what to call it. He asked Channing, who thought for a second.

Grady, who'd overheard the question, called from a few feet away. "Call it the 'Tanner effect,' Channing. After all, you've got a Nobel. It's Jerry's turn."

Jerry paused and Channing smiled and took the dish from him. TANNER EFFECT SAMPLE/STRESS ANALYSIS. He scribbled the date in the corner and handed it back to Jerry.

Jerry called to Grady, "Can you guarantee that the Nobel won't be posthumous?"

"No."

"Then I'm not sure if I want it." He tucked the small round culture dish in his jacket pocket to take to Metallurgy. But instead of taking it directly there for analysis, Jerry stood amid the debris and slowly looked around. "It's here and we can't see it," Jerry said, after a few moments. "It's right in front of us."

Channing was shaking his head. "It's not the same. There was no one here. There was no experiment going on here."

Suddenly, Jerry knew. It was there in bright lights for the first time: the thing that had been gnawing at him all morning. "Holy shit!"

"What?" Grady turned.

"That's it. Come here. Look." He trotted across to the blackboard at the corner of the lab. Many lab researchers used it to jot down experiment information. Jerry thrashed across the tray, finally finding a minuscule piece of chalk.

"Now look." He sketched the Schyler experiment in a floor map. It was crude but it approximated the upstairs lab. A rectangle became the lab table. He drew an S for Tim and a J for Jeff. He put a third circle in at the position of Jack Schyler. He drew ever increasing concentric circles around each of them until a space equidistant between the three was covered with overlapping designs.

"There were two things that we were missing. The first of them we should have figured, but perhaps we were too close. The second—well, if this is right, we're lucky. Anyway . . ."

He chalked in the area of the table and the metal sample. "We were assuming that Jack Schyler had nothing to do with what happened because he was considered talentless as a test subject. We were wrong. The two test subjects set up a resonance in the metal that squared what either one of them had done originally. Jack *had* to be the third element. With his help, the force cubed. That's what knocked out all of the power. All three of them were sending at the sample. The signals overlapped, cubing the force and causing all of that chaos."

Channing pointed to the lab. "I'm sorry, Jerry. I don't understand. How does all of that relate to an empty lab? And how come we couldn't duplicate what happened? If all of them were in the same positions as we'd had them in before, we should have gotten the same results. We didn't."

"Yes," Grady agreed. "And what principle or hypothesis are you working on, Jerry? Forgive my ignorance but my art history and political science didn't carry much theoretical physics with them."

"It's what's called the 'beat phenomenon.' Each person sends a signal. Each signal creates a bubble in the energy, cosmic or otherwise. The bubble thus created interacts with another bubble, and at the point of intersection something new is created. It combines the force of the outward expanding bubbles in such a way as to square them. If there is a third force, then the intersection is cubed and on and on. The energy works at the point of intersection. Reich said it could be sent like a radio signal from that point. He developed an Orgone box to trap and enhance it. He was discredited, but people have been using that principle for ages—covens and the earliest cabala mystics. It's so simple. How could we have missed it?"

"Jerry?" Channing's tone was one of patience melded with confusion. "Reich never supplied scientific data to back up his theory. Almost all of his experiments were suspect. And even if this was what happened in the lab, how could it have happened here? There was no one in this lab." Channing paused, trying to recover his composure. "And you still haven't said why we couldn't duplicate it before, assuming that Jack Schyler was a part of the operation."

"There were other experiments going on at the same time . . . in other places in the institute. We never included them in the reconstruction. They were overlooked. The forces generated by the others billowed outward and some of them intersected with the energy that Jeff and the Schylers were exerting on the steel.

The three of them acted as a focus for the signal; it intersected with the sample in just the right way. If there were four or five or even one other PK operation going on in the institute that day, then the power generation was enlarged by the factor of the number of participants. That was more than enough power than was needed to destroy the sample and knock out the lights."

Outside, the first pellets of rain were starting to beat against the sides of the institute. "This lab was empty. But other experiments in the other labs set up a proper beat. It's a strong signal that exists as the sum total of all of the ripples that intersect in the vicinity. See?"

He pointed to the chalked-in area on the board. "A large number of signals intersecting created a new signal, infinitely stronger than any of the contributory ones.

"Group magic and witchcraft use it. So does voodoo. They just call it by another name. Witches call it coning power. All they do is get into a circle and move the energy in such a way that the person at the center of the circle is able to fire off a concentrated blast. It has to be the same energy that we have here. It's only the applications that change. We want the energy to be used for the destruction of steel. Some groups want it to destroy their enemies. Some use it to cure the sick. It's all the same energy, just shaped differently. And, Channing? This makes a theoretical paradigm meaningless. All we have to do is find the proper spacing of the subjects and put the strongest of them at the epicenter of the pattern of people; the center person then can move the energy off in the direction of a target. The chances are that whatever destroyed the bridge and nearly wrecked the dam were simply focal points of energy. They wouldn't have to generate a great deal of energy if there was a well of minds somewhere else to tap. If that man—what was his name—Lewis? If he had anything to do with the bridge, the chances are that he was the lens for an energy flow sent from another location."

Channing was starting to nod in agreement. "Sent by distant seeing or its equivalent."

Jerry rushed on excitedly. "It turns the whole ball game around. All we have to do now is find the right distances between subjects and choose the strongest of them for the lens role."

"Then we have to find where each experiment was going on in the building at the time."

Jerry pointed again to the crude sketch on the blackboard. "And repeat them with the Schyler experiment. Then we feed the information to Daniel and he tells us exactly what the pattern of people has to be for the breaking of steel at a number of locations. If we mix that with the volume that Rosemary McGee turned up yesterday on resonances, the chances are that we have a game plan."

All four of them could feel it, even Grady. For the first time in more than a month, there was a flicker of hope. They would have something to fight back with when they needed it, and that would be soon.

14

There are moments when one feels free from one's own identification with human limitations and inadequacies . . . life and death flow into one and there is neither Evolution nor Destiny . . . only Being.

—Albert Einstein

Almost all of Paulson's advisors agreed that the wheat deal was turning out to be an act of political suicide. Tilden had spent two weeks hammering at it and the outcome was a drop of six points on all of the polls for Paulson. It boiled down to money, as it usually did. When the news of the wheat deal broke, the commodities market exploded instantly. Wheat furures soared; taking a cue from the market, distributors and retailers raised their bread prices. Sensing a panic in wheat and a drought thereafter, consumers across the country denuded the bread shelves in a matter of days. Paulson was not able to fix a ceiling on wheat prices, which came close to doubling in two weeks. With the Soviet wheat deal tied to the price that Paulson set earlier, it looked to the media and to the American public that the Soviets were getting cheaper wheat than America was. It was that fact that Tilden was battering. "American wheat for America" became the battle cry that was taken up by millions.

As Paulson's staff frantically tried to negotiate the logistics of shipping fifty million tons of wheat halfway across the world, they found that the shipping industry was rallying to the side of Tilden's forces. Shippers balked at the agreements that would put grain on their fleets. Stevedores' unions refused to load the wheat; ship's crews refused to cross picket lines. The unions threatened to shut down every port on the East and Gulf coasts if the wheat deal was not cancelled. The West Coast ports, slated to ship to Vladivostok more than thirty million tons in the month of June, were plagued with demonstrations and labor disputes. Paulson had to act quickly. He did. The action he took was the most efficient way to get wheat to the Soviet Union. It was also an act that potentially sealed his political doom.

He ordered the secretary of the Navy to move both U.S. Navy cargo transports as well as available vintage "Victory" ships to all of the shipping ports. He used Regular Army port and stevedore units to load them. The decision was met with violence at some of the ports and with serious talk of impeachment in the Congress. Thus, delays in shipments were not something that Soviet Premier Kharkov could call contrived. They were as real as the political dispatches that arrived daily in the Kremlin from Eastern Europe, from India, from China. By the end of the second week in June the demands for wheat were as great on Kharkov as the pressures not to sell were on Paulson.

It was just past nine in the morning on a hot, humid day that Grady arrived at the White House. He was escorted to the den, where Paulson sat with the usual sheaf of briefing papers in front of him. He looked ragged, tired and generally irritable. Grady thought that that was a reasonable condition for a man who was watching his political career dissolve before him.

"Sit down, Mike. Coffee?"

"No, Steve. I've done about four cups already today, and it's what? Nine-fifteen? I'd better hold off for a while."

"Okay. Let's get to it. How many ships sailed out of Portland?"

"Just one, so far."

"And we scheduled how many?"

"Six, for yesterday. The army port units are bound to be a little slower than the civilian stevedores, at least for a few days, until they get the hang of new equipment and procedures. With luck we'll be close to schedule by the end of next week. My people tell me it will be the same for the Gulf and East coast ports. The overall delay in schedule won't be more than two weeks. Ironic, isn't it?"

"Isn't what?"

"We didn't need to fabricate a delay. We got one ready-made."

"We got a lot of things ready-made, Mike. What has Moreland managed to put together? On the phone you said that he had something."

"Well, they think so. Tanner's come up with a method for moving his psychics out into a pattern. Each pattern varies according to what the nature of the target is and the distance from it. It looks to me like a broadcast system. By yesterday afternoon, they'd managed to alter a piece of steel just over five miles from the institute. In their second experiment, Moreland and Tanner had half the group assemble in the same . . . formation, so to speak, surrounding the target."

"One attacked and one defended?"

"Yes. And it seemed to work. At least nothing managed to change the metal. Tanner keeps warning me that they don't know if they can duplicate any of this.

He says they're flying by the combined seats of their pants."

"So am I, Mike."

Grady outlined the real problem with the Tanner effect. "Unfortunately, it requires that psychics be on or near the target site. That would mean knowing in advance where the next attack was going to take place. Unlike Russia's offensive capability, Tanner's brand of psychokinetic signal projection is fairly short-range, so far. More time is needed to perfect a detailed and comprehensive approach."

"Forget it. Time has nearly run out." Agitated, Paulson rose to his feet and paced the room. Grady followed suit. "What else can you tell me?"

Grady shook his head sadly. "You see, the chances are that the Golden Gate catastrophe was the result of this man Lewis acting as the epicenter or sender, with others at some distance helping him. We haven't managed to find any others. We can't even be sure that he didn't have a technique developed that enabled him to work alone. There's nothing saying that the Soviets are even using the same system that Tanner has!"

"You're saying we're still effectively defenseless?"

"As of now, we are."

The pacing increased furiously as they debated the Tanner experiment. They were interrupted by the arrival of the Director of Protocol, Jake Carpenter, who looked gray. He carried a long strip of wire service copy.

"Mister President?"

"Yeah, Jake?" Paulson had the look of a man wary of too much bad news in too short a time. "I hope it's important."

"It is, Mister President. Reuters just carried this on a relay from their Moscow office."

He handed Paulson the news story, which had red

underlines heavily scored beneath key lines. Paulson skimmed it.

The story was brief. Moscow had experienced a total power blackout. Power had been out for over an hour and Reuters thought the story newsworthy when Kremlin representatives refused to comment on the cause or the time needed for repairs. The last line of the story intrigued Paulson most. "Reuters was also unable to contact its offices in Kursk or Leningrad. Informed sources in Moscow seem to think that the power failure is not limited to Moscow alone."

Paulson stared at the line for a minute before he passed the sheet across to Grady. "What does this look like, Mike? Insurrection? Sabotage?"

Grady quickly skimmed the story. "If it is, we'll have a lot more information soon. If Moscow just blew a fuse, we won't hear anything."

But Moscow hadn't blown a fuse. It was minutes later when Carpenter was back. This time, he carried a sheaf of wire copy. The information astonished Paulson and Grady. Power was gone in Kursk, in Leningrad, in the Crimea. Power failures were erupting all across the Soviet Union.

Paulson raced through the wire copy. "Jake, keep getting these up here as they come in. Keep me informed."

"I don't think I'll be able to do that, Mister President."

"Why not?"

"Well—" Jake pointed to the bottom of the last sheet. "This was the last one to come in through the Reuters' wire. I checked their Washington office from down in the pressroom. They said that the Soviet Ministry of Information had slapped a press security blanket on the whole thing. It looks like Moscow is really trying to keep the lid on."

Paulson and Grady exchanged looks. What the hell was going on?

"Mike, can we tell anything from satellite shots? You know—how extensive the blackout really is? What impact it might have on them?"

"Sure, but I don't know what it would tell us about insurrection or sabotage, though. All we could see would be the affected areas, not *how* they were affected."

"That's good enough for now." Paulson looked at his watch. "I have a meeting in ten minutes. Call me with whatever you come up with, sometime this afternoon. And keep your pulse on this Moreland and Tanner development."

Grady sped back to the Defense Department. Satellites that continuously orbited over the Soviet Union were ordered to scan the night skies. They would register the size of the infrared signatures of the cities. Computers would then compare the shots sent to the ground by telemetry with shots of the same areas a few days earlier. Marked differences in the signatures would allow Grady to infer the extent of the power failure.

It was just past two in the afternoon when Grady's staff reported in. Every major city in western Russia was blacked out. It had started with Moscow and moved outward like a wave, sweeping across city after city, stopping only at the Urals and at the Gulf of Finland. Soviet media was still mute about the failure. Not only were correspondents prevented from sending stories out of the country, they could not even contact their home offices. Something big was brewing, but not enough information was coming from their intelligence operatives. Grady frantically called the President. Paulson answered laconically.

"Yes, Mike? What have you got?"

"The whole damn country is blacked out! We're still gathering the facts, but we don't know how or why."

"No wonder Kharkov just made a priority request for a hot-line call. I'll be picking up in a minute."

Grady looked to the door of his office. One of his staff was coming in. The man held out a clipboard with a pad on it. A single sentence had been printed across it.

Grady read the sentence. "Wait—this just came in! We have a satellite report that their Dnieper Dam just failed. We got a shot on one of the last satellite passes. She's the biggest they've got and she is capable of producing more than Hoover."

"What the hell is going on there?"

"You said you'd settle for effects. Causes are speculative, right now. We don't know if someone blew it or it just fell down."

"You're always so damn logical—I have to go. I'll get back to you—"

Grady suddenly found himself holding a dead line.

Paulson picked up the red phone apprehensively.

Igor Kharkov was not known for pleasantries; he went right to the core of the problem.

"Mister President, as I am sure you are already aware"—Paulson was not surprised to hear Kharkov's crisp King's English; the Soviet Premier had been a foreign minister in London for a number of years.— "a major problem has arisen with respect to the generation of electrical power."

"I know, Mister Premier. We received earlier reports on it this morning. We also just got word about a problem at the Dnieper Dam."

There was a pause; Paulson could hear the Premier conferring with someone.

"Yes, Mister President. That's true. The dam failed just over half an hour ago. But let's not play cat and mouse. You are aware of the timing of the events perhaps better than I."

Paulson flushed. "Mister Kharkov, would you care to explain that remark?"

There was a slight blipping sound and a rustle somewhere in the phone connection. Paulson thought that the signal shifted from one satellite to another, high overhead. Or perhaps there was someone monitoring the call with the Premier. Perhaps it was both.

Kharkov's voice boomed over the phone. "Do you think we are fools, Paulson? Do you think us that naive? The design of your plan is transparent. There is resistance to a wheat sale at home . . . considerable resistance. You send the ships to sea then carry out your plan of sabotage. You wish to hold on to your position so badly that you destroy the Soviet Union to do it? You were going to wait until the U.S.S.R. was on her knees, with her power systems a shambles, then direct the ships home. I warn you, Paulson."

There was a tone of more than anger in the Premier's voice. It was something that bordered on panic. He was being pressed and pressed hard by the forces around him. Unlike Paulson, Kharkov did not have the protection of a democratic electoral system. Kharkov held the Central Committee together with power; the power of the KGB and the might of the armed forces. It was his sabre-rattling generals who were doing the pressing. Paulson was sure that there were two or three of them in the room with the Premier. The uncharacteristic bluster and accusatory tone were not in keeping with the behavior Paulson had seen in their two meetings since the American President took office.

"My government and the Russian people will not stand for this kind of intimidation. Already, there are at least twenty thousand dead of hunger and there will be thousands more dead from the collapse of the dam on the Dnieper. My generals are demanding that the

Soviet Union launch a pre-emptive nuclear strike. As your systems would detect a missile launch almost instantly, you would be forced to retaliate. Oblivion. You see?"

"You have offered no proof of this charge, Mister Premier. You simply make allegations and threaten a nuclear holocaust."

"I *have* the proof, Mister Paulson. I had it from Andrei Sholodkin not ten minutes ago. The samples that he retrieved from the power plant in Leningrad were altered. You remember your ultimatum to Gregory Luboff? The samples from Leningrad were altered . . . psychically. You are making good on that threat? You just launched a first strike, Mister President. You did. And now, both of us stand at the edge of the abyss."

There was a distant sound on the line, like the wind moaning through the lines. The conversation was being shifted from circuit to circuit.

"Mister Premier, I need not make a strong case for the sabotage of the Golden Gate Bridge and the ruthless murder of the Vice President and the attack on Hoover Dam. Those are already known to you, I am sure. Let me remind you, though, that those attacks were the first strike of which you speak. We did not retaliate then, and we have not now." Paulson paused for a second. "I suggest that as I am not fully conversant with this kind of weapon and I dare say, neither are you, we arrange a meeting of our respective experts. Let them jointly investigate all of this. I don't know if it is the best solution, but at least it is better than the alternative. Our Doctor Moreland and your Doctor Sholodkin could meet at some neutral location, acceptable to both countries, in say a few days. Would that suffice to show the good faith of the United States?"

There was a muffled sound on Kharkov's end of the

conversation. He was covering the phone with his hand, while he conferred with someone.

"Mister President?" Kharkov's voice was restrained, careful. "We accept the proposal. But this must be done quickly, very quickly. Where would they meet?"

Paulson's mind raced through the possibilities. "Zurich," he said after a second. As the financial and banking center of the Western world, Zurich was the sanctum sanctorum of world political and military neutrality for centuries.

"Yes. Zurich. That would do."

"Might I suggest, Mister Premier, that we each contact our experts and make the arrangements?"

It was a minute later when the conversation ended. Paulson stared at the phone for a long time. It took that long for the realization to sink in. A four-minute telephone call brought the world back from the brink of a nuclear holocaust. He and one other human being had just given the civilized world another chance. A slender chance.

All of it depended on what two old men said to one another in Zurich in a few days.

As the Premier and the President spoke, the S.S. *Western Victory* steamed on a northwest course in the North Atlantic. She was two days out of New York and carried American wheat destined for Russia. A carbon copy of her sister ships in the World War II *Victory* fleet, the *Western* was more than forty years old, slow, cumbersome, rusty and uncomfortable. Moreover, her officers and crew were U.S. Navy and not merchant seaman. They were used to a newer generation of ships, with decorated cabins and air conditioning in the quarters.

Lieutenant John Christoffson hated the ship and the mission as much as he loved the navy and the sea. He signed up for extra bridge watches to avoid having to spend much time in his tiny, sweltering cabin. His four years at Annapolis had taught him that boredom and tediousness were overcome by a surfeit of work. It would make the endless days spent cruising at a snail's pace of twelve knots move quickly.

It was close to seven P.M. in that part of the Atlantic, when Christoffson assumed the midwatch from an ensign whose name he hardly remembered. He set to work, checking the pencil entries in the captain's log and preparing to have them made a permanent record. After he set course and speed with the helmsman, he adjusted his officer-of-the-deck armband and moved out to the wing bridge.

It was the part of the evening that he liked the most at sea. In the west, a twilight glow darkened into ebony, while above, the first of millions of stars started to dot the crystal clear sky. The sea was slate gray and dead calm, like a carpet of glass. The only breeze was created by the ship's movement. Below, in the officers' ward room, there was laughter and conversation which spilled out through the open ports and wafted up to John on the wing bridge. The party was serving two purposes. It was a get-acquainted affair for the ship's officers and a small celebration for the captain's birthday. John was the only officer on deck.

From the wheelhouse behind him, John could hear the whistling of an old sound tube. Electric intercoms were considered luxuries when the *Western Victory* had been built. He came back into the wheelhouse and unplugged the tube as it started to whistle for a second time.

"Bridge."

He recognized the voice on the other end as a chief petty officer he'd met the day before. The man was the assistant to the engineering officer. "Bridge? Engine room. Look, we've picked up a steam leak just to the

rear of stanchion . . . ah . . . sixty-three. She's starting
to pop rivets. We're shipping a bit of water in the
engine room."

"Start pumps and organize a party to start shoring.
I'll inform the captain."

"Aye-aye, sir."

He plugged the tube and started to activate the one
that connected the bridge to the ward room. Before he
could finish, there was another signal from the engine
room: "Bridge."

"We got trouble here. We picked up a second leak
and someone just said there's a third. We're shipping
water fast. We have to cut speed."

"Stay with it."

John uncupped the other phone and called into it.

"Captain to the bridge. Captain to the bridge." He
thought for a second, then added, "This is an emergency." He didn't wait for an answer from the wardroom. He turned to the officer-of-the-deck's runner who
stood in the corner of the wheelhouse.

"Sailor, lay down to the wardroom on the double.
My respects to the captain and would he report to
the bridge, immediately. Tell the engineering officer to
get below to the engine room on the double." He wondered about mentioning the nature of the emergency
to the sailor and thought better of it. There was no
sense in starting rumors.

Again the whistle from the engine room. She was
shipping water fast. The chief sounded frightened. He
asked if speed had been cut. The water was getting
ahead of the pumps. He also asked for permission to
damp boilers one and two. John sensed the chief's
urgent tone. He allowed them to be damped.

He turned back to the helmsman. "All stop."

"All stop, aye, sir." The helmsman cranked the
signal to the engine room and the small arrows on the

round face of the crank snapped into place almost simultaneously.

Suddenly, there was a rumble below, far below. It frightened John. He blew into another tube. "Radio room? Start sending our position immediately. This is an emergency." He didn't wait for a reply. Then he opened the sound tube to the engine room—and threw his hands in front of his face. He had been hit with a plume of steam. He stumbled toward the door to the wing bridge, more shocked than hurt. At the side of the door he opened a small glass cabinet and pressed a red button. A klaxon started to sound. *Where the hell was the captain?* John moved through the door quickly, to see if any damage might show on the foredeck. It saved his life.

Five seconds later a huge torrent of sea water engulfed the engine room. When the sea water hit the superheated steam of the as yet undamped boilers, the *Western Victory* blew herself out of the water.

No SOS had been sent. There had been no time. Lt. John Christoffson was blown clear of the bridge and far out into the water. Luckily, he was thrown clear of the secondary explosions in the ship's fuel bunkers and the tremendous suction created by the rapid sinking of the remains of the ship. Stunned, he swam automatically away from the ship, until flotsom started popping up nearby. A small three-man wooden raft appeared. It had obviously been pulled under by the suction and wrenched loose to float back to the surface. Exhausted and in shock, Christoffson dragged himself aboard and started to paddle toward the frothy grave that moments before had been the *Western Victory*. He could find no one. Christoffson was the sole survivor.

By first light, the area of the calm sea where the freighter had sunk was strewn with debris and haloed by a huge pattern of wheat chaff, which had poured from the shattered holds. It was this very halo that attracted the attention of a passing plane just before dusk. They sent a ship to pick up Christoffson, but as with Melville's ship *Rachel* in *Moby Dick,* they were able to find no other lost children.

15

Energy projected into any kind of construction, psychic or physical, cannot be recalled, but must follow the laws of the particular form into which it has been for the moment moulded.

—Seth

For nearly an hour Jerry had been watching the sun come up. The gray streaks had sliced across the night sky, then lightened into pink. In the tree outside the bedroom window, a whippoorwill tuned up for its day's call to a mate. In the distance, Jerry could hear the plaintive, haunting call of a loon. It was elusive and at the same time insistent, like the problem that he wrestled with at the institute. They were so close to an answer and yet, it seemed to just barely elude them.

He looked back to the sunrise and then down to Eve. She slept soundly, with her arms curled protectively around the fetus. She was close to term now and was starting to feel fatigue more critically. He worried about her, knowing that despite the ferocity of her protestations, she wasn't as strong as she pretended to be. He knew how desperately she needed to take this baby to term . . . and that a large part of the need was really his. He gently brushed a strand of hair from her face and she stirred but didn't awaken. The phone rang.

and Jerry surprised himself by snapping it up a split second into the first ring. Eve moved but didn't fully waken.

The voice that he heard was distant, crisp and efficient.

"Delta, Delta . . . Mike-Romeo . . ." It was the authentication code for a secured call. It would have to be Grady.

"Jerry?" It was Grady. "Sorry to call so early. But . . ." He paused as if to look for the right words. After a few seconds, he gave up with a grunt and spun out the tale of the Soviet power disaster.

Jerry could feel a cold knot of fear start to form in his stomach. It was all happening too soon. They were escalating the stakes in the game—whoever *they* were —and Jerry knew that he didn't yet have any chips to call the bet.

"I want Channing to be ready for that meeting in Zurich. I'm trying to arrange it for the day after tomorrow."

"I don't see any way Channing can bluff Sholodkin, Mike. And I also don't know why the Soviets would want to sabotage their own power systems in order to set up this confrontation. It just isn't in their interest."

A persuasive tone crept into Grady's voice. "I don't think we can call this thing a confrontation—not of the conventional sort, at any rate. It's more like a summit. That's why I want you to go with Channing. You two teamed up to convince the President pretty effectively . . . me too, for that matter. And, there's the question of Channing's age. Having a younger man along will take some of the strain off him."

Jerry looked down at Eve and paused a long minute before answering. The chilly memory of Eve's miscarriages and the hope they both had for the current one battled in the back of his mind. Besides, he was a scientist, not a politician.

"If we're in a race against time as far as counter-measures are concerned, perhaps it would better for me to keep trying to plow ahead with things at the institute."

"Jerry?" Grady's voice carried a slight edge. It wasn't animosity. Rather, it was something more like tension. "Can you hold?"

"Sure."

There were a series of mechanical and electrical clicks and beeps as Jerry's end of the conversation was relegated to a microscopic, electrical siding. Nervously he ran a hand through his hair and looked down at Eve again.

Her blue eyes greeted him.

He reached down and placed a hand against her stomach. It was warm to his touch. "You heard?"

She sat up with some difficulty and stretched. "I was asleep . . . not deaf. When do you have to leave?"

"*If* I agree to—"

She shook her head with the absolute certitude of a trial judge overruling an objection. "You won't have a choice."

"What do you mean?" He held the receiver away from his ear for a second.

"You'll go wherever he wants you to go. Besides, odds are you'd be back in a few days. I'm not due for over three weeks."

"But Grady wants the institute turned over to Deladier while we're gone. I—"

Again, Eve shook her head, overruling him. "That'll have to be a calculated risk."

Her face muscles relaxed and she cocked her head to his side, her eyes blindly staring into the distance. She was experiencing a precognitive vision. "There's more . . . a map with little green dots of light. They keep blinking on and on, so many of them . . . no choice . . ."

"Jerry?"

It was Grady's voice. Jerry quickly pressed the receiver to his ear but kept his eyes on Eve. Her faraway expression faded while he listened to the latest development.

After he hung up, he looked to Eve.

"You were right again. There won't be a choice in the matter. Grady just found out that one of the grain ships sunk in the Atlantic—popped apart like a Tinker Toy."

"Like the bridge and the dam?"

"He doesn't know. But it seems there was a Soviet trawler less than twenty miles away from the grain ship's last reported position—satellites confirmed that —so Premier Kharkov knew about it before we did. Incredibly, the Russians accused us of sinking the ship."

"It's crazy, Jerry. Why would we?"

Jerry shook his head. "We wouldn't. There's no reason in the world we'd want to sink one of our own ships. Not now . . . not under these conditions. Paulson denied it. Kharkov said he was being pushed very hard by his generals and as a result, he moved them to what Grady called a 'higher state of readiness.' "

"A war alert?"

"Just about. Paulson was forced to respond in kind. So everything's hanging on the edge. I'll have to go to Zurich with Channing." He stood up to stretch cramped muscles.

"In your vision, you talked about green lights and maps. Any idea what that means?"

Eve shrugged. "I'm sorry. I guess I'm not very good at interpreting what I see. When it actually happens, you'll know it," she finished lamely. She was thinking of her own nightmares of fire and darkness and blood. Seeing the future was no comfort if such terrors could

not be averted—she would have to wait for her nightmare to come true and hope to survive it.

She sat silently on the bed, staring at the wall, while
a worried Jerry Tanner left her alone. His own nightmares would begin soon enough.

Rosemary McGee sat quietly at the console. She
thought for a second before she allowed her fingers to
play deftly across the keyboard. In the distance, micro-
circuits activated and the huge MRI computer sprang
to life as it recognized an access code. She paused a
few seconds, then punched in a series of coded numbers. The machine retrieved the information she'd called
up almost instantly. The display glowed in green on
the scanner in front of her.

The information was a summary of the research
carried out over the preceding weeks. She'd been over
all of it hundreds of times already, but there was always
the chance that something had been missed. All of it
was there: the distances; the effects on metals; the
stress indices of the test subjects. Each page remained
until she tapped the key that wiped it and replaced it
with the following page. As the last page evaporated
from the screen, Rosemary typed in the code that
correlated the earlier information with all that she'd
gathered on resonances and vibration frequencies. The
figures had not changed. She sighed and stretched.

After a few minutes, she ran the second program
and the third. They all read the same way. Jerry's
cluster of psychics, which included the Schylers, Eve,
and Maria Munoz, generated a signal that was effective
at short range. But as the distance between the group
and the target increased, the effectiveness plummeted.
Daniel was not providing an answer.

She pushed her chair back from the console and let
her eyes play across the banks of machinery that packed
the room. Though she was disappointed, there was

still a sense of excitement for her as she sat at the console. She'd almost forgotten how much she'd loved working with computers, especially one as sophisticated as Daniel. When she'd gone to work for Anton, she'd been pulled away from them. But being close to him had filled the gap . . . erased the need for challenge. It had also gotten her away from Hughes, whose adolescent womanizing had been a constant irritant and had gotten in the way of her work. Now she felt a challenge again. *Oh, God . . . what does that say about Anton and me?*

He'd been growing more distant, more secretive, even with her. They'd not made love in more than two weeks. Where was it going? She brushed the hair back from her face and pulled her chair back to the console, smiling for a second at the glowing face of the machine.

"Well, Daniel, me lad . . . *you* don't give a girl any grief, do you? You just answer all of the questions—as long as I know what to ask."

Again, she punched in the series of programs and as she was about to type in the RUN command, her fingers paused above the keys. She debated adding a step to the program and, deciding she would, she allowed her fingers to fly across the keys in a new pattern. The step was only a check, one that she'd gone through the first time she'd run the programs weeks ago. The computer staff called it a central processing corollary. Daniel was ordered to hold the programs in memory and search his system for related information that was already there. It only took a few seconds for Daniel to fly through the billions of bits of data. Rosemary expected an INSUFFICIENT COROLLARY DATA to flash across the screen as it had when she first had run the check.

It didn't.

Rosemary blinked at the screen. "What? What the hell is—"

The numbers patiently winking off and on once a second said: CODE 944.

The blinking was a coded apology of sorts that told the programmer that there was significant data available but that it was under another access code, one that would have to be punched in before Daniel could carry out her earlier command.

She stared at the numbers, almost mesmerized. Daniel now contained information relative to Jerry Tanner's project that had not been there two weeks before. How had it gotten there, when she was the only one working on the problem?

Behind her, a door opened. She started and turned in time to see Tom Hughes. He smiled broadly, covering his surprise.

"Well, good morning."

"Oh, morning, Tom. You startled me."

"Sorry. I didn't expect you. Have you spent the night or did you just come in early?"

"Came in early. I've been running Jerry Tanner's stuff through."

"Oh. And I thought you came in for an early morning rendezvous with me."

"Tom!" There was an impatient edge in her voice.

"Sorry. I should have known it was too early for a line like that. Want some coffee?"

She shook her head. "No. I've been living on it for a couple of days."

"Suit yourself." She watched as he walked across the tile floor to a small utility alcove and started to spoon coffee into a flow-through machine. She looked at the blinking numbers and then back to Tom. If there was anyone at the institute who would know what the CODE 944 meant it would have to be Tom. She waited until he poured himself a steaming mug.

"Tom? Daniel's feeding me a nine-four-four on the Tanner programs. Who's running related programs?"

Hughes turned from the coffee machine and stared at her quizzically. "What? You mean besides Anton?"

She was stunned for a split second but tried to cover it by yawning elaborately. "Oh, I'm sorry, Tom. I must be sleepier than I thought. I'd forgotten Anton's work. I was so tied into my own. Stupid of me. The nine-four-four is his and I'd forgotten. He and I are the only two working on it, right?"

"Right."

"Maybe I will take that coffee."

"Sure. Be ready in a minute." He headed back to the coffee machine.

Rosemary looked back at the console. Why had Anton never told her? Never even mentioned it? What the hell was going on? She grabbed a black vinyl loose-leaf binder and flipped through the pages until she found Anton Deladier's access code. She typed it into the machine and Daniel wiped out the blinking code. Page after page of data flashed across the screen.

She couldn't tell much from the quick glimpses she was getting, but it seemed to start with Jerry's work and move further into theory. She typed in the order for a print-out and obediently, Daniel started to operate the chattering high-speed printer, creating hard copies at a rate of sixteen hundred words a minute.

Tom brought her a coffee cup. "One cream, one sugar. Right?"

She nodded and sipped at the coffee.

"Don't let Anton know you forgot all the hours he was putting in on this. I'm sure he wouldn't appreciate it."

She smiled. "It'll be our secret, Tom."

There was a leer in Tom's smile that repelled her. It said, *I'm sure you'll find some way to repay me.* It was the same leer that had driven her out of the computer center in the first place; that and the desire to be near Anton. She'd almost forgotten how distasteful it was . . . almost.

They chatted aimlessly for a few minutes. Tom looked for an opening, while Rosemary simply waited for the printer to stop. When it did, she took a last sip of coffee and got up. "Thanks for the coffee, Tom. I've got to get this stuff upstairs."

Outside the computer center, Rosemary moved down the hall in the direction of the elevators. Under her arm, she carried the thick run of the new data that Anton had compiled. She could feel the anger and the confusion build inside of her, though she'd managed to cover it in front of Tom.

As the elevator moved swiftly and quietly upward, she looked at her watch; Anton would be in the office. His research might have saved her weeks of work. His information was needed by an America under siege. Why would he work secretly on a project that everyone in the institute was going loony trying to solve? And even if there was some real reason—some flawlessly rational explanation to the why of it—she doubted that he could say anything that might rekindle the fire that was going out inside of her.

She forced the hurt and the anger back inside, took a deep breath and strode into Anton's office.

Anton was seated at a strangely empty desk, perusing a folder. He looked up at her and smiled.

"What a pleasant surprise. How are you, love?"

Her smile was a bit strained. "Tired. I got in very early this morning to run some things by Daniel."

He got up and came from behind the desk. He moved to where she stood and slipped a hand around her waist. His grip was like steel sheathed in velvet. "So. He's my rival . . . Daniel is. I'll have to damage some of his capacitors so that you won't spend more time with him." He looked down at the sheaf of computer paper that she gripped tightly. "Is that Daniel's love poetry?" He laughed.

She slipped deftly from his grip. It was a move designed to tell him that something was wrong. He did not miss the connotation. She moved to his desk and dropped the papers on it. They landed with a thump. "I don't think it's Daniel's work, Anton. It's yours."

He moved slowly around the desk and flipped over the first page of the run. His head snapped up to her almost immediately. "How did you—"

"How did I manage to find it, Anton? Simple, really. I tricked Tom Hughes."

"Hughes? Hughes mentioned . . ." There was a rising anger in his voice that infuriated Rosemary all the more. She could feel a screaming scene coming on and that was what she didn't want. She wanted answers, important answers, no matter how painful they might be.

"Don't be angry with Tom, Anton. There's no reason to be. He was being honest, you see. He'd assumed that you'd shared everything you'd done with me, with your mistress . . . with the woman you love. It would be a natural thing to do, wouldn't it, Anton? Wouldn't it?" There was a quiver in her voice that she could not disguise.

Anton's eyes were narrow and cold in a way she'd never seen. "Who knows about this?"

"Does it matter, Anton? I don't think it really does. The most important thing is that I didn't know about it. You carefully avoided telling me. And all of that time, I was going crazy trying to make sense of Jerry Tanner's experiments. Why didn't you tell us?" Her voice started to crack. She paused to regain control. The last thing she wanted to do was to go to pieces in front of him. "Why in God's name didn't you tell *me?*"

He didn't answer immediately. But, in a way, he

didn't have to. It was the change that came over his face, the terrible change that heralded what he was going to say. His dark eyes widened with a fire long repressed. His hand clenched into a fist and it slammed down on the computer paper as his words came out in an agonized, almost guttural, hiss.

"Because *you* are working for *them,* you stupid bitch!"

Rosemary stumbled back a step. She could feel a tear well up and spill over each eyelid. There was no holding them back, not now. Dear God. She'd never heard him speak that way to anyone. Why to her? Why?

Through her tears, she could see his expression change again. The rage vanished as suddenly as it had come. It was eerie. His composure returned and in seconds he was the Anton she'd always known. But both of them knew that anything he could say now would come too late. It was over, and inside she felt like stone.

Anton ran a hand through his thick, dark hair. "Rosemary, I'm sorry. I . . . I . . . just didn't know what I was saying." He leaned toward her over the desk. "You must understand. You have to. It's the only chance I have. I'm on the track of an answer. I *know* the answer. It's here."

He grabbed the sheaf of papers and gestured with them, his viselike fingers bending the computer paper.

"Channing wouldn't let me work on it—wouldn't give me credit—not for all the years of work—not for all of the ideas that were really mine. No. Nothing for Anton. Nothing except the job of shuffling his paperwork. I had to win this time. I had to. And I have. He'll have to listen now. Him and his prissy little protégé, Tanner. Both of them will listen. And it will be today. It will have to be today. You hear." His angry voice rose shrilly. "If you'd have known, you'd have told them. I know you like Tanner. I've seen the way you look at him. And so, I couldn't tell you. You see, don't you?"

Rosemary brushed the tears away from her cheeks with the back of her hand. "You didn't let me choose, Anton. You didn't trust me. Yes. I would have told them. Because what we're doing is more important that what you and I—had." She could see that the word stung him. Good. She wanted it to. "There are millions of lives hanging in the balance, Anton. And I can't allow your conceit and ego to put them in greater peril. No matter how much it hurts you and us, I can't just stand by and let you do that."

She shook her head. "I can't." She could feel her control slipping. It was like the beginning of a long skid on an icy road. All she could do was watch it. "I loved you, Anton. But I have to respect you, too. And—and since the start of all of this, it's been getting harder and harder. And now, this." She pointed to the computer paper on the desk. "I have to give this to them. I have to do it today." She took a deep breath, and turned to go. Anton's voice stopped her.

"Do it, then. It won't do anyone any good—not without me. They won't know what it means. I'm the only one who knows that. I—"

His words were cut off as she slammed the office door behind her.

She managed to make it through the outer office and down the hall to her own office without crying, though she was sure that her tear-ravaged make-up betrayed what had gone on. She closed her door and leaned against it for a long minute. Inside, she could feel deep, racking sobs start to bubble up.

"Rosemary?"

"What—?"

Maria Munoz was sitting across the room from her. The old woman got to her feet.

"I'm so sorry. I'd wanted to speak to you and I—" The old woman stopped in midsentence and strode across to Rosemary. She took the younger woman by the shoulders, with a surprising strength. *"Ay . . . pobrecita."*

They stood there for a long minute, while Rosemary let the tears and the sobs escape. It was after Rosemary had blown her nose and seated herself at her desk that they spoke.

"I'm sorry, Maria. I—"

"It was a confrontation of sorts with Anton Deladier?"

Rosemary's nod was automatic. She knew that surprise showed in her face.

"It had to do with what he knows . . . that no one else does. There is a great hatred inside of him. No?"

Another nod.

"I knew there was something. I started feeling it when we were at Hoover Dam. It was something dark, something painful. It took me some time to understand that it was him—that it was Anton. I think . . ." Maria's face grew distant for a second, as if she were reliving the moments at the dam. "He is a man on the edge of madness, my dear. I had come to speak of it to you. But now it seems that you already know the things I was going to say."

Rosemary pushed her hair back from her face and took a deep breath.

"I was running some programs through this morning when I found a great deal of test data that Anton was running on his own. He's getting different results from the things that Jerry and Channing are putting together. I don't know what all of it means, but it seems significant." She got to her feet. "Can you call Channing's office? I'll go to the computer center and run another read-out. I left the copy in Anton's office."

The old woman nodded and reached for the phone.

Rosemary shuffled toward the basement home of Daniel, still wrapped in her own sadness.

Jerry got up from the conference table and moved to the huge picture window that looked out to the green farmland. In the distance, a dark squall line was marching across the sky. The heat of June would be broken by a summer storm, Jerry judged, in less than an hour. He turned back to look at Channing, who was sipping coffee.

"What time did Grady say the helicopter would be here?"

"Seven in the morning. That air force jet of his will be airborne by nine. It puts us in Zurich about ten tomorrow night. The meeting with—" The old man paused to push away a yawn—"Andrei will be at ten the next morning. The scheduling's good. It will give us a chance to shake off the jet lag." He started to assemble the papers they'd spent more than an hour working on.

Jerry shook his head. "It isn't much, is it?"

"What isn't?"

"Those papers you're putting into a neat pile over there. It doesn't say we've done much, not since that meeting with Paulson and Grady, at any rate."

"I think you're wrong, Jerry. It really is a great deal. We may not be able to duplicate Andrei's long-range results, but at least we can get short-range results. That's a great deal more than we knew when we started. We've mastered a theoretical principle. That doesn't happen frequently and you should get the credit; you and Eve and Morey and the others." Channing shook his head as he looked at their jointly assembled notes. "Besides, I don't think Andrei's that much farther ahead. I think he stumbled on a technique no more than a year ago. It has to have been right after their weather alteration experiments blew up in their faces. Weather control would have been the perfect weapon for them to beef up their wheat growing season and harass ours. They must have pulled Andrei in like the cavalry, expecting miracles. He gave them what looked like one. All of it might have come together except for the problem with the Soviet power grid. Thank God that happened."

Jerry shook his head and started back to the conference table.

"I don't know if I want to thank anyone for that. I still don't see what all of that means, except that it puts us over a nuclear barrel."

Channing held up the papers. "They're over as big a barrel as we are. We'll meet here, at six-thirty. Is that all right?" Channing pushed himself to his feet and nearly lost his balance before placing a hand on the edge of the table to steady himself.

"Channing? Are you all right?"

The old man nodded. "Just tired. I need sleep."

Jerry knew that was a half-truth. What Channing was apt to call "tiredness," Chet Kumasaka would call extreme exhaustion. Grady's reasons for asking Jerry on the Zurich trip became more clear.

Jerry rolled down his sleeves and fastened the cuff links that Eve had given him for their fifth anniversary. They were small, embossed replicas of a card from the tarot deck. It was the first card in the Major Arcana: *The Magician*. It was a card of power. Jerry remembered Eve's words when she'd given it to him. "A card of power for a man of power." He laughed to himself. Clearly, he was no magician. He was nothing like it. If he were, he'd have many more of the answers he sought.

He looked to Channing as he prepared to leave. "I still can't get a clue. The Soviet power grid—the ship at sea. That Soviet trawler that Grady said was shadowing it? Who here would do it? Could do it? Did they do it to themselves? And if they did—*why*, for God's sake?"

Channing smiled and for a split second Jerry could see the old man's charm. "A great scientist once said, 'scientific investigation reveals few answers. It only reveals more interesting questions.' So, let's take it one step at a time. We'll meet Andrei and take things from there."

"Six-thirty, here, Channing?"

Channing nodded.

In the distance, Jerry could start to make out the dull rumbling of thunder. The squall line was moving closer now and faster.

"Channing?"

"Mmmm?"

"Who was the famous scientist? The one who spoke of questions? Was it you?"

The old man grinned for a second. Then, as if with a second thought, his face sobered. "No. It was Andrei Sholodkin."

16

*If Man has not yet learned to fully control or cope
with the fragments of Godhead that reside in his
own mind, the reason for the lack of control is
clear. He has proven himself too immature to cope
with power of all sorts. How he gains, maintains
and loses it are things baffling to him. It may be
that until he masters the concept of power, he will
not grow sufficiently mature to master the power
of his own mind.*

—Swami Vishta

Jerry passed Anton Deladier in Channing Moreland's
outer office. They exchanged a polite greeting but there
was something in the man's eyes that put Jerry on
edge. It wasn't anger or threat; it was more like despera-
tion. Jerry reasoned that Deladier was a man forced to
watch as events passed him by. He pushed away the
thought and kept moving. As he passed Alice, who was
on the phone, he waved and winked. Harassed, she
managed a smile in return and went back to her caller.

On the other end of the line, Maria Munoz tried to
get her call through to Channing but Alice was firm:
she'd put through the call after Deladier and Channing
finished their meeting. The loudness of the click on the

other end of the phone was a punctuation to Maria
Munoz's frustration.

Jerry was halfway to his lab when he saw Maria coming in the other direction. He started to smile but the
smile evaporated when he saw the look in the old woman's eyes. It was a volcanic look; a look of such repressed anger and frustration that it stopped him in his
tracks.

It only took a few minutes to recount her conversation with Rosemary.

"And she thought it was important to the distant influence work?"

The old woman nodded. "Very. She said she couldn't
be sure, of course. It is not her area of expertise. But
she said that the computer obviously considered it
related and important. Deladier has the print-out. After
the argument they had, she did not want to take it from
his office. She went downstairs to get another print-out.
I've been trying to get through to Channing, but that
robot in his outer office will not let me speak to him
until his meeting is over."

Suddenly, Jerry remembered Deladier and the look
he'd seen in the man's eyes. He could feel a chill sweep
across him. He reached down and took the tiny old
woman by the shoulders. "There's more, isn't there,
Maria. You wouldn't be this upset if there weren't.
What is it? Has it something to do with Channing?"

She nodded tersely. Her look was that of courage,
underlined with fear. "It's just a feeling. I'm worried
about him. It—" She shook her head, unable to ver-
balize more.

"Go back to the lab and stay there. Tell Morey and
the rest of the staff to stay put until they hear from me.
I'll go back to Channing."

She nodded and turned away. Jerry watched her for
a second, as if he were rooted to the spot. He turned
and dashed off in the direction of Channing's office.

He could hear the yelling as he came through the outer office door. Anton's voice shrieked in rage. It was a tone that froze Jerry where he stood. It triggered the memory of the man in the mental institution almost a decade earlier; the man who'd died while attacking Jerry. He stood for a long second, staring at the inner office door.

Alice was beside herself. She rushed across the room to him.

"Oh, dear. Oh, Doctor Tanner. That argument's been going on since you left. It's been getting louder. I'm frightened. What are they fighting about? One of them locked the door. But, oh, my goodness!"

Jerry shook his head, as if to shake the paralysis of a traumatic memory. He pushed Alice a few feet back and sat her down in a chair. He ran across to the inner office door and pounded on it. Inside, Deladier's voice grew wilder. Jerry couldn't make out the words, only the tone.

He tried the handle. Locked. He pounded with his fists.

"Channing? Channing? Open up. What the hell is going on?"

He was about to pound once again, when the oak door burst outward. The blow knocked him into Alice's desk. He bounced off it and skidded to the floor. By the time he got to his feet, his entire right side was starting to tingle with pain. He caught a glimpse of Anton Deladier, gripping an attaché case tightly and striding out into the hall.

Jerry took a step toward him but stopped as a voice from the inner office called out.

"Jerry?"

It was a throaty whisper. It was Channing—in pain.

He ran into the office and saw the old man. Channing was stooped over the edge of his desk. A rigid left arm kept him from falling over; his right arm was curled around his left shoulder. His face was ashen and in torment.

"Je—"

Jerry ran forward as Moreland collapsed across the wide desk. Surprised at his own strength, Jerry lifted Channing clear of the desk and placed him gently on the floor. The old man, still semiconscious, started to whisper. Jerry leaned close, but could only hear a mumbled word or two before Channing slipped into unconsciousness. Then he leaned further and listened to the man's chest. It only took a few seconds to confirm what he feared. He opened Channing's tie and ripped open the front of the old man's shirt. He thumped the sternum once, twice, and yelled to Alice.

"Alice? Alice?"

The woman stood in the doorway, her hands pressed to her mouth. She was glassy-eyed and she mumbled like a woman repeating the words of a litany.

"Oh, my God. Oh, my God. Oh, my God."

"Alice!" Jerry shrieked. It seemed to pull her out of shock for a second.

"Alice. Get Chet Kumasaka. Now. Get him here. Tell him to bring a resuscitator. Channing's had a coronary."

She turned and grabbed for the phone as Jerry started to press Channing's chest in a steady, methodical rhythm. Outside the windows of the office, the summer storm had just started to lash the institute with gusts of wind and sheets of blinding rain.

In the computer center, Rosemary was furious.

"What do you mean, he pulled it?"

Tom Hughes resented the interruption, especially when he was getting ready to go home. "I mean just what I said, he came in about forty-five minutes ago and pulled the program. He took the cards with him— said there were some alterations that had to be made.

It's not my place to question that. Now, what are you so furious about?"

She ignored the question and turned instead to the console.

"It'd still be in memory from the run I did this morning. Wouldn't it?"

Hughes nodded, quizzically. "Yes. Anton mentioned that I should wipe that portion of the memory. He said he'd have the new program in at the beginning of next week."

She turned and looked up at him. Her deep blue eyes burned with a cold fire. "Did you wipe it yet?"

"Ah, no. I hadn't gotten around to it."

"Good."

She moved quickly to the console and snapped on the activation switch. She was starting to type in a set of instructions, when there was a loud clap of thunder somewhere quite near the building. There was a split-second flicker in the fluorescent lights of the center. Rosemary's eyes were drawn to the bank of three "traffic lights" that were mounted high on the nearby wall. The green light, which indicated that the computer system was at full power, flickered and winked out. In a split second, it was replaced with the amber warning light. Rosemary's eyes moved back to the console, where a flickering message echoed what the lights had already told her. The system was going down. Drained of power, Daniel would, in a matter of seconds, become so much dead metal and circuitry. Rosemary swore to herself. Even if the power was restored instantly, it would take more than a half-hour to reactivate Daniel's delicate switching circuits.

The Central Hudson Nuclear Power Complex was the newest in the United States. Its planners and builders had worked for nearly a decade to perfect its design. Its nuclear reactor was of a new and complex design, necessitated by the complicated and intricate set of interlocking environmental protection regulations issued by the state and federal governments. Operational for just over a year, it fed the immense power needs of much of the Northeast, sending energy north to Boston and south to the ever-hungry New York City complex.

At the core of the generating system was Agnes. She was one of the most advanced examples of nuclear power reactor design in the Western world. Working through hundreds of safety and switching systems, Agnes produced massive volumes of raw heat from the nuclear fires that raged in her core. This raw heat boiled water into steam that pushed turbines and produced the gigawatts of power that the Eastern corridor's midsummer power hunger demanded.

Chief operating engineer Wallace Burroughs stood, white-coated and pensive, in the antiseptic reactor control room. Attached to his clipboard was a power adjustment request that Central Hudson had just received from the Western Jersey Power and Light Company. Western Jersey served Warren, Sussex and Hunterdon counties and with the recent building boom in the exurbs of New York, they'd been the first to patch into Central Hudson's new facility. An adjustment request was routine and Burroughs moved across to one of the two massive consoles in the control room. He passed the request to the computer engineer who manned the power flow console.

"Looks like Western has a bunch of outages. They're in the middle of a cluster of thunderstorm cells out there. Set up a three percent downward adjustment. They'll cut the downed areas out of their system. And"—he looked back to his ever-present clipboard—"set up for a two percent increase into New York metro. Run the shift in"—he glanced at his glowing digital watch—"ninety seconds." The engineer started to nod absently, his fingers already playing over the keys that would activate a standard set of computer programs. They, in turn, would take two percent of the allotted wattage and shift it from the partially crippled Western Jersey operation and feed the power to the hungry air conditioners of the New York City area.

Burroughs crossed the control room to the other console. This was one that he was more familiar with. It was the monitoring system for Agnes herself. With a two percent increase in the system at one end and a three percent reduction at the other, Agnes would have to be adjusted to compensate. It was all quite routine. Burroughs handed the request to Chandris, his new reactor technician. The chief engineer had to admit that the young man was quick and bright, despite the fact that his blend of Hindi and British speech patterns took some getting used to.

Chandris read the request and acknowledged. As power shifted, he would ease the control rods in a fraction. The rods in turn would absorb a flow of neutrons, lowering Agnes' power output to make up for the one percent differential. Forty seconds later, both console operators activated their programs. The transition should have been routine and instantaneous. It wasn't.

The power reduction to Western Jersey came about as planned, as did the shift of two percent of the wattage to New York City. In seconds, the printer behind Burroughs was chattering a response from the New York systems, confirming the increase in flow. Seconds later, Western Jersey's also confirmed the decrease. The problem that arose with surprising speed was not in the shifting mechanisms but in Agnes herself.

It was some ten seconds after the transition that Chandris called out to Burroughs in clipped tones. "I do not have a confirm on neutron flow."

Burroughs was on his feet and moving in the direction of the console as he spoke. "Repeat insertion command."

Chandris turned from the dials to look at his superior. "I have, sir. Three times. Still negative reduction."

"Have we got confirmation of rod insertion."

"Affirmative. But I get no confirmation of neutron flow reduction."

"Let me in there."

Burroughs slid into the console as the small, slender Indian slipped out. His eyes moved across the dials. "That's crazy as hell." The comment was made more to himself than Chandris. He looked across to the switching console. "Harding? You confirmed that shift, right?"

Twenty feet away at the control console, Harding's eyes were riveted to his screen. He nodded and called out. "That's affirm. I just rechecked."

Burroughs looked again at his control board and chewed his lip. Agnes was being cranky in a dangerous way. Burroughs' monitors read that the control rods had been inserted the fraction that would reduce power the necessary amount. Yet, inside the bowels of the reactor, the flow of neutrons had not diminished as it should have when the cadmium rods were inserted. Either one set of readings was wrong, or there was something wrong inside of Agnes. Burroughs turned to Chandris, who hovered just behind him. "Did you use secondary insertion?"

"No, sir. There was no indication of malfunction of the primary. The only thing I noted was the stasis in neutron flow."

Burroughs turned back to the console and stabbed at the button that would recycle the insertion process. Several hundred feet away, electrically controlled motors were supposed to respond to the command, easing the dozens of control rods in ever so slightly to cut back on the heat and power flow. Burroughs watched as a green light flashed to life, confirming the insertion. He waited ten seconds, eyeing the meters that measured the energy flow in the atomic hell of Agnes' core. They did not move. He tapped the glass ever so slightly with his fingertip. Nothing. Without hesitation, he reached across and snapped a switch that activated the mechanical backup motors that would confirm the insertion with mechanical pressure. The green light below the switch did not blink on. It was trouble.

Burroughs got up from the console and moved to his desk, ordering Chandris to watch the core temperature. If Agnes was still producing energy at the same rate and there was a malfunction in either the mechanical backup insertion system or the electronic primary, the result would be an increase in heat at the reactor core. As there'd been none that Burroughs could detect, the chances were that the steady neutron flow reading was in error. He reached for the phone to report the anomaly to his superior. As he dialed the number, he realized that he might be in for a long night. They'd have to check out the manual system, the neutron flow monitors and at least five other systems before the end of the shift.

He hadn't finished dialing the number when he heard Chandris' voice from the console. The clipped tones of the report started a cold ball of fear building in Burroughs' stomach. "We have a hotspot."

Burroughs slammed the handset back into the phone cradle and spun toward the console. "Where?"

"Fuel bundle A-sixteen. I'm reading nine hundred eighty degrees. It's jumped forty in . . . ten seconds."

"Give me emergency shutdown—now!"

Chandris' hands flew across the switches. In the distance, Burroughs could start to hear the grating blare of a klaxon as it screamed out an emergency warning to the complex.

"One thousand degrees . . . one thousand twenty . . . one thousand thirty . . ."

"Confirm emergency shutdown." Burroughs' voice was shrill.

Chandris' voice was mechanical and aggravatingly calm. "Negative function on primary. Board indicates negative function on mechanical secondary. Starting manual override." As Chandris pushed buttons, the wail of yet another klaxon penetrated the control room. Outside in the complex, reactor teams and white-suited nuclear medicine groups were scurrying to their assembly points.

Burroughs looked to Harding, who sat transfixed at the console.

"Report an emergency shutdown message. We're pulling out of the grid, as fast as we can." He turned again to Chandris. "Confirmation?"

"Still waiting."

"Increase coolant flow ten percent."

"Coolant flow increased. Temperature stabilized at one thousand thirty. Falling now . . . one thousand . . . nine ninety . . ."

"Have you confirmed manual shutdown?"

"No—yes! Board confirmation."

Burroughs took a deep breath and exhaled audibly before he turned to Harding on the other console. "Divert heat excess to the cooling towers."

He headed back to the phone, knowing that Agnes was now safe, cold and totally inoperative. His concern shifted to the power grid. What the hell would happen to it with Agnes pulled from the middle of the power flow? The answer would come quickly.

With the millions of watts of power supplied by Agnes gone, the Northeast power grid started to falter in minutes. The outage had happened at the worst possible time: the homeward-bound commuter hours, when power demands were greatest. The power drain surged north and south along power lines; power stations en route noted substantial demand increases for energy within seconds of Agnes pulling out of the system. Four minutes after the pullout, the upper Hudson Valley was plunged into a power blackout as engineers pulled out of the grid before their dynamos overloaded.

The power drain rolled outward like a ripple in a pond. Six minutes after the pullout, New York's Con Edison plant at Storm King Mountain pulled free of the system to save her dynamos. This created more of a drain on the existing power generators in the grid; a drain that could not be corrected. Twelve minutes after the pullout, Boston and New York went dark. Now it became a game of dominoes. It was impossible to meet power needs, and as each system in the grid pulled out, the need became greater, until it was insurmountable. Less than a half-hour after the initial problem with Agnes, seventy percent of the power systems on the East Coast were dead. The ones that were still operational served small communities, where operating engineers had cut local systems free of the grid in time. For the twelve minutes that followed, engineers in power plants as far west as the Mississippi fought frantically to save their power integrity. They had only a moderate degree of success.

17

There are powers next to which nuclear violences are but faint puffs in the air.

—Richard Bach

The position of acting secretary of defense was one that Grady considered confining. He could no longer be the gadfly of international relations. He had to play by the rules that governed all of the members of Paulson's Cabinet. There was decorum to be observed, precedents to be followed. However, despite what he considered to be a "short tether" in the position, it did offer him advantages that his former position did not. One of those benefits was the ability to see situations as they emerged, within the defense community. As acting secretary, and he always stressed the acting, he sat atop the most efficient communications network in the Western world. His office in the Pentagon was privy to the fall of a sparrow, if the sparrow fell in Free World air space. Many times it knew of the falling sparrow before the sparrow itself knew. It was this communication capability that told Grady of the collapse of the power grid in the eastern U.S. only minutes after the engineer Burroughs reported it.

As he got the second report about the spread of the power failure, Grady put in an emergency call to the

President. He got through to Paulson with a speed that he found impressive, and he explained what had happened in the Hudson plant: the apparent inexplicability of it; the multiple failure of backup systems; the confusion of Burroughs about the affair.

"What conclusions can you draw?" Stress was evident in Paulson's voice.

"It's early for conclusions. We're not really sure of anything yet. But, and this might sound far-fetched—it sounds like the Russians are playing tit for tat."

"Their power grid for ours?"

"Possibly. And there are other things, Steve. I want to avoid a phone briefing, if possible."

"Oh, I see." Grady's phrasing had been purposely opaque. It was a code that had evolved between them. Something vital—crucial was going on and, despite the secrecy of the phone line, Grady was clearly saying that they would have to meet personally. "Come over then. I'll see you as soon as you get here."

"Ah, Steve. I think Site Y would be the best place." There was a substantial pause before Paulson responded. Grady knew that the vast impact of the mentioning of Site Y would take some time to assimilate.

"As serious as that?"

"Yes."

"All right. Look. I don't want to make any shifts in defense status. We'll set it up as an inspection tour that was missed in the daily itinerary. The last thing I want to do is let the media blow it apart. We'll get out a statement to the effect that we're looking into the power thing and I'll go to Site Y. Let's make that in one hour."

Paulson was gone from the other end of the phone before Grady could respond. The Irishman could expect little else, after he'd dropped Site Y like a china plate on a concrete floor. *Site Y. Dear God!* The thought of the place made him whistle through his teeth. What was it that the staff called it? The Hole? It was buried in the deep rock of a Maryland mountain, impregnable and simultaneously Pyrrhic. He'd only been to the underground national command post twice: once as acting secretary of defense and once on a tour with Paulson. He'd reasoned that while the place was built to be impregnable to nuclear attack, it would also serve as a concrete and granite mausoleum, which would house the President and his staff while the land hundreds of feet above their heads was blasted and scorched by a nuclear holocaust. For a fraction of a second, Grady wondered if he'd overreacted in suggesting it. A look at the red-bordered security reports that littered his desk told him he was right. It was all starting to happen with alarming speed.

Grady picked up the two satellite shots and looked at them again. In the first, the Soviet trawler *Vladivostok* sliced her way across the spreading residue of wheat chaff that was the only marker for the ill-fated *Western Victory*. In the second shot, taken only moments later, the *Vladivostok* was gone. The Satellite Command duty officer had thought that odd and bucked the photos up to the Joint Chiefs, where their significance might be determined. Less than an hour later, on the next pass of the same satellite, a series of high-resolution shots were taken and the information telemetered to a ground base. So the shots along with a hastily prepared report were given to Grady by the chairman of the Joint Chiefs. Small grease pencil circles marked the spot where the trawler had been. The only trace of the hundred-fifty-foot-long vessel was some floating debris and a widening oil slick in the midst of the wheat chaff. The Soviet ship had vanished as quickly as had the American one. How? Grady had scratched his head, in the same way his staff of experts had.

Now all hell was starting to break loose in the Soviet defense system. Satellite reports and intelligence dispatches were rife with troop movements in the Fulda area of Germany: the classic invasion route. In addition, there was missile activity in Novaya Zemlya and the Black Sea Fleet was moving toward the Mediterranean at flank speed. Despite Kharkov's assurances to Paulson, it was obvious that the Soviets were escalating their war alert status. By the end of the hour, Grady was sure that both shoes had fallen. He was wrong.

The reports of the collapse of the power system that started with Agnes in the Hudson valley and moved westward with lightning speed led Grady to only one conclusion. In the midst of the chaos, Kharkov or his generals or whoever was running the show in the Kremlin was preparing to launch a first strike at the U.S. While the sinking of the *Vladivostok* was still a question mark, as was the loss of the *Western Victory*, Grady could not allow himself to dwell on either of them, in light of the later Soviet troop deployments. They were a clear preparation for war. We were forced to do the same.

Grady reasoned that there was only one more step to take before he boarded the helicopter for Site Y. There might only be a handful of people who could prevent the impending holocaust—if it could be prevented at all.

He reached for the phone.

"Get me Doctor Channing Moreland at the Moreland Research Institute, in Hunterdon, New Jersey. We have a secure patch there." He thought for a second. Also . . . have that patch extended through to Site Y. This is a Flash Override precedence call."

Eve Tanner hung up the phone and swore. Crissy, who'd been walking into the kitchen, stopped short and looked up at her thoroughly aggravated mother.

"Mommy?"

"What? What is it, Honey?"

"You told me not to use words like that."

Eve sighed. Caught in the act! She could see a flash of neon letters that seemed to light above her head. Letter by letter, they spelled H-y-o-p-o-c-r-i-t-e. But damn it, she'd been trying to get Kim Kumasaka for three hours and the frustration was getting to her.

"I'm sorry, Crissy." She looked at her watch and out through the kitchen window toward the rain. It wasn't a cloudburst any more. It had settled into a steady, occasionally heavy rain. At the intersection, fifty yards away, passing cars had turned on their headlights to cut through a rain-filled, early dusk.

She shook her head. There was no sense in trying to call Kim again. Besides, she'd made the commitment to Jerry more as a device to give him peace of mind than anything else. There was no reason in the world that she couldn't drive into Warrensburg herself for the checkup.

She looked down at her little girl, who was reveling in something like righteous indignation at being able to mention swearing to her mother.

"Crissy? Get your raincoat and something to read in the car. We're going to drive to the doctor's."

Crissy looked up with her head cocked querulously to the side. "I thought we were going with Mrs. Kumasaka?"

"That's why I was swearing. I can't get her. We'll drive in."

"Oh, okay." There was an ambivalence in Crissy's tone and that, Eve thought, was unusual. Normally, she enjoyed the drive to Doctor Stoner's. She'd giggled to Eve that she got a kick out of seeing all of the fat women sitting in the waiting room. Eve had reminded her that *she* was one of the fat women. Crissy had giggled, "Yeah. I know," and then they'd both laughed. But there was something different this time, something Eve could not pin down in Crissy's reaction.

Crissy was halfway down the hall moving to get her coat, when Eve called to her. "Crissy? Is anything wrong?"

"Nope." Even in the single word response, it seemed that there was something offish. Eve shrugged. There was no sense in pushing it.

They were on the road ten minutes when Eve realized just how severe the storm was. Traffic crept through the sheets of rain, and it seemed the sky had slipped into full night two hours earlier than normal for June. She made sure that Crissy was belted into the back seat, though she was unable to do the same for herself. Lap seat belts were out of the question after the third month of her pregnancy.

After ten minutes more of creeping along the rain-soaked road, Eve realized that the delay was not only the fault of the rain. The lights at the large intersection, where the access road she was on intersected with the interstate, had been knocked out. They were a complicated arrangement of traffic signals even in the best of weather. There were delayed greens and turning arrows, funneling traffic into the large superhighway. And at this time of day, the traffic was normally difficult. With the signals dark and no police to pick up the slack in traffic direction, cars slid slowly across the intersection like slow-motion bumper cars at an amusement park. She assumed that the failure was limited, not knowing that the power at the Tanner house had failed minutes after she'd left. She moved the station wagon through the intersection and onto the entrance ramp of the highway, assuming that power would be normal in Warrensburg. Entering the interstate committed her to the trip. There were no exits short of Warrensburg. It would be a twenty-five-mile nonstop run, and as she looked at her watch, she realized that even after her early start, she'd barely be on time for her appointment.

It was forty minutes later when she pulled off onto the Warrensburg exit ramp. Looking at the outskirts of the town, she realized that the power failure had been more extensive than she'd thought. Warrensburg was in total darkness. Cars crept through intersections without traffic lights to regulate them. Occasionally, a harassed policeman directed traffic. But with the small police force that the town had and the large flow of commuter traffic that it normally experienced, it was a losing battle.

They were three blocks from the doctor's office when Eve slipped into a parking space. The rain had let up a bit and, despite the dark sky and streets, she thought that they would make faster time on foot.

"Crissy?"

"Yes, Mom?"

"Let's go. We'll walk the three blocks."

Crissy wrinkled her nose and looked out the window. "But it's raining out there."

"You've got your raincoat and so do I. We've got an umbrella. Let's go."

Crissy shuffled. Oh, all right." She wasn't exactly enthusiastic.

In the three-block walk through the gloomy streets, Eve and Crissy were passed twice by wailing fire engines. The second of them was followed by a police car. Crissy pulled closer to Eve, clearly frightened. She had never liked fire engines and wailing sirens. Neither had Eve.

By the time they got to Doctor Stoner's office two more police cars had passed. The lights from inside the old, serviceable professional building were reassuring. Stoner and the other two M.D.'s who rented the building had installed an emergency lighting system that was fed by a small, gasoline-powered generator in the rear of the building. It was like an oasis of light in a darkened neighborhood.

As Eve and Crissy walked into the waiting room, they could see that there had been a number of cancellations. There were only two other women there, both in advanced stages of pregnancy. Eve thought that if she'd known the trouble that the visit would have caused, and if she wasn't three weeks from term, she too would have canceled. She checked in with the harried receptionist, who'd spent more than an hour on the phone with patients calling to cancel.

The woman looked up at her and smiled.

"Hello, Mrs. Tanner. I'm surprised you came in. This power failure seems to have gotten the whole county. Doctor can see you in about fifteen minutes. Mostly everyone else has canceled."

Eve smiled. "Thanks, Joan."

Joan smiled up at her. "Let me tell him you're here." She grabbed the phone and punched one of the buttons. She paused, then punched another . . . and a third. "That's crazy."

"What?"

"The phones. They were working a minute ago. Now they're dead. I don't understand it. They almost never go out in a power failure. Well, take a seat. I'll go in and tell him."

As Eve waited, she could hear another police siren wail its way past the front of the professional building. The sound frightened her. She began to think that it might have been a better idea to turn back. She shook her head. It was nonsense. There was no going back, not once she'd gotten on the interstate. Still, she couldn't shake a slight wisp of fear from her mind.

Twelve blocks away, a third police car screeched to a stop beside a fire engine. Less than a block away, in the blighted area of town, a fire raged that the trucks could not get to. They'd been hit with stones thrown by children in the streets. There had been a distant report from a pistol and the thud of a bullet as it hit

the side of the bright red pumper. As the six police-
men moved out ahead of the fire engine, they could
hear the sound of shattering glass. Store windows were
being caved in by thrown garbage cans. With the
power out and the burglar alarms stilled, the streets
ahead were filling with people carrying chairs and
tables, food and stereos. The looting had begun. Warrensburg would be hard pressed to stop it.

Channing Moreland was alive, though as Chet
Kumasaka looked down at him, the old man looked
more like some cyborgian nightmare than a Nobel
Laureate. The machines to which he was attached
monitored his heart rate and boosted it when necessary. The latter decision was monitored by a small
medi-computer, running on the institute's auxiliary
power generators. A slender nasal tube fed him vital
oxygen, and a half-dozen other devices were attached
to monitor and boost vital signs.

Chet looked at the tape that fed into his hand like a
Delphic priest seeking the answer to some obscure
problem in metaphysics. In a way, he was amazed that
the old man survived at all; amazed at the durability
of the human heart. Had the old man been stricken
in most other places in the country, where the power
was knocked out, the chances were that he'd have
been dead in minutes. A myocardial infarction acted
that way—quick, deadly. But now the peaks and
valleys of the EKG were regular. The battered heart
was already starting to repair itself. If there were no
complications, the chances were that in a matter of
weeks, he'd be making decisions again. At least, that
was what Chet could hope.

He assigned one of the nurses to watch the vital
signs and moved to the hall, where Maria and Rosemary waited. As Chet approached the two women

from one direction, Jerry trotted toward the group from the other. He called out to Chet.

"Well?"

Chet nodded to him. "So far, so good. He's stable. We'll know more in the next twenty-four hours. I'm optimistic."

Maria looked up at the white-coated M.D. and grimaced in frustration.

"And why shouldn't you be optimistic? I said that when you got him here. He will be fine. He—" A slight flicker crossed Maria's face, like a pain, distantly felt. When she spoke, her voice was softer, almost sad.

"He . . . will live." She stopped as if she wanted to say more, but didn't dare. Her tone was one that Jerry and Chet had heard before. It was the tone of one who has seen the future—a mournful, certain future. They paused for a second, each afraid to ask her meaning.

It was Jerry who knew Maria best. He was sure that if there was more to be revealed, she would reveal it. He looked at her as she stood sphinxlike, mute. He knew she would say no more. Though there was something ominous in her tone, he could not pursue it. He turned to Rosemary and Maria.

"I just got off the phone with Grady. He was pretty close to the vest with what he said, but they've advanced the departure schedule. He's going to have a helicopter here at one A.M." He stopped for a second and looked to Chet. After what Grady had said in their brief conversation, there was no way he could add the man to the list of people who knew what Grady had revealed. "Chet, we'll be in the conference room. If there's any change . . . ?"

Chet nodded. "I'll buzz if anything pops."

On the way to the older, Tudor part of the institute, Maria and Rosemary explained what they knew of the

research Anton had done. By the time they settled
into seats around the conference table, Jerry was filled
with questions and more than a little anger.

"If you knew this morning, why didn't you bring it
to me?"

Rosemary's eyes were dark-circled with fatigue and
red with emotion. They formed a strange counterpoint
to the calm in her voice. "I screwed up. I thought perhaps you or Channing knew about it, and then, when
I realized you didn't, I waited to talk to him. Knowing
how he felt about you two, I thought he might tell me
more. I—well, he didn't."

Jerry spun a razor-sharp pencil in his hands. "He
exploded."

Rosemary nodded.

"And you couldn't get a duplicate print-out from
Daniel?"

"Not without full power. I don't even know if we
can do it then. They're magnetic impulses. When the
power falls, Daniel fixes them in memory until the
power is returned. But with only the wattage that the
auxiliaries produce, we can't get the read-out printed
without the distinct chance that what we need will be
erased. We have to wait."

Jerry tapped the pencil against the desk nervously.
"Has security managed to get to him?"

Maria shook her head. "I called. No. He drove out
a few minutes after he left Channing's office. With
the phones out and all the rest of the power gone, they
can't find him. He might be at his house. They just
don't know."

Jerry pointed to the sheets containing the information Rosemary could remember from her early-morn-
ing session with Daniel. "This is what we've got,
then?"

The two women nodded. Jerry whistled through his
teeth.

"It's aggravating." He understated the case. It was more than aggravating. Deladier's research was a brilliant compilation of what Jerry had done but with a whole spectrum of new elements. It seemed that a geometrically arranged group of trained sensitives *sent* a signal consisting of a visualized event; all seeing it the same way at the same time. In one version of the program there was an operative who acted as a lens: a focal point for the signal. In another fragmentary version that Rosemary remembered from the printout, there was no need for a focus. In effect, the first method required a radio receiver and the second did not. That would account for the bridge disaster being different from the helicopter and the dam disasters. But it seemed that from the second set of notes that Rosemary had assembled, the number of senders would have to be massive to manage to destroy something without an operative acting as it seemed Trevor Lewis had. If Sholodkin had a number of operatives that large, why would he have needed Lewis in the first place? Why not just do it from a distance and avoid the possibilities of tracing the operative in the way Eve and Grady had traced Lewis? It didn't fit together.

"This is all that you can remember?"

Rosemary spread her hands out, palms upward. "I'm sorry, Jerry. I just didn't go about it right. I should have run a duplicate print-out when I had the chance. I just . . ." She shook her head. For a moment, it looked as if she might cry. She brushed her hair back from her face and cleared her throat as she pushed the emotion away. "Like I said—I screwed up."

Jerry nodded understandingly. It was amazing that she'd managed to assemble as much as she had from a brief look at a report that was totally out of her field. There was nothing to blame her for, nothing.

"I'll send a security car out to his place. It's only

a few miles. If he has it with him, they'll get it back. We can make sense of it by the time that chopper gets here at one in the morning, so I'll have the ammunition I need for the meeting with Sholodkin."

He paused for a second, allowing himself to consider the enormity of it all. Grady had warned him everything was ready to blow up. There was only one thing Jerry could infer from that: nuclear war! The end of everything. Sweet Jesus—and all of it might hinge on his meeting with an old Russian in Zurich. The fate of the civilized world. He pushed it away, trying to insulate himself from the numbness that started to creep across his mind. It was a defensive reaction. Considering the end of the world was something that could easily create numbness.

"I—" He stopped, frozen for a second. It struck him like a fist. He had never felt anything like it before. He could feel the pain, the blast, the blackness. In his mind, two signals seemed to fire at once. And then there were more. He reached up and put his hand to his head, as if to push the pain away. He couldn't. It overwhelmed him.

The fire flickered in the distance. The smell of alcohol mingled strongly with another smell—the smell of death. His stomach was twisted in a terrible cramp and his head throbbed. There was a sticky warm wetness in his groin, as if he'd somehow soaked his slacks with urine. He tried to move, but something seemed to pin him down. And there was pain . . . and a voice . . . "Jerry? Jerry? Oh, God! Now, Jerry!"

Jerry pushed himself to his feet like a man coming out of a deep, drugged sleep. For a second, he wavered, then he put a hand to the edge of the table to steady himself. The firestorm that boiled up in his brain was gone with the same terrifying suddenness that it had arrived. When he spoke, his voice was a

throaty whisper, still agonized from what he'd seen—
or felt. "Eve? *Eve?*"

Rosemary stared up at him, her eyes wide. Maria
breathed deeply and closed her eyes for a second.
When she opened them, they were wet with tears. It
was a look that Rosemary had never seen in the old
woman before.

Maria pushed herself up from the chair with some
difficulty and moved to Jerry. She took him by the
shoulders and forced him to look down at her.

"You must go. You must go now. It is the way it
has to be."

Jerry looked down at the old Spanish woman who'd
been right about so many things for so many years. He
couldn't fight it. It was as if she'd joined him in the
nightmare, or whatever it was that left him shaky
and soaked with perspiration . . . as if she had to force
him to feel the terror and the pain again. Her eyes
burned into his with a fiery intensity that told him
not to dismiss it, not to let his scientific detachment
dissolve the vision.

But deep inside, Jerry was sure—surer than he'd
ever been of anything in his life. He could *not* let it
pass. Maria's stare simply reinforced the incredible
sense of urgency that all but overwhelmed him. He had
to go now. *Now!* There was no other way. He patted
his pockets for his car keys and tore his glance away
from Maria's. The old woman nodded slowly, like a
grandmother approving a grandchild's first steps. Stopping suddenly, as if remembering something important, she pointed to the yellow legal pad on the corner
of the table. "Write down the number, Jerry."

Jerry looked at her quizzically for a second.
"What?"

"The number. Grady's coded number. I think we
will need it."

Jerry scribbled down the number, then repeated it aloud to himself.

He dropped the pencil and started for the door. Maria grabbed him by the shoulder and he almost took her off her feet before he stopped. She pulled him down and kissed him hard on the lips. "God be with you."

In seconds, he was gone and both women could hear his footsteps as he dashed down the hall and headed for the door to the parking lot.

Maria looked away from the door and breathed deeply. She looked down at her aged, leathery hands and saw that they trembled. She took a deep breath and sighed deeply, slipping quietly into the chair and turning herself inward for a second. She closed her eyes and took several more deep breaths, feeling a bit of her strength return with each one. When she opened them, she found herself looking across the table to a thoroughly bewildered Rosemary.

"Maria?"

Rosemary's voice carried the tone of a child asking a parent to make sense of something strange and mysteriously frightening.

The old woman folded her arms against the breasts that had nursed a half-dozen children and buried her chin against her chest, as if to hold in the reserves of strength that she was starting to expend. It was the power that showed in her eyes that unnerved Rosemary. It was unlike anything she had ever seen.

Rosemary shook her head as she herself started to shake with a fear she could not identify.

"Maria, I—what?"

"Hush. There can be no fear, not for either of us . . . not now. There is much we must do . . . much you must do."

"I? But what?"

Maria shook her head slowly, deliberately. She managed a smile.

"Why do you ask what you already know? You thought it only moments ago. I could feel that you were thinking it in your office when you cried."

Rosemary shuddered as if a cold blast of air had slammed into her on a warm summer day. Her eyes met Maria's, and after a second, the fear passed. When she spoke, her voice was calm, almost mechanical.

"Anton."

"Yes. And now . . . you must leave."

Inside, Rosemary could feel the rightness, the certainty of it. It was something for which there were no words, not even the fragments of thought. What had to be done spread somehow in front of her with the brilliant and mindless certainty of a blossoming flower. Yes. It was right. She left the room without another word and hurried down the hall to her office to get her raincoat and her car keys.

Maria sat in the chair for several minutes without moving. Her eyes closed, and in a few seconds, a set of images started to coalesce. For a fleeting second, they were dim and vaguely muted—like a distantly remembered Cézanne. Then they snapped into sharp focus.

She stood at the center of a great, white hall. Ahead lay a corridor. Another stretched out behind. As her eyes gazed left and right, she could see that the hall was like the center of a great wheel, radiating spokes, each of which seemed to branch away into others endlessly. And yet, as she looked at each of them, they dissolved like watercolors in the rain. She shrugged the others away: roads not taken, choices not made. A lifetime had led her to where she stood. Ahead of her, the last corridor moved away and forked into a dim recess over which she knew she had no control. They would do the rest.

She blinked. The vision was gone.

She looked down at the sheet of paper on which Jerry had scrawled Grady's number. She picked it up and folded it into neat quarters. There was time before the final set of choices had to be made. She smiled to herself. The choices were no longer hers and she allowed that thought to comfort her as much as what she'd seen in the dim recess of the last corridor had chilled her. It was up to the two of them now . . . and to Grady and all of the others who would play out the drama's last scene. For now, she could wait quietly in the moment between the toss and the catch.

18

Life's battles don't always go to the strongest or fastest; sooner or later, those who win are those who think they can.

—Richard Bach

Eve Tanner could feel the cold tile against her side. She'd just gotten off the examining table when the blast threw her to the floor. It had all happened too quickly and she was having trouble sorting it out through the incredible cramping pain that seemed to start in her low back and work across to her abdomen. Her legs were wet and sticky underneath the paper examining gown. The pain grabbed her like a vise and with it came a dread—a terror. God, sweet God. She knew what it was. The wetness was fluid, amnionic fluid. The membranes had ruptured as she fell. It had started a chain of chemical events over which she had no control. She tried to pull her left arm into a position where she could see her watch, but she found that she could not move it. It had been wedged between the examining table and the remains of the autoclave that had once stood in the far corner of the examining room. Stoner! Where was Doctor Stoner?

She craned her neck to the side but couldn't see much in the darkness. All she managed to do was to touch off a sharp. pounding headache, on the right side of her head. For a second, it seemed to match the uterine cramp that was just subsiding. It was only as the contraction eased that she started to think with any clarity. *Crissy!* Crissy had been in the waiting room.

"Crissy! *Crissy!*" She shrieked.

Nothing. Then, faintly, she could hear a muffled voice call back to her. It seemed a long distance away. "M—Mommy? Oh, Mommy? . . ." The child's voice dissolved into terrified sobs.

Eve tried again to move, but she was pinned, immobile under the lower arm of the collapsed examining table. There was no pain in her arm but there was clearly no way she could move it. "Here, Crissy. Here, honey. I'm here."

It took all the courage she could muster to keep her own voice steady. She peered into the gloom and for the first time she became aware of a flicker of light filtering in through the remains of the examining room window. It was the light of a fire that was starting to lick its way up and across the back portion of the building. Dear God! she thought. The gas generator. It had blown up somehow—the explosion had touched off a fire. Though she was safe from it for the moment, she would have to get out from under the table. It was then that she remembered Doctor Stoner. He'd been washing his hands at the sink against the back wall.

She squinted toward the light; toward the hole in the wall where the sink had been.

The explosion would have—

She let her eyes trace the line of the blast. Then she saw him, or what was left of him. He was a crumpled rag doll, thrown across the room by the force of the gasoline-fed blast. His head seemed tilted at an odd angle. He didn't move. He had to be dead.

"Mommy? Where are you?"

"Here. Come to my voice. Move carefu—" She could feel the beginnings of another contraction. How long had it been? A minute? Ten? She had no sense of time. All she could think of was Crissy and the first wisps of acrid smoke that started to slip in through the hole in the back wall. The fire was starting to build. She had to get out and soon. "Cri—"

She couldn't manage to call out as the pain of the contraction built. It was too soon . . . too soon for them to be this intense. A terror started to creep through the pain. The baby.

It wasn't fair. Not now. Not this way. When she'd lost the others, there'd been an emptiness: a hollow pain as if she had been neatly opened and had a part of her soul sliced away. But those painful incisions had always healed, with time and perspective and a great deal of love. But none of those babies had lived long enough for her to feel, for her to watch as it moved and grew.

No. It wouldn't happen, not again, not ever. This baby was hers and there wasn't a power on earth that she would allow to take it from her.

"Crissy. Follow my voice. Get to me."

"Mommy?"

In the dim, flickering light and the thickening smoke, Eve could see Crissy start to turn the corner.

"Here. Here, on the floor."

It took her a few seconds to get Crissy to pass close to Doctor Stoner's body. When the little girl moved across the floor, her head averted, Eve could see that it was an act of total trust and incredible bravery for a seven year old.

For a second, Eve was filled with a pride in Crissy the like of which she'd never before felt. But there was no time to bask in it, not even fleetingly. Eve probed her left arm with her free right hand. There was a numbness, probably because of the downward pressure of the table, pinching a nerve or cutting off the blood supply. She tried curling the fingers of her right hand under the lip of the table and pulling upward.

It didn't move. It was not that the table was that heavy. It was more a question of leverage. She stopped pulling and reached up with her free hand to hold Crissy. After a minute, she looked up at the tear-stained, terrified face. She gestured her head in the direction of the table. It triggered a wave of pain that she tried to ignore. "The table. We have to lift it. We have to do it now. I can't lift it, not from this position. See if you can get your hands under the edge of it and lift when I do."

Crissy leaned down and dug her tiny hands under the edge of the tabletop.

"Now." Eve grunted and yanked upward. The effort tripped a sledgehammer in the side of her head. She pushed upward until she thought her head would burst. "Lift . . . Lift. Now!"

It started to move—a fraction . . . another.

It was not enough. Eve shrieked as the weight came back down on her arm. Crissy started to sob. "No. No—" Eve's breath was coming in hot, dry gasps. "You can't cry. We'll do it. We just can't cry . . . not now."

She needed something: a wedge, a lever she could pry under the edge of the table. She looked past her daughter and her eyes darted frantically around the demolished room. The smoke was getting thicker.

"There!" she heard herself say. "That." She pointed to what looked like a steel rod a few feet out of her reach. It looked like something that might have braced a wall; something torn free by the blast. Crissy grabbed the half-inch-thick bar and together she and Eve wedged it under the table. They managed to get seven or eight inches of it underneath with a stretch of two

feet or so protruding. "Stand up and—" She stopped
for a breath. She could start to feel the beginnings of
another contraction. But there was no stopping. The
fire was starting to lick up toward the window opening. As it did, the draft through the hole in the building started to pull the smoke and flames into the room.
Eve coughed and the cough started the contraction
in earnest. "Pull it up. I'll push."

Crissy yanked as hard as she could. Eve's free arm
lunged into the steel rod. It moved. Yes. Enough. She
slid her arm out and screamed at the same time.
The pain was unbelievable. She was free.

After the contraction ended, Eve managed to get
into a sitting position and was getting to her feet when
she heard the distant wail of a siren—a fire engine or
a police car. A few seconds later, she started to hear
movement in the front of the office. Flashlight beams
cut through the smoke in strange halo patterns. Someone was coming. There'd be help.

She opened her mouth to yell when she heard the
laugh.

Her blood froze. It was all that she could do to
clamp her hand over Crissy's mouth.

*The dream. Sweet Jesus . . . it was the dream. The
fire and the monsters.*

It was her dream and Crissy's dream—the nightmare. The laugh was the same: guttural, cruel.

The lights came closer and with them came the
voices.

"There ain't nothin' here I tell ya'. Ain't nothin'."

"Shut the fuck up, you dumb shit. It's a doctor's.
We can score all kinda good stuff here."

The second voice was shrill, tense, a counterpoint
to the deep booming sound of the first. "You don't
need to score nothin'. The shit we got in our pockets
can keep you in smack the rest of your life. You

crazy, man. You hear them sirens? That's the pigs, man. I'm goin'."

The glare of the flashlight turned the corner and played across Eve and Crissy.

"Well." The voice deepened. "What we got here?"

The second light turned the corner. The voice seemed shriller, more piercing now. "Just some honkey bitch and a kid. There ain't nothin' else. This place was blown to shit. And there ain't no smack."

Eve pulled Crissy close, as they crouched to the wall in the glare of the flashlights. *The boot came at her. There was an explosion of pain.* She tried to push away the thought of the dream, but it sat indelibly in her mind's eye. She started to cry.

Outside, the sirens got louder, car engines roared closer. Brakes shrieked and cars screamed to a stop: first one, then a second and a third.

And then there was someone thrashing in the dark reception room, stumbling, crashing.

"Come on, you dumb fuck. Now. Out the back. It's cops."

"Eeevvvveeeeeeeee!"

The voice was a roar in her ears and for a second she couldn't be sure if was real or not. "Jerry, here!"

In a second the men with the flashlights were gone, crashing their way to the back door.

Jerry turned the corner, still in his shirtsleeves.

In a minute, the room was filled with police. They hadn't been after the men with the flashlights. They'd been after Jerry. He'd roared down the highway at over ninety and careened through Warrensburg, almost running over two patrolmen and sideswiping a police car. They'd taken off after him and in the mad, high-speed chase that followed, he'd led them to Stoner's office.

Eve felt him grab her a second before the room slid into blackness.

Grady looked at his hands as they gripped the cool metal of the balcony railing. He knew that if he let go of the rail, his hands would shake. In the same way, he knew that if he felt his forehead, he'd find it beaded with perspiration. His eyes moved up to Paulson, who stood to his left on the observation deck overlooking the War Room. Paulson looked down at the war board display and the flag-ranking officers who manned the headsets. They were the Joint Chiefs: sober, ashen-faced career soldiers. Some were in slacks and sport shirts. Some were in uniform. All were there.

They stood and watched the board and the polar projection map while they listened to reports on the headsets. The chances were awfully good that the display board showed a military design for the end of the civilized world.

Below them stood Air Force General Edward Forrester; he looked up to Paulson and Grady. "Mister President?"

Paulson nodded, tightly.

"We have telemetry from SKYSAT Niner." Forrester stopped and pressed the headset to his ear. SKYSAT was the finest piece of surveillance satellite technology that the United States had ever developed. There were twelve of them in orbit, feeding computerized mosaics back to NORAD and the Pentagon every forty minutes.

The general mumbled a response into the mouthpiece that hovered an inch from his lips. As he spoke, a series of black dots appeared on the map of the Soviet Union. As Paulson watched, the electronic dots turned red. They glowed up at him and Grady, like a threat ready to be made good.

"We have confirmation. Soviets silos at Novaya Zemlya are open. They were closed on the last pass."

"Conclusions?" Paulson's voice was like an overwound bowstring.

"Full war alert, Mister President. They've jumped over a gradient. They are at Alpha One. Forty minutes ago, they seemed to be at Alpha Three. Two was jumped."

Paulson grimaced. "And above Alpha One?"

Forrester pulled off the headset, mussing a shock of white hair.

"Full retaliatory strike . . . or a pre-emptive first strike."

A few feet from the general, Fleet Admiral Gregory Kingsford pressed the earpiece with one hand and raised the other. Grady's eyes shifted to the admiral, then for a split second to the map, where a series of green dots had started to glow. They appeared to be in the Black Sea.

"Mister President, the Black Sea Fleet has started dispersal maneuvers. It appears to be a full scramble system: the kind the Russians use when they anticipate being nuked. The scatter pattern assures that a single hit won't get much more than a few ships."

"What about the Atlantic coast?" Paulson was like a machine.

Again, the admiral pressed the headset and pointed to a second screen on the far wall of the huge, underground War Room. The screen flashed to life. This time, the map was the more familiar Mercator projection; the kind from which schoolchildren learn geography. Grady wondered if there would be schoolchildren by tomorrow . . . or even by later tonight.

A series of green dots flashed to life in the area that represented the Atlantic Ocean. The dots stretched out along the coast like green pearls. Paulson didn't need any explanation from an admiral to see that there were concentrations of dots parallel with the major cities of the East Coast.

Kingsford used an electronic pointer to slide up and down along the line of dots. "There are eighteen Soviet subs in the pattern. Of that number, twelve are new *Kiev*-class boats; like our *Poseidon*-class ones. Each carries fourteen nukes, of an average strength of ten to twenty megatons."

Grady leaned forward toward the rail and squinted at the board. Something was strange about the configuration; something he couldn't quite piece together yet. "Admiral?"

"Yes, Mister Secretary?"

Paulson glanced at his old friend, as if surprised to hear him speak. In fact, Grady was tired of speaking. He'd opened the meeting with an extensive briefing for Paulson; one he clearly didn't want to give.

"Are they all on station?"

"Ten of the eighteen are stationary, Mister Secretary. The other eight are moving at top submerged speed. We consider that the ten are on station and in an attack configuration. The others, we think, will be in a matter of . . . oh, say, less than an hour."

"What is their procedure?"

"Well, Mister Secretary, when and if they get a launch signal, they let their birds go and go deep. Then, after confirmation of strike, they move further out into the Atlantic, to some rally point and await further orders."

Paulson put a hand up, reaching vaguely in the direction of Grady to interrupt him. "Excuse me, Mike." He looked down to Kingsford. "Admiral?"

"Yes, Mister President?"

"There's no submerged radio communication for a sub, right?"

"Yes, Mister President. Not at this time . . . not as far as we know."

The admiral stumbled verbally for an instant. It was a question he did not expect. But Paulson seemed to be on the same frequency as Grady. Each could see it in the eyes of the other, as their eyes met for a split second. Paulson turned back to the admiral, who stood ten feet below near the corner of the war board display. The admiral had taken off his headset and smoothed back his hair, though the close-cropped salt-and-pepper gray didn't seem to need it.

"How do they get the launch order, Admiral?"

"Normally, the same as we do, Mister President. It's a miniaturized wire-link transponder. A signal is beamed from Moscow to a satellite and a single series of high-speed pulses is beamed from the bird to the floater. Then, they retract it, so there's no trace. It's probably a foot or less around the floater in any event. There's little chance to trace it. It's only released at coded times when the right satellite is overhead. Any one of a dozen of them could be the sender." Kingsford's tone was slightly defensive. The chief of Naval Operations wanted the President and the acting secretary to understand that there was little chance to detect or intercept such a signal . . . through no fault of the navy, of course.

Paulson glanced at Grady for a split second, then turned back to the admiral. "There are other means, though?"

"Sir?"

"Other means, Admiral. Other means. Other ways to send the signal?"

"Well, Mister President, there are a number of experimental ones that both we and the Soviets have in the arsenal. None of ours are operational, at least not at this time. And we have no clear intelligence data to indicate that any of theirs are either. No, sir. I think the odds are that the signal would come as I mentioned it would: a floating transponder released and retracted at regular coded intervals."

"Thank you, Admiral." Paulson turned to Grady. The Irishman noticed that Paulson had loosened his tie and opened the collar button of his shirt. The President's gray suit was rumpled and there was a hint of stubbly shadow on the ruddy farmer's face. Steve was ragged, tired, frustrated. He was under more pressure than perhaps any man in the history of the West. And he was holding up. Grady's respect for his long-time friend grew. "Mike, could they have created the Hudson Valley thing with .·. . ah, sensitives aboard the subs? Or could they be getting a launch message that way. Is it likely that this Sholodkin would have been that astute?"

Grady paused for a minute, then nodded. "It could be either or both. Moreland told me he thought they were adapting their people to a whole matrix of sending modes. And back in the fifties, the Nautilus experiments with telepathy seemed to indicate that a telepathic signal could penetrate a sub under polar ice. There would be no need for a transponder."

"What's Moreland's condition?"

"The doctor there—name's Kumasaka—says he's stable but unconscious."

"Where's Tanner?"

"At the institute, at least that's what I was told when I checked the last time."

"Could Tanner get some of his people to jam signals that might go to the subs? It could buy us some time."

Grady nodded and turned to move in the direction of a secure phone. Suddenly, he stopped. His eyes were drawn back to the war board. There was a flicker, a sort of blink, as if some distant communications or power system cycled for a fraction of a second. Grady peered at the pearls that dotted the Atlantic coast like green fire. *Yes, by God! That's it!* He'd noticed before, but it hadn't fully registered.

"Excuse me, Steve." He pointed to the map. "Admiral?"

"Yes, sir?"

"Eighteen subs. Right?"

"Yes, Mister Secretary."

"There are nineteen dots there. You've got an extra sub. Who the hell does that one belong to?"

Kingsford grabbed for the headset. After a few seconds, he looked up.

"We don't know, Mister Secretary."

Rosemary flicked on her high beams as she turned onto the narrow, country road. She snapped off the windshield wipers and peered through the windshield. The heavy rain had let up, almost stopped, and the windshield wiper blades had been squeaking in a rhythmic litany on dry glass. It had started to raise the hackles at the back of her neck before she snapped it off.

No. It wasn't the squeaking that did it. It was everything else. It was Maria reading her thoughts . . . and the drive out here and the glow in the sky in the direction of Warrensburg. It all terrified her. She wasn't even sure how she could get the program from Anton. It was something that Maria had not mentioned. There was just the certainty that it would be gotten.

But no, almost in sight of Anton's farm, she was terrified. The radio reports of looters sprawling out in marauding bands into Hunterdon chilled her, and the thought of what the radio was saying about the state prison was nightmarelike. Prisoners out of their cells when the power was lost rioted, slaughtering guards. There was no electric alarm system. Dozens, perhaps a hundred, had gotten over the wall and fled into the rainy night. It was then that she'd turned the radio off. There was no sense listening to more. There was no sense to anything except to get to the man who'd been her gentle, tender lover only days ago. Get to him and get the program back.

She turned off the access road and into the long, mud-rutted driveway that led to the farmhouse. Anton had liked his privacy when he'd bought it. She tried not to think about the times they'd met there. It was a million years ago, another reality, another life.

She skidded to a stop at the end of the driveway. Anton's car was there!

She went to the front door and found that it was half open. Inside, Anton Deladier sat on the large, colonial couch, staring at a wood fire that lit the darkened room in flickering light. It was hot for a fire. She could feel herself start to sweat from the oppressive heat that mixed with her fear.

Anton looked up at her. *"Ma chérie. Ma petite.* We share the end . . . together. It is like the last pages of a pulp romance."

"Anton, I—" She could see it on the coffee table in front of him. The stack of computer paper sat like a talisman, out of her reach. She moved toward him. "It's Channing. . . ."

"Channing? Dear Channing. He didn't know how wrong he was until I told him. Now he knows—all of it—now that it's too late. He was a fool, more than a fool. The ones that are left . . . if there are any left when all of it is done. They'll blame him. They'll see it all."

"Anton." She took another two steps toward the table. There were other papers on it. On top of the neatly folded sheaf of computer paper was a battered envelope. It had the look of something that had been folded and refolded many times. "Channing's had a coronary. He almost died. Everything's going crazy. The power is out and Jerry has to go to meet Sholodkin in the middle of the night." As she spoke, Anton unfolded the envelope and took a paper out. He glanced at it, then up at her.

He looked horrible. Deep circles arched under his eyes. Even in the firelight, his face was ashen, drawn. His eyes were red and wild. Yet there was a frightening calm in his voice.

"Please, Anton, you have to—"

He shook his head to cut her off. He held up the crumpled paper in one hand and patted the computer run in the other. "It was this." The paper shook ever so slightly in his hand. "It led me to more. It led me to the answer." Again he patted the paper on the table. "While Channing was running off crazily and not listening, I had it all . . . right here. And he wouldn't listen."

"Anton, please? Listen."

"There is no time to listen, my love. It will all be over too soon for anyone to listen to very much. It's here, you see. It's here." The paper was quivering faster now. He reached into his jacket pocket and took out a small, disposable lighter. He flicked it once or twice as if to insure that the flame worked. "It was all said hundreds of years ago. It was what I told Channing, what I could have told him so much earlier, if he hadn't been so wrapped up in his friend, Sholodkin. It was Nostradamus . . . he had said it all. He had the answer."

He looked up at her and his face split into a manic smile. *Dear God. He's insane. He's totally gone.* She could feel her legs get weak. Her stomach started to feel like hardening concrete. How could she get it? How?

She watched, transfixed, as Anton brought the lighter dangerously close to the edge of the paper and flicked it again. The tip of the flame wavered in the draft from the fireplace. It was only a hairbreadth from setting fire to the paper. "All of it." His voice was higher, with a strange shrill tone. "All of it will be fire soon . . . so soon. And it's right that this goes to the flame first."

"Dear God, Anton, please don't. If there's any chance that it can help—any ch—"

She stopped in midword. She could hear a truck engine outside screeching to a halt. There were voices, shouts from men outside. In a few seconds there was a crash at the door. Anton's head snapped toward the door and Rosemary lunged for the paper.

She grabbed it out of his hand. He dove forward to stop her and she skittered out of the way. The shouts were in the hall now, heading for the light of the fireplace in the living room.

Anton grabbed for her again and she backed up across the room, almost losing her footing. A deep, animal groan started in the back of his throat. *"Nooooooo!"*

She bolted for the other side of the room and changed direction, remembering the back door. She tore through the darkened kitchen. If she'd not been so familiar with the room, the chances were that she'd have stumbled and fallen. But Anton's kitchen was like an old friend, even in the dark.

The terror of what she heard behind her blended with anger. She'd failed. She'd come away without it. The computer run still lay on the coffee table and the program itself . . . God only knew.

"Out the back. She went out the back."

She could hear the male voices in the house yelling to one another. The voices came closer. She kicked off her heels and ran in the direction of the woods, with the scrap of mysterious paper balled tightly in her fist. She ran blindly through the saplings and the rain-soaked underbrush. Just over fifty yards into the wood-line, she stopped and pitched forward, sliding under a bush. For a long minute, she lay there on her stomach, feeling the blood pound in her temples and her breath coming in quick gasps. When she caught her breath, she started to shake. Waves of chills washed across her and with them came sobs that forced her to press her hand to her mouth lest they be heard. She could hear the noises coming from the farmhouse: glass shattering, angry voices and then a shot . . . a second. She shook ever more violently. But it was not the cold or the fear . . . it was the realization. She knew what she had to do.

It seemed an eternity before she heard the truck engine roar to life. They were going. Who were they? Looters? Escaped convicts? She realized that it didn't really matter. All that mattered now was that they hadn't chased her into the woods and now they were going. She waited until the sound of the truck was out of earshot before she moved from under the bush. She had trouble getting to her feet at first. Her knees were shaking too much. When she did, it took a great force of will to make herself move in the direction of the house. She pushed away the fear and the pain and set out to get what she'd come for. She'd get the program.

The kitchen was a shambles of broken glass, and she skirted around it, being careful not to slash a foot. She got to the living room and froze. On the floor, in front of the fire, lay Anton. A huge, red stain was spattered across his chest. His eyes were already starting to glaze. The expression on the dead face was one of surprise.

Hypnotized, she stared at him for a long minute. Past the revulsion and the fear, there was nothing. She was stone inside. For a split second, she worried that she might always feel it: that cold, dead sensation. She tore her eyes from the body and looked at the coffee table. *It was gone.*

She started to move through the room looking for it.

The last thing she looked at was the fireplace. The last shreds of the computer run were embers in the center of the firebox, just a few feet from where Anton's body lay. Had he died to toss it in the fire? Was that why they shot him?

She shook her head. It didn't matter, not now . . . not ever.

She took a shambling step in the direction of the fireplace and stubbed her toe on something cold and hard. She looked down in a moment of pain and looked at it.

The briefcase. Anton's briefcase!

She dropped to her knees and grabbed it, clawing at the latches. Inside, neatly folded into an envelope, was the typed version of the program from which Anton had derived the print-out that now lay as ashes in the fireplace. It was then that she realized that she still clutched the battered ball of paper in her left hand. She unraveled it and read it. The last line was underscored several times. She read it and then read it again. It took a full minute to make sense of that was there.

"My God."

She tossed the paper into the briefcase, still numbed by the meaning of what she'd read. They'd been so wrong. So utterly wrong. The very thought of the words she'd seen scrawled on the bottom of the sheet by a wild, possibly even psychotic hand, screamed at her to run, to get back to the institute no matter what. There was an outside chance that it wasn't too late.

She snapped the case shut and got to her feet, still feeling the shakiness inside. She prowled around the living room looking for her purse amid the broken tables and smashed lamps. She couldn't find it. She started to retrace her steps into the kitchen and stopped. There was no time. The spare key—the one in the small box. She'd use *it*.

She ran through the house and out the front door

to the driveway. The pebbles cut through her stockings and stabbed at the soles of her feet. She was sure that the pain had been there as she'd run into the woods, but she'd had no time to feel it then. In a way, she couldn't allow herself the time to feel it now. She opened the door and tossed the case on the seat. It cost her two fingernails to feel along the inside of the fender for the small magnetic box, which she yanked from its magnetic hold on the steel and started to slide open. It wouldn't budge. She swore at it and banged it against the fender. After four or five tries, the rusted box slid open enough for her to pry out the ignition key.

She fired up the engine and roared out of the driveway onto the long access road. There was a slender chance. Perhaps, there was none at all. All she knew was that she had to try. She pushed the accelerator to the floor.

Jerry sat in the right seat of a Warrensburg police cruiser. The patrolman at the wheel snapped on the siren and the roof light, then pushed the cruiser to eighty as it came onto the interstate access ramp.

Jerry was frazzled. The ride to the hospital was agonizing. He held Eve all the way. The pain of a contraction pulled her up from unconsciousness; she told him that they were more regular and more intense. They were coming at almost one a minute now as the police car threaded its way through the snarled downtown area of Warrensburg and pulled up to the hospital emergency entrance. Jerry, two interns and a nurse flew down the hall with Eve strapped to a Gurney. They got to the examining room with only a minute or two to spare.

It was a boy: small, red, squalling. Once he was sure Eve and the child were all right, Jerry managed to persuade the staff to let Crissy stay with her mother.

He ran back down the hall and out to the waiting police car.

What was it he had felt back in the conference room. Was it a psychic flash? An intuition. He remembered Eve's words as they'd sat in the den together; it seemed a million years ago. *You will when the time comes. You will when something's important enough.* Whatever psychic ability he'd had all his life, it had lain sleeping, and, as with Arthur or Holge Danske, it awoke only when it was sorely needed.

And how had Maria known? Had she shared the vision? He forced the questions away as the police car passed an exit sign. He looked across to the driver.

"Slow down. That's the exit up ahead."

19

The spring is wound tight.
It will unwind of itself. . . .
    —Jean Anouilh

Grady barked the codes at the operator. He was furious. *Kingsford, you asshole!* How could it happen. A sub sits in the middle of a pattern of other subs and no one sees it? It was madness. He made a mental note that tomorrow, if there was a tomorrow, he'd have words with the admiral. The series of clicks and electronic beeps on the phone line was exceptionally long. Computers routed the call through military lines, seeking out a patch where the power was still intact. It seemed to ring for only a second before it was picked up. The voice on the other end was old and female.

"Good evening, Mister Grady."

"Wha—? Who is this? Where's Tanner?"

"He is busy now. This is Señora Munoz. I will pass a message to him. It is about ships—no?"

"No. Ah, yes. How—?" Grady shook his head. There was no time to wonder about it. He had seen the things that the old woman and the others were capable of doing. He simply did not have time or energy to question.

"Yes. Submarines. There are a pattern of Soviet subs

off the coast. They're in international waters but we think there is a possibility of them—" He didn't quite know how to say it. To mention more was to violate every page of the National Security Act. "Well—"

"An attack?"

"Possibly." His voice rang cold and metallic in his own ears. "The chances are that they will get a signal . . . an attack order, perhaps psychically. I was going to ask Doctor Tanner if he could—I don't know—jam it?"

He could hear the old woman breathing on the other end of the phone.

"No."

"No?"

"It cannot be done."

"Are you sure? Are you positive?"

"Yes. But—" Again, there was the breathing. "There is something else. Another submarine . . . and—and there is something that can be done."

"What?"

"You wouldn't understand."

Grady could feel an anger flare inside of him. What the hell did she mean he wouldn't understand? He forced the anger down.

"Mister Grady?"

"Yes?" Again, his voice was metallic, calm.

"Do not attack."

"What do you mean?"

"Do not attack. No matter what happens, do not attack. It would start the end of everything. No matter what happens, do not attack. Please trust me. Please?"

Suddenly, Grady wanted to laugh, not at Maria or even at himself. It was the madness of all of it. The chances were that in a matter of hours, a nuclear holocaust would obliterate ten thousand years of mankind's development, and it all came down to this. A phone conversation with a possibly senile old woman; an old woman who warned the most powerful retaliatory force in the world not to attack. And yet, he knew deep inside he would have to trust her. To counterattack was to end everything. To wait might be to end everything. But still, it might not.

"Very well. I'll speak to the President."

Maria hung up the phone and leaned back in the leather chair at the head of the conference table. She folded her arms and leaned back against the coolness of the leather. She closed her eyes and instantly was aware of the chill and the darkness and the certainty of it. *It would be now . . . soon, very soon. The old friend would visit—gloved in marble, shod in lead. She'd push him off, divert him for a time, as she'd done before. It was too soon.*

She let the thought dissolve and let her mind move outward into the dark, chill water. It would be hard. So hard, and yet, it had to be done. It would be now. There were only moments. She had to hurry.

Jerry ran up the steps two at a time and skidded to a stop at the front door of the institute. A shrill voice from behind him was calling his name. He turned to see Rosemary McGee stumbling up the steps. She looked horrible. Her feet were cut and bleeding, her dress was torn. She was mud-covered and gasping for breath. She clutched an attaché case with both hands.

"Rosemary? What—?"

"N—no time." She gulped a breath and held the case out to him.

"It's here. The program's here. Anton's dead. But he had this."

He took the case from her and, arm protectively around her, led her inside to the now vacant receptionist's desk. She fell into an empty chair while he unsnapped the case. She gingerly unfolded the paper that Anton Deladier had almost incinerated in the last moments of his life.

"It's here. It connects to what I remember from the print-out, what was strange about the whole thing. It all fits now. This is a list of predictions that have all happened: the bridge, the dam, the Vice President, the Russian power failure . . . and ours. It's laid out here. The last one—" She stopped and breathed for a second. When she spoke again, her voice was calmer.

"The last one is a quote. Anton raved about it being from Nostradamus. He said it was the key to everything. It was why Channing and you and all of us had been wrong."

She handed the paper to Jerry. The last prediction was a wild scrawl. "The dragon will force the eagle and the bear to destroy each other . . . the dragon in secret . . ."

Jerry was thunderstruck as the truth slammed into him. Nostradamus. It was what Channing had tried to whisper to him as he'd slipped into the agony of his coronary.

He looked up at Rosemary's mud-smeared face. "The eagle is the U.S. Nostradamus called it the rising sun of the west. The bear—Russia. The drag—" *China! The dragon was China.*

"Then China's out to cripple both. . . ." It connected. It was the reason that Jerry failed to get distances. He didn't have enough psychics. He would have to have hundreds of them, even thousands, working together flawlessly. Channing knew that Sholodkin didn't have them either, so they'd gone off looking for another technique. The technique was right all along. It was the numbers that were wrong.

He turned and started to run toward the stairs. He yelled over his shoulder.

"I've got to get Grady."

He took the stairs two at a time, heading for the conference room. Rosemary was only a few steps behind.

Grady was winded from the run back to the observation deck, where Paulson waited for him. Below, the screen still carried the map of the East Coast and the eighteen emeralds still glowed in a pattern in the Atlantic. The nineteenth now glowed red.

Paulson looked to Grady. "Well?"

He paused for a second. "They'll try. They said to concentrate on that new bogey, the one they've got in red there. They think they can do something about that one. As far as delaying the attack signal . . . no chance."

Paulson turned and looked down at the officers who stood on the tile floor below. "Kingsford? Have you got a make on that other sub yet?"

The admiral was holding a phone to his ear. "Getting it now, Mister President. A—a *Hunan*-class Chinese sub. They resemble the *Kiev*-class Russian boats. They carry a bank of twelve nukes . . . all IRBMs."

Paulson murmured to himself. "They don't need more than spitting range to hit the East Coast." He turned to Grady. "But a Chinese boat? Why, Mike? Is she there to shadow the Russians? What the hell is going on?"

Grady chewed his lip. "Tanner's people assure me that's the crucial one, the key. They also asked, almost begged, for one more thing."

"Yes?"

"Don't attack. They said that to attack was to end everything. Tanner's people say we have to trust them. Don't attack. That was made clear."

"What do you think?"

"They haven't been wrong yet. I—"

The voice from the floor below was almost a shriek. It was Admiral Kingsford's voice, terrified. "Launch. We have a launch!"

Grady and Paulson spun in the direction of the board. The red dot had started to blink. "The Chinese boat?" Paulson's voice was high-pitched.

"Yes. I'm plotting trajectory now. If it's the East Coast, impact will be in ten to twelve minutes."

Another voice from the floor rang in Paulson's ears. It was the Joint Chiefs' chairman.

"Mister President? I ask for immediate release of nuclear weapons and I request permission to order the SAC bombers to start in from their fail-safe points."

Paulson was shaking and gray. So it had fallen to him. And it was to be now. "Very well—"

Grady yelled at him. "Steve! No! They said don't attack. The only chance we had was not to attack. You couldn't stop that Chinese bird, anyway. She's too close in. We have to wait. We have to."

Paulson looked to the board and the generals who looked at him. The entire room below him was frozen, like a single frame from a motion picture.

The chairman of the Joint Chiefs of Staff looked up. "Mister President, speed is essential. You have to authorize countermeasures now—right now! I urge you to release the nuclear weapons. We might have only minutes before there's an all-out launch. I—"

Kingsford cut him off. "Trajectory indicates target is Washington. Impact time . . . fourteen minutes."

Grady reached up and spun Paulson toward him. He grabbed the man by the shoulders. His face was only inches from the President's as he spoke.

"Steve, no. I believe them. Wait. Just wait. You

can't stop the bird;—Washington's gone in any event. Wait, for God's sake!"

Maria rocked slowly back and forth. Her mind flashed upward, faster now. There were wires and— Yes, there. She had to . . . had to . . . had to . . .

A fire exploded in her head. She tried to reach up to the right side of her head, but her hand would not respond. It only shook spasmodically. The old friend had arrived; death had arrived and she'd fooled him. She'd finished. She spasmed once . . . twice, and her head pitched forward to the top of the conference table.

On the war board, the red light turned white and swelled out until it covered several inches of the board. Kingsford was shrieking. Paulson could barely hear him. "Detonation! We have a detonation. Ah, seventy thousand feet. The bird blew up."

Grady's eyes still riveted themselves to Paulson's. "Wait. Wait, Steve. Whatever the hell they're doing up at the institute, it's working."

Paulson pulled away and looked down at the board. A colonel at a nearby console spun around. "We have another launch."

Paulson could start to feel his stomach turn to jelly. "Where?"

The colonel got up from the console and pointed to the display board. "It's coming up now, sir. Sector seven. There."

The nearest green dot to the white circle on the board started to blink.

Kingsford turned to the officer. "What kind of bird?"

The colonel was shaking his head as he looked back to his console. A thousand miles overhead, a satellite flashed telemetry information through to the computers of the war room. The computer came up with an estimate, and it flashed on the screen in seconds. It was the estimate that caused the officer at the console to shake his head.

"She's not a bird. I say again—not a bird. She's an antisub device."

Paulson leaned over the railing. "What?"

"Sir, an antisubmarine airborne torpedo. It's been launched from the nearest Russian boat to the—"

The colonel at the console interrupted again. "Impact!"

On the board, the white circle grew infinitesmally larger.

Kingsford pointed to the board. "Looks like a Red sub's blown that chink boat out of the water, sir."

Paulson shook his head. "Why?"

"I don't know, sir."

An aide rushed along the deck toward Grady and Paulson. Grady turned to the man.

"What?"

The man, an air force major, skidded to a stop on the polished floor. "Sir, Doctor Tanner is on the line from the Moreland Institute. He told me not to get you to the phone, just to tell you. He said: China. That it was China and not Russia. That they were setting up a confrontation. He said it was about food . . . about wheat."

"Did he say anything else—anything?"

"Yes, sir. He said Mrs. Munoz was dead—she died a few minutes ago."

"Thank you, Major."

Unsure of what to do, the man retreated back down the observation deck.

Grady turned back to Paulson. The man was wiping

a film of perspiration from his forehead. He looked older by years than he had only moments before.

"Wait—they said to wait. Sweet God . . ."

Below them, the board flashed suddenly to the polar projection.

An air force general looked up after pulling off his headset.

"Mister President?"

"Yes?"

"Sir, NORAD reports a Soviet missile launch near Novaya Zemlya."

"What kind of missile, General?"

"Checking, sir."

The same major who retreated back along the deck was running forward to Grady and Paulson again. "Mister President. We have a Flash Override hot-line call from Premier Kharkov."

Paulson's eyes did not leave the board. "I'll take it here."

It took them a few minutes to string out the phone line and another few minutes passed before Paulson was on the line to Premier Kharkov.

"Mister Premier." Paulson's voice was calm again, measured, careful.

As he spoke, the air force general called from below. "That bird is an IRBM—intermediate range ballistic missile. Looks like impact near Tien Shan . . . China."

Paulson nodded and went back to his conversation.

The name of the place rang in Grady's ears, jangling his memory. Tien Shan. *The open lands program. The rural émigrés . . . an army of them. Gone in the fireball.*

Grady listened to Paulson talk with the Russian Premier for more than an hour. Despite the fact that a cloud of nuclear hell was cooling over the Chinese border, there were no further launches from China or Russia. When Paulson hung up, he turned to Grady.

"Tanner will have company on that flight to Zurich."

"Who?"

"You and me. We're meeting with Kharkov and his foreign minister . . . and Academician Sholodkin. We're about to put together the fastest summit in history."

20

*"It is across the void, the valley of darkness . . .
that Man must make his ultimate leap . . . into
belief. . . ."*

—Sören Kierkegaard

MYSTERY SUMMIT YIELDS PACT
Reuters: July 1

After the surprising and sudden mystery summit
in Zurich last week, President Paulson and Soviet
Premier Kharkov today jointly announced the
formation of a sweeping new SALT agreement.
Though all of the terms of the summit have not
yet been disclosed, the bilateral reduction of nuclear arms, which seems to be the key to the
agreement, is certain to brighten the prospects for
Paulson's re-election.

CHINESE BLAST AT TIEN SHAN PROBED: INDIA FILES FORMAL U.N. PROTEST

The Indian govenment today filed an official pro-
test with the United Nations Security Council in
New York, concerning the recent explosion of
a small nuclear reactor in the midst of China's

361

open lands program in Tien Shan Province. India
is demanding reparations from the People's Republic for the deaths of an estimated seventy
thousand Indian workers. Indian officials involved
closely with the program have denied any knowledge of the reactor's existence at the site of the
rural émigré community. China, in the midst of an
obvious power shift in the wake of the nuclear accident that claimed an estimated one million
Chinese lives, has agreed to discuss the possibility. . . .

EPILOGUE

It was a sultry day in August and the weather was warm for Frankfurt. In Gruneberg Park, the two old men sat in their shirtsleeves and watched the chess players move the wooden pieces around the huge board. The small, bald Russian lit a cigarette and coughed.

Channing shook his head. "I warned you about those."

Sholodkin looked up at him. "I smoke. You don't. Who has coronary? And who is still strong as bull? Huh?"

Channing, paler and thinner than at their last meeting, shook his head. "Then smoke your head off. But seriously, who was the man Lewis? We knew he was a Russian, but who was he?"

Sholodkin took a deep drag on the Chesterfield. "His name was Gregor Balchev. He had worked with me for two years and his skill in psychokinesis was greater than anyone I have ever seen. He was, you might say, my prize student . . . until he defected."

"Did you know where he went?"

"No one did. The KGB scoured Russia for him. As he did not turn up in the West and there was little valid intelligence coming from China, we had no way of knowing. He simply disappeared a few weeks after

363

I met with you in January. He must have been made a considerable offer. He always seemed happy in Leningrad."

"And the weather program?"

Sholodkin took off his glasses and rubbed the side of his nose.

"It was madness. It blew up in their faces. They were using—" He stopped and looked up at Channing and smiled. "Well, no matter what they were using, it didn't work."

Channing stared at the small Russian for a second. "Security? Still?"

"Still. I cannot even reveal what failed. God knows what they'd had me do if something succeeded. But they called me in when it failed. They were looking for a system that would bypass spy satellites and nuclear weapons. What we developed, you know now. That brilliant young assistant of yours, Tanner, he developed the same thing and we both came up with the same problems—distances. It was from that that I moved to the idea of numbers. When your ship was sunk and then our trawler the same way, none of it made sense. We had done nothing. There was no reason for you to have. China was the answer. It was then that one of our sensitives came up with the rural émigrés at Tien Shan. There were perhaps ten thousand of them . . . all trained for years. We think that your Golden Gate catastrophe was a single experiment, using Gregor, or Trevor, alone. When he did not survive, we think that Premier T'sing decided to move with an earlier plan—a long-range assault. There was no danger of apprehension."

"What about the helicopter?"

The Russian shrugged. "We never knew. Perhaps there was another Chinese operative? We might never know. In the same way, we might never know how Deladier got that list of predictions." The Russian stubbed the cigarette underfoot. "And you. How is it that you retire before me?"

"I didn't retire, not exactly. But I had to get time for us to work together. The new institute in Zurich will be hard work, right?"

Sholodkin nodded and let his glance move to the chess players.

"So, Jerry Tanner is the new director and a woman named Rosemary McGee is the new deputy. Is she good at her job?"

"Very."

"We shall see. I see her in Zurich next month. Then we shall see. She will have much to do when we start on the accelerated food growth project."

Both men watched as the chess players set up the wooden pieces for another game.

"What about China, Andrei?"

The Russian shook his head. "No problem. Not for now. They need food as much as we do. They will stay in line . . . for now."

On the board a few yards away, the white player called his first move.

Channing smiled as he looked from the board to Andrei. "Did I tell you I was a grandfather?"

The Russian blinked. "You and your wife never had children. Or have you hidden one from me?"

"Well, not actually a grandchild. A sort of step-grandchild." He took his wallet from his jacket pocket and extracted a small photo. "Here."

The Russian took the photo from him and peered at it. Channing pointed to the infant that he held in his arms. It was a boy.

"Child is handsome. You are ugly as usual."

Channing laughed. "He's Jerald Channing Tanner. He's as close to a grandson as I will ever have."

The Russian turned to him. There was a tenderness in his eyes and a smile creased the craggy face. "Is good for you, my friend. We old men need such things."

Channing looked at his watch. "We'll have to go. The conference in Zurich won't wait for us."

Sholodkin turned back from the chessboard. His face was flushed in a sudden flash of pique. "Of course they wait. We are the only ones who know what to tell them to do. What is good of being old and famous if you cannot make bureaucrats wait, huh? We watch this last game. Then go. Yes?"

Channing waved a hand as if in surrender. "Yes."

On the board, a young German, perhaps a college student, was responding to black's move. It was queen to bishop seven and check—fool's mate.

The two old men laughed.

"A BOOK TO HAUNT
YOUR MEMORY AND YOUR DREAMS."
—ROBERT BLOCH,
AUTHOR OF *PSYCHO*

The Sibling
By Adam Hall

An absolutely gripping psychic thriller about a
brother and sister whose fierce love and mur-
derous hate would terrify the world for all time.

Drawn together by a mysterious passion, pulled
apart by strange forces from beyond the grave,
both are condemned to relive the rites of a long-
forgotten past and must answer the voices of
ancient gods demanding sacrifices that can end
only in death.

16522 $2.50